A flying bomb.

A lethal shower.

A fatal twist of rope.

Three gruesome deaths.

Three diabolical M.O.s.

And a pattern of murder only a brilliant L.A. cop can fathom....

"They're not dumb. . . . There's this cop, Santomassimo. . . . I think he knows. . . . I sense he knows. . . .

"Quinn's pretty bright, too. . . ."

Click. The recording light went on. . . . The reels turned. . . .

"I could have loved her in a different life. . . . Now it's too late. . . . Maybe I'll dedicate this to her . . . in memoriam . . . for Kay Quinn. . . .

"I think my work's getting more defined. . . . These next scenes have to be worked out carefully. . . . I need my notebook . . . my storyboard. . . .

"Yes . . . my storyboard. . . .

"For Kay Quinn . . . deceased. . . ."

FUNERAL MARCH

Frank De Felitta

BANTAM BOOKS
NEW YORK · TORONTO · LONDON · SYDNEY · AUCKLAND

To the memory of
Irwin R. Blacker:
simply the best

FUNERAL MARCH
A Bantam Book / February 1991

All rights reserved.
Copyright © 1991 by Penny Dreadful Inc.
Cover art copyright © 1991 by Tom Hallman.

ISBN 0-553-28927-6

Published simultaneously in the United States and Canada

Bantam Books are published by Bantam Books, a division of Bantam
Doubleday Dell Publishing Group, Inc. Its trademark, consisting of the
words "Bantam Books" and the portrayal of a rooster, is Registered in U.S.
Patent and Trademark Office and in other countries, Marca Registrada.
Bantam Books, 666 Fifth Avenue, New York, New York 10103.

PRINTED IN THE UNITED STATES OF AMERICA

OPM   0 9 8 7 6 5 4 3 2 1

Click . . . A tape recorder began . . . recording . . .

"I was hooked on movies as a kid . . ."

Click . . . "Who the hell cares?" . . . Whirr . . . The tape reversed . . . back to the beginning . . . Click . . .

"I have to explain so many things . . . my storyboard is about being alone, about my art . . ."

Click . . . "Fuck this crap." . . . Click . . . The voice resumed, more determined.

"It's about the master I follow. The great master. A genius. You can't understand anything if you don't understand him. Truly understand him. The way I do."

Click . . . Shadows moved. Time went by. There were noises, vague and disquieting, in the tiny apartment. More time went by . . .

Click . . .

". . . Let me mention my library . . . The first film book I ever got was the Frank Capra book, The Name Above the Title. *Still have it. Right over there. I was ten years old. My uncle gave it to me for my birthday. Then I bought the Chaplin books—still here—right by the video—and the von Stroheim—and I got the memoirs of Douglas Fairbanks from*

*some faggy little dealer in Venice. Jesus, I hated that guy.
But as you see, I've got over 4,000 volumes. No, I guess
you can't see it. You can't see a damn thing. You don't even
exist.''*

The tape stopped.

''Who the fuck cares about a library?''

Click . . . The tape rolled again . . .

*''It's not exactly easy, you know. So that's why I'm making
this verbal outline, this description. So you'll know what I
went through. What was involved. You'll know it wasn't easy
to get to my present state.''*

*A shadow moved over the tape recorder. ''I need a beer.
Is there a beer in this fucking place?'' The shadow came
back to the heavy seat. For a long time, there was no motion.
Then the tape recorder began from where it had left off
recording.*

*''I had this addiction . . . I can't think of any other word for
it . . . I was born with it, and it bloomed like a cancer as I
grew, except that I liked the disease . . . It's hard to explain
. . . I was . . . I am . . . addicted to movies.*

*''I don't mean I like movies and that I see a lot of them,
although that's true. I mean, my brain thinks in film shots. I
edit and re-edit reality. When I talk to people, I see CLOSE
SHOT: JAMES, then CAMERA DOLLIES IN TO EXTREME
CLOSE SHOT, or DIFFERENT ANGLE—ROSEMARIE, or RE-
VERSE ANGLE or CAMERA TRACKS WITH PORSCHE AND
WE SEE THE DRIVER NERVOUSLY LIGHTING A CIGA-
RETTE. See what I mean? I'm a biological camera. It isn't
always pleasant. I've been to a psychiatrist and I know this
is not normal.*

*''And my brain edits and re-edits. MONTAGE OF HIGH-
SPEED TRAFFIC ON THE HARBOR FREEWAY or CAMERA
INTERCUTS BETWEEN COP AND BLACK STREET-
DEALER. Things I see, things I experience, they get
trimmed, heads and tails, fragmented and put back together
in the seamless, continual nightmare that is my life.*

*''So I was hooked on movies as a kid. Old movies, black
and white. THE THREE STOOGES, LAUREL AND HARDY,
THE KEYSTONE COPS. My family was uptight. Baptists of
the worst sort, but with money, real money, and we lived in
Nebraska, and you know what kind of people live there.*

Narrow, tight-fisted bastards. My life was cheerless, joyless, but I knew that cinema was my way out. I learned cinema syntax before I could write English. If you want to be fancy, I saw some kind of metaphysics in those old melodramas and comedies. Cinema became my religion.

"By the time I was eight, I had the reputation of being a weirdo. I had no brothers or sisters. My father and I never got along. The prick never indulged me. I made my own films, on nickels and dimes that I generally stole from my mother's purse. I made costumes. I wrote scripts on the backs of paper bags. I made the kids in the neighborhood memorize the action. And what epics they were, THE SAGA OF CHARLES STARKWEATHER, the mass murderer whose escape through the Midwest created such a terror. I know it seems sick now, especially now, but . . . What was I saying? . . . Other epics, grand visions I had . . . THE BATTLE OF ANZIO . . . because I was a bug on World War Two . . . A remake of THE OXBOW INCIDENT . . .

"And I made these films with great care. I made the establishing shots, the high angles, low angles, reverse shots, and I made those little shits do it again and again until they did it right. I didn't care if they cried or had to pee or their mothers were calling. I WAS MAKING A FILM.

"Ever edit regular 8mm? I nearly went blind. I worked on a rickety card table in the basement. Imagine? The basement. In a twenty-room mansion. And there, among the spiders and mildew and the family laundry, I used a blunt scissors and film glue, and a viewer I made myself. And I'd show these films when they were done. It was the only thing I ever did in that damn house. Somehow they knew they couldn't suppress my films. I'd show them to my parents and uncles, and some of the kids' parents. I'd make all the sound effects, including the music, myself, beating on a waste basket for a drum, banging on a piano, shrieking and screeching, whispering all the dialogue. Looking back, I realize I embarrassed everybody. Insanity was a great shame among us. But I didn't see it that way. I hated them for their narrow-mindedness, their inability to feel, to see . . . I didn't care what they thought . . . I had this vision.

"Moviemakers—and let's face it, that's what I was, even by the age of eight—tend to play God. Their natures are

manipulative. I'm extremely manipulative. I manipulated the neighborhood kids, and I tried to manipulate the adults through my films. I need to dominate, or I get . . . I become real . . . That's why I've never had a stable relationship.

"I felt a great deal of rage, growing up in Nebraska. I was shut out. Nobody believed in me. Nobody really wanted to have anything to do with me. I wasn't a good student and I wasn't a good Baptist. Obviously, something was wrong with me, right? And I despised my family and the people I was surrounded by, especially my teachers because I sensed their hypocrisy, their limitations, and they recipro- cated that feeling . . . They called me little Charles Stark- weather and things like that . . . because deep down they were afraid of me . . . People are always frightened by that rare thing, a calling, a natural talent . . .

"You have to come to terms with this, this etiology—the origins—of my project. You have to listen carefully, you have to get at the roots, and it's not as simple as you think.

"I was driven by megalomania. I'll admit it. But think about it. Movies. It's not like making a ceramic pot or a haiku. It is a massive enterprise, the rewards are extraordinary, a shot at immortality, and the competition is cutthroat. Everybody in it is crazy with megalomania. They think they're endowed with exceptional talents. And really, so few of them are . . . so very few . . . They are amoral . . . above the moral law . . . Well, so was I . . . almost from the beginning . . .

"I was afflicted with this cinema way of life, this drive. And I've been destroyed by it. I was deserving of having so much more, I was qualified . . . the way few are really qualified . . . to execute my dreams . . . to execute these visions . . .

"Execute . . ."

Click . . . The tape recorder stopped. Everything was motionless. A bottle of beer was opened.

"Fuck this crap."

A hard, harsh laughter filled the room.

". . . Execute . . .

"CUT!"

1

The sun rose over the mountains, and a golden glow crept from the Pacific Coast Highway to the dew-wet, packed sand just south of Carbon Beach, Los Angeles.

A man jogged down the long stretch of wet mud where the surf trailed lightly away, leaving fingers of kelp, and where the private houses ceased briefly, providing a narrow corridor to which the public had access. The jogger was a man who respected the rights of private property. He owned two homes, one in the Palisades and one in Spain. He also owned a condo in New York City. He was president of the third-largest advertising-public relations-management agency in Hollywood and had vigorously campaigned, wherever he lived, to keep the drifters, the homeless, and the riffraff out.

This morning, he could see that teenagers had had a drinking orgy on the small stretch of public sand at

the north end of the beach. The residual evidence of
the blowout disturbed his sense of calm.

Now, running in his long, gray sweatpants, gray
sweatshirt, his curly black hair neatly tied in a red
band, he savored the morning vapor still in the air. To
his right lay the vast Pacific, calm, eternal, gently
ebbing; to his left, the homes and apartments of the
wealthy. Beyond, and spread grandly above it all, stood
the J. Paul Getty mansion, an eighty-room eminence
reigning majestically over the hills and bluffs of Porto
Marina Way, a charming stretch of the California
coastline. The jogger would have wished for a house
in these hills with its commanding view of the Pacific,
but he knew that the land was unstable. Homes had
literally slid from their foundations, and had had to be
removed by the city—at the owner's expense.

He ran harder now, barefoot, with mud and sand
oozing and splattering under his toes, pushing all
negative thoughts from his mind and concentrating
on the bracing, revitalizing exercise.

Far away he heard something like a fly droning. He
looked, but saw nothing—only his footprints, which
stretched back about a quarter of a mile, and then lost
shape, melting into the glistening mud of the Pacific.
It was six-forty-five in the morning. In his mind, he
drafted two memorandums to his attorneys. A nasty
fight for international distribution of a client's package
of film videos was headed for litigation.

Again came the sound of a huge fly droning. He
shielded his eyes from the sun now blazing over the
flat tops of the beach apartments. He saw a model
airplane, perhaps two feet long, doing figure eights in
the sky directly above him. It was the kind that was
guided by remote control.

Damn those kids! he thought. His eyes searched
the nearby embankment and building tops, but he
couldn't see who flew the plane.

He jogged on. The interruption had almost broken

his stride. It is important to maintain a pace as unbroken and regular as film sprockets running over a toothed wheel. Otherwise, fatigue sets in. Instead of release, there is frustration. He jogged harder and harder.

And now the airplane circled the green shingled roof of the nearest apartment house.

"Get that piece of shit off the beach!" he yelled.

He stumbled over a pocket in the wet beach. Kelp and a channel of retreating light surf splattered up onto his sweatpants. His mind focused on the legal case, where a firm of sharp attorneys from Cincinnati, of all places, had blocked distribution of his film videos in Holland, Belgium, and Denmark.

Of late, in spite of strenuous diet and a retreat to an exclusive resort in the high desert, he had gained almost twenty pounds. Alcohol, a friend for so many years, now made him look old. And looking old was lethal in his business. Do what you might with dyes, lotions, tucks, they sensed it in you. Like chickens pecking a sick hen to death. Especially now, past the age of fifty. Then they steal your concepts, corrupt your business relationships, and laugh at you.

The model airplane dipped, dived, and roared, spitting drops of gasoline over the sand in his path.

"Goddamn you—!"

The plane passed so close, he ducked. He stumbled. He stubbed his left toe on the mud. Now, ludicrous and out of breath, wobbling and angry, he kept on jogging, but he felt heavy. He felt impinged upon. And he could not see the operator of the plane.

Some people were stirring behind their windows, perhaps awakened by the plane. Two actresses, an attorney, several advertising vice presidents, the son of a wealthy industrialist, and a college president lived on this stretch of the beach. Film people. Media people. He knew how important it was to be seen in the rhythm of health, of vigor, of striding forward into a fighting future.

But he believed he had broken his toe. Pain was shooting up to his knees.

Behind him, he heard the airplane whine. It sounded as though the metal was straining. He turned to look. Incredibly, the plane was streaking straight up, perfectly vertical, up into the sky. Then the pitch changed. The metal gleamed in the sun, a wing catching light. It gained speed, twisting and trembling, accelerating downward.

The airplane zoomed at his head.

He ran, fell into the surf, and ran some more, limping. He ran as fast as he could. Piles of kelp and a child's toy bucket and shovel impeded him. Disoriented, he saw the airplane fly across the sand, barely three feet above the ground, banking, turning playfully. Covered with mud, he ran, then crawled on hands and knees, then struggled shakily to his feet.

He was vaguely, dreamily aware of a little boy, Bobby Brady, who was twenty-one months old, who waddled to the rail on the balcony of the last apartment and grasped the iron bars.

"Again," the toddler squealed, delighted. "Again! Again!"

Now the jogger looked through the brightness and mist, past the bluffs and hills, his eyes roving downward to a stretch of undeveloped embankment abutting the highway, and finally made out the silhouette of a man's shape standing, actually quite close, legs apart, operating a remote control box.

"*DAMNED IDIOT!*" the jogger shouted. "*WATCH WHAT YOU'RE DOING!*"

But the man, if he heard, made no response. He caused the plane to bank, turn, and race back up the beach, six inches above the mud.

Disbelieving, the jogger stared at the airplane, which grew larger in geometric acceleration. Wisps of smoke came from its engine. He could even see the detail of the tiny rubber wheels. But at the last second, he dived into the surf. Staggering in the knee-high water, he turned back to see the airplane climb high again, over the apartment roofs, gracefully flip over on its back, and dive back at him.

"Again!" shrieked little Bobby Brady, "Again! Again!"

From inside the apartment, a dull shadow moved. Bobby's mother was coming out to investigate.

The man's shape on the embankment pushed a small lever, and the airplane gained speed.

"YOU FUCKING MANIAC!" the jogger shouted. But he was running now. Running harder than he had ever run in his life. The pain in his foot was forgotten. So was his dignity. He ran without stride, rhythm, or beat, like a demented beast. But behind him came the throaty roar of the airplane. It came toward his ear now and the roar grew into a scream.

Horror-stricken, he turned. He saw the decals mounted on the plane's wings, the tiny struts, the mock cockpit that gleamed fiercely in the bright morning sun. He smelled the gasoline vapor and heat of the metal in the sun.

An oily, orange flash leaped over the sand. Smoke, mud, white water, and bits of gray sweatshirt flew over the beach. Fragments of brain, fingernails, and a denture plate showered between the pilings under the apartments.

Bobby Brady's mother rushed out onto the patio, screaming. Instinctively, her face struck by grit and darkened instantly by oily smoke, she grabbed Bobby. She kept on screaming, in a daze, but Bobby knew what he had seen. He clapped his pudgy hands but he did not laugh.

"Again," he whimpered weakly, his eyes round with shock and confusion. "Again . . ." he repeated atonally. "Again . . ."

The day was hot. The morning vapor had burned off, and the sand had dried. Gulls hovered over the apartment patios, and a little girl tried to raise a red kite over the bright pounding surf. Under the embankment, a crowd watched a thing that looked like an elongated sandbag, covered in a police blanket. Los Angeles police stood, arms folded, guarding a perimeter of steel stakes and red ribbon around the thing.

Plainclothes detectives stepped under the red ribbon and searched the sand and the upward slope of the embankment for something which even they could not define. Two more plainclothesmen, also technicians, combed the sands, one with a metal detector and earphones.

Thirty-five beach residents stood, curious, waiting in the same somnolent way the police waited. Something had to happen soon. And when it did, they would see the sawed-off torso of the late jogger.

An ambulance pulled up to the edge of the Pacific Coast Highway. Al Gilbert was the medical examiner and he had bad indigestion. He had consumed a full roll of Rolaids that morning already and it was only eleven. It was an ulcer. He knew it was an ulcer. Being a doctor, he also knew they put tubes up your ass and leaked barium into your gut, and that was just to find it. Gilbert knew the symptoms. It was probably bleeding. A wound in the stomach lining, and could probably kill you like a dum-dum bullet. Gilbert's mind revolved automatically around bloody visions. Just habit.

Gilbert sidled awkwardly down the sandy slope, using his left foot to brake.

A knot of policemen stood around a hole about ten feet wide and six feet deep. Bits of charred body, flannel cloth, and small slivers of metal were spread inside the ribboned perimeter. Spots and dribbles of blood, and long strings of gristle speckled the hot sand.

Gilbert's nose wrinkled. There was a smell already. Or was that the kelp decaying in the surf? He looked down into the hole. It began approximately where the head of the body should have been.

"Yuck," a voice behind him said. Gilbert jumped.

It was Detective First Class John Haber. Haber was pushing sixty and had glaucoma. You could see it in the milky blue of his eyes and the offset way he looked at you. Haber grinned slyly.

"Smells like a barbecue, don't it, Doc?" Harber said.

"Yeah. Not much to examine. What'd he do, step on a land mine?"

Haber didn't answer. Gilbert turned to look at the waiting crowd, which was edging closer now, sensing the moment of the grand unveiling, the climax of the morning's blood ritual. The normally mild-mannered inhabitants of surrounding homes had unpleasant gleams in their eyes.

"I want your crew to pick up the pieces, Detective Haber," Gilbert ordered. "Every piece. Every hair folicle and every fingernail. Bag them."

"Yes, sir."

"Is Santomassimo here?"

"Yes, sir. There was a witness. He and Sergeant Bronte are in her apartment now."

Gilbert looked away from Haber, away from the crowd. He stepped closer, once again, to the edge of the grizzly hole. The crowd leaned forward with him. Gilbert's shoe knocked loose sand down into the hole, and something like a patch of cloth—a designer label for a $600 jogging outfit—began to slide into the bottom.

"One thing's for certain," Gilbert observed.

"What's that, sir?"

"The brain was blown out before he could receive the information."

"Information?"

"Yes, Haber. That it was being blown apart."

The metaphysical nicety escaped Detective Haber. Gilbert went back to the base of the embankment while Haber's crew began sifting the sands with large, flat small-mesh sieves. Disappointed, the crowd settled back. And waited.

In the Brady apartment, Linda Brady was drinking scotch. Newly promoted Lieutenant Fred Santomassimo and Sergeant Lou Bronte waited. Santomassimo was in his mid-thirties. His face was long and sad with the brooding eyes of an El Greco visionary. Right now he was impatient. The woman's nerves were so shot, she kept spilling her scotch down her chin with each swig.

"Could you describe what the victim looked like, Mrs. Brady?" he asked.

"Christ, no! I just stepped out the door when it happened."

Lou Bronte was five years older than Santomassimo. His face was rounder. Unlike Santomassimo, he looked like a baker or an accountant, a seemingly dull witted, yet deceptively clever fellow, the kind you see in Italian comedies. Right now, Bronte was quiet and very sober. Santomassimo was unusually tense.

"Pow!"

Santomassimo jumped. He turned. Bobby Brady waddled out from behind Bronte's footstool, making a diving motion with his hand.

"*Pow!!*"

Santomassimo and Bronte stared at the toddler. What vision of destruction, Santomassimo wondered, had been acted out before that mind still without language? Something that had seemed to the toddler a piece of amusement, like watching Daddy get drunk? Although Santomassimo already knew there wasn't a Daddy around and it was Mommy who got drunk. Santomassimo turned back to Mrs. Brady.

"But you think he was hit by a toy plane?" he asked.

She brushed her sandy brown hair off her forehead. The gray eyes glistened, but from the scotch, not tears. A red flush of abnormal excitement had appeared on her throat and shoulder, something between fear and an enthusiasm that disturbed Santomassimo.

"Sure? What am I sure about? I stepped on the deck, because Bobby was excited about something. I think I know what hit him. It was a model airplane. I could hear it. They should outlaw them. Every weekend, people drive here to fly them. And up at Zuma Beach, too. They stand up there on the embankment and play World War One. Dogfights. Zooming. Diving. Figure eights. They're a real pain in the ass. They start at dawn and go on till night. Grown men, some of them. Pay no taxes here."

"But this morning there was only one plane? You heard only one plane?"

She nodded. The scotch was working. "Yeah. One plane. That's because it's Monday, Lieutenant. Only time we get any peace around here is during workdays. Weekends forget—" She burped. "Planes. Frisbees. Ghetto blasters. The whole stinking mess."

Bobby crept behind Lieutenant Santomassimo.

"POW!" he yelled.

Santomassimo instinctively jerked and wheeled toward the toddler, but whatever instinct had ordered him to do he just as instinctively suppressed it. He exchanged glances with Bronte. Santomassimo gently pushed Bobby away, redirected his attention on the child's mother.

"I assume you're an early riser, Mrs. Brady?"

She downed the rest of the scotch and looked for the bottle, now on the bookshelf where Santomassimo had left it after pouring her the first drink.

"You assume right, Lieutenant," she said.

Bronte leaned forward, pushing Bobby away from his knee, where he was leaving drool marks.

"Have you ever seen joggers that early in the morning, Mrs. Brady?" Bronte asked.

"Sure. They run all the time. Day and night. *Stop that, Bobby!*"

"It can be dry cleaned, Mrs. Brady," Bronte said.

"Have you noticed one particular jogger who runs *every* morning?" Santomassimo asked.

"They all run."

"But they'd be your neighbors," Bronte pointed out.

Mrs. Brady turned to Bronte. She was in her mid-thirties, and still attractive, but awfully unhappy. It was in the lines around her eyes and the rigid sparkle of her pupils. "I don't know my neighbors," she said. "I bought this condo with my divorce settlement. Bobby and I have only been here two months."

"Okay. Thanks for your help, Mrs. Brady," Santomassimo said. He felt vaguely depressed, and didn't know why. He rose to leave. Bronte quickly followed, smiling a polite farewell. Santomassimo paused, dug out a card, and gave it to Mrs. Brady.

"If something occurs to you," he said. "Anything at all. I can be reached at this number."

Bobby, chastened, waddled around the room, from the bookcase to the television set, from the telescope and starfish and green fisherman's netting tacked to the veneer of the wall, to the ice chest of the bar. He kept making diving motions with his hand. His mouth kept silently forming the same word: "*POW!!*"

Lou bent down, hands on knees, and smiled at Bobby. "You saw it all, didn't you, Bobby? Too bad you can't talk."

"And by the time he talks, he'll have forgotten," Santomassimo said.

"Bobby has an excellent memory," Mrs. Brady said defensively. "He just can't talk yet."

Now Santomassimo realized why he was vaguely depressed. It was not the faint aroma of scotch on the pretty woman's lips. It was the decor. Cheap when it didn't have to be. Transient, somehow, as though her life would be transient from now on. Santomassimo wandered across the living room, looking at the picture of Mrs. Brady and Bobby on the bookcase. In the bedroom, where the door was partially open, he saw a bra draped over a chair. Her slippers were there, too, beneath the chair. The bed was rumpled on one side only. She still slept on one side of the bed.

Santomassimo stepped out onto the deck. Below, the police technicians were climbing in and out of the large hole, like enormous beetles, carrying back debris for the sieves. The crowd was larger now, mostly teenagers and some mothers with children.

Linda Brady came onto the deck with Lou Bronte.

"Some welcome," she said. "Right off my front porch. Maybe Bobby won't forget. What happens if he does remember? What's in his subconscious now,

Lieutenant? How will it affect him? Maybe it'll make
him a killer, too."

"I don't think you have to be worried about it, Mrs.
Brady," Santomassimo assured her gently.

"Well, what about the hole in the beach? And all
his—guts—or whatever they are? Does the city clean
up this mess? Or do we have to fight the county?"

"It will all be taken care of, Mrs. Brady."

Down below, Al Gilbert was peeking under the
blanket. Even at this height, it was obvious that
threads of veins and flesh came out of the neck. The
crowd watched in a stunned, satisfied silence.

Lieutenant Santomassimo went down to the beach
with Bronte. Al Gilbert walked up to them.

"We sure are lucky today," Al said.

"Yeah?" Bronte looked hopeful. "Why?"

Gilbert pointed up the beach to the north. "Another
hundred yards that way, this would all be the Malibu
sheriff's problem."

Santomassimo grinned. "Sure, Al. And about a half
a mile south of here, it would be Santa Monica's
problem. But the victim had the bad taste to get blown
up on the tiny stretch of beach in between, so it's now
LAPD's problem."

"You're right," Al Gilbert said. "Fucking bad taste."

Santomassimo climbed up the steep embankment
to the Pacific Coast Highway. Waiting for him on top
was a tall, obese man in a light gray business suit,
blue shirt, and dark tie. Santomassimo recognized
Steve Safran KJLP's nose for news. The day had grown
even more humid and Safran was sweating heavily,
his shirt and portions of his jacket were plastered to
his skin. Behind Safran was a slim, wiry cameraman,
his face hidden behind the viewfinder of a shoulder-
braced mini-cam. The red light was on. Safran had
his man recording. Santomassimo turned away.

Safran ran after him, one hand pushing the cameraman.

"Lieutenant!" Safran said. "KJLP News. Can you give us a statement?"

"I've nothing to say at this time."

Santomassimo paused, scraped at the sand with the toe of his shoe. It was full of specks and bits of mica, tiny clots of dirt, and God knew what half-decomposed litter mixed into its constituent chemicals. It was not the kind of soil that held footprints.

"An explosion of that dimension," Safran puffed. "Do you believe it to be the act of a terrorist?"

"I don't know what caused it, Mr. Safran. What you see is what we see." Santomassimo turned and walked off.

Safran followed, then stopped, catching his breath. He made a gesture, trying to catch Santomassimo's attention, unsuccessfully, and the gesture turned to one of explicit disrespect.

"Thank you, Lieutenant," Safran said, and beneath his breath added, ". . . prick."

Police technicians were now sifting the dirt along the embankment, above the body and the hole. The beach was clean, except for the dead jogger's footprints and bits of biological matter. On the embankment, however, there was scuffed-up soil. Santomassimo exchanged glances with Detective Haber, in charge of the detail. The crowd of gawkers practically leaned over the red plastic ribbon barrier.

"You've gotta give them what they want," Santomassimo observed. "That's the secret of show business."

"Right, sir," Haber smiled. "They'll be taking what's left of the corpse to the lab in about an hour. That should please 'em."

The technicians shoveled the embankment sand into large flats of wire mesh. After sifting the sand thoroughly, they dumped the remaining litter into plastic containers. The containers were then marked with grease pencils, identifying the position of the residue on the embankment. Small piles of purified sand accumulated at the policemen's shining black shoes.

Haber sensed Santomassimo's impatience and wondered if it was a criticism.

"We've sifted every likely vantage point, Lieutenant," Haber said. "Even across the highway and parts of those bluffs on Porto Marina Way."

"Anything?"

"Bottles. Bottle caps. Glass. Cigarette butts. Condoms. Used, of course. Bits of a dead cat."

"Tire marks?"

"No."

"Footprints?"

Detective Haber turned to look at the crowd. Santomassimo followed his glance. The crowd shrank slightly back, instinctively sensing the anger of authority.

"Sure," Haber said sarcastically. "Thousands."

A technician bent over like an Arkansas cotton picker in the hot sun. The sand poured through the mesh. Pebbles were left, broken bits of a brown beer bottle, a piece of pipe, probably for hashish, a starfish dead and hard as a slat of wood, and a single piece of yellowed, probably once buttered popcorn.

The technician popped the kernel into the green plastic container along with the dead starfish, glass and pipe stem.

Sergeant Bronte climbed up the embankment. Mopping his jowls with a monogrammed handkerchief, he joined Detective Haber and Santomassimo.

"We've covered every house on the beach," he said. "Some people heard the explosion, but as far as they know, nobody else jogged at that hour, and nobody saw him." Bronte consulted his notebook. "One man— Elmo Richardson, a retired bank executive—was in his sauna and thought it was a sonic boom."

"Peachy."

Unruffled, Bronte flipped over the page of his spiral notebook.

"Officer McGivney found a car parked on the road. A quarter of a mile to the north, and as far as the residents can tell us, it belongs to nobody who lives there."

"That's something."

"It's a spanking new Cadillac Biarritz. Convertible. A marshmallow cream sundae. The kind you feel honored to touch. And there's a pressed suit inside, and a tie and very expensive-looking shirt."

"Anything in the suit pockets?"

"The car is locked, sir."

"Call headquarters for a break-and-search."

"They're on the way."

Santomassimo wondered. A Biarritz? They don't give those away with book club memberships. If it belonged to the corpse, he was wealthy. Maybe into the mob for money? Cocaine? Santomassimo started walking up the Pacific Coast Highway, alongside Bronte. Neither man spoke. There was a moist heat on the broad road, and traffic had picked up. Santomassimo gazed from left to right, from the house-dotted hillside to the east of the road to the staggered roofs of houses actually on the beachfront. Anybody could have stood here, operating a remote control bomb. Hidden among the cacti and thistles. Or perhaps not hiding at all. Perhaps the killer had done the job cooly, calmly, letting himself be seen.

Mrs. Brady had said a model airplane. She knew the sound of them. *A fucking toy airplane.*

It was a freaky M.O.—a crazy way to kill.

The Biarritz was everything Bronte had promised—a white, sparkling beauty with the convertible top firmly locked. Now, to his disgust, Santomassimo saw that elements of the crowd had spotted the arrival of the break-and-search team and had followed along the embankment, coming out where the Cadillac stood baking by a clotted drainpipe.

A police locksmith fit a steel needle into the door lock. With a few deft probes, he sprang the lock. The crowd was pleased, inspired at the speed with which a car could be opened. Some almost seemed ready to applaud. One woman with a Nikon took a picture.

Lieutenant Santomassimo held back the locksmith and signaled for the fingerprint man. A short, balding veteran came with brush, powder, and black satchel, and began dusting the door handle. When he blew the dust away with a rubber bulb, a confusion of latent fingerprints were visible.

Santomassimo put on white cotton gloves and gingerly avoiding the prints, opened the door. The beach erupted with the wail of the Cadillac's alarm. The crowd shrank back, and then, laughing sheepishly, drifted even closer toward the car. Santomassimo leaned into the car, reached under the dashboard, and turned off the Klaxon.

When he sat in the driver's seat, it felt good, hot and good, like the secret of luxury made tangible in soft leather and chrome materials. The glove compartment opened at the touch of a finger. Inside was a thick cloth-bound folder. Santomassimo paged through it. It contained the Cadillac maintenance records, the owner's manual, insurance certificate, and the vehicle registration form. Santomassimo turned the registration form right-side up.

William Hasbrouk, 2334 Plantation Drive, Pacific Palisades, California 90053.

A good address, Santomassimo thought. Goes well with the car.

"Take care of the removal of the corpse while the people think the circus is up here," Lieutenant Santomassimo whispered to Sergeant Bronte. "Keep the car off limits."

"Yes, sir."

"When you're through, we'll take a drive into the Palisades."

Bronte nodded and grinned, then casually slipped away from the scene and walked down the road to transmit the instructions to Detective Haber. Santomassimo stayed in the car, pretending to examine it, long enough for Bronte to signal, and then Santomassimo went down the road to meet him.

3

Santomassimo drove an open-topped Datsun. It was long and low, Bronte braced himself when he saw a pothole coming, but it rode over it smoothly. Santomassimo had a tiny white Christ of excellently carved ivory attached to the dash. It see-sawed gently with each turn of the wheels. Normally, the sergeant would be chauffering the lieutenant, but Santomassimo loved to drive.

The Pacific Coast Highway overlooked the entire magnificent white sands from Malibu to Santa Monica, glittering as though specks of diamonds had been scattered on the beach. Tall Italian cypresses guarded the estates of great walled houses rising on the Palisades.

Santomassimo drove with a relaxed control, the low blue Datsun taking the Palisades curves easily.

Half-facing Santomassimo, Bronte lounged against the door smoking, his tie flapping in the wind. Bronte waited. He knew that Santomassimo never let go of a train of thought. He would just get off the train in strange places.

"Jew?" Santomassimo asked suddenly.

"Hasbrouk?"

"What do *you* think? Arab?"

Bronte paused as Santomassimo pressed the stick carefully into third gear and took another steep curve, past stone lions rampant on a gated driveway.

"You're thinking terrorist?" Bronte finally asked.

"I don't know. I don't know what I'm thinking. But whoever killed him sure wanted him obliterated."

Bronte scribbled down a note into his notebook and put the notebook back into his inside coat pocket. He, too, had his methods of thought. Half-formed intuitions littered his notebook, in the margins of data, to become hypotheses much, much later. At least on those cases where they found the killer.

"You're sure that was Hasbrouk on the beach?" Bronte asked.

"I'll bet on it."

"Remember the case of Mustafa Mabout?" Bronte asked. "Used to fly to Las Vegas on Tuesday and come back to the studios on Friday with suitcases of cash to meet the payroll?"

"Where did they find him? Benedict Canyon?"

"Part of him."

Bronte made another notation in his notebook. He leaned back and savored the salty, hot breeze as Santomassimo drove.

"Very strange way to kill somebody," Santomassimo suggested.

"A bomb?"

"A flying bomb. In a toy. Hasbrouk's footprints show he was jogging normally about a quarter mile down the beach, then he stumbled, then later he fell and began running, and then he ran erratically to where the hole is now."

Bronte lit a second cigarette, leaning toward the dash to keep the flame alive. "Whoever did it played with him. Humiliated him. Sadistic, really. Hasbrouk was defenseless as a baby."

Santomassimo nodded.

"*If* that was Hasbrouk," Bronte wondered aloud.

Santomassimo did not answer. Bronte had worked with Santomassimo two years, long enough to work out a *modus operandi* with him. They asked questions, expecting no answers. It kept their minds on the same leash somehow.

"All those people on the beach," Santomassimo said. "You'd think one of them would have investigated somebody operating a model airplane that early in the morning."

"Executives. Actresses. Film people, Fred. For them, the bizarre is not something to get excited about."

Santomassimo drove a long time, thinking about the beach people. The difference between the public dream that was cinema and the brutal strugglers behind the scenes. He wondered what the jogger had done for a living.

"My Aunt Rosa saw *The Ten Commandments* eight times," Santomassimo said, smiling. "It was a small neighborhood theater in Brooklyn. Every time she waited for the miracles. It was an obsessive, hypnotic kind of thing. DeMille took her in completely. Sometimes I wondered if it should be legal."

Bronte chuckled. "I know what you mean. My son watches the videos. Every week his hair is a different color. Pomades. Earrings. *Earrings.* On a grown boy with normal instincts."

A dark mood settled over Santomassimo. He stopped the Datsun at the base of a small rise, where a short but steep driveway went up past a concrete wall and signs warned of guard dogs, neighborhood watches, and police-wired alarm systems. Bronte also got tense.

As though they were at a dead man's house. If the Biarritz and the house were both owned by the corpse.

"Let's see who's home," Santomassimo said.

The estate was much larger than one would have guessed from the road where the Datsun was parked. The house was a manorial size and was situated at the far end of a large, well-tended lawn, a kind of plateau over the Palisades and the Pacific Coast Highway and beach below. Delicate water sprinklers crisscrossed white jets of water over neat beds of red roses and blue delphiniums.

Santomassimo rang the doorbell. A houseboy of Latin extraction opened the door. Santomassimo showed his police credentials. From the reaction, Santomassimo guessed the boy was an illegal.

"We'd like to talk to Mr. Hasbrouk," Santomassimo said.

"Mr. Hasbrouk not here. Mr. Hasbrouk at work."

"Where does Mr. Hasbrouk work?"

The houseboy, who, to Santomassimo's practiced ear, was not Mexican but Guatemalan or even Colombian, hesitated between protecting Mr. Hasbrouk and wanting to get the police away from 2334 Plantation Drive.

"Downtown," he finally said.

"What address, *por favor?*"

The houseboy licked his lips, looked at Sergeant Bronte, and then back at Santomassimo .

"The Sheffield Building," he articulated. "On the top. A suite."

Bronte wrote down the building's name."

"What's the name of the company?" Bronte asked.

"Hasbrouk."

"Yes. Hasbrouk," Bronte acknowledged, irritated. "What's the *name* of his company?"

"Hasbrouk."

"I see. Hasbrouk Company."

"And Mr. Clentor."

"Hasbrouk and Clentor?"

"Yes. Two men. One company."

Santomassimo turned back from watching the gardeners blow leaves and clipped grass from the wooden deck, using gas-powered blowers. One had the feeling up here of sailing, of leaping forward, as with great gliding wings, out over the endless, sparkling ocean, as though one were liberated from things like pain, divorce, and killing forever.

"Did Mr. Hasbrouk jog?" Santomassimo asked suddenly.

The houseboy retreated, his eyes suspicious.

"Run," Santomassimo said. "Did he run? To be healthy?"

"Oh. Yes. Every morning. Six-thirty. On the beach."

"Thank you."

Santomassimo went back down the steep drive and got into the Datsun. He drummed his fingers on the black leather that wrapped the steering wheel. Lou Bronte got in beside him.

"The houseboy didn't know Hasbrouk was dead," Santomassimo said.

"Why would he know? Who would have called?"

"Well, I was thinking . . . maybe the killer . . . What's the fastest way to the Sheffield Building?" Santomassimo asked.

"At this hour, just take P.C.H. and the Santa Monica Freeway."

The Datsun wheeled around in a very tight circle and rushed downward toward the glitter and noise of the traffic on the coastline.

The Sheffield Building turned out to be undergoing additions. Scaffolding reached to the third floor and hard-hatted construction crews guided pieces of aluminum onto the facing. Apparently, a restaurant on the ground floor was going hi-tech. Santomassimo saw lots of steel globe lamps and metallic bands for a salad bar. It looked like a place Bronte's son would eat in.

There was also a security guard inside the first floor. Santomassimo and Bronte showed their police credentials. They waited at the elevator while in the restaurant a designer directed the angle of black-and-white tiles for the new, enlarged floor.

"Has the Sheffield Building gone *finocchio*?" Bronte asked.

"What hasn't? It's the new look. Everything is aluminum and black-and-white tile. Ersatz. Know what I mean? In lieu of taste, everything is black and white. It's emotionally cheap."

Yet another designer instructed workmen in the placing of original etchings and gouaches to be lighted from below by bulbs embedded in the wall. Santomassimo remembered when restaurants sold food, not ambience.

The elevator doors opened. They stepped in. Santomassimo pressed the top button, *Hasbrouk & Clentor*. The elevator glided upward with astonishing speed. When the doors opened, they were not in a hallway but already in a carpeted reception area of a massive suite.

A slender blond receptionist looked up. She looked very intelligent. Or was that opportunism in her eyes? She was stunningly outfitted in a gold blouse with small shoulder pads and a white skirt under an equally white desk. A single peony in a vase decorated her IBM computer.

"How may I be of assistance?" she asked.

Lieutenant Santomassimo walked closer, Bronte a step behind. They held out their police credentials.

"Lieutenant Santomassimo of the Los Angeles police," Santomassimo said. "We need to speak privately with Mr. Clentor."

She hesitated, and in her lovely black eyes Santomassimo saw all kinds of calculations and questions, but her smile never faded.

"Just one moment, please," she said, and lifted a softly rounded telephone receiver.

"Mr. Clentor?" she said gently. "I'm sorry to interrupt your call. The Los Angeles police are here. Lieutenant Santomassimo and Sergeant Bronte. They want to speak with you."

She listened, then hung up.

"Please go in," she said, and gestured to a walnut door.

The name *Miles Clentor* was embossed in gold leaf on the wood. An identical walnut door on the other side of the reception area read *William Hasbrouk*. Santomassimo knocked lightly and walked in without waiting for an answer.

Miles Clentor was a large walrus of a man, affable in the jowls, but menacing in the very small, darkly sparkling eyes. He grinned, showing evenly capped teeth, and shook Santomassimo's hand in a manly manner, and then Bronte's.

"Well," Clentor said. "Two of you. And no uniforms. So this isn't about that parking ticket last Thursday?"

Neither Santomassimo nor Bronte laughed. They sat without being invited. The office was the largest Santomassimo had ever seen. They could have played touch football between the plate glass windows, if the pile of the carpet wasn't so thick to have hindered running. Clentor must have had the same designer as the restaurant down below, because the fixtures here were also steel and aluminum, globes and strips, with odd juxtapositions of black-and-white tile, even on the wall over a fireplace mantel.

The view from the windows behind Clentor's desk included the entire downtown of Los Angeles, Dodger Stadium, all the way west to Westwood—the Cinema

Tower poked upward in a mild blue haze—and even to the Santa Monica cliffs. On a clear day, Clentor probably saw both the mountains and the ocean.

Clentor waited, his hands folded on his desk.

"Have you heard from Mr. Hasbrouk today?" Santomassimo asked gently.

Clentor maintained his smile, but slowly retreated in his leather chair.

"I don't like the sound of that, Lieutenant."

"I'm afraid it's possible that Mr. Hasbrouk was killed this morning, Mr. Clentor."

Clentor stared back, white-faced.

"—Bill—?"

"By a bomb," Bronte added. "A remote control flying bomb. In a toy airplane."

Clentor slowly collapsed against the chair, still staring at the two men.

". . . But you're not certain it was Bill?"

"We got a few fingerprints from Mr. Hasbrouk's car—not very good ones. We'd like our technical people to examine his office for any latents. It is necessary to compare them with the victim's fingerprints."

"Why didn't you just look in his wallet?"

"It was a big bomb, Mr. Clentor," Bronte said.

Clentor tried sitting up in a dignified position. He had a crooked smile, which Santomassimo had seen too often: a rictus of shock, an inability to comprehend the immediate present, an embarrassment in the face of death. His voice, though soft, sounded strangled.

"I gather you're pretty sure it *was* . . . Bill."

"At this point, we're not sure of anything, Mr. Clentor," Bronte said.

There was an impasse while Clentor absorbed the substance of what they had told him.

"Just . . . blown up—?" lentor said in a stupefied amazement. "—Entirely—?"

"There are *some* pieces," Bronte said.

"My God!—A toy airplane! Killed by a toy? How is that even possible?"

"Well, it wasn't the toy, Mr. Clentor," Santomassimo reminded him. "The toy was the vehicle. It was what was in the toy that killed him."

"*My God!*" Clentor repeated.

Santomassimo leaned forward, trying to fill Clentor's vision with himself, trying to gently but firmly break through the shock.

"Can you tell us something about Mr. Hasbrouk?" he asked. "What kind of man was he?"

"Bill? He was a wonderful man. A great partner, and a friend."

"Was he married?"

"His wife, Barbara, died three years ago."

"And since then—?"

Clentor squirmed on the chair. He toyed with a silver cigar box, his eyes misting over, growing red-faced. His voice was still firm. The anesthetic of shock, Santomassimo figured, was wearing off in phases.

"No. No women. Bill was that rare thing in the industry. A one-woman man. When Barbara died, that was it. No more romance. Not that he was too old, you understand. Bill was fifty-six. He was vigorous. In fighting trim. That's why he jogged. He had lots of excellent years ahead of him."

"Any children?"

"No children. It was just the two of them. And the industry. You could say business, the partnership, became his mistress after Barbara died."

Bronte cleared his throat. "Hasbrouk. Is that a Lebanese name?"

Clentor smiled. "Yes, but he was a Jew. A staunch supporter of the State of Israel."

"How did you get along with him, Mr. Clentor?" Santomassimo asked.

Clentor smiled again, but this was a warm smile, a beatific smile. "We got along perfectly. We were a perfectly matched pair. We came out of college in St. Louis and opened this agency at the age of twenty-eight. We've been together, through strikes, lawsuits, threats, and bonanzas, more than twenty-five years." The smile dropped like a mask from a Halloween trickster, revealing a horror-stricken, helpless man. Death appeared in the center of Clentor's eyes. He realized his partner was debris. "My God! Killed by a toy! I . . . I can't take it in . . ."

"Are you married, Mr. Clentor?" Santomassimo asked.

Clentor was crying openly now. He could only gesture at a portrait of his wife and their two children on his desk. Finally, he gained control.

"Happily so," he said, wiping his eyes with a linen handkerchief. "As you can see, we have two children. Both in college now. One's in law school—My God— Poor, dear Bill—I—can't . . ."

Clentor suddenly looked at them both with dead, level eyes. "I want you both to know that Bill Hasbrouk was a model human being. Not an enemy in the world. He was straight arrow. All the way." Clentor stared at them. Santomassimo sensed Clentor's penetrating mental control now, and guessed that the man deserved his top floor suite. "Who the hell would want him dead?" Clentor demanded.

"Mr. Hasbrouk was involved in lawsuits?" Santomassimo asked.

"Of course."

"Big money?"

"All our lawsuits are big money."

"Nothing out of the ordinary?"

"We aren't laundering cocaine money, Lieutenant Santomassimo."

"Lots of big money from strange places floats into film production. That's how it gets back into the United States."

"The film business is still ninety-five percent honest. We belong to that majority. We're an old-time firm, Lieutenant. Besides our management services, we promote films, package videos, handle distribution of commercials. Our name is gold."

"I'm sure it is. I have to consider everything, Mr. Clentor."

"No apology required."

Santomassimo and Bronte exchanged glances. They rose. Clentor looked up, startled. Either he expected more intense questioning or he was afraid of being left alone.

"We don't know who killed him, Mr. Clentor, and we don't know why," Santomassimo said. "But if the victim does turn out to be your partner, we may need to visit you again."

"Anything you need, you ask. You want to examine his office, tell Sheri to open his door. My God! His door—! He'll never walk through that door again—"

Clentor began crying again.

"We have to leave you now," Santomassimo said gently. "We're very sorry we had to be the ones to tell you."

Clentor waved at them with his handkerchief. Santomassimo and Bronte went to the door. Clentor's office must have been soundproofed because only when Santomassimo opened the door did the receptionist hear him sobbing. She rose, confused, and, giving them ambiguous looks, ran past them into his office.

They heard her soothing words and his crying all the way to the elevator.

Santomassimo drove, but less quickly, out to police headquarters. It was not smoggy, but the weather had turned unpleasant. A chill quality, like transparent metal enveloped the area. Abrupt changes in the weather always made him feel alienated from the city.

"What are you thinking?" Bronte asked, seeing Santomassimo's troubled brow.

"The way the killer toyed with him. I don't know. Humiliated him. Like a poison needle on a toilet seat."

"Yeah. Weird."

"The killer made a joke of the guy's existence. Why? Is this some kind of sport?"

Santomassimo maneuvered the Datsun to narrowly avoid running over a squirrel.

The squirrel, Santomassimo thought, had had more chance than Hasbrouk.

4

The Palisades Division Headquarters was crowded and the noise was deafening. Battens had been lowered from the ceiling but they only seemed to reflect voices and sounds of typewriters and radios in different directions.

Inside the large squad room marked DETECTIVES, Santomassimo bumped into two policemen wrestling a long-haired weight lifter into the double doors. Captain Wilton B. Emery appeared long enough to drop some documents onto Santomassimo's desk. Bronte went to his desk beside the watercooler to fill in the documents concerning the beach murder, but an elderly couple—recently robbed and visiting from out of state—were crying on the chairs in front of him.

Jim Bishop, a 20-year veteran, intercepted Santomassimo at the back of green filing cabinets. He was tall, dark-haired, with very small brown eyes. The

police uniform was always a little tight because of the
pressure of his gut.

"There's been a rape behind Pali High, Lieutenant,"
Bishop told him. "Captain Emery assigned me to
investigate. I'll need a partner."

"What about Sergeant Grisholm?"

"Sergeant Grisholm broke his forearm in two places
last night. Somebody hit him with a crowbar behind
Frascino's Restaurant."

Santomassimo glanced past the police technicians
carrying their macabre plastic bags from the beach
down to forensics in the basement for analysis. Bronte
was busy with the elderly couple, showing them a
thick book of identification photographs. The two
tourists were arguing about who had forgotten to buy
traveler's checks instead of bringing cash to California.

"What about Franklin?" Santomassimo asked.
"Why can't he go?"

"Franklin's been sent to investigate the Security
First National electronics burglary."

"He doesn't know anything about electronics."

"Still, the division has to interrogate the people and
the records. Before calling in the Feds."

Santomassimo sighed, looked at the schedule board.
There were two other detectives on duty, Mike Randolph and Henry Travis, but he knew that Randolph
was on an aggravated assault that had taken place at
3 AM behind the Safeway, and Travis was still at the
construction site behind the real estate offices on the
Coast Highway, combing the debris for remains of a
missing cocaine distributor.

"Let me check my desk, Jim," Santomassimo said.
"I'll meet you in ten minutes. Bring a patrol car
around."

"Right, sir."

The documents on Santomassimo's desk included a
deposition for a court case indicting a realtor who had

absconded with hefty deposits from seven different buyers. The realtor was long gone, but the victims were now suing the real estate company, and their lawyers wanted Santomassimo's notes.

There were two more court documents to fill out: an aggravated assault north of Sunset Boulevard, involving two bikers, and an arraignment, which had been mishandled by the division headquarters. Santomassimo sent to Records to see how the original documents had been filed.

A man had been picked up in Arkansas, and Captain Emery wanted Santomassimo to handle the extradition details. There had been a hit-and-run south of the beach. The San Francisco police believed the runaway car had been involved in a robbery in the Mission District. They wanted Santomassimo to double-check the license number, which had been improperly filed in the computer network. Because of the work overload some of the computer work was being done by new additions to the department.

A naked peeping tom had been spotted masturbating under the moonlight while peering into an apartment window.

"What a weirdo," Santomassimo chuckled.

At that moment, a policeman pushed a recalcitrant teenager to a desk and down onto a chair. The teenager got up to run away and Bronte reached over and slammed him back down. Santomassimo saw, beyond the teenager, Al Gilbert in the hall, drinking deeply from the watercooler and washing his face and neck. Detective Haber sat down at his desk and the telephone rang. Santomassimo watched Haber's pencil scrawl quickly over a pink sheet and then Haber abruptly left, taking the rookie cop, Terwilliger, with him.

Crime was increasing geometrically in Los Angeles. Santomassimo saw less and less charm, more and more sleaze.

Captain Wilton B. Emery, chief of detectives of the Palisades Division, poked his head out his office window.

"Fred," he called. "You will fill out these F6s, won't you? I know they're not exciting, but the parole board needs them."

"Soon as I get back from Pali High."

"You're going on the rape case?"

"With Bishop."

"What about the beach job?"

"Nothing left but a big hole, sir."

"Yeah. I saw the plastic bags. What did you do, excavate the whole damn place? Never mind. It's a clean way to go."

Captain Emery thought for a while, perhaps about mortality, maybe even about his own, or maybe it was only a spasm of indigestion, but something was bugging him.

"Stick around, Fred. Travis just pulled in from the construction site. I'll send him with Bishop."

Santomassimo studied his superior narrowly. "What's up?"

"That particular business with the airplane has a peculiar stink to it. I want you and Bronte to stay with it." Emery consulted his watch. "I know it's getting late, but I'll see you downstairs in forensics when you've got something to show me."

"Sure, chief," Santomassimo said, knowing it was going to be a long night.

It was dank in the basement of the Palisades Division Headquarters. Santomassimo watched as a man's forefinger was carefully rolled onto an inkpad and the end of the finger pressed into a tiny blue square on a police card. So did Bronte. The finger had no hand, arm, shoulder, or body. It was a piece of the jogger. A kid on a three-wheeled dune buggy had found it on the coast highway.

Santomassimo and Bronte then walked down the corridor to the forensics laboratory. It was a large room where the heating ducts and tubing protruded from the ceiling and dust continually fell, interfering with delicate tests. Yet the building had won an architectural prize. The architects, Santomassimo thought, didn't have to work here.

Echoes of men and women, municipal workers, police employees of all grades and descriptions, passed down the dark corridors outside. It was cold inside the laboratory. The architects probably never even visited the place.

Stan Liebowitz waited for them at a small bench, smiling smugly. Sooner or later Santomassimo and Bronte had to come to him. Liebowitz was the chief forensic scientist. He was a small man with a squashed head and thick spectacles. He looked like a very nice toad. Right now he held a model airplane in his right hand, painted silver, nondescript. Liebowitz used a pencil in his left hand to push the propeller, situated at the plane's nose, in and out on its shaft.

"Good evening Lieutenant Santomassimo," he said. "Good evening Sergeant Bronte."

"Good evening Mr. Liebowitz," Santomassimo answered. "What's the airplane?"

Liebowitz smiled again. He was a lonely man. He enjoyed attention. Slowly he pushed the prop in and out on its shaft. "This is a typical early version of the Luftwaffe's Messerschmitt, generalized in some of the detail. This one is made by Ravel Toys and comes in chrome or plastic," Liebowitz said. "The carrier of the bomb was made out of steel, so perhaps it was purchased in a specialty shop, not a toy store."

"Looks harmless," Bronte observed.

"The prop moves freely in and out," Liebowitz continued. "Behind the shaft, a detonator is rigged. Behind the detonator, about six ounces of plastique.

Nothing happens until impact. Then WHAM! The victim disappears."

"The killer must be quite an expert with these models. Guiding the plane with that pinpoint accuracy."

"Who knows?" Liebowitz said. "Practice makes perfect. Maybe he practiced at home. On the beach even."

"Maybe."

"You got anything at all on the victim?"

"If it *was* Hasbrouk he was a perfect human being." Bronte said. "Loved by all. No bad habits."

Santomassimo turned. The fingerprint technician was coming forward. He had the card of prints in his hand. Santomassimo had never asked what they did with things like fingers and toes. They couldn't just throw them in the furnace by the heating ducts, could they?

"He's the fellow, Lieutenant," the technician said. "The prints from the Biarritz, the prints from the office, the prints from the finger, all identical."

"Well," Liebowitz chuckled. "You got half the case solved."

"Huh?" Bronte grunted.

"You know who the victim is."

It was nearly nine o'clock in the evening before Santomassimo gathered up what evidence and leads he had to present to Captain Emery. The lights blazed in the parking lot and in some of the offices, but inside, down in the basement in Forensics it was dark, with small floodlights focused on a long metal table. On the table was the residue from the beach, laid out on a black grid that represented each segment of earth that the police technicians had sieved.

Besides Santomassimo and Bronte, there was Detective Haber and hard, uncomfortable Captain Emery. Their bodies cast multiple shadows on the table from the lights everywhere overhead. It was like working in a little Dodger Stadium at night.

Emery kept shifting his weight. He was in his middle forties, and had faced a lot in his twenty-three years on the force. Emery hated weirdness. Violence he understood, greed he was familiar with. Weirdness shook his equilibrium. Killing with a bomb-carrying toy airplane was worse than weird. Santomassimo, sipping black coffee from a Styrofoam cup, went down the long table. His other hand pointed out bits and pieces of garbage, subdivided by linear tapes. It even smelled bad, like the foul excretion of a sick world, made tidy and catalogued by the rational systems of police work, which had not the slightest idea of what, exactly it was dealing with.

"Fourteen different brands of cigarettes," Santomassimo recited. "Eight brands of beer and ale, two wines, both cheap, four quarters, a dime, two plastic rings, a 14-karat bracelet, bits of *The Los Angeles Times* sports section, lots of rocks, mostly granite, pebbles, condoms—"

"Used?" Captain Emery asked.

"Yes. One displays traces of blood. On the exterior."

"That's good," Detective Haber chuckled.

Santomassimo, Captain Emery, and Bronte stared at him. His chuckle stopped and his smile vanished.

"The fags are using rubbers," Detective Haber said soberly. "That's good. Isn't it?"

"Yes," Santomassimo said.

Captain Emery leaned forward, breaking the slight impasse. Detective Haber's attitude toward the gay community had recently come under public scrutiny. What Santomassimo's attitude toward gays was, Captain Emery did not really know, but he knew Santomassimo's attitude toward Haber. Santomassimo liked a smooth-running department, and public scrutinies interfered.

"What about the victim, Lieutenant Santomassimo?" Captain Emery asked, without hope. "Anything at all new there?"

"No, sir. We've checked into his background. Exactly what Clentor said. Pillar of the community. Health enthusiast. High-ranking member of the synagogue."

"What synagogue?"

"Beth Am. In Beverly Hills. He kept loyal to it when he moved to the Palisades."

"A Jew. A bomb? Suggest anything Middle East?" Emery asked.

Lieutenant Santomassimo shook his head.

"According to our few but informed local Israelites, Hasbrouk was politically unimportant to them. A donor, but not a massive one. No political connections. Not worth the trouble to blow up. Quote, unquote."

"Film in-fighting?"

"They kill you in the law courts, sir. Not with bombs."

"What about his partner, Clentor?"

"Clean. His time from home to office all accounted for. He was gassing up his Mercedes the moment Hasbrouk was being blasted."

Captain Emery got up gingerly, then reached for the model airplane Liebowitz had procured. He guided it through the air, as though visualizing it in flight.

"What the hell kind of M.O. is this, anyway?" he blurted. "What is he, a prankster? A toy freak? You ever come across an M.O. like this before, Lieutenant?"

"No, sir," Santomassimo answered.

He looked at Bronte and Haber. They also shook their heads.

"Well, what about bizarre M.O.s?" Emery exclaimed, impatient. "Can't we run a computer check on—on—weird ways of killing—?"

"We did that, sir," Santomassimo said. "It's not a normal category of filing, but—"

"But what? What did you find?"

Captain Emery's face was the color of chalk as he leaned over the detritus at Santomassimo. Santomassimo had never seen him so worked up. The case seemed vile to the captain. It was a personal affront to the way murders should be committed.

"There was a man in Bishop who clubbed whores to death with a twelve-inch dildo. I wish I were joking. He's doing life in Chino."

"What else?"

"In Sacramento, a woman ran a boarding house. She fed her guests Seconal in their soup, then, when they fell asleep, blinded them with her darning needle."

"Disgusting."

"She's at the State Facility for the Insane at Camarillo."

Captain Emery turned to Haber and Bronte, whose bodies were in the penumbra of the focused floodlights. They were opaque, shadowy, completely still, and no help at all. Captain Emery gestured at the debris, the airplane still in his hand.

"Does any of this shit mean anything to you?"

"Maybe later," Bronte said. "Not now."

Captain Emery stared down at the grid, then suddenly back at Santomassimo.

"Lieutenant Santomassimo," he said softly. "Tell me honestly. Do you expect him to hit anybody else?"

"You tell me, Captain. You tell me the motivation. All we have is a kinky *modus operandi*. I mean, who, or what, are we dealing with?"

"You want to know, Lieutenant?" Captain Emery asked. "I'll tell you."

The man looked down with Captain Emery as he put the toy airplane on the far end of the table. It looked ready to take off. Ready to fly high, circle, and swoop down on the debris, and perform its remote controlled extermination. The men looked a long time.

Over a landscape of bottle caps, pieces of rubber, coins, and one still yellow, still firm piece of buttered popcorn.

"A nutcake," Captain Emery finally admitted.

It was Santomassimo's custom on Friday night to go to the movies. *The Fires of the City* was a smash hit at the Bruin in Westwood. It was about a pair of policemen who interrupted a gang war, only to find themselves mixed up in the cocaine trade, and with supernatural elements of Haitian voodoo as well. The audience, mostly young couples, cheered as the cops blazed away with uzis in the jungle. But reality was never like that. Life was never so clean, so violent, in the police business.

Santomassimo vaguely watched the firefight of helicopters over a Florida marina as he chewed popcorn. But his mind was filled by the case at hand. What had Hasbrouk done that he deserved to be annihilated? Who had engineered his final moment with such diabolical *humor*? What was Hasbrouk's private cinema? The reality they can't show you on the screen, the violent disintegration of the brain?

And whatever happened to the soul? Aunt Rosa in Brooklyn believed that on the day of the Resurrection the body had to be whole. Hasbrouk's remains were by now either dumped in the Forensics crematorium or buried by Miles Clentor. Jews buried their dead fast.

Santomassimo drove to the Cafe Mediterranean on Santa Monica Boulevard. It was an Italian place, with excellent espresso and real *dolce pan,* licorice twists that Americans still didn't know about, and even seafood salads with a tomato sauce you couldn't get anywhere west of Naples, not even in Manhattan's Little Italy. They even got the fish from the Mexican coast, where it was not polluted.

Fortunately, the Cafe Mediterranean was not infected by the same epidemic of chrome, black-and-white tile, and aluminum globes. Like a bulwark of warmth and old European taste, here were huge bottles of Chianti, the necks three feet tall, garlic on strings, salamis, an ornate mirror frame from Tuscany, and every variety of pasta imaginable for the diner's inspection.

Since his divorce two years ago his life had settled into a disciplined pattern. Certain things had changed since then, physical things, for which Santomassimo had no rational explanation. He drank only espresso now, whereas before the divorce he had drunk tea. He had reverted to Italian food, but only at good restaurants. Milk chocolate had been his passion, and now it was bitter chocolate. And he no longer saw romances, only thrillers and police films.

Divorce is a sobering experience. That was when he learned about women.

"*Dolce*?" asked the waiter, gesturing to the sweets in the counter.

"*Dolce*? Yes, Phil. *Dolce far niente*. Sweet it is to do nothing."

"But you're not doing nothing, Lieutenant. You have that look. A bad case?"

"All kinds of bad cases."

The waiter, Phil, brought a marzipan roll with a napkin on a decorated plate.

Santomassimo read the final morning edition of *The Los Angeles Times*. There was nothing about the beach killing. Strange. Captain Emery might have delayed giving them a statement until too late for their deadlines. But the fat television reporter, Steve Safran, had probably not only mentioned the killing but shown his video tape on the eleven o'clock news. Safran was a relentless pursuer of the strange, the violent, and the uncanny. His late evening spot was always good for a shudder.

Santomassimo stirred the espresso with a tiny spoon

and watched the sea breeze rustle the dark shapes of palms outside on Santa Monica Boulevard. A movie was letting out across the street. *Killer's Harvest*. God knew what those images stirred up in the perfectly ordinary looking people leaving.

He considered going to see that film, because he did his best thinking at the movies, but he was fatigued.

"Another espresso, Lieutenant?" the waiter, asked.

"No. But thanks. I'd better get some sleep. I'll take a few of those Italian lemon cakes if you have some fresh."

"Made this afternoon."

"Terrific."

Santomassimo carried his lemon cakes in a little white paper bag to his blue Datsun.

He drove down to the coast highway. Here was his landscape: deserted, silky on the water, luminescent where the city lights reflected off the underbellies of clouds out over the pier. It was lonely, exciting, and full of secrets. The immensity of the black Pacific felt like a premature peek at death.

He parked his car in the basement of his condominium complex on Sunset Boulevard, just up from the Pacific Coast Highway, practically within view of the beach . . . and the murder scene. He took the elevator up to his apartment, ate one of the Italian cakes, and looked out over the terrace toward the beach. The view was partially hampered by other condos, and palm trees, but his imagination made up for what his eyes failed to discern.

He wondered what Bronte was thinking. They were both Italian, and that made them colleagues in a way that no one else in the division could be. But Bronte was always rumpled, a family man, easy to underestimate. Bronte was bothered by the beach murder. Bizarre killings are the worst cases to solve not only because of their random nature, but also because there is only one kind of clue to their motivations.

A second corpse. A third. Fourth.

Click.

"Technique . . . That's what it boils down to . . . Technique . . ."

Click.

"Goddamn fucking technique . . . Oh, Jesus . . ."

Click . . . The tape continued . . . recording . . .

"Moviemakers are endowed with extraordinary technique. I don't mean crap like slow motion and camera dissolves. I mean . . . how to redress a room so that you shoot in the same direction and make it look like two different ends of the room, how you never have to depend on nature or the way things are in reality. You fake EVERYTHING. You make normal people believe anything. By simply cutting two pieces of film together, you make an audience believe a guy is on the Amazon when he's really in Burbank.

"See, it's what people believe, what they can be made to believe. And it can be very, very real. I'm going to have to tell you now what I mean. I warned you it wouldn't be as simple as it seemed. And you're going to have to listen. You don't have much choice, do you?

"I escaped from Nebraska. Escaped is the operative word. I stole $200 from my father's wallet and took the train to Ohio, where my uncle worked as a gypsy film cutter, making cock movies. Well, the old fart didn't even recognize me. I had to tell him my mother's birthday and crap before he even let me in the house. Well, I showed him my films. I'd never stopped making them, you see, all those 8mm films and even a black-and-white 16mm film I made from outdated stock I got from a mail-order house. That one cost me $150. So I showed them to my uncle. He was a bad alcoholic. I'd never seen anybody twitch like that, all red and puffy under the eyes. And the only thing that potbellied creep would talk about was what a great editor he could have been if the unions had let him in.

"But in his eyes—after I took the black-and-white 16mm film off the projector—I saw the most wonderful thing in his rheumy little red eyes. Fear. I saw it and recognized it. The

same fear I had seen on the faces of the people in Nebraska. Because people, especially older men whose lives have slipped out of control, are afraid of natural talent. And I knew, however imperfect my films, however jumpy the cuts, and cheap and amateurish the direction, that he saw a raw, naked ability in there, a quality and drive he had never really had.

"He just got drunker and drunker. He started crying, slipping around the kitchen in his stocking feet, showing me his old awards for editing. He slobbered over moldy film in dusty cans he hadn't looked at in twenty years. It was repulsive. I almost vomited. But he gave me the address of somebody he knew in New York. An editor named Jerry Green.

I hitched, walked, and stole rides to Manhattan. I guess I should have been intimidated, all those weird people, the rich and the wretched and the tallest buildings in the world, but all I did was walk straight to Jerry Green's little production house, with my suitcase in one hand and six cans of my films in the other.

"Well, Green was okay. I mean, he was a fat little Jew with those stupid yellow knit shirts with the crocodiles on them that cost a fortune, and like my uncle he liked to reminisce about the old days when he had a fire in his belly. But eventually he put my films on his Steenbeck—he even had a way of looking at the 8mm—and we watched, there in his pristine white cubicle, all of my films. He didn't say much. Just handed the films back to me in their original cans.

"But this was the miracle. Even though he looked through his Rolodex and didn't come up with more than three or four names that might help me, he talked to me like an equal. Do you understand? No condescension. No bullshit. He knew I'd had shit for equipment. He knew what Nebraska was like. But as far as he was concerned, I had made it. I was part of the brotherhood.

"Well, he let me sleep on the floor of his office, which was pretty generous, considering he didn't really know me and had expensive things in there which I could have stolen. He wasn't married and I don't think he had any unnatural feelings about me. Just lonely. And gradually I began to learn what Manhattan is like.

"See, I had this romantic idea that I was doing it the right way. You sleep on studio floors. You walk from office to office and get condescending looks. You're poor and one sandwich has to last the whole day. You get robbed—I was robbed twice—and you smell bad. And the weather gets bad. You meet people who once wanted to do films and now they're wasted on cocaine or alcohol, or maybe they sell their bodies at night to pay for the film stock for the next day. But in the end, you prevail, right? Isn't that the American story? Sure it is.

"So I was in hell. But my faith never wavered. I just felt time was getting short, that was all. I was past twenty-four in fact. Orson Welles was twenty-five when he directed Citizen Kane. Of course, I knew I wasn't Orson Welles. On the other hand, there were times I felt I was better than Welles—more consistent . . . I was tormented by visions, sequences, whole passages of films I wondered if I would live long enough to make. These images came upon me with a force that is impossible to describe. Since I had no camera, no crew, I wrote them down as scripts just in case I should forget. I must have written thirteen scripts in only four months, plus pounding the pavements, reading in the library, seeing films at the museums, and working part-time as a dishwasher, fending off some of New York's night life, because in all honesty, I was always better than average looking. I just want you to get an idea of the sheer intensity of the life I was living.

"And my parents? I think they wrote once. I never wrote to them. They were baffled by this craze of mine. They were embarrassed by it. New York? Making movies? It was like communism or sex with dogs. They didn't even talk about me with their friends.

"It gets pretty fucking cold in December in New York. It's a terrible place to have put a city that big. Jerry Green had to move me out of his studio on account of his moving into a small sound studio. I lived for a while with somebody I'd met washing dishes—separate beds, so keep that out of your mind—but my half of the rent was putting a heavy burden on me. I kept catching colds, especially in the chest, because I couldn't afford a winter coat. There were icicles inside our room, and frost patterns on the window glass. I

*was almost twenty-five. I felt like my talent had reached a
point where if it didn't mobilize itself soon, it would start to
die. I began to feel for the first time that what had happened
to my uncle and to Jerry Green, and all the wasted individ-
uals you see hanging around film crews in the city, could all
happen to me. I wasn't invulnerable any more.*

*"I got very paranoid, and began moving my scripts
around and hiding them from my roommate, who could
hardly read English, much less a script.*

*"So listen to what happened. I did it. I got a job on a
cheap non-union shoot in New York. A job, did I say? Let me
explain. I was one of twelve or thirteen unpaid production
assistants. None of us got paid. Experience was our pay.
Almost instantly, I realized the truth of it, that they needed to
take on people who'd work for nothing, who'd take up the
slack and do the shit details. There were plenty of young
people out of schools interested in working on a 'real' film,
and they were desperate, just the way I was, and fighting to
be exploited. They did it for free. God knows what the girls
had to do to get the jobs. But they did it for free, worked any
hours they were asked. And I was just one of them.*

*"I swept up and got coffee for people. I helped move
furniture into the rooms where the filming was going on. I
carried cable—not the cameras, nobody trusted me to get
near the expensive equipment—I remember the film cost a
million and a half and there was this big staff, and everybody
knew it was a turkey. The gaffers and camera people were
such losers. Such egos. They fought all the time. And deep
down I knew, I felt, that they didn't know as much about film
as I did. I had seen the classics, I had grown up on celluloid,
and these clowns were commercial makers, masturbators,
grown-up children with expensive toys.*

*"They really should have been put in jail, the way they
treated us. Like slaves. Not one person called me by my
name. I worked sixteen hours a day, six days a week,
coughing my lungs out, and the snow coming in through the
flaps in my shoes, and all the while I was tortured by the
visions that were coming to me, that I had to scribble down
at night and at odd moments, that growing fear that maybe
I was dying and would never get my ideas made. Never*

make reality out of what was inside me. Never change other people in a permanent way.

"It was so horrifying—"

Click . . .

"I can't go on with this . . . My head is . . . coming apart . . ."

Click . . . The tape rolled on . . .

"Where was I? Oh, yes. How could I forget? I tried so hard to forget. All my dreams, and they trample on them with dirty boots.

"One morning we shot in a bar called The Nightingale, and the owner bitched about the dirt the crew made on the corner (we shot there way past midnight). So the production manager dismissed everyone but the production assistants and told us to wrap-out. Understand this is three or four in the morning. He puts a broom in my hand, and orders me to sweep the crap down the street. I said, 'You want me to sweep the gutter?' He said, 'Yeah, it's a health hazard, the city'll get on our case, so start sweeping.' And I objected. And he got angry. He shouted, 'What do you think you're here for? We need you to do this! It's your job on this picture!'

"Always that veiled threat; we can find someone else to do this, the city's full of eager film students, there are plenty of people who want to work on movies. And I don't like you much anyway.

"So I got in the gutter. I swept it. You know New York. They have mounted policemen. Ethnic parades. Every goddamn day there's some other immigrant group celebrating its arrival to these blessed shores. Are you listening? It was very dark and all kinds of zanies were wandering around and I was sweeping huge chunks of some enormous animals's frozen feces—I can still see the fucking pieces of straw sticking out golden stiff—and half-frozen vomit—must have been recent from The Nightingale. I could have puked. I stood there, thinking: I was born, raised, and driven by some irrational, overpowering dream, maybe even, who knows, a genuine talent, for this? To sweep the gutter on Second Avenue and Thirteenth Street and clear the worst excrements into the clotted drains? I ruined my health, risked everything, to be treated like this? To be turned into something subhuman? Horrible . . . Humiliating . . .

"Technique . . ."

Click . . . The tape recorder was still. Far away were the sounds of the big city, and the gleam of the world's biggest ocean . . . After a long pause, the tape recorder began recording again, and the voice was calmer . . .

"The L.A. police . . . shit . . . I didn't even make The Los Angeles Times . . . I guess there are so many killings out here one more or less doesn't count . . ."

Click . . . The tape reversed . . . stopped, went forward, erasing . . .

"Better not put that on tape. The cocksuckers . . ."

Click . . . The tape continued . . .

"Technique . . . " The voice now continued, happier, being recorded. "Yes. Technique." It's not easy, doing this. Let's just say, in the light of recent success, which far exceeded anything I had even dreamed of . . . Let's just say I have this need, again, tonight . . . to direct . . .

"I am, after all, a director . . .

"CUT! CUT!"

5

The Windsor Regency was the jewel in the crown of downtown Los Angeles's new architecture. In the central atrium was a bar, dance floor, reception desk, steps leading to a sunken restaurant, and escalators to the mezzanine. Bellhops pushed hand trucks, mountainous with luggage, and the noise of conventioneers rumbled and clinked, echoing off the surrounding walls. For the surrounding walls zoomed upward thirty-five stories, each floor lined with hanging ferns like a Hanging Garden of Babylon, up to and including an absolutely open sky window, where palms shook in the roof garden.

Strategically placed spotlights and wall lights kept a perpetual daylight inside the atrium. It was timeless, like Las Vegas, but the colors were subdued, dignified, for the clientele here came to generate wealth, not lose it. It was like being in a pyramid turned inside out, eternal, a place of events on the cutting edge of history.

Nancy Hammond was twenty-three years, five months, and two days old when she checked in at the desk. She wore her blonde hair short but swept back over the ears. It was her first visit to the West Coast. The severe and professional cut of the maroon jacket, with the laminated card *Pier Industries, Inc.* did not hide her excitement. Even after she received her key, she went to the agenda board, a gilt-edged velvet rectangle mounted on an easel, and read: *October 1– 3: Secretarial Convention of Import/Export and Trading Firms*. Relieved that she officially existed, or at least her convention did, she went with the bellhop into the sleek glass elevator and rode upward to her room on the twelfth floor.

The other bellhop, who worked the north face, Armando Lupe, later testified that he had noticed, very early that morning, while rolling a coffee wagon down the wide, softly carpeted, hushed corridor, a whirring noise from Room 1207. It had seemed odd that workmen would be making adjustments, since Mr. Ates had spent the night without complaint.

It had sounded like a drill, or somebody scraping rough, braided cord over metal.

Armando had been curious, but Mr. Townshend was waiting in Room 1201 for his morning coffee. Mr. Townshend was sharing coffee with a new friend. Mr. Townshend would not like to be kept waiting. Mr. Townshend was a senior vice president of Hewlett-Packard Corporation, and so Armando had kept rolling the coffee cart onward.

When Nancy Hammond came onto the twelfth floor, there were people from yet another convention anxiously looking at her lapel plastic. She and the bellhop wormed their way through the crowd, and the door to Room 1207.

She was not sure what to tip. Whatever the bellhop

thought, he smiled nicely and said, "Have a pleasant convention, Miss Hammond." The bellhop left. Nancy swirled around the room. The view over the brilliant city below was fantastic. There was a light fog, and it made the lights radiate.

It seemed impossible that any city could stretch so to infinity. Chicago was large, but it had dark areas, the lakes, parks, and railroad terminals. Los Angeles below went out to horizons that belonged to science fiction. There was a taste of future in the air, something impossibly subtle, and glorious beyond all definition.

She was so excited she telephoned her mother in Evanston. She talked twenty-three minutes, then looked yet once again at the leather-bound agenda in her briefcase. Tomorrow was the presentation from IBM and after that a tour of more computer ware from Toshiba, followed by dinner on the beach.

The prints on the wall were subtle beige, and matched the patchwork pattern on the bed. It was glamour, she thought. It was excitement. There were even spotlights at odd places in the city, like premier openings to magnificent films.

She did not drink, but made an exception when she saw the miniature—and complementary—bottle of California chablis in a small refrigerated chest. It was a sparkling chablis. Nancy did not like champagne, but she felt transcended in the Windsor Regency.

Then she saw the gleaming tiles and brilliant mirror in the bathroom—somebody must have left the mirror lights on for her—the door slightly ajar, and the delicately wrapped miniature soaps and shampoos. There was a sensuous promise in those expensive soaps. She undressed, slipped into her white terry robe and then, savoring the moment, looked again out the window at Los Angeles.

So big, she thought. So mysterious. So much energy. So quiet for such a big city. Like an ocean. One could sail on the energy of an ocean of light like that.

She pulled the drapes shut. The wine made her feel agreeably warm inside. She turned on the television. It seemed like there were a thousand stations, only half of them in English. Some of the Japanese stations seemed to have Korean subtitles. There was an old black-and-white film of Delhi and a mariachi band on a Mexican ranch. Then she found the MTV station. She moved in syncopated rhythm to its rhythm-and-blues inflected drums.

She danced, letting the robe slip, into the bathroom. Her body glowed softly in the mirror lights. The mirror was flattering, but accurate. The young breasts, slender waist, the hips—all part now of that same undefined future, breaking now upon her like a distant, ineffable wave. Nancy opened a bath gel. There was an aroma of jasmine.

She reached into the tub and adjusted the shower control. Somebody had left it on extreme cold. She turned it halfway to hot, then turned on the water. She bent toward the mirror to examine her face for blemishes. Sometimes excitement brought on blemishes. But so far, so good. The mirror grew steamed from the hot water. She saw her own face dissolve away.

Nancy Hammond pulled the shower curtain aside, stepped into the shower. She reached down to pull the tub lever so that water wouldn't collect. Suddenly, before she could smell smoke, she saw a blinding flash that collected in the back of her brain. Then nothing forever. It was her ineffable future.

Room 1207 was clogged with police technicians and their paraphernalia. Doorknobs, windows, and furniture were carefully dusted for fingerprints. A policeman vacuumed the floor. Two other policemen redirected the curious out of that part of the twelfth floor. More technicians crowded in the bathroom, measuring, photographing, tracing.

Lieutenant Nathan Hirsch of the Central Division questioned a Mexican maid.

"Now, Carlotta," Hirsch said carefully. "You're telling me you didn't clean the bathroom at all this morning?"

"Was no reason," Carlotta said defensively. "Was clean. Sink. Shower. Towels."

"But wasn't there a Mr. Ates, a financial investor, here last night?"

Carlotta colored. "The soap still had paper on it. The toilet seat still had paper across it. Paper not broken."

Santomassimo and Bronte quietly entered the room. They stood in the background. Hirsch saw them, which threw him off stride, and then he recovered. He turned to the manager, a sallow fellow with spectacles, nervously scratching his knuckles.

"Isn't it a rule of the Windsor Regency that when anyone checks out you clean the bathroom, whether it's been used or not?" Hirsch asked him.

"Yes, or course. I—Carlotta, we clean all bathrooms, don't we? Whether they've been used or not? Comprende? Hotel rules."

Carlotta's dark eyes flashed darker. "Only I'm glad I no clean, Mr. Cornell. Or is me is dead. No priest, no nothing. Boom."

Neither Hirsch nor the manager could refute logic so unassailable.

In the other end of the bedroom two plainclothes detectives interrogated the bellhop, Armando Lupe.

Hirsch rose from the sea-green upholstered chair, moving slowly. He stood at the threshold of the bathroom and gradually the technicians sensed his presence and stopped working. They looked back, gauging his mood, waiting for orders, like loyal dogs.

Hirsch walked into the bathroom. He was aware of

Santomassimo and Bronte coming in with him, but he still said nothing.

A detective turned away and gingerly extracted an electric wire from a hole in the drain pipe. Both ends of the wire were stripped of their rubber casing.

The other end of the wire was plugged into a floor outlet beneath the sink. The detective unplugged the wire and waved it triumphantly at Hirsch.

"It's ingenious," the detective said. "The killer drills a hole in the drain pipe—we found metallic shavings— Then he puts the live end inside and caps the drain." He demonstrated by reaching into the bathtub. He pushed a lever, and capped the drain. He turned back, smiling at the faces staring down at him. "The other end he plugs into the light socket right in plain sight, gambling she won't notice it, and she doesn't. She steps into the shower, finds a buildup of water in the tub, bends down to release the drain, and her convention is over.

"Shit," Lieutenant Hirsch suggested. And added, "Royal fuck. Swollen balls. Weird games. That's all I need."

"It's a random hit, isn't it?" Santomassimo observed. "The killer wouldn't know who was checking in here, would he?"

"Maybe. Maybe not," Hirsch muttered. "I don't know who had access to the hotel registration book."

Lieutenant Hirsch, slightly in bad posture due to fourteen hard years of pounding a beat, turned to face Lieutenant Santomassimo. Santomassimo was natty, as usual, dressed in a clean, neat black suit, like the early Marcello Mastroianni. Bronte looked like something more out of early Fellini: rumpled, awkward, provincial. But Hirsch knew not to underrate Bronte.

"Hey, Santomassimo," Hirsch said, as though just seeing him for the first time. "This ain't your territory. Did I call for you? Or were you coming to the convention anyway?"

"Just interested, Nate. Heard it on the radio and had an intuition to come."

"Yeah? Why?

"The M.O. It's weird."

"Yeah. A fucking nut," Hirsch agreed. "Aren't you guys supposed to be investigating a freak killing on the beach? A gangland execution or something? I hear it's getting busy up there."

"You read the newspapers."

"Saw it on *News with Steve Safran* last night before I went to bed. How does that guy get on these cases so fast? Does he make the appointment with death?"

"I believe he must, Nate."

Lieutenant Hirsch grinned at Sergeant Bronte's nervousness. "Yeah," he drawled, "jogger killed by toy plane packed with explosives. I hear they've set up a community watch at Palisades beach. You don't think it's the same nut, Fred?"

"Maybe," Santomassimo answered.

Bronte dug Santomassimo in the ribs. *"Let's get the hell out of here,"* he pleaded.

"Hold on, Lou," Hirsch said. "I'm talking to Fred." Lieutenant Hirsch put a fatherly arm on Santomassimo's shoulder, notwithstanding that Santomassimo was four inches taller. Hirsch led him to the mirror, where they sat on the marbled counter top.

"Consider the similarities, Fred," Hirsch said in a mock logic lecture. "Random killing. Victim has no connections to killer. Girl is one tiny part of a three-hundred-person convention. She is assigned Room 1207 purely by luck. All of it bad."

"Keep going."

"Okay. Guy on the beach. Early morning jogger. Maybe the killer laid in wait. Maybe it, too, was random. A handy target. A sport. A game. The M.O.s, Fred—my God! A toy plane. A hot wire in a shower. The odds against two crazies, simultaneously active, must be about as great as my winning the Oscar for best leading actor with dentures. Even Los Angeles has *some* stability."

"A little."

Bronte now came to the marbled counter and intruded himself between the two men.

"No, Fred!" He turned to Hirsch. "Now look, Lieutenant Hirsch, you're not going to push this case on us. Just because we were curious. We've got thirteen cases in addition to the Palisades Beach dive-bomber."

"Calm *down,* Sergeant," Hirsch said. "Be respectful. I'm not pushing anything. Besides, it's still Lieutenant Santomassimo I'm talking to." Hirsch turned from the chastened Bronte. "What do you think, Fred?" Hirsch whispered. "It *is* the same killer. Isn't it? Huh? Don't look at Bronte. Look at me. *It's the same killer,* isn't it?"

Santomassimo stared at the end of the wire, lying on the tile on a piece of cloth the detective had placed there. The copper end gleamed, like a snake's eye, brilliant in the mirror lights, menacing, inscrutable.

"Yes."

"Oh, shit, Fred," Bronte wheezed, rubbing an agitated hand through his thinning hair.

"It is, Lou," Santomassimo said quietly. "you know it is, too. But so what?" He turned back to Hirsch. "You offering me this case, Lieutenant?"

Hirsch put up his palms defensively. "No, no, Fred. I haven't the authority to do that—unless, that is—you requested the transfer. I'd be agreeable to it, and I'm sure I could make Homicide see the logic of it. What do you say, Fred?"

Santomassimo considered Hirsch's offer thoughtfully while Bronte fumed. Finally, Santomassimo nodded resignedly.

Hirsch exploded in a gleeful chuckle, slapped Santomassimo on the knee, and stood up. His voice suddenly became authoritative, urgent.

"Wind it up, boys," he ordered. "The case now belongs to the Palisades Division."

Santomassimo and Bronte rode down from the twelfth floor. Below them rose, through the curved glass and ferns of the elevator, the entire atrium of the Windsor Regency, an acre of luggage, carts, people, bar hostesses and men with slide projectors, microphones, and charts, setting up for the next day's conventions. The noise echoed and re-echoed, until it sounded like a Roman circus.

"I couldn't believe it when you were so curious to see this homicide," Bronte finally let out, "but I'll be damned if I understand why you want to take it."

"What does your head tell you, Lou? Was this done by the same killer or not?"

"I don't know."

"I think Lieutenant Hirsch was very decent to let us have the case, don't you?"

"I don't think Captain Emery will like this."

The elevator doors opened. Women in business suits, their lapels pinned with laminated cards, came in, filling the elevator with aromas of perfume. Santomassimo stepped out, while Bronte bumped and struggled past the women.

"Hirsch has dumped you with a piece of compost!" Bronte shouted, changing the last word at the last instant in the interest of public politeness.

Santomassimo ignored him. He was pushing through a group of secretaries, many from Pier Industries, almost all in tears, some sitting, shocked and dazed on leather couches while the staff of the Windsor Regency brought them tea.

It was very quiet around the registration desk. There were three desk clerks, all in red and gold, but even the few visitors nearby looked down, ashen, and Santomassimo felt the funereal taste of the day in their quick, surreptitious glances at him. They looked at him as though for help, to save them from the brute fact of death, and a vile, violent death at that, perpetrated through the hotel's own fixtures.

They also had the guilt that Santomassimo had seen often: a secret pleasure of standing alive when death had so arbitrarily tossed somebody down the tubes.

The chief desk clerk, Silva Portrera, had no memory of Nancy Hammond. But then, more than two hundred women had checked into the Windsor Regency that day, not to mention another two hundred, male and female, attending the concurrent airplane safety, and orthopedic surgeons conventions in the Blue and Gold Suite and the North Tower Ballroom.

Portrera was a tanned man in his early forties. Police made him feel guilty, even though he had never even parked in a red zone. It was a spiritual thing. Life was hard in Los Angeles. The police worked for people for whom life was easy. Nevertheless, he put on his best, most obsequious smile when he saw Lieutenant Santomassimo coming.

The scandal of the murder was in the process of permeating the hotel, through the entire atrium, the ballrooms, even to the lowest corner of the sunken restaurant. Portrera could see the information spread in little waves through the Windsor Regency, and he disliked the morbid little smiles and gleams of intense interest in the eyes of self-assured strangers savoring the news. The lieutenant seemed to see the same thing with the same disgust.

Portrera's hands shook under Santomassimo's eyes. There was no reason, and it embarrassed Portrera, which made the shaking worse. Should he have refused a room to the young woman on the grounds that she would soon be dead in the bathroom?

"I need to see whatever information you have on the

gentleman who occupied the room last," Santomassimo said.

Portrera flicked through the registration cards,
picked one out, and handed it to Santomassimo.

"This is the man who occupied Room 1207 the day
before Miss Hammond checked in," he said.

Santomassimo studied the card. Without looking
back, he handed the card to Bronte, whom he sensed
behind him. Bronte squinted down at the card.

N.B. Ates. 121 Holly Drive, Fresno, California. Party
of one. No car. No license plate. Oddly, no home
telephone. Representing himself. Bronte copied down
the information in his notebook.

A memory—something less than a memory—an
image—suddenly flitted to the edges of Santomassimo's consciousness, elusive, alive, taunting, unreach-
able. His brow furrowed in deep thought, but it would
not come.

"There's no credit card slip attached," Bronte said
to Portrera. "Doesn't the Windsor Regency require
credit slips?"

"Whenever possible, sir," Portrera replied. "But
many people don't have credit cards."

"People who stay in a place like the Windsor Regency?"

"Sometimes people like to be private."

"Private?"

"Yes, and if the guest has luggage, or is known to
us personally, we'll accept cash on a one-night basis."

"One night. Okay. I get it."

Bronte turned to Santomassimo, but the lieutenant
was lost in thought. He probably had heard nothing in
the last minute, Bronte realized, chasing down after a
slippery notion. Bronte cleared his throat.

"Anything else, sir?" Bronte asked, clearly and
loudly.

"Hmmmm? Oh. Yes. Yes . . . Mr., ah, Portrera. I

don't suppose you could give us a description of Mr. Ates?"

Portrera smiled dully. The adrenalin from the excitement of the news of the murder was gone, leaving him fatigued, his mind embarrassingly numbed.

"I have been in the hotel service fifteen years, Lieutenant," Portrera said quietly. "Two years at the Windsor Regency, since it opened. The faces I see are faceless. Thousands of noses, lips, eyes, hair. Gray, black, white, blond. Blurs of features, but no faces anymore."

"Thanks."

"Figure it out, Lieutenant," Portrera said. "Two hundred people, four hundred people a week, fifty weeks a year, fifteen years. You haven't got that many faces in your identi-kit folders."

"I think we do."

The manager, Mr. Cornell, had been hovering by the edge of the registration area in a blaze of golden-white glitz caused by the reflective specks in the counter. Santomassimo beckoned and he came forward brushing back his black hair.

"Yes, Lieutenant," Mr. Cornell said. "How can I help you?"

"Have you checked all the bathrooms in the hotel?"

"Yes. Lieutenant Hirsch, before he transferred the case to you, told me to. Our maintenance crew has gone systematically out from the north side. So far, no problem."

"I want you to instruct your staff not to speak to the television crews or newspaper reporters."

The manager nodded to Portrera, who took it as a command, and Portrera lifted up a receiver and began telephoning the staff supervisors.

"Your hotel doesn't need rumors," Santomassimo said, "and neither does the Los Angeles police."

"Quite right, Lieutenant."

"Also, the last four rooms of the corridor, which

includes Room 1207, will stay cordoned off pending the completion of police examination. So you might want to reshuffle some of your guests."

Portrera and the manager exchanged glances. Santomassimo guessed the hotel was completely booked, and now there would be four highly irate conventioneers. Eight if the rooms were shared. It gave Santomassimo an unjustifiable twinge of pleasure.

"We will cooperate fully with your investigation, Lieutenant Santomassimo," the manager said.

"I know you will. Thanks."

Santomassimo and Bronte left, feeling the same sensation they had felt on the beach. Nancy Hammond had been exterminated instantaneously, like Hasbrouk. In the prime of life. Unsuspecting. It was a quirky death. With just that odd sense of cruel, random precision.

Outside the Windsor Regency, Santomassimo saw instantly that any plea for discretion was ludicrous. There was a crowd that blocked both the near sidewalk and the sidewalk across the boulevard. The faces had the same awed, congealed curiosity that the beach crowd had had. And no wonder. In a sudden, complete silence, two ambulance drivers wheeled out the corpse of Nancy Hammond.

The corpse was wrapped in a clean, brown blanket, and then a plastic sheet that completely covered her, leaving only the generic human shape on the stretcher. Santomassimo knew she was nude underneath. If the crowd only knew, he thought. Nancy Hammond was lifted, stretcher and all, into the ambulance's rear. The drivers slammed the doors and locked them. The crowd sighed.

Lights blazed everywhere on the boulevard: traffic headlights, patrol cars, shop windows, the Windsor Regency floodlights implanted below the rubber trees outside. More light spilled out from the crowded atrium. Suddenly, the brightest light of all, a hot blue-white, struck Santomassimo full in the face.

It was the fat reporter, Steve Safran, guiding his cameraman deftly through the crowd.

"How about a statement, Lieutenant?" Safran shouted.

"Go f—" The camera was recording. "I have nothing to say at this time."

The cameraman was tensed into a human tripod, bent slightly backward, hips jutted forward. It would have been obscene had he not had a video camera on his shoulder and his face to the eyepiece.

Safran came closer. The microphone, attached to the lower end of the camera, pointed at Santomassimo's mouth. Safran grinned. Dogs have that look when they've cornered something.

"You're way out of your jurisdiction, Lieutenant," Safran shouted.

"Yes."

"Are you assisting the Central Division, Lieutenant Hirsch?"

"In a manner of speaking."

"Are you taking over the case?"

"The case is being transferred."

Santomassimo felt distinctly uncomfortable under the portable lights. The crowd, too, had turned its attention to him. He was almost as interesting as the corpse had been.

"It tells us there's a connection between the murder at the Windsor Regency and the Palisades dive-bomber," Safran suggested.

"I cannot speculate publicly."

"Come on, Lieutenant. You didn't come here to look at the roof garden."

"Excuse me. I cannot say any more at this time."

"Lieutenant Santomassimo—"

"I'm sorry."

Santomassimo pushed right between Safran and the

cameraman, Bronte following. Santomassimo felt the hot portable lights on the back of his neck, and heard, with decreasing clarity, Safran describing the brutal electrocution in room 1207. Santomassimo checked his watch. Safran had a few minutes, but would probably get it on the eleven o'clock news.

People made way, but what infuriated Santomassimo was that they gobbled Mars bars and Snickers and tossed the wrappers into the gutter, like they were watching a film. Someone slurped Coke through a straw, peering at what action there was right through the ambulance window. Santomassimo even thought he saw a hand with gleaming, yellowed, buttered popcorn.

The Palisades Division Headquarters was located on Sepulveda Boulevard and Santa Monica Boulevard, two blocks west of the San Diego Freeway, about three miles away from the quick slope to the rocks and sand of the beach itself. Eucalyptus trees grew behind the parking lot. It might as well have been on the moon. It was dominated by a pale yellow haze of smog.

Santomassimo entered into the tumult of the night crews bringing in suspects, the typewriters and word processors clacking, voices yelling, traffic roaring outside on the main road, and he could faintly smell the sea breeze. It was vaguely unpleasant, an infinite kind of feeling. Like something bigger than life and much meaner.

He sat at his gray metal desk and began typing from his handwritten notes on the murder by electrocution at the Windsor Regency. He finished the bottle of Pepto Bismol and dropped it thunderingly into his empty wastebasket. The insidious care with which the homicide had been carried out turned his stomach. He had come across nothing like it. Except for Hasbrouk's last jog down the beach.

Captain Emery's door opened.

"Santomassimo. Get in here. Right now."

It was a bad sign when the captain called him by his last name. Santomassimo crossed himself, more in irony than devotion, but nevertheless did not fail to kiss his thumb. He rose, straightened his tie, smoothed his hair back, and tucked in his shirt. It had been a hell of a day, and the day wasn't over yet. He wasn't even paid overtime. He went down to the captain's door and raised his hand to knock.

"Santomassimo?" Captain Emery's voice called from inside. "Get your ass in here!"

He opened the door, closed it carefully behind him, and approached the captain's desk.

Captain Emery's face was the color of a tomato with mildew problems. He was leaning far over the desk at him, but all the lieutenant saw were the captain's eyes with new shades of color in them.

"By what *fucking right* do you transfer a case from Central Division to Palisades?" Emery yelled. "Without so much as asking me? What am I, a piece of goddamn shit? *I AM YOUR SUPERIOR OFFICER, LIEUTENANT! YOU CONSULT ME! YOU ASK MY AUTHORIZATION!!*"

"Sir, I—"

"*SHUT UP!* Don't you believe in picking up telephones any more, Lieutenant? Did you think the killer had them hotwired? You couldn't go across the street? Tell Bronte to call me from a booth? Send a carrier pigeon?"

"I believe—"

"You're not talking now, Santomassimo! I AM! And I am saying that you ask my fucking permission before you let that goat balls Hirsch sweep his problems through my door!"

Santomassimo knew to wait for the fury to subside. Captain Emery seemed lost for words to express the full extent of his anger. The captain sat down, looking suddenly very old. It must have been the poor lighting, because he abruptly swiveled in his chair and viciously dialed a number on the telephone.

"Who are you calling, sir?" Santomassimo said as quietly, but as clearly, as he could.

"Who do you think? I'm bouncing this baby right back in Hirsch's face."

Santomassimo stepped forward and pressed the telephone's button, disconnecting it. Captain Emery stared at Santomassimo's fingers as though a papal sacrilege had been committed.

"Wait, Bill," Santomassimo said. "Before you do that, let me say something."

Once Captain Emery had thrown the telephone at Detective Haber. It had ripped the cord jack from the wall and sent the flower vase, paper, paperweight, and assorted pencils and pens flying out the open window. Santomassimo now saw Emery's hand grip the logbook on the desk.

"All right," the captain said with a terrifying, trembling calm. "Say something."

Santomassimo felt the veteran's eyes on him. It was every performer's nightmare. He blanked momentarily, and then it came to him, smoothly. He even bent forward toward the captain.

"We've been together twelve years now," he said carefully. "We worked the same beat together, same neighborhood, Korean, Filipino, Latin American, black. All those changes, and we were there together. We even got our stripes at the same time. You went a lot farther than I did because you were smarter . . ."

"Don't oil my ass, buster. It tickles. What's your point?"

"Okay. All right. I know, on the face of it, you're right. Sure you're right. We've got a casework load that would cripple a department twice our size. We don't need one last straw."

"This is very persuasive, Fred."

"The Windsor Regency murder is our baby, Bill."

"Fuck a duck. Fuck two."

"And you know it."

"I know no such thing."

Irritated, Captain Emery leaned backward, close to the division map on the wall. It covered from east of Santa Monica to Will Rogers State Beach, alleys, the Coast Highway, and all the housing developments, knolls, even the railroad track. Santomassimo knew it by heart. There wasn't an acre that hadn't had a beating, a robbery, a rape, or a murder. He leaned farther over Captain Emery. Emery didn't like it but he was trapped against the wall and its map.

"Come on, Bill!" Santomassimo pursued. "Random victim? Kinky, motiveless? Something just a little . . . what? . . . *cat-and-mousing* with some unsuspecting person . . . ?"

"Committed twenty miles apart. Los Angeles is a big city, Fred. Lots of freaks."

"Look at the M.O.s. Tricky. Dramatic. Death comes from outer space. Immediate. Extermination. A toy plane, a hot wire in a shower. And consider: technically adroit, plotted with care, with a sick imagination. A bit of genius."

"You're dreaming."

Santomassimo grinned. Captain Emery watched him with hands folded behind his neck, a posture that Santomassimo knew meant he was being drawn into the hypothesis.

"This is just a beginning, Bill," Santomassimo said. "He'll kill again."

"I don't buy this, Fred."

"Of course you do. There'll be more killings, Bill. Just as kinky. Crazy killings. Harbor Division. Foothill Division. Van Nuys. Devonshire. This guy will have the whole Los Angeles Police Department playing Keystone Kops."

Captain Emery pretended to be involved in unscrewing a recalcitrant thermos top. It leaked and he licked up the coffee bubbling at the top. Santomassimo stood silently.

"I'm waiting, Lieutenant," Emery mumbled encouragingly.

Santomassimo sat on the edge of the desk. Captain Emery's eyebrows raised, but he said nothing.

"The important thing here is not *where* he plays his game," Santomassimo said, "but *why* he plays it. That leads us to *who* he is. And I think to find that answer requires a concentrated effort under *one* roof."

"You just don't take it upon yourself to transfer a case from one fucking division to another! What about Downtown? What about Homicide? What about the commissioner? Don't you think they should have been consulted?"

"It's a hot potato, Bill. Hirsch was glad to get rid of it. He said he'd square it with Homicide. And they'll let us have it. With their blessings."

Captain Emery paused, fearing the truth of Santomassimo's assessment. Finally, sighing wearily, he stammered, "And why should we assume this honor?"

"Well . . . let us say . . . Maybe I think I'm getting a handle on the killer."

Captain Emery looked hard at Santomassimo, eager and slightly suspicious.

"Handle, Lieutenant?" Captain Emery asked. "Are you keeping something from me?"

"I sense a connection. The Malibu dive-bombing and the murder in the Windsor Regency."

"Right. He killed somebody."

"I mean . . . a pattern, Captain. A pattern."

"Like what?"

Santomassimo moved off the corner of the desk. He stepped back into the shadows, and came around to the side of the captain's desk. He sat down in a beat-up black leather chair, the captain's old chair, icon of the good old days in the old headquarters before all the remodeling. Santomassimo leaned on the desk, toying with the broken thermos.

"I can't tell you, Captain. I don't know. That's the hell of it. I've got something running through my head. You know? Like an old memory that you can't quite grasp. It's got a familiarity to it."

"Is that what I tell the commissioner? Lieutenant Fred Santomassimo, loyal and award-winning lieutenant with twelve years service, sees a connection, a pattern, can't figure it out at all, but by golly, it keeps running through his thick Italian head? Is that what we tell the commissioner?"

Captain Emery saw Santomassimo's sudden anger only in the abrupt motion of Santomassimo's fingers, which twisted off the thermos top. Automatically, Emery reached for a paper towel and put it under the lightly bubbling container.

"I needn't remind you," Captain Emery added, "that your appearance at the Windsor Regency was noted by Steve Safran, the dark prince of KJLP news."

"Yes, sir. We had a little encounter outside the hotel."

"I believe you publicly announced that the case had been transferred."

"Yes, sir. I may have given that impression."

Crestfallen, Santomassimo leaned away from the desk, back into the shadows, the old leather chair complaining with squeaks.

"I think, sir," Santomassimo conceded, gesturing to the telephone, "that you do what you have to do."

"Yes."

Santomassimo stood up, tucked in his rumpled shirt again. Captain Emery picked up the telephone. The captain hung up again and abruptly walked his lieutenant to the door. He put a hand on Santomassimo's shoulder.

"I'll give you twenty-four hours," Captain Emery offered. "Does that help you? Twenty-four hours?"

"Thanks, but what the hell is twenty-four hours?"

"It's the best I can do, Fred. We're so overworked. I can't spare you on wild ideas. And that damn television reporter Safran. No matter what you say about hot potatoes, the commissioner really doesn't want to be drawn into an interdivisional squabble."

"Can't blame him."

"He has political ambitions, you know."

"The commissioner? Who in his right mind would vote for him?"

Emery smiled. "Twenty-four hours, Fred. Then I'll have to give the Windsor Regency case back to Hirsch. It creates a city-wide impression, you see. Incompetence. Or division rivalry. Especially with a kook on the loose. All kinds of crap the public doesn't need to know about."

"I appreciate your going out on a limb, Bill."

"That limb is exactly twenty-four hours long, Fred."

Santomassimo smiled. "Thanks. I'm sorry about not having asked you, but—"

"Do it again and I'll hot-wire your asshole."

Click . . . The tape recorder rolled onward, recording . . . The needle wavered gently within its range . . . The voice was controlled, bitter. . . .

"I mentioned my unsatisfactory experience in New York. Mercifully, I was fired from that job following a fistfight with the assistant production manager. I had a cousin in Orlando and I needed a place to get my head together. He had some money and a desire to get into films. So I went down there to help him on a documentary he was making about the wildfowl of the Everglades.

"We holed up in this motel on the edge of the swamps with all our gear and conflicting egos. There was my cousin, and me, and the sound man, and a girl who sort of ran around getting in everybody's way and providing sexual innuendos. There was lots of drinking, and the people who lived in the shacks of the Everglades, half Seminole or something, asked us to leave. The sheriff came at midnight

and we moved to a different motel, this one with bigger cockroaches, on a different lagoon, where the rednecks came to drink beer and scratch their armpits and rub themselves as they stared at the girl, who ran around in a red halter.

"Let me tell you, it made Manhattan seem like Club Med. There are insects in Florida they don't even have names for yet. They're big and they crawl into bed with you and suck blood. My body was covered in rashes and I came down with a fever so bad I was quoting whole pages of Citizen Kane in my delirium. I woke up long enough to scream. I still have the shakes from it. It must have been malaria.

"I sweated so bad, I had to keep wiping the moisture out of the eyepiece of our Eclair. I was literally shooting through fog by the time I got to the end of a long pan. That's how steamy it was. Leeches were crawling into my boots, which were ripped, and at night our feet stank like garbage. And my cousin, a wimpy snot, danced around with a red bandana and a director's eyepiece—symbol of artistic authority—and his ideas were straight out of the CBS School for the Visually Illiterate. I mean, he was doing voice-over narration about Little Baby Flamingo and Daddy Flamingo.

"We got about twenty-thousand feet shot, and by then my cousin was running out of money. He fired the sound man and fucked up the Nagra tape recorder. He fucked the girl, too, in the motel at night, which I didn't care about, except it kept me awake and I was losing my grip on all those fine visions that had come to me in New York. I tried to write them down, but the heat and stinking humidity made it hard to concentrate.

"I kept lugging that fucking Eclair through the mud and nettles. I lost twenty-five pounds and wished I'd joined the Army. I hated flamingos. I hated Florida. I hated my cousin. I almost hated film.

"Then the girl left, her arms full of psoriasis and maybe pregnant. My cousin now was insufferable. He thought he was the reincarnation of Robert Flaherty, but his ideas were puerile. Many were called, you see, but few have the gift. You can tell who has the gift. They have that tortured look.

"We filmed and recorded for four months. Can you believe

it? Four months where the water mocassins wouldn't go, crawling on our bellies to get a five-second shot of Mama Flamingo sitting on her stupid eggs.

"He still hadn't paid me for the last two months. We couldn't stand the smell of each other. One night late in August with the crickets screaming derisively, it was three o'clock in the morning, and I was lazily smoking marijuana, seeing the films in my head that I was having so much trouble remembering in the heat of day. Suddenly, the door flew open and I saw a glint. I thought it was a cockroach, because they have this metallic sheen in the moonlight, at least in Florida. But it wasn't a roach. It was a gun.

"I dived under the bed, screaming. There was a shot. Then I heard a second shot and my cousin started screaming. Then a third shot, and he stopped screaming. I caught a glimpse of a crazed figure, a dark guy with jeweled barrettes in his hair, and then the figure ran away and I went over to my cousin. I was sure he was dead, because of all the blood pumping way out into the air from the back of his head, and from the way his body trembled all over.

"Well, my cousin survived, but he didn't remember anything anymore—brain dead, they called it—and all his hair fell out. I didn't know what to do. I decided to try to edit the five miles of footage that we had my own way. You know, as a portfolio item. Something to show people in Los Angeles. They would see that I had a flair for image and continuity. I sold the Eclair and the other equipment and spent three months editing. I rented an editing room in Orlando and lived in it, twenty-four hours a day, eating almost nothing, drinking black coffee. I got stomach cramps, the shits, acne, and my fingernails turned yellow form the damn glue in the splicing tape. But I began to see things in that footage. I—I saw rhythms, rhythms that led into larger rhythmic compositions, visual motions that revealed a cruelty in nature.

"And something else. Art. Yes, that fucked-up, three-letter word that nobody really knows about. Art. I imposed art. I added bits and fragments of jazz scores, and strange sounds played backwards, human vocables, all kinds of things. I made a personal essay on the struggle for life. It was beautiful, savage, a little bit painful even, and undeniably original.

"My nerves were shot and I looked like a concentration camp victim. I was hysterical, ragged, disintegrated psychologically and physically, but I did it. I edited the fucker into a symphonic documentary that also observed the conventions of dramatic structure. I bought a one-way ticket to L.A. When I got there, I bought a used sync block and glue and rented a scraper.

"But Florida had defeated me. When I opened the cans to match the negative to my workprint, the negative fell into powder. Mold. Something greenish. It fell through my fingers like sweeping compound.

"Well, I thought about suicide. I just couldn't face years and years of this moral darkness . . . this fear . . . this wasting of my talent . . . Because it goes, you know . . . Talent decays like negative or anything else, and it doesn't come back . . . I didn't have the strength to see that happen . . .

"In a weird way, I envied the crazy who had shot my cousin for no reason at all. I began to believe that crazy guy was really the artist. I can't explain it any better. I admired him.

"And he kind of invaded my personality.

"I became obsessed with watching films again. Violent films. But with this different perspective: with the changes in reality, the manipulation of the audience's psychic reality. The art of film, see, isn't the organic progression of dramatic emotion, all that horse turd they teach you in school. It's the unvocalizable, the ambivalent, disturbing changes in reality that afflict the audience. Cary Grant and Eva Marie Saint cling from the nose of President Lincoln at Rushmore. They fall. To their deaths? No! Into the upper berth of the Twentieth Century Limited, kiss, kiss, the end! See. The audience has been tampered with. They've been used and changed. You don't believe me. You think directors are benign people with entertainment on their minds. Bullshit. Anybody who doesn't recognize the depth of cruelty and sadism in making a film isn't fit to talk about it.

"The director makes his biggest creation out there, in reality, in the deep dreams and violent impulses of millions of unsuspecting, good people.

"That, to me, is the mark of genius, of power and true, unforgettable genius."

Click . . . "I need a fucking beer . . ."
Click . . .
"You don't need a camera and film to be a truly great director . . . You need people . . . locations . . . props . . .
"Above all, people . . . Good, ordinary people . . .
"CUT!"

Two blocks south of Hollywood Boulevard, with no view but the rising walls of expensive apartment complexes, was a small, one-story peeling relic of the old Hollywood days. The home looked like an abandoned motel, but it was not abandoned. Geraniums grew, and ferns, and the litter was bad only in the gutter, not where the car was parked in the forecourt. It was night. A pearly light glimmered down from enormous palms where street lights shined through the rough fronds.

On both sides of the small house were vacant lots piled with debris, mostly rusted cans, but also mattresses, tires, and cardboard boxes stained with ancient foodstuffs. A single off-white van was parked under the street light. It was an older van, the kind that bearded visionaries once lived in during the 1960s. Now the van, having been repainted several times, bore the neatly inscribed red letters, complete with the Barnum style of flourish, NICE COLLEGE BOY MOVERS AND HAULERS. Under the sweeping flourish was a telephone number and the name, CHARLES PIERCE, PROP.

Inside the living room was a moth-eaten carpet on the floor, once gray, now mottled charcoal. The furniture belonged to the late 1950s, the kind that landlords buy, or old people hang on to, with angled leg supports and plenty of veneer. Only here the veneer was cracked. Under a lamp with a dangling chain was a large decorated chest, about the size of a human coffin. The floral design was nearly faded, but it must once have been the pride of a fine artist, for the birds of paradise were intricately worked against improbable tropical boughs.

Charles Pierce had been cut from the first string of UCLA's football squad. Still, second string at a place like UCLA was pretty damn good and his confidence was riding high. His moving business had taken off a lot faster than he had anticipated. Instead of providing enough for a bit of rent and some good times, he was taking on two, now three assistants and was about to buy a second truck. Only tonight his assistants had stayed home. The caller had said specifically it was going to be a small move. And a short distance.

Pierce, hands on hips, smelled the mildew and mold, but barely perceived the shipper in the shadows of the room. He sensed the shipper was depressed. Or introverted. Or something. Maybe he was being forced to move. There was that air of unhappiness that Pierce had already noticed in his young business. Lots of people were forced to sell and move and he was not immune to the sadness of it all. He tried to be cheerful, though the night weighed down on him with a claustrophobic gravity.

"You've got some pretty nice pieces here," Pierce said in what he hoped was a jocular tone. "I mean, a lot of them can be fixed, like that sofa over there, and the club chairs. It's all worth moving. Definitely. Only I can't get it all into the van in one trip. It's just a little bit more than you said on the telephone."

Pierce gazed down at the hand-carved trunk.

"Now this," he added, in sincere admiration, "is a real beauty. Must be an antique."

The shipper said nothing. Pierce bent down to peer into the chest's interior. It smelled of delicious old resin, perhaps a pine oil, something to keep out wood worms, but whatever it was, it made him think of faraway places, long sea voyages.

"God, it even smells nice—"

The rope caught him between syllables. Hemp suddenly squeezed his vocal cords. For an instant, he saw a profusion of red-and-blue spirals of stars in an extremely black sky.

"What the hell—?" he wanted to say, but the vocal cords were already crushed.

He kicked backward, punched rearward with his elbows. He was a good fighter, but somehow he couldn't quite reach the shipper who was digging into his side with—what? his heels?—and pulling—how? on the rope.

Pierce's fingers could not even get in under the rope to ease the pressure on his windpipe.

"God—" he managed to blurt.

God didn't answer. Pierce's lungs filled to bursting with nothing. He lost track of what was shadow and what was furniture. He could hear the thunder of his blood pounding, and could smell the interior of the chest. Then his brain died.

He gurgled, and bodily fluids oozed up from his ravaged, bruised throat. He felt none of it. There was no pulse.

Santomassimo left Captain Emery's office, picked up his jacket in his own office, and got into the blue Datsun in the parking lot.

Santomassimo was agitated. He went cruising. He drove all the way east to Hollywood, thinking. Several detectives watching the hookers on Vine recognized him. He kept driving. He stopped in at the El Adobe and had two margaritas. A former governor was at the far end of the bar. The commotion disturbed Santomassimo's train of thought, and he left.

Soon he was in the quiet streets where the old studios were, and the great film processing laboratories. A light fog hung over the deserted courtyards. Security agents stood in booths or patrolled the grounds with dogs.

Between Melrose and Hollywood, half the film industry worked and slept, and not just the old studios, but also in the sleek suites where hundreds, maybe thousands of agencies, some new, some old like Hasbrouk and Clentor, functioned.

There was old Hollywood and new Hollywood. The former had the dark grandeur, the palpable ghosts of the great men of genius, still brooding over Los Angeles. The latter had the hot ambition of young, irreverent men dividing up the world markets with sophisticated technologies. So what? What did Hollywood have to do with anything? Santomassimo was thinking of the connection between the beach murder and the Windsor Regency murder, and being in Hollywood tonight was stimulating.

Santomassimo stopped at a Tiny Naylor's for black coffee. He eyed the young girls in denim jackets and fishnet stockings, red hair bands around black, curly hair and redder lipstick on young mouths. Watching them, precocious before their time, dark and glittering in their special way under the cheap night-lights, Santomassimo admired them, their romantic rebellion.

But what did Hasbrouk have to do with Nancy Hammond?

Because there *was* something linking them. Has-

brouk and Nancy Hammond. Not just the irrational.
The bizarre. There was a hidden theme. It was a
violence with a sick sense of showmanship.

The clubs looked packed on the Strip. Santomassimo cruised down the steep La Cienega. He thought
hard about the killer, but the elusive idea fluttered like
a dying butterfly on the edge of his consciousness.
The margaritas wore off. He found himself driving
through Miracle Mile, a single espresso bar the only
lighted storefront in an otherwise dark and forbidding
wall of glass buildings. It was like a necropolis at this
hour.

Driving west, Santomassimo saw the shafts of blue-
white floodlamps probing the sky. Expensive cars
rolled on the Century City boulevards. The bright light
shafts were visible all over the west side. Posters and
banners were hung along Santa Monica Boulevard.
Apparently, there was going to be a Russian film
exhibit, part of *glasnost*.

Santomassimo checked his watch. It was eleven-
fifteen. He had exactly twenty-one hours and twenty-
five minutes to provide Captain Emery with a logical
connection between the beach explosion and the
Windsor Regency electrocution. Like watching films,
driving in Los Angeles usually stimulated his imagination, but nothing materialized tonight.

He dug into his experience of the foul garbage
heaps of human motivation but the elusive idea still
remained out of reach.

He drove home. The full moon dappled rays on a
quiet sea. The Pacific was like an endless black milk.
It had no end, no beginning. Sparkles of light danced
on the waves, and the boats of the marina stood still
as though frozen. There was a glow on the horizon
from the city lights.

The piers were deserted. Brake lights of automobiles
glowed in the cramped driveways of the fish restau-

rants on the highway. The sea had a funny mood, Santomassimo thought. It was sinister tonight.

He drove into the security-gated parking lot of his apartment building. He got out of the Datsun and rode the elevator up.

His apartment had one bedroom, living room with kitchen exposed, and was the antithesis of what a cop's apartment should look like. An art deco settee stood against a cream-white wall, softly underlit, and a John Marin watercolor, framed in slender gold, caught the low light above it. In the corner was a curved 1930s cabinet, with tiny crystal windows, holding dark bottles of rum and whiskey.

There was a lounge chair opposite the settee, by the mahogany bookcase, overlooking the balcony and the ocean. The chair was deceptively heavy, carved with a ball and scroll on the feet and a bar of ornate wooden vegetal motifs along the top. It had been purchased in an estate auction by Santomassimo's father for $350 in 1938. Santomassimo knew it was now worth over twelve thousand.

The chairs in the apartment were from an Italian set, made in Naples and exported to the West Coast by a family of vegetable sellers, one of whom later became important as a record producer. They were tall, dignified, with splayed slats and somewhat worn velvet seats. They had the austere dignity of a family that has come into money but has never forgotten its peasant origins. The insurance appraiser had priced the set at $25,500.

From a small but rich monastery near Monte Cassino had come four wall sconces. They were made of brass, alive with curvilinear tendrils, even berries and acorns. They were ecclesiastical items. The appraiser had placed them at about $3,500 each.

Santomassimo had a collection of lamps, bought in Los Angeles during the Depression by his father, but all made in Italy, mostly in Milan. They were floor lamps, very tall, with slight fluting on the vertical pole, and were tri- or quadruple-socketed under tissue-thin stretched cloth. The light switches were gold link chains that hung down with small armatures to make them hang out from the shade. He had refused fourteen thousand each from Captain Emery's cousin, a dealer of fine furnitures.

The carpet was Tunisian, long, thick and slightly asymmetrical in its geometric pattern, though only Santomassimo knew where the asymmetry lay. Perhaps it was for good luck. The Tunisians were as superstitious as Italians. Hell, the Italians had colonized it long enough. It was *premiere qualita* and certified as such, and the weave and pattern were quite rare. A dealer on La Cienega Boulevard, looking at a slide transparency of it, instantly offered Santomassimo eighty-five thousand for it.

His family had owned a prosperous antique store until Santomassimo's uncle had swindled them out of it. All that was left was the furniture and Santomassimo's instinctive eye for taste and value. Santomassimo had grown up philosophical about the greed of mankind and the criminality that grows there. He adored art deco and was intolerant of bad taste. And, unfortunately, much of Los Angeles was built on bad taste.

At a walnut table inlaid with intertwined grape leaf patterns, the whole ringed about with a generalized Arcadian scene of darker cherry wood, Santomassimo picked at a frozen Gourmet Delight Lean and Trim Instant Asparagus and Chicken au Gratin. The table was probably worth in excess of $145,000. Dinner cost $2.95. The contradiction between the furniture and the dinner did not arise in his mind.

Santomassimo was playing a kind of mental chess. This was chess on a non-euclidean board. One had to make contact, through the bizarre M.O.s, with a killer's mind. And he even had the odd feeling that the killer was doing the same with him. But where did that feeling come from?

It was late. Santomassimo went to his bedroom. It was even more ornate than the living room. Santomassimo looked at the portrait of his parents on the wall, the formidable countenance of his father, a short, barrel-chested man of immense dignity and perhaps too much trust of his fellow man, and the softer, subtler look of his mother, her raven hair swept up in a bun, yet never looking severe, but almost regal, a natural beauty. They looked back at Santomassimo. They couldn't help.

The waves were louder. He went to the window. The glassy, milky smoothness, the heaviness of the beast, was broken. Ripples broke into swells, coming from Japan for all he knew. Boats rocked gently in the marina far below. It was suddenly busy on Sunset and busier on the Pacific Coast Highway. The movie houses had let out. Santomassimo sat back on his bed and turned on the bed lamp. He crushed the pillows behind him, picked up *Old Prints of Germany, Part One: Schongauer and Durer.* His eyes drifted off the page as his mind cornered his idea.

There *was* a connection. Hidden in the grass like a snake.

He tossed the book aside and reached for the television remote control. The images of a bland newscaster alternated with scenes of fires, a flood in Pakistan, riots in Spain. The local news was full of a big heroin bust at Los Angeles International Airport. Nothing about the Windsor Regency. Maybe Steve Safran got himself fired, Santomassimo hoped.

But no, there he was, young and florid, pontificating on a crime wave in Los Angeles. It was a quirky, philosophical essay on the meaning of murder in the big city. Safran had a high opinion of himself. Santomassimo changed channels. A Korean was machine-gunned out of a tree in a black-and-white film, and a hand grenade was thrown into a smoking hole in the earth. He changed the channels.

Gounod was a composer well known to Santomassimo. Gounod was a highly popular composer of the 19th century and a particular favorite of his father's. Gounod still featured heavily in Santomassimo's record collection. Right now, he was listening to Gounod's "The Funeral March of the Marionettes," the signature music of a famous television program whose opening visual featured a fat, jowly man who stepped into his own shadow profile.

Santomassimo stared, oblivious of the plot developing with understated, maniacal skill.

It was the theme, the marching, diabolical theme, that chased the snake out of the grass. Santomassimo was dumbfounded.

"Holy Mother of Jesus," he softly swore.

7

It was late morning and the Santa Monica Freeway downtown was still bottled like a bunch of marbles in a jam jar, with no place to go.

Santomassimo's Datsun inched past a construction truck that had turned over, spilling sand and concrete over two lanes. There was also a crash near the Coliseum. Santomassimo drove down the shoulder, took the first off ramp, and went by city streets.

Los Angeles around the Coliseum was caught uneasily between the immigrations—Hispanic, Vietnamese, Korean, and Thai—and corporate speculation. There were still small stores, little ethnic restaurants, a Black Pentecostal church, and a Salvation Army Mission, but there was also a gourmet cheese shop and several boutiques catering to the Japanese executives.

New and used cars were for sale in gleaming lots with red pennants. The streets were cluttered with billboards, telephone poles, and a few ancient, pre-war dusty trees. But there was also development down here: pink stone buildings, with tiny saplings, and top-of-the-line clothing stores.

It was the area of the church on Alvarado where the evangelist Jim Jones had recruited believers before taking them off to Guyana and eventual mass suicide. There was the Hillel Center with exhibits of Judaica and artifacts from the Holocaust. There was a great Spanish Baroque church, ornate as a wedding cake, the great outpost of Roman Catholicism in a commercial, multi-religious landscape.

The University of Southern California had also expanded recently. It was a wealthy institution, with ties to the Mideast, Hollywood, professional football, and the military. It had been a long time since Santomassimo had been in this part of downtown. Now there were high-rise luxury hotels for visiting academics and businessmen. The campus itself, a conglomerate of pink brick buildings, seemed laid back in the dense haze, like a stone flower waiting for a bee.

Santomassimo paid to park. He felt like an insect in a trap. He was out on a limb with Captain Emery, and down to nine hours to demonstrate a plausible connection between the Palisades Beach and Windsor Regency killings. What he had been doing this morning could turn out to be a perfect and ludicrous waste of what little time he had.

He walked down the sidewalks between science buildings. Tall, good-looking young men leaned desultorily on rakes, talking, leaving the leaves alone. Athletes, Santimassimo guessed, on scholarships. He himself had graduated from Los Angeles City College before the Police Academy. He had been a fullback on the football team. One look at the size and definition of the young men with the rakes reminded him that this institution produced world caliber athletes.

Students crisscrossed the lawns, the sidewalks, and

the road down the center of the campus. It must have been between classes. They seemed too young to be in college. They were nicely dressed, with short hair, both men and women, and the girls all seemed blue-eyed, blond, and vivacious. It was a kind of time warp in which rebellion, drugs, and Vietnam had never happened. It was like an academic Disneyland.

Santomassimo walked past the statue of Tommy Trojan, just now decorated with white paint by a flying squad from UCLA. Campus groundsmen busily scrubbed the paint away. Banners everywhere declared revenge on the Bruins. Santomassimo walked to the cinema department.

Once the cinema department had been housed in yellow barracks that formed a miniature courtyard with one diseased banana plant and a single bench for students at lunch time. Now the entire department had moved into a vast complex, dark gray buildings, sound stages, a new laboratory. It was the sixth most productive studio in the country.

A man in a gray suit perked up as Santomassimo came into the central building.

"May I be of assistance?" he said genially.

"I want to see Professor Quinn," Santomassimo said. "I called, and was told—"

"That class is in session. May I have your name, please?"

"I just want to speak to him for a few minutes—"

"Name, please."

The man smiled even more genially, his pencil poised over a roster on a clipboard. He was a little man, psychologically. This was his one power play. Right now. Extracting names from visitors.

"Fred Santomassimo."

The man laughed. "I couldn't pronounce that let alone spell it."

Santomassimo pulled out his police identification and showed it. The man had it half copied before he realized a police lieutenant was standing in front of him. The genial smile hardened and he put down the pencil.

"Third floor. Room 334. Enter by the back door and remember that the lecture is in progress."

Santomassimo rode up to the third floor. Evidently the floor was devoted to lecture halls, since he saw neither library nor technical equipment. Several students and a faculty member passed, who nodded, no doubt figuring Santomassimo must be either new faculty or, given his dark jacket, a young administrator, perhaps even a dean.

Room 334 had a gray metal door. Santomassimo looked around, but saw no other door, and no way to know if he were at the rear of the lecture hall or the front. All he saw was a small card slotted into metal slats, reading: PROFESSOR QUINN. Then, below, in smaller type: HITCHCOCK 500. Santomassimo carefully opened the door.

He emerged about halfway up the slope of plush seats. The lecture hall was dark. There were about two hundred students in the hall, good looking, but not quite so well-dressed as the others on campus. There was an air of exhaustion and, simultaneously, burning intensity. This was no casual department. He ducked low and slipped quickly into a seat in the rear.

Professor Quinn turned out to be a woman. She was very pretty and wore a gray jacket with a Lavalier mike pinned to her lapel. From where Santomassimo sat in the darkness, he judged her to be in her late twenties. She spoke easily, but slightly abstractly, as though reading from notes, and very brief notes. The students wrote quickly with illuminated pens. It was like being in a cavern of fireflies.

On the screen was a grainy, enormous image of a vaudeville-type face, a clown face, and unpleasant face with insane eyes, all made up in black greasepaint.

"To truly understand the mind of Hitchcock," Quinn

was saying, leaning slightly on the podium, "one must look beyond the plot. One must look beyond the characterizations, and beyond the mechanisms of rising tensions, at which he was, indisputably, cinema's greatest master. One must look in a very strange place. One must look at his delectable, mischievous wit."

Santomassimo fingered his lips, listening carefully.

"It is that sense of playing games with the audience," she continued, "that marks out Hitchcock's uniqueness. He was an elfin, practical joker with consummate cinema technique, and he fooled his audience. He frightened them. He delighted them and manipulated them. People watching a film by Hitchcock are thrilled, entertained, and absorbed, but they are also uncomfortable. Because the sources of Hitchcock's wit go very savagely deep into the human subconscious."

Santomassimo watched her go toward the screen. She tapped on it with a pointer, more for emphasis. She spoke completely without notes now, but her voice flowed as lucidly as before.

"Think now of the long tracking shot in *Young and Innocent*, which you have been studying in the film laboratory. Without a single cut, the camera circulates through the dance floor, seeking the killer. And there is *one* clue to his identity. *Only one*. A physical mannerism, a nervous twitch, a tic in the eyes. Do you remember how cleverly Hitchcock had established that?"

Some of the students looked blank, even embarrassed. Others were with her. Santomassimo had hated lectures while he had been at LACC. This one had him captivated.

"Recall, then," she continued, absorbed in the remembered imagery, barely conscious of the students staring at her or writing. "The camera tracks past the dancers. Finally, it moves right into the band itself.

All the musicians are made up in blackface. Do you see the wit? The toying? All is revealed. All is simultaneously disguised. Now the camera moves to the very top of the bandstand, moving inexorably, into the drummer's eyes."

She gestured at the vaudeville face that dominated the platform.

"A huge closeup. The power of the closeup. Suddenly, we see the eyes—*twitch*—"

The students laughed. Santomassimo smiled, too.

"When I saw the film for the first time," she added, "I still remember that the audience screamed. Not that they were frightened. It was the *diabolical cleverness* of those twitching eyes."

Santomassimo looked at his watch. He was in the right place. The class was nearly over. He would have to intercept her immediately before she disappeared out the rear of the hall.

"I want to show you now, just in the last five minutes, a single clip from his American *oeuvre*, *Vertigo*. You'll be analyzing it scene by scene in the film laboratory, but I want you to see one other thing. And that is the technical mastery, the attention to visual detail, which became a permanent part of film language."

A young man in a jacket one size too large for him threaded a reel of film into a projector inside the glass-enclosed booth behind Santomassimo's head.

The film began to roll.

Santomassimo spied the student next to him writing in a quick, abbreviated script form.

LONG SHOT: MAN IN BELL TOWER
  A man in a gray suit looks down.
HIS POV
  A dizzying whorl of descending steps.
THE MAN

As the man grasps the railing, he looks sick, stumbling.

HIS POV

THE CAMERA PULLS BACK. BUT THE LENS ZOOMS FORWARD. THE STAIRS FLATTEN BY THE PRESSURE OF PERSPECTIVE CHANGE, DIZZYING, INEXORABLY DISTORTED.

The student's quick script form made only a bit of sense to Santomassimo. What *was* unmistakable, however, was the old sensation, on the film screen, of a man looking down a deep flight of stairs that did not change in size and yet seemed to recede and come closer simultaneously, in a way that was impossible in the normal world. It was dizzying, unnatural, perverse, and disorienting.

"This forward zoom," Quinn explained, "is operated while the camera moves backward. Contradictory perspective systems. Today it's known as a retrograde zoom. But until Hitchcock, it had never been done before in the history of cinema. All the audience sees is the warping of space. This perspective squeezing expresses the hero's vertigo, but also reaches into and disturbs the audience's subconscious. It confronts the audience with a kind of experience it fears."

She smiled. The students were impressed. Hitchcock's scene had left them with pens poised, momentarily forgetting where they were.

"Lights, please," she said.

The lecture hall lights went on.

"The film laboratory has five prints," she concluded, "so there should be no excuses on the exam."

The class laughed nervously. There was an excellent rapport between Quinn and the students. She took off her Lavalier mike and that was it. Class was dismissed. In the chaos of rising bodies and collected notebooks, chatter and even a small dog tangled up in a chain leash, Santomassimo jumped up and ran down the aisle after her.

A faculty member with two slide carousels for the next class came in, blocking his way. Santomassimo struggled past him, out into the corridor. All he saw were students crossing to other lecture halls, carrying film cans, many haggard with sleeplessness.

"Miss Quinn," he called. "Professor Quinn!"

She barely heard him. She turned and saw him walking quickly up the hall, holding what appeared to be a laminated police identification.

"Excuse me, Miss Quinn," he said. "Lieutenant Santomassimo of the Palisades Division. Can I talk to you?"

She had extraordinarily clear green eyes that right now stared at him suspiciously.

"What about?"

Santomassimo was jostled by a group of young filmmakers carrying tripods, bursting out from the stairwell. He could hardly hear her. He also didn't care to discuss two murder cases right now among them.

"Could I buy you a cup of coffee?" he asked.

She looked at her watch. "No. You can buy me lunch."

Taken aback, Santomassimo smiled awkwardly.

"Where? Is there a cafeteria? A commissary or something?"

"How about Chinese?"

"Yes. Chinese. Why not?"

He followed her to her office, which was cluttered with film scripts, volumes on the semiology of film, and four huge gray metal bookcases filled with glossy film publications. On the wall was an enormous poster. It featured the silhouette of Hitchcock's face filling out an inked profile. She caught him staring at it as she picked up her purse from the desk.

"Is he why you've come?" she guessed.

"I would rather we waited until we were alone to discuss it."

She smiled enigmatically and led him to the elevator. He followed her out of the building. It was hot outside, and the smog irritated his throat.

"I must warn you," she said as they walked off campus, "if you're investigating a student for a security clearance for a job, I'd be happy to cooperate, but I always advise the student that he is being investigated."

"It has nothing to do with a job, Professor Quinn."

There was a small Chinese restaurant, The Slow Boat, which was dark as a cave inside, with small bamboo curtains around a little waterfall on terraced stones, and a tiny stone temple in the goldfish pond. The prices were low, and yet there were no students. Faculty were here, but also executives from the new corporate buildings nearby.

They sat in a small booth and Santomassimo felt even more awkward. Professor Quinn had eyes that simply did not go away.

"I must ask that everything I tell you be confidential," he asked cautiously. "Can you agree to that?"

"Yes."

A Chinese man in a gold coat smiled and put glasses of ice water before them. Santomassimo waited until he was gone. Kay kept watching Santomassimo. Santomassimo dug his fingers into the tablecloth and then stared directly into her green eyes. They were extremely Irish.

"You must have heard of the murder on Palisades Beach," he began.

"Bill Hasbrouk," she said. "Yes. It was a great shock."

"You knew him?"

"I knew of him. Some of our students were represented by him."

"Students? Handled by a wealthy firm like Hasbrouk and Clentor?"

She smiled. "Understand the strength of our cinema department, Lieutenant Santomassimo. Take the writing program. It was set up by Professor Blacker and in the last fifteen years our graduates have earned over two billion dollars in the cinema profession. But Blacker is no longer here and anyway I'm in film studies. Some of our best students worked with Hasbrouk and Clentor after they graduated."

"Do you think anybody would have a reason to assassinate Mr. Hasbrouk?"

"No. He was a very decent man."

Santomassimo sat back as the waiter came a second time. They ordered garlic chicken and *mu shu* pork. The waiter bowed, smiled, gathered up the menus, and left.

"Are you aware of the method in which Mr. Hasbrouk was killed?" he asked.

"A flying bomb, wasn't it?"

"In a toy airplane. Does that suggest anything to you?"

"Nothing."

Santomassimo took a deep breath. "As you know, a part of his company dealt in advertising," he said.

"It still suggests nothing to me, Lieutenant."

"There is a second murder, Professor. I don't know if all the details have been made public. The victim was a young woman, a blonde, killed at the Windsor Regency Hotel yesterday."

Professor Quinn looked back, waiting.

"You've heard nothing about it, then?" he asked.

She smiled apologetically. "I don't have much time to read newspapers. I'm teaching two seminars in addition to the lecture class, writing an article—tenure is very difficult, Lieutenant. If I don't finish a book by next September and get a publisher's contract—"

"I understand."

"Do you? It's either/or. No book, no job. And it has to be a good book. It has to be a marvelous book."

"What's it on?"

"The representation of cruelty."

"Hitchcock?"

"He figures largely in it. Of course. His humor was a form of cruelty."

"It's that combination—of cruelty and—I guess you're right. A sense of black humor. Of making being murdered look ridiculous, humiliating, even fun. That's what led me to you—I need your help, Professor Quinn."

The waiter brought the *mu shu* pork and deftly spread the small pancakes on the plate, then set down ceramic bowls with plum sauce and then the pork in white dishes. The garlic chicken came in a ceramic bowl with flowers hand painted on it. Santomassimo waited until the waiter left. Then they ate. Professor Quinn was very good with chopsticks. Santomassimo tried, then resorted to the fork on the tablecloth.

"The girl in the Windsor Regency," he said. "First time on the West Coast. A secretarial convention. She was killed in her hotel room. In the shower."

"I'm sorry, I really don't see—"

"The man who last occupied the room was N. B. Ates."

"Ates."

"N. B. Ates. Norman Bates."

"Let me understand this. The girl was killed in the hotel room, in the shower, and the previous occupant was N. B. Ates, which makes you think of Norman Bates, who was played by Anthony Perkins in *Psycho*. Which in turn brought you to me."

"And the victim of the airplane was in advertising. Cary Grant, in *North by Northwest*, was in advertising."

"It seems very tangential to me, Lieutenant."

Santomassimo smiled at the waiter who was approaching the table, shook his head, and the waiter went back to his position near the goldfish pond.

"But surely the beach murder fits a pattern," Santomassimo insisted. "A jogger on the beach, on a broad piece of land, blown up by a toy plane packed with six ounces of *plastique* . . ."

Professor Quinn said nothing, thinking hard, digging at the garlic chicken, but absorbed in Santomassimo's idea.

"An expensive toy plane," he continued, "powered by a gasoline engine and steered by remote control into Mr. Hasbrouk's body."

She looked up sharply. Santomassimo's familiarity with violent death was different from her familiarity with the *depiction* of violent death. And yet, he was proposing there was little difference for somebody.

"Possible," she conceded. "But not probable. Cary Grant was chased across a deserted stretch of prairie land by a crop duster. As you say, he was in advertising. But he wasn't killed. In fact, the plane hit a fuel truck and was demolished. Grant lived."

"I'm thinking that somebody wants to improve the original. Replicate it. I don't know."

"The girl was a secretary?"

"At a big secretarial convention."

"Well," Kay conceded a second time, "Janet Leigh was a secretary in *Psycho*. But she was stabbed. In seventy-eight superb camera setups. Not electrocuted."

"Maybe he's changing the script. Stabbing people in crowded hotels often leads to getting caught."

"I don't know, Lieutenant. I just don't know. Maybe. It's the sort of thing Hitchcock would have appreciated."

"What?"

"Homage to the master. In the form of murders."

They fell silent. Professor Quinn had slightly angular features. Her hair seemed to pick up highlights from the floodlights reflecting off the goldfish pond. He instinctively waited for her.

"You know," she said softly. "Hitchcock is a kind of god to many people. You don't understand what film people are like, Lieutenant. Not just people in the film business. People studying films. I know. I did my doctoral thesis on an analytic comparison of the British and American versions of *The Man Who Knew Too Much*. I guess that sounds pretty specialized to you. But the people I met—and there are thousands, Lieutenant, thousands—they get—"

"Hypnotized?"

"Let's just say that Hitchcock buffs don't kid."

"I guess he *is* pretty famous."

"His face is known all over the world. His films still work, still frighten, still toy with minds. It's been over a decade since his death, and he is now—by latest count—the most studied film director in history."

"Did you ever get to meet him?" Santomassimo asked. "When you were writing your thesis?"

"No. I wrote, but—and then he died. Maybe it's better. I'd have been terribly intimidated. Like having an audience with the Pope." The professor paused and blushed. Santomassimo said nothing.

"This . . . killer," she continued, "if what you suggest is accurate . . . is raising Hitchcock to some kind of fourth dimension . . . emulating him . . . embellishing him . . ."

"In reality."

"Extraordinary."

"That's why I need your help, Professor."

She was taken aback. "Help you?" she asked. "How?"

"Figure out the killer's next hit."

Professor Quinn looked at him as though wondering if he were serious. She laughed, then saw he was entirely serious. "You've got to be joking, Lieutenant," she objected. "Alfred Hitchcock made *fifty-three* motion pictures. Twenty half-hour television films. Except for *Mr. and Mrs. Smith,* each one dealt with murder and mayhem."

"I know it's a lot, but—"

"You're talking at least seventy-five acts of violence. It would be impossible to predict the time, place, and methodology of his next . . . *hit* . . . based on Hitchcock's *oeuvre*."

Frustrated, Santomassimo took the bill and dropped a credit card on top of it. The waiter carried them away on yet another ceramic dish.

"Well, could you at least get me a list of the crimes in the master's—whatever you called it?" He asked. "The locations. The methods."

Professor Quinn studied Santomassimo with mock severity. "You're going to make me pay for this lunch aren't you?"

Fred smiled, said nothing.

Professor Quinn's faced relaxed somewhat. "Tell me, Lieutenant, what made you come straight to me?"

"I didn't. You were fifth on my list. I started at The American Film Institute, but their Hitchcock specialist was on vacation. Next I hit Paramount, and then Universal. With no luck . . . Paramount's archives have a paucity of Hitchcocks, but Universal is a veritable mausoleum of his films . . . Only trouble is, it takes more than a badge to enter the tomb . . . I was told to make an appointment with the man at the very top, whose calendar is totally booked for the next three weeks. A nice girl there suggested UCLA, who in turn suggested that at USC there was a Professor Quinn whose dissertation had been on Hitchcock, and who was currently conducting a seminar on him. So, here we are, having lunch."

"The information you want could easily have been found in books," Professor Quinn said dubiously. "Did you ever think of that?"

"I haven't the time to read books."

Professor Quinn sighed, relenting. "I suppose I could go through the synopses. I have the complete collection in my computer. Is tomorrow all right?"

"How about right now?"

The professor stiffened at the urgency, looked at her watch, and relented. "All right. I've got a half hour before my seminar. We'll have to move fast."

They left the restaurant, dodged traffic, and got back onto campus. Santomassimo followed her, through milling students carrying Arriflexes and Eclairs, up to her cluttered office.

She quickly pulled three spiral-bound indexes from the shelves, put them on her desk, and sat in her chair. She began typing quickly into a small, white computer. Santomassimo watched, fascinated by her speed. She transcribed some facts, and others she obviously remembered. The dark green computer screen developed steadily, four columns: *Film, Method of Murder, Location, Profession.*

Santomassimo browsed among the densely packed books. *The Coroner Cometh: An Analysis of the Structure of Alfred Hitchcock's Later Films. The Master's Voice: Interviews with Alfred Hitchcock. Suspense and Language: A Semiotic Study of North by Northwest.* Santomassimo opened the last book. It was in a language like engineering.

"What's semiotics?" he asked.

"The science of signs. Language is a system of signs. So is cinema."

Santomassimo walked to another bookcase, past the rows of manuscripts, unpublished Ph.D. dissertations, bibliographic compilations, and studio notebooks, all relating to Hitchcock's long career. He saw a book titled *Marx and Cinema: The Thriller Genre.*

He pulled out the volume and opened it. The text was dense, and words like *dialectic, ideology,* and *reification* appeared. There were also lots of Russian and German names quoted. Santomassimo closed the book and put it back.

"Heavy stuff," he mumbled.

Santomassimo peeked out the tiny window. It was slightly shaded, making the hot, smoggy day just that little bit grayer, almost as though a rain might be coming. But it wouldn't rain here. Not among the hot concrete and pink stone buildings. Students were walking toward the library. Suddenly, he began to sense the anxiety that underlay the people here. He could almost smell the undercurrents of ambition, frustration, even confusion. The groves of academe, he thought, were not so secure as he had thought.

"Lieutenant," she said.

He turned. The computer's printer was squeezing out pages. The columns of murders were neatly typed. She gently tore the papers from the printer and handed them to him.

"I hope it helps," she said sincerely.

"Thank you. I mean that, Professor. I want to thank-you for your help."

"My first name is Kay."

She gave him a card with her name and title printed on it. *Kay Quinn, Ph.D. Assistant Professor, Film Studies. University of Southern California.* Below it was her campus telephone number. He put it carefully into his wallet.

"Thank you, Kay. My teachers were never so help-ful," he said. "Or so lovely."

She laughed.

"Anything I can do for you, Lieutenant Santomas-simo. Give me a call."

They shook hands. Her hand was warm. He nodded farewell, suddenly awkward, and went into the corri-dor, remembering her green eyes.

But the Gounod march was still in his head. He peered into the film laboratory. It was a very large room with soft lighting in translucent panels in the ceiling and long mahogany desks below. At the desks were about a dozen students, each staring at a video screen, punching buttons, taking notes, peering into the image, playing scenes back and forth.

At a counter stood a tall, lanky young man, and behind him were hundreds and hundreds of copies of films, neatly shelved.

The teaching assistants wore jackets and walked among the desks, helping the undergraduates. Santomassimo recognized the stocky young man who had operated Professor Quinn's projector.

One of the younger students, a girl with a blond ponytail, struggled with a scene from *Psycho*.

CLOSE SHOT: KNIFE ENTERS SHOWER CUR-
    TAIN DIAGONAL UP
CLOSE SHOT: KNIFE ENTERS SHOWER CUR-
    TAIN DIAGONAL DOWN
CLOSE SHOT: VICTIM'S EYES—TERRIFIED
CLOSE SHOT: KNIFE AGAINST NAKED BELLY
CLOSE SHOT: WATER FROM SHOWER
CLOSE SHOT: VICTIM'S EYES—TERRIFIED
CLOSE SHOT: DRAIN: FLOWING WATER TURNS
    DARK WITH BLOOD
CLOSE SHOT: VICTIM'S EYES—GLAZED, DEAD
    IN SHOWER

It was an immensely powerful scene. Santomassimo was astounded at the number of cuts, the assemblage of so many fragments of violence into the terror of the victim's last moments. The blond girl kept staring into the screen, as though hypnotized. The entire room was filled with mesmerized students, supervised by the teaching assistants.

There was something hideous in staring at the fragmented murder scenes, Santomassimo thought.

Because the director was too clever. The pieces got in under the brain's defenses.

Did Nancy Hammond have even those few seconds of terror? he wondered, walking out of the building. Or was her death mercifully instantaneous? Had the killer toyed with her, as Hitchcock did with his audience?

Captain Emery's office was cleared of its clutter. The thermos was gone and the top of the desk had been emptied of memoranda, wire baskets, even the telephone. The old black leather chair was pulled up to the side, providing support for what Santomassimo had unrolled across the desk: Professor Kay Quinn's chart of Hitchcock's films, the murders, locations, professions, enlarged now onto glossy cardboard, filled in with felt-tipped pens.

Detective Haber held down one end of the chart. Bronte held the other. Captain Emery swiveled uncomfortably in his new chair, alternately eyeing Santomassimo and the chart. The chart was bright, almost luminescent, strangely hypnotic, under the captain's directional goose-necked lamp.

Bronte and Detective Haber exchanged glances. Santomassimo had not only gone out on a limb, he appeared to be on a different tree altogether.

"This is the summary of all the plots," Santomassimo said, gesturing at the chart. "At least the murders. From the beginning, in England, to *Vertigo, Psycho, North by Northwest, The Birds—*"

"We can see that," Captain Emery interrupted.

"Well, look. Here, for example, is *Dial M for Murder.* Place of crime: a London brownstone apartment. Weapon: a pair of scissors. Victim's occupation: car salesman. Professor Quinn, from the University of Southern California, helped me organize this chart as to place, victim, profession, and *modus operandi* in each of Hitchcock's films, fifty-three in all."

"I wondered where you were this morning. Did you know that there was another rape? In the canyon."

Santomassimo stepped back. He gestured at the chart. "How we set up surveillance is, of course, the major problem. We certainly don't have the manpower. We don't even have a clue as to where and how he might strike next."

Bronte stifled a cough. Detective Haber stifled a grin. Finally, Captain Emery sighed. He turned to Bronte and Haber and when he spoke his voice was unusually gentle.

"Would you please excuse us?" the captain said.

Startled, Bronte and Haber looked at Santomassimo, then at Captain Emery, who smiled strangely, giving nothing away. They left. The ends of the chart rolled up. Santomassimo methodically put a stapler on one end, a tape dispenser at the other. When they heard the door close behind them, Santomassimo looked at the captain.

"I feel like crying, Fred," Captain Emery said softly. "I feel like fucking crying."

Santomassimo's face hardened. "I feel strongly about this, Bill. More strongly than I've ever felt about a case."

"That's what I mean," the captain said. "The one possibility in a million that you may be right." He rubbed his eyes. "My problem is, how do I present this shit to the commissioner? You know what he would do, Fred? I'll tell you what he would do. He would take my badge, gun, and police credentials and insert them up my ass and escort me to the bursar to collect my pension."

Santomassimo shrugged. "Fuck the commissioner. You know I'm right."

"*Possibly* right, Fred."

"The evidence speaks for itself."

"Does it? Does it really? Let's examine it. A nut kills two people in very wild-assed ways. You seize on a very convenient package that fits the killings. Except they *don't* fit exactly."

"Sure they do."

"They don't, Fred. Look. In the first case, the jogger wasn't supposed to die. Isn't that what the film said? The guy escapes from the airplane, doesn't he? And in the second case, poor Nancy Hammond was electrocuted. According to your own chart, the victim in *Psycho* was stabbed."

"Their occupations fit."

Captain Emery's expression showed a mixture of exasperation and a desire to get Santomassimo's conception out of the office and out of his own mind. But it wasn't going away. The captain wheeled around on the axis of his new chair and stared at the chart. His nose was inches from *Weapon: a pair of scissors*.

"All right," he said. "Let's look at *Dial M for Murder*. Victim, it says here, was a car salesman. Know how many car salesmen there are in greater Los Angeles?"

"I know. I know. Look, I didn't say it would be easy, Bill. I just said I was right."

"Not right enough. I can't—won't—put my ass on the line for this, Fred. Take this back to your professor

and tell her to publish it. Where it does the most good.
But you gotta do better than charts and theories."

His mind decided, Captain Emery smiled, relieved.
The telephone rang. He held up a forefinger, a sign
for Santomassimo to wait until the phone call was
over.

"Hey—Callahan—" the captain shouted jovially into
the receiver. "How's my boy? How're things going
down in crimesville?"

Captain Emery chuckled. Then he picked up a
pencil and made notations on his pad, which he
retrieved from the floor. Santomassimo saw the color
of the captain's face retreat, leaving a sick pallor.

"Okay," Captain Emery mumbled, lips barely moving, his eyes dazed. "Okay, Tom. We'll look into it."

He hung up slowly. Then he looked up at Santomassimo, suddenly seeming very much older than he had
a few seconds ago. He cleared his throat in a numbed
sort of way.

"That was, um, Captain Callahan of the Newton
Division, Fred. They have a case—a real nasty case—
He and Homicide think maybe it belongs to us."

Captain Emery kept clearing his throat and drum-
ming his fingers on the desk top. He looked very lost.
Then, as though walking into a bad dream, he
abruptly rose, and he and Santomassimo went out the
door and ran to the parking lot.

It was brightly lighted inside Lyons Second Hand
Furniture Company on Western Avenue. People
thought a film was being made until they saw the
patrol cars. A red plastic ribbon cordoned off the crowd
on the sidewalk. The faces alternately were pale blue
and livid red in the flashing lights of the squad car.
Inside the warehouse police technicians applied white
powder to a motley assembly of old and repaired
furniture. Others searched the stairway, and still oth-

ers went into the office, looking for signs of break-in and robbery. There were none.

Uniformed patrolmen looked through the garbage cans in the alley and interviewed people living in the apartments behind Lyons.

Al Gilbert went slowly into the furniture store. He was quite sure he had an ulcer. He had had an endoscopy. Shoved a black tube down in his throat until it felt like it was coming out his asshole. They had found no bleeding. But why else did he feel this gnawing, burning hole in his gut? There weren't enough Rolaids in America to coat his stomach. Now, in the entrance to Lyons Furniture, it burned even worse. Why had Captain Emery ordered him to come to this case in downtown Los Angeles?

Maybe it was the job, he decided. That was why his stomach lining was gone. He went to the cluster of policemen and looked down at an ornate walnut chest.

He admired the handiwork on the exterior. It was exuberant, the kind of craftsmanship that had died out about the time he was born. Inside the chest, for display purposes, was a rug with green and broad blue bands, some dried flowers, and also a little white teddy bear to give it that homey touch.

And a well-dressed young man, dead, stuffed into the corners.

Gilbert examined the neck. He touched the flesh of the chest. The skin had that clammy wilted-lettuce feel that nauseated him. The musculature had tightened, the posture of the crumpled corpse going rigid in rigor mortis.

Gilbert turned and looked up. Captain Emery was staring down into the chest. So was Fred Santomassimo. They briefly nodded greetings. Gilbert looked down at the corpse. The face was young, perhaps a twenty-two-year-old face, surprised, and kind of sadly disappointed at being dead. Gilbert blew his nose. Bronte came across the cavernous furniture store floor, rumpled and agitated, notebook, as always in hand.

Gilbert stood up. He kept wiping his fingers on little moistened towelettes he carried, tearing them out of tiny plastic packages.

"Good evening, Captain," Gilbert said. "Evening, Fred."

"Last time we met you were getting a suntan," Captain Emery said.

"Yeah. Well, this poor bastard is pale as a vampire's date."

Santomassimo bent over, studying the grimace, that death had smeared across the face of the young man.

"What's the cause of death?" Santomassimo asked. "Strangulation?"

"Damn right. See?" Gilbert bent down and pressed the dead man's collar apart. Santomassimo was taken aback by what appeared to be a rust-red necklace of flesh—bruised flesh—and then purple-and-blue abrasions around the red. "I can't be a hundred per cent sure until I get him on the table," Gilbert said.

"He might have been strangled by a pair of hands. The rope used as a blind."

"You think it could have happened that way?"

Gilbert shrugged. "I'd like to look under the fingernails. Pieces of somebody's skin, or something. Maybe there was a struggle."

Captain Emery covered his mouth and nose with a white handkerchief. Gilbert smiled without warmth.

"As you can smell, Captain," he said, "this is no fresh death."

"How old?"

"I'd go as far as to guess that it could have happened four, five days ago."

Captain Emery sighed with disgust, but he could not take his eyes from the corpse. Death has a weight, an undeniable reality. It holds down the fabric of the living by showing the future. Violent death gives the lie to the proposition that good wins. Santomassimo walked from the chest and snapped his fingers. A distant patrolman looked up.

"Is the owner here?" Santomassimo ordered. "I want to talk to the store owner."

Inside a glass-enclosed office the patrolman conveyed the order, and a detective interrupted his interrogation of a nervous-looking man with a chopped off, bushy mustache. The store owner came down the corridor of chests, desks, hat stands, sofas, a china cabinet, and two bidets, carrying his book of invoices, clutching them, as though clutching to the only reality he could depend on.

All Santomassimo said was, "Any break-ins in the past few days?"

The owner, William Mabley, clenched his invoices even harder. All the police, all the detectives, uniformed and plainclothes, were looking at him. The reputation of Lyons was ruined. He felt faint. Were those photographers' flashes? Was he going to be in the papers?

"No," Mabley managed to say. "Lyons is protected by a touch-sensitive and light-sensitive electronic alarm system, wired directly to a private security agency. In addition, we have vertical iron grates on all the glass, also wired to the agency."

"How long have you had this chest?"

Mabley consulted his book of invoices. His hands were trembling so badly he nearly tore the pages.

"Victorian bedroom chest," he read. "Inventory number 3245. Value of twenty-five hundred dollars. Insured for that sum by Pacific Indemnity. Shipped to the store from a house in Hollywood—probate sale—mostly junk—came to us on—" he turned the page—October 5th." Mabley looked up, his pupils like pinpoints, dots of darkness in the bright store lights. "That would be two days ago, Sergeant."

"Lieutenant."

"What address in Hollywood?" Bronte asked, coming up behind Mabley.

Mabley looked at the invoice. "2338 Selma Avenue."

Bronte wrote it down and tucked his notebook into his interior coat pocket.

"I'll check it out, Fred," he told Santomassimo.

Bronte left. Gilbert kicked an antique armoire for no reason other than an animal dislike of the store and its putrifying contents. Mabley raised a hand but kept silent. He turned to Captain Emery and Santomassimo.

"We get stuff from all over," Mabley said. "Private sales, estate auctions, probate liquidations, dead storage auctions—"

"Couldn't you fucking smell something wrong in this batch, Mr. Mabley?" Captain Emery demanded.

Mabley laughed humorlessly, a cold giggle. "Smell? It's old furniture, Captain. We get all kinds of smells around here. Camphor, mildew, dust, rotted upholstery, rat turds, dead rats. Gets to a point, we don't smell anything."

Captain Emery raised an eyebrow. He turned away in disgust.

"A decomposing human being, Mr. Mabley," he advised, "has a distinctive and unforgettable odor."

Santomassimo went to the plate glass window. The sun was setting. An eerie orange glow permeated the streets. The adjacent apartments looked like terracotta. People were on their balconies, staring down. A squad car came quickly up the boulevard, its siren howling, and the police pushed a reluctant crowd from the curb.

"Who's that?" Captain Emery barked.

"I made a little request, Captain," Santomassimo said.

Santomassimo went to the door. The patrol car double-parked in front of Lyons's door. A policeman opened the passenger door for Kay Quinn. She was wearing a sweater and green skirt. Not so formal as in the lecture hall. She seemed confused by the crowds, the police, and the bright lights. He greeted her on the sidewalk.

"Thanks for coming," he said. "I've put myself out on a limb with the Hitchcock theory. The captain is on the verge of believing."

She smiled, still confused, but less so now, and trusting Santomassimo.

"I'll be as authoritative as I can, Lieutenant," she said.

"Good." Santomassimo paused, a look of concern in his eyes. "It's pretty gruesome in there, Kay. If you're at all worried I'll have the driver take you home."

"Don't be silly," Kay laughed. "Gruesome is what I deal in."

He escorted her toward the door. An all-too-familiar brighter-than-bright, blue-white light hit him in the side of the neck. It was Steve Safran. By Safran's side was a cameraman from KJLP news.

"Another murder, another division," Safran shouted, the microphone pointed at Santomassimo. "Why are you handling the case?"

"We've just been invited to look in on Captain Callahan."

"Come on, come on," Safran insisted. "What's going on? This is a part of a serial killing, isn't it?"

Santomassimo took Kay by the arm and pushed his way toward the door. "I really can't go into details," he said. They went inside. Safran went to the door, where he and his cameraman were stopped by a uniformed policeman.

"Who's the lady?" Safran shouted. "What's *she* doing here?"

Santomassimo ignored him and ushered Kay into the knot of policemen standing around the chest. It was twilight inside the store now. The store owner, William Mabley, stared suspiciously at Kay.

"Who is she?" he asked. "She's not from the police."

"Move aside, please, Mr. Mabley," Santomassimo said. Captain Emery was staring at Kay. The captain found her attractive. Extremely atractive. But he was staring because he found her an intrusion and didn't know why Santomassimo had brought her.

"This is Professor Kay Quinn," Santomassimo said, looking directly into the captain's eyes. "I wanted her to see the victim. I wanted to hear what she has to say."

"Why couldn't this wait? Did you have to bring her here?"

"She's a Hitchcock expert," Santomassimo said.

Captain Emery looked at Santomassimo and saw the deadly seriousness in his lieutenant's face. He knew better than to interfere. "Okay. Fine. Go ahead, Fred. Show her what's in the chest."

Captain Emery signaled, and Al Gilbert and the rest of the police moved aside. Suddenly self-conscious, Kay paused at the edge of the huge carpet on which the furniture—including the ornate chest—was displayed. Santomassimo took her once again by the arm.

"Oh, dear God—" she gasped.

A wave of nausea hit her. She swayed. The rictus of death had made the corpse grin, a knowing, almost lewd leer, and one eye had opened enough so that half the pupil was fixed in her direction.

She tightened her grip on Santomassimo's arm.

"*Rope*," she said hollowly.

Captain Emery, not understanding, leaned forward to hear her better.

"Rope?" Captain Emery said. "Of course it's a rope. We don't yet know if the cause of death was actually—?

"No," she said. "The film. *Rope*. A whole film done

in five single takes by the greatest master of suspense. Oh, God—!"

She caught herself and fought her disorientation. The young man, suddenly ageless now that he was a dead thing, kept staring back at her, at one of those angles that always look at you no matter where or how you move. Kay felt a pressure and darkness around her and knew she was going to faint.

"John Dall . . . and Farley . . . Granger . . ." she said, fighting the encroaching darkness, ". . . strangle a . . . student friend . . . with a rope . . . and . . . stuff . . . his . . . body . . . into a . . . chest . . . Jim . . . my . . . Stew . . . art . . ."

The darkness won. Kay Quinn felt Santomassimo's strong arms around her and then she fell into a quick void.

She woke in Santomassimo's arms. They were standing outside and she was leaning against him. He guided her toward a tavern across the street. Zippie's was small and grungy, very dark inside, with few clients. It smelled of disinfectant and old beer and cigarette butts, but nevertheless it had more fresh air than the furniture store. A few sour women turned toward them, watching from the bar stools as he helped Kay into a booth.

"Here you go," he whispered softly, making a pillow of his coat. "Lay your head on the table."

"I'm so embarrassed—"

"Shhhhhh. I'm sorry I put you through this ordeal."

"You warned me."

"Yes, but—I thought it was important that *you* identify the film. Not for me, but for Captain Emery— to convince him. Only you could do it, and it worked. He's on our side now."

"Great." Kay smiled lamely. "I think I need a drink, Lieutenant."

Santomassimo nodded. He rose to get two stiff

drinks. As he went from the booth her hand instinctively reached for him.

"Hurry back," she pleaded.

He came back with two tumblers of Zippie's best
brandy.

"Oh, God—" she blurted.

He slowly massaged her neck and shoulders. It was
a good feeling. She was nicely assembled, strong and
athletic. Right now she was tight as a drum. Slowly
she relaxed. He picked up her brandy.

"Here," he said. "Drink this."

Kay nodded but trembled as she raised her pallid
face. She allowed him to bring the tumbler to her lips.
It burned. She coughed and made an effort to
straighten up.

"Drink it all," he encouraged.

Kay took another sip, then shook her head. The
stuff was stronger than smelling salts. She pushed
his hand away. "I'm all right, now," she said.

He put the tumbler down. Her eyes watched his
hand, his wrist, his arm and shoulder, and then
his face. She looked so vulnerable. Her eyes were
looking for something in his. He sat down across from
her and her eyes still kept looking into his.

"Reality is pretty grim, isn't it?" she said.

He nodded. "It grabs all the senses. That's for damn
sure."

"Yeah."

Kay picked up her brandy. He watched her finish it.
She was very pretty. Even her hands were delicate, yet
strong. He was convinced she was a skiier or a swim-
mer. Kay's eyes filled with sadness.

"Do you know who . . . the victim was?" she asked.

"Yes. His wallet was in his trousers. His name was
Charles Pierce. He had an undergraduate ID from
UCLA. A physical education student. Some gymna-
sium numbers. Might have been an athlete. Just an
unlucky kid who happened to fit the part."

Kay shivered.

"This man is crazy," she said.

"Yeah, crazy."

"I mean . . . *Really* crazy."

"*Really* crazy."

"He's got to be stopped," she insisted.

Santomassimo leaned forward to tell her about the captain and the options open to them, when a shape blotted out Zippie's internal floodlights. The shape sat down at a table just opposite the booth. It was Steve Safran.

Safran eyed them both, a little smile on his rosebud lips. He still had a cable for a microphone on his shoulder, but the ubiquitous microphone and cameraman were nowhere to be seen.

"Mind if I join you?" Safran asked, pulling his chair closer to their booth.

"We do," Santomassimo said.

Safran ignored him. He kept staring at Kay. Then he snapped his fingers, remembering.

"Hi, Professor Quinn," he said. "Remember me?"

"No."

"Two years ago. You did a spot for me. *Women in Cinema.* Remember? I put that series together myself. I believe you talked about Alfred Hitchcock."

"I might have."

Safran leaned toward her, enjoying Santomassimo's discomfort.

"What did you call it?" Safran asked. "The Hitchcock Imperative?"

"I remember."

"Are you working with the police on this case?"

Santomassimo gently but firmly interceded. "She's with me, Safran. She's a personal friend."

Safran laughed, leaning back against the edge of the table, his head back. He tossed one fat leg up over the other, watching them both. "Yeah, sure. Just enjoying a tête-a-tête over a dead body. Hell of a place to take a lady on a date, Lieutenant."

Santomassimo stared hard at the puffy, pink face of the news reporter. The face was porcine, insolent, yet the eyes glittered with a relentless fascination, even a certain kind of unpleasant brilliance.

"Buzz off, Safran!" he said.

"Gosh, Fred. You're so excitable. Tell me. Why are the police keeping such a tight blanket on this? Is it *that* explosive?"

"You know what you should do, Safran?"

"No. What?"

"Go see the commissioner. Tell him I sent you. That's where all the official statements come from."

"The commissioner has no statements to make at this time," Safran said. "That's all I've heard for days." Suddenly Safran's expression turned angry. The obese reporter moved closer to Santomassimo as a waitress placed a glass of beer before him. Safran drank. Then he wiped his lips, still angry. "Face it, Lieutenant. There's a big and very inquisitive public out there who want to know. And have a right to know. And I'm going to tell them, with your cooperation or without, understand? Just as soon as I put a few more pieces together."

Santomassimo had a sudden urge to shove the beer glass down Safran's throat. There had been a manslaughter case like that in Barstow. Bam—the whole glass, right down into the moist red mouth. But he refrained. Instead, he stood and put a hand on Kay's arm.

"Come on, Kay," he said.

She rose shakily. He steadied her. They edged out of the booth, brushed past Safran, and went to the door past two drunks arguing over a baseball score. Safran remained on his chair, tilted at his table, near their empty booth. He kept watching them. A small smile was on his round face. He reached into Zippie's hors d'oeuvres bowl, little fat fingers nosing the ceramic for food. He found popcorn.

Yellowed with butter, salted popcorn.

Santomassimo took Kay to his unmarked police car. The crowds were still peering over the police cordon at Lyons furniture store. Captain Emery was inside the office, arguing with another police captain.

As Santomassimo opened the door of his car for Kay, Bronte ran up perspiring heavily.

"There *was* a break-in at the Hollywood house," Bronte said. "The killer jimmied the back door lock. I sent a team to work it over."

"For all the good it will do young Mr. Pierce."

Bronte glanced at the ubiquitous notebook and brushed strands of moist hair off his forehead. "Fred, we found out that Mr. Pierce had a small moving and hauling business. Nice College Boy Movers and Haulers. He apparently had a call about four days ago. So the killer must have lured him there."

"Killed him and stuffed him."

"Yes, sir."

"Because he'd seen a film like that."

"It appears so, Lieutenant."

"Do we breed these maniacs, Lou?" Santomassimo asked, angry and frustrated. "Does every country have them?"

Bronte had no answer. Who did? For all they knew the killer was in the crowd, enjoying his reviews. Santomassimo turned to go, but noticed that Bronte stood there uncertainly.

"What is it, Lou?" He asked. "You got something else for me?"

"Well, it's pretty strange—"

"What?"

"This."

Bronte took a Plasticine envelope carefully from his coat pocket. He handled it as though it contained the world's rarest diamond dust. From it he pulled a piece of popcorn. He showed it to Santomassimo.

"I found this myself," Bronte said. "On the floor of the chest. After they unbent poor Mr. Pierce and carted him away."

Santomassimo took it gingerly between his fingers, examined it, held it to the light. It was just what it was, a piece of popcorn.

"So?" he asked.

"There's another piece back at headquarters," Bronte said, not without pride at his memory. "In the garbage screened from the Pacific Coast embankment."

Santomassimo handed the popcorn back to Bronte, who deftly dropped it back into the Plasticine envelope.

"I'd like Professor Quinn to see what we have at headquarters," Santomassimo said.

"You're the boss."

"Meet us there, will you, Lou?"

Bronte nodded and went across the street to his car. Pierce's corpse was removed, but the crowd kept surging around the door. All these patrol cars, they reasoned, there *must* be something neat going on.

Santomassimo drove with Kay to Santa Monica Boulevard, then straight for the beach. It was a deep twilight, an indigo sky where a few stars were visible out over the brightly lit Santa Monica pier below. The palms rustled in front of the high-rise hotels.

"Are you feeling better?" he asked gently.

"Much better, thanks."

He smiled. "My Aunt Rosa always said confession was good for the soul, but if there wasn't a priest nearby, a shot of good brandy worked almost as well."

She laughed. "That *was* a dreadful sight. I'm sorry I blacked out. Dealing with murder on the screen is one thing. It's art. It's intricate, subtle, clever. But seeing that young man's face in the chest—"

"Brutal. You're right. There's nothing subtle about death."

"Who was that reporter?"

"Steve Safran? Oh, he's just doing his job. Lots of people get vicarious kicks when real people are killed. People like Safran feed them."

They drove westward along the Santa Monica Freeway. It was a dreamy feeling. The unmarked police car drove well, and Santomassimo was a fast, good driver. He turned on the tape deck and Smokey Robinson's milky smooth, upbeat melody came out. Kay settled back, closed her eyes, and smiled.

"I didn't know police cars had tape decks, Lieutenant," she said.

"They don't. And you can call me Fred."

When he pulled up in front of the Palisades Division she got out of the car, and then hesitated. She laid a hand on his arm.

"There won't be any more corpses, will there?" she asked.

"No. Just bits and pieces of things. To jog your mind."

They went inside. Bronte was already there, sipping black coffee, using a wooden stirring stick to remove the residue of melting plastic that coated the top of the coffee.

"Hello, Fred. Professor Quinn. This way."

They went down to the long room with the table. Bronte went inside first. Only a goose-necked lamp illuminated the debris from the beach. Santomassimo turned on the room lights. Kay saw the detritus, looked back at him and Santomassimo nodded, gesturing for her to go to the table. He joined her where the small airplane stood as though poised to fly over the landscape of broken beer bottles, candy wrappers, and sandy garbage.

Bronte waited until she was through looking at the

toy airplane. Somehow everything was becoming too real for her now.

"Over here, Professor," Bronte said.

Slowly she looked. In a grid near the corner of the table, its position on the Pacific Coast embankment marked with a grease pencil, was a single piece of yellowed popcorn. It still had not decayed. Bronte took the second piece from his Plasticine envelope and placed it adjacent to the first. The popcorn pieces stared back, a perfect pair, like ragged little eyes.

"See? Not bad, huh, Fred?" he said. "I remembered noticing the popcorn the other day."

"You're saying the killer dropped them?"

Bronte shrugged. "All I know is, there are two of them now. Count them. One. Two." Deftly, like a magician, he produced another Plasticine bag with a third piece of popcorn. "And now you see three."

Santomassimo stared at the third piece of popcorn in dumb amazement . . . Bronte grinned. "It's from Hirsch's sweepings at the Windsor Regency. Nancy Hammond wasn't forgotten."

"It's like a signature," Kay suggested.

"Signature?" Santomassimo asked.

"Hitchcock was famous for appearing in his own films, just for a second. Difficult to find him, but the audience kept waiting. It was a game. It was his signature."

Santomassimo looked to Bronte for guidance.

"Fred," she insisted.

"Yes?"

"Where does one eat popcorn?"

"At the movies."

A terrible silence filled the room, an audible shroud over Bronte, Santomassimo, Kay, and the toy airplane, the debris of the beach, the goose-necked lamp, and three insolent pieces of buttered popcorn.

*　*　*

Santomassimo drove Kay to her apartment. It was in a Spanish-styled complex below Westwood. Bouganvillea grew along a white terrace and enormous purple glads surrounded the entrance. When he stopped the car, she made no move to open the door. She was lost in thought about the murder.

"Come on," he said quietly, "I'll see you to your door."

She looked up at him with that vulnerable look. Then she smiled. "No, please, don't bother. I'll be all right."

He reached across her to open the door. The door swung open and she began to get out. Santomassimo let his arm lower so it rested on hers. The arm was warm. She hesitated.

"I . . . want to thank you . . ." he stammered. "For helping us."

"I want to help you. I want to see this maniac locked away, Lieutenant Sant—"

She cocked her head slightly and looked at him inquisitively. "Santomassimo?" she concluded in a different tone of voice. "What kind of name is that?"

"Italian."

"Does it mean something?"

Santomassimo colored. "Great Saint."

Suddenly Kay laughed, a sweet laugh of surprise. "Great Saint!" she said. "Wow! That's some name for a cop!" Equally suddenly she studied him seriously. He felt her eyes searching his face. For what? He wondered. What wasn't there that wasn't obvious? "But then," she said, "you don't look like a cop."

"Really?"

"It's your eyes. Much too warm and understanding for a cop."

"Not for an Italian cop."

A cat ran across the lawn, chasing shadows of bougainvillea. She watched, then turned to him. Her face had softened. It was like lovely silk under the street light.

"May I ask you a personal question?" she asked.

He nodded.

"Are you a married Italian cop?"

"I was."

"Divorced?"

He nodded.

"You don't mind my asking?" she asked.

"You're a professor. Professors ask questions. Just like cops."

She laughed, then moved to get out. This time his hand closed on hers. Her hand was even warmer than her arm. She stopped moving, her face slightly averted.

"May *I* ask a personal question?" he said.

"Of course."

"Same question."

She turned to look at him. The breeze stirred through her hair. Santomassimo felt momentarily suspended in the green of her eyes. She withdrew her hand, smiling sympathetically.

"No," she said. "I'm not married."

She got out of the car. They smiled at each other.

"Goodnight, Great Saint," she said very softly.

"Goodnight."

He watched her go to the security gate, unlock it, and walk past tall palms and lilies up a delicately railed stairwell to her apartment. He kept watching for a while, even after she was gone. Then he drove away. He knew he would not sleep that night.

Click . . . The tape recorder rolled on, recording . . . the figure sat hunched by a window that overlooked old, decaying Hollywood, the great film laboratories and the film rental houses, the billiard halls and the adult movie theaters . . . It was quiet for a while . . .

"Why Hitchcock?"

There was another long silence . . . The figure opened a bottle of beer, raised it to his lips, drank, and wiped his mouth with his hand.

There was a noise outside. Instantly, the figure turned off the tape recorder. There was a wait. The footsteps receded and, with it, a thick coughing and clearing of phlegm from a diseased throat. Then the tape recorder began again, recording.

Click . . .

"Why Hitchcock? It's a difficult question. Why anything? Why was I born? Why did I appear in a godforsaken place like Nebraska with this talent, this curse, call it what you want, that won't quit? Why has my life been ruined by it? Why have the studios, even the small ones, shut their doors in my face?

"Hitchcock because he chose me. I didn't choose him."

There was a long pause. The figure did not move. The figure seemed oblivious to the turning reels, recording nothing but ambient sound, the distant traffic, inchoate apartment plumbing sounds. After awhile, the voice began again, distantly, as though it had thought about hard things to face and now came back to the present once again.

"I was suicidal. I think I mentioned that. After the negative turned to green dust, I sort of wandered around. I even worked selling soap door to door. Can you believe that? Me, with a bunch of housewives in the Valley? I worked ten times harder than I ever worked before. I quit after three weeks, flat broke . . . I was a failure as a salesman.

"And then, miraculously, a wonderful thing happened. My mother and father passed away. In Italy. On vacation— Naples—bad clams. But even dead, they managed to screw me. The inheritance would come to me in dribs and drabs— tiny morsels to appease my hunger for food and drink, but not my hunger for artistic requitement. I was the only heir to a fortune of millions, which I could neither sell, barter nor control until I achieved the age of forty-five. Can you believe FORTY-FUCKING-FIVE? That is TWENTY FUCKING YEARS!

Click . . . The figure sat back in the chair, panting hard . . . the breathing stertorous, accompanied by a tiny mewling sound. Gradually, calm returned. The figure leaned forward to the tape recorder . . . Click . . . The recording went on . . .

"Still . . . it wasn't so bad now. With the breathing space the trust checks permitted, I had the luxury of looking around without having to earn my daily bread. I became entranced by Los Angeles. The city was a sprawling monster. I liked the sunlight and the attitude of the people. It's like we were all hustlers, all seedy, all decayed, but, hey, we could make it look good, we could put on this huge party that would be called Los Angeles. And we could make films, talk about films, see films. Films were in the air. People believed in films. They believed in what films told them, more than they believed in schools or religion, or what schools tried to teach them. Film's a gas. For everybody, me included. Especially me.

I lived above a tobacco shop on Santa Monica Boulevard, and all night I could hear the cockroaches jumping around in my pantry. I could have afforded better, but I didn't care. I had this fever to make films, see, worse than ever before. So I didn't care about anything else.

"And I began watching the old films again. Black and white, mostly, or the early color films. I guess you could say I was escaping again, but I wasn't escaping from, I was escaping to. There it was, my old world, the most real world, the cuts, dollies, zooms, and the subtle points of narration, all the things the audience missed but which I caught.

"And Hitchcock was the greatest. Is that so hard to understand?"

Click . . . The figure rose . . . Far off, there was the sound of a toilet flushing . . . The figure came back . . . listened to what had been recorded . . . Click . . . The tape recorder went on, recording . . .

"When I saw those Hitchcock pictures, I realized he was creating illusions. Sure. I know. All directors create illusions. But listen, damn it. There's more to this crap than meets the eye. Your eye, anyway. When Hitchcock created illusions, he let the illusion show, but it worked anyway. Can you absorb that? Like a magician who shows you just how he's going to do the trick and then goes ahead and does it and by Christ you believe, you really believe that the fucking rabbit came out of his jockstrap or wherever—Hitchcock did that. It was just a movie, see. It was make believe. These were dumb actors. Cattle. Mouthing lines. Bizarre stories.

You could see the artifice of the tension, the suspense. And it worked every single fucking time.

"Because that was his vision. Murder was a joke. Because life was a joke. I understood that. That's why his films are comic and sinister at the same time.

"I used to watch the faces in the audience, torn between laughter and suspense and I despised them for being the passive playthings they were.

"I wanted to be Hitchcock. I wanted to be the director I was born to be. I wanted so much. And all I could do was listen to some failed writer lecture about screenwriting, which I knew better than he did anyway.

"No. With Hitchcock, you're dealing with a force unique in our time. His stamp is on every picture he ever made. Wyler, Cukor, Zinneman, are all good, but compared to Hitchcock, they're invisible. Hitchcock is obsessive. Hitchcock knows that death is a hoot because life—talent, ambition, all the hopes and desires of our hearts—are worthless in the long run. Hitchcock made visible the cruelty that underlies our lives."

There was a short pause. The voice hummed, indistinctly, an old tune, a march, from Gounod. Then it broke into laughter. It settled down, cheerfully, enthusiastically.

"And let me say, by the way, that it hasn't been easy, getting people to do what I want. Actors are bad enough, with their little egos and mincing ways, but at least they know what the script is. Charles Pierce didn't know a damn thing, but he was excellent. I'd say he was the best. Hasbrouk was a nondescript corporate man. I don't think he showed much flair at the end, wallowing around in the surf and mud like a beached seal. There wasn't a shred of dignity, of panache. The girl, on the other hand, was good, very good. Nancy Hammond. A cute little twitchy blonde, with that nice, all-American look, that glacial frigidity, that almost naked sexual desire. I really lucked in when they arbitrarily assigned her that room. Hitch would have liked her. The perfect secretary. Definitely his type.

"There's so much that goes into these scenes. Timing, planning. Exterior. Interior. Time of day. Motivation. Angles. The dawning awareness of the victim. I have these outlines, drawings, storyboards. I don't slap things together like that *director I call twenty-takes-a-day-Charlie. One-two-three kick. Sure, he gets in under budget. That's why he keeps getting all those assignments. But he might as well be making knishes because there isn't the slightest bit of artistry, precision, subtlety, frisson to his work. Because the zooms, the dollies, the closeups—it all has to be right, inescapably, perfectly right. I can do that. I've done it. I'll do it again. Beautiful, beautiful scenes.*

"Actually, it's better without cameras . . . Better than sex . . . Better than the best dope you can buy . . .

"Better . . . even . . . than Hitchcock . . .

"OH YEAH . . . CUT!"

9

KJLP was a young station, only five years old. Its broadcasting studios were located on Sunset Boulevard, behind the old Directors Guild building. Its exterior walls were pale green and new chrome doors and hi-tech furniture in the lobby did not hide the fact that the structure itself was old and cracking around the foundations. It was a very popular station, however, featuring a format of unusually aggressive news reporting and rock-and-roll videos.

It was eleven-fifteen. Steve Safran sat on a dais, wearing a checkered sports coat with a Lavalier mike in his lapel. Two cameras were trained on him, while the floor manager, fiddling with a headphone, followed along on his cue sheet. Safran read his editorials in a voice of assured authority.

"Three innocent people killed, the same police division involved in all three murders, though the bodies were found in Pacific Palisades beach, downtown Los

Angeles, and West Los Angeles. What's going on? Los Angeles wants to know. I want to know. They can't keep this from you, and they can't keep this from me. When will the police commissioner tell us?

"Or is this Russia, where the police are unaccountable?"

Safran paused melodramatically.

"This is Steven Safran, KJLP News."

The floor manager made the sign of cutting his throat, and the red light went out under the lead camera. The other cameraman began rolling up cable while an assistant moved the ponderous recording machine back against the wall. Technicians moved the backdrop, a huge map of the city streets of Los Angeles, to the wings. Safran, mopping his face, came from the desk onto the floor.

"What did you think, Bill?" he asked the floor manager.

"I don't know, Steve. You're slamming the police pretty hard. Maybe you should ease up."

Safran laughed, taking off his microphone. "They need it, Bill. Read my fan mail. My fans know something stinks. I'm a plumber. I flush the truth out of smelly places."

Safran saw Monica, the girl behind the console. She beckoned to him, indicating a white telephone receiver in her hand. He went up into the control booth.

Inside, the director, Frank Howard, hunched over the man at the console.

". . . and dissolve to . . . credit roll . . ."

Howard pointed to the toggle switch, the technician flipped it, and the names of the KJLP news staff began rolling up a television monitor screen. Without missing a beat, Howard gave Safran the thumb-and-forefinger success sign, then quickly pointed to the music track switch. The technician deftly segued into the KJLP theme.

Safran, pleased at the large type and position of his

own name in white letters on the monitor, took the receiver from Monica.

"Safran here," he said, as Monica toweled off his face.

The voice did not come at once. When it did, it seemed to come from far away. It was not the call of one of his fans. The voice was slow, yet troubled, and very intense. It had a dead sound, as though the voice came from an improperly miked studio.

"I have information," the voice said.

"Yeah? What kind of information?"

"I mean, I liked your news show, Mr. Safran. I think you're onto something. I think you'll be interested. That is, if you really are interested in the killings."

Safran gently moved Monica away. He turned to face the corner, where neither she, the director, the technicians, nor any of the crew coming in now for the next program, could hear him.

"Sure I'm interested," Safran said in that instinctively quiet voice one used to keep somebody on the line. "You know I am. You were right about that. What kind of information?"

"It's the information the lieutenant won't tell you . . . what he refuses to divulge . . ."

Safran leaned into the receiver. "What do you know about Santomassimo?"

"Oh, fuck it . . . I . . ."

"No—Don't hang up! I'm interested. I'm very, very interested!"

There was a long silence. Safran heard a slow breathing at the other end. Monica, puzzled, looked at him, but Safran just turned away and huddled into the corner even more tightly.

"What is it?" Safran gently persisted.

"Before I tell you that, let's talk . . ."

"Okay."

"About money."

Safran swallowed. "What do you mean?"

"What would it be worth to you?" the voice asked impatiently.

"Oh, I don't know. Depends if it's really usable. Maybe a couple hundred bucks?"

There was another long pause. This time Safran heard barely audible expletives. The voice came back, slow and steady.

"How about a couple of thousand?"

"Forget it. No. Wait. What are you, a cop? Are you working with Santomassimo?"

"Never the fuck *mind* who or what I am. I know about Professor Quinn, too, Safran. I know why she's got a role in this melodrama. But you'll have to pay to find out."

Safran was sweating again, partly with excitement, partly with an odd shivering malaise that he couldn't explain. "Look," he said. "I can't raise that kind of money. I don't *have* that kind of money. Would you settle for five hundred?"

"Make it a thousand."

"Wait—"

Safran tried to figure where he could get that kind of cash at this hour.

The director, Frank Howard, was putting on his coat. Safran turned to him, covering up the receiver with his hand. "Frank," he said crisply. "Don't go yet." Then he spoke into the telephone. "Okay. I can do it. Meet me in front of the studio. You know where we're located?"

"No, Mr. Safran. *You* will meet *me* where *I* tell you."

"Go ahead."

Safran listened. It was hard to hear. The voice began to ramble, and the swear words were dreadful. Finally it came around again, focused, and proposed a location. Safran frowned, puzzled.

"What? Why there? I mean, Jesus—"

In the Hollywood apartment the figure taped the conversation. It was a cluttered apartment. There were books, folios, a musical instrument, bits and pieces of film stock, still photographs, and an old rewind on a board. Photographs of Alfred Hitchcock were on a desk, like an altar. By the refrigerator were publicity stills of his films. On the wall were huge posters: *North by Northwest, Rope, Sabotage, The Birds*.

The figure smiled, enjoying Safran's eager impatience at the other end. The figure toyed with the telephone cord.

The posters glowed softly with their sheen. They seemed to have more presence than the rumpled figure in the darkness by the window.

"Why there?" he mimicked into the telephone at Safran, "I mean, why . . . shit . . . because . . . because . . ."

The figure craned his neck to look at a long poster that gleamed in the night light coming in through the open window. It had the big type: *Foreign Correspondent*. Then in smaller type, Hitchcock's name. The image: a man falling to his death from a church bell tower.

The figure returned to the telephone. For the first time the voice sounded friendly, even relaxed.

"Because it's private," he told Safran cheerfully. "Something for you only."

St. Amos's Church was a bulky structure, many additions and repairs having altered its silhouette over the years. Against the night clouds stood the bell tower, a black shape over the tenements of central Los Angeles.

Safran drove to the curb in front of the church. The car was a small Volvo, highly reflective. Safran still wore his plaid sports coat. He felt like a sitting duck. He was in the middle of gangland territory. St. Amos's had once been a prosperous church. Now even the sign announcing next week's sermon was askew on the shabby little lawn.

Safran walked quickly to the front steps. St. Amos's shadows swallowed him. The doors were open and he walked in. For a moment he stood, blinking in an utter darkness.

A glimmering light, the source of which he could not see, flickered palely on a crucifix on the wall and on gilded frames of paintings of the Passion. Dried, dusty flowers were set by a small door. Hymnals were stored in locked glass cases under a boarded window.

He saw now the trails of moisture on dark walls and chips from the stone. He crossed to the small door and opened it. It was the sacristy. A few candles burned low on a private altar. Evidently someone had died recently. Flowers were once fresh, but now drooping. Kneeling pads were badly worn below the few pews. On the altar was a small brass cross and against the stubby votive candles a black-bordered death card.

Safran silently shut the door. He looked behind him once again, and saw a darker door. He went to it. The door was wooden, bowed and cracked with age. He hesitated, then gingerly pulled on it. It resisted, then swung out with surprising ease. The hinges must have been well-oiled. He poked his head inside and looked up.

The staircase curled upward to the bell tower about 150 feet above him.

Safran kept staring. He mopped the sweat from his face, hands, and wrists. He didn't like the idea of squeezing his bulk up the narrow passage. It induced a certain claustrophobia. On the other hand, KJLP would make national news by cracking open the serial killings. And that was where the voice had instructed him to go.

Safran stepped into the staircase. The concrete stairs were worn and his slick shoes barely found a grip on the slightly sloped stone. At first there was no banister, and he had to push against the enclosing cement walls. It was like crawling up a rock intestine. Then he pulled himself upward by grabbing an old banister. The floor of the bell tower's stairwell receded under him.

He stopped. He heard no one, saw nothing but concrete and spider webs. The fear of ridicule seized him. KJLP was a great place for pranks. Or was it somebody on the police force? Was Santomassimo the kind of man to do a thing like this? He listened. Ancient wood creaked on the stairwell. Then it was quiet.

Safran loosened his tie and unbuttoned the top button of his shirt. It was cold but he was sweating and finding it hard to breathe as he climbed. A draft was coming through the open top of the bell tower. It swept down into the stairwell like a winter wind.

The bell tower was a ten-by-ten-square-foot cupola. St. Amos's black iron bell took almost the entire area, leaving a narrow walkway around it. Safran saw it all from a low angle, his head just protruding from the stairwell. The wind was fierce and he became dizzy.

"Hello!" he called. "You there?"

There was no answer. Safran climbed onto the floor of the cupola. He grabbed the remains of a rusted iron rail and hauled himself up. He was breathing very hard now. Some perverse instinct made him look down the stairwell.

The staircase twisted dizzyingly away, darkly, all the way to the bottom, 150 feet under his shoes.

Safran held hard onto the rail. It wobbled under his pudgy fist. A sickening emptiness had come into his stomach, a sudden nausea. He turned and picked and pulled his way around the narrow catwalk to the far side of the bell.

It was less windy on this side. Below, an extraordinary blaze of lights—red, yellow, and with black lines—stretched to infinity: Los Angeles at night. The city was radiant in a spectacular outpouring of energy. Even the skies had winking lights as aircraft of varying sizes flew in low toward the airports. The carpet of jeweled lights and colors faded gradually into a multicolored haze at what seemed the far end of the planet.

"Mr. Safran?"

Safran whirled around. He looked, and saw no one.

". . . uh . . . yes, yes," he said, still trying to see into the dark corners of the cupola. "I'm here. I've got the money."

He took an envelope from his pocket and held it in the air. "See?" he said.

"Just put it on the floor."

Safran stared at the direction of the voice. He saw only cobwebs and black shadows, but his ears were honing in. "Where are you?" he demanded. "Come on. Show yourself. I don't like dealing with a disembodied voice."

The voice was both languorous and impatient. "Put the money on the floor. Then you'll see me."

Safran bent over and put the envelope on the floor.

"All right," he said. "It's on the floor."

Safran lay the envelope on the warped boards. The wood was so old that it had long ago splintered around the nails, now rusted and protruding. Safran was staring at them when he heard a strange sound.

He heard a quick patter of running feet.

The image of mice came to him and he recoiled upward in disgust. But the sound wasn't mice. Mice don't scream. Not loudly. And now Safran, turning, heard a terrible murderous *joyous* scream. A black form, a shape of darkness, hurtled from around the edge of the bell and slammed into him. Safran was knocked off his feet, grasped once at the railings, missed, and tumbled into the open air of the deep shaft.

His scream also did not sound like mice.

But Safran had the oddest final vision: he was falling

hard yet staring intensely, focusing on whoever had
hit him. His concentrated vision seemed to move
forward at about the rate that he fell away. It gave a
weird, disorienting effect. Safran slammed into the
concrete, his eyeballs registered different parts of the
stairwell, and then he had nothing left to see anything
with.

St. Amos's was quiet for a long time. The bell tower
remained silhouetted against the clouds lighted from
below by city lights, and only the colors changed, and
only a little bit: pink, ochre, yellow-gray, and patches
of darkest indigo where the stars were also visible.

Then the bell struck the hour of one.

A police ambulance pulled up to the curb, and patrol
cars, and an unmarked car. People quickly gathered.
A church was a neat place for a cocaine bust went the
rumor. Police technicians went into the stairwell,
worked, and came out ashen faced. One of them
vomited behind the ambulance.

Santomassimo stood on the lower stairs, over the
somewhat liquified, spread shape of what had been
Steve Safran. Santomassimo glanced upward. It was
an awfully long way up. A fly could fall without harm,
a mouse would break a leg, and a man, a fat man like
Safran, would splash. He had splashed. Technicians
worked on the walls of the lower stairwell too.

Captain Emery appeared in the doorway and looked
over Bronte's shoulder. He stared a long time at the
jumble of clothes, belly, wrist watch, protruding bone,
and puddles of blood. Then, feeling Santomassimo's
expectant gaze, he looked up to the lieutenant, and
with a degree of embarrassment whispered, "*Vertigo*?"

"Maybe."

"Bell tower. The jumper."

"This fellow didn't jump, Captain."

Captain Emery looked back down at the remains,
still portly. "No. Not likely," he conceded.

Santomassimo rubbed his eyes. "If I remember right, the victim was Kim Novak and she did not play a reporter. The jobs don't match."

"So what are you saying, Lieutenant? The theory is no good?"

"I'm screwed if I know, Bill."

The medics hauled, stuffed, and coaxed Safran's remains into a black bag and then they zipped the bag and wheeled it out to the ambulance. Photographers came in to record what was left.

Santomassimo waited at the door. A police car turned through the crowd. Kay Quinn climbed out of the rear seat, wearing a cloth coat thrown over hastily assembled skirt and blouse. Her feet were still slippered. She seemed dazed by having been woken, and also by the fear of another murder site.

Santomassimo took her arm gently.

"Thanks for coming again," he said. "I've had the victim hauled away. There's nothing for you to see, so don't be nervous."

The captain came out with Bronte. Emery looked at Kay with surprise, then suspicion. He licked his lips, swallowed, and then gestured for Bronte to stay where he was. He beckoned Santomassimo to step under the oak with him.

"You're bringing this woman into this case more than is warranted," Emery warned.

"I don't have a case without her, Captain."

"Oh? Since when does the department depend on civilian help to this extent?"

"As of this moment, she *is* the case, Bill. She's all we've got, and we need her."

Emery thought about this, then said, "There are reporters, Fred. TV news people. They worked with Safran. They're watching our every move. It isn't discreet, bringing in Quinn."

"I can't help that, Bill. She's crucial."

Emery looked hard at Santomassimo. "It's just her expertise?"

Santomassimo felt himself blush in spite of himself. "That's all it is, Captain."

Emery sighed. "All right. Bring her forward."

Santomassimo walked back to Kay and put a hand on her arm.

"The dead man is Steve Safran," he said. He heard her slight intake of breath: "Yes, the man we saw in the bar. The television reporter. He was pushed from the bell tower."

She followed his pointed finger and looked at the ominous silhouette. Three starlings, pure black shapes, dived low through the cupola against the clouds.

She looked a long time. A strange realization moved her lips into something close to a smile.

"Captain Emery thinks the connection might be *Vertigo*," he said. "In the film, there was a death at a bell tower—"

Kay started to laugh. She tried to control it, but couldn't. It was not a laugh of warmth and humor. It was wrong, humorless, a distraught release of pent-up tension. It shook its way out through her as she tried to talk.

"Don't be silly," she said. "It can't be *Vertigo* . . ." She gritted her teeth, laughing. "It's *Foreign Correspondent* . . . Joel McCrea was supposed to fall from the bell tower . . . *he was the reporter!*"

"Take it easy, Kay . . ."

She pulled away from him. Her laughter came hard now, only half human, hurting. "Fred, it was . . . really Edmund Gwen . . . the killer who fell . . . Don't you see?"

The medics were closing the rear door of the ambulance. Before they did she pointed at the glistening black plastic bag, neatly zipped, bulging. Her laughter escalated until tears streamed down her face.

"That's not Kim Novak in that plastic bag," she

declared. "It . . . It's . . . Edmund . . . no . . . Oh, my God! . . . I don't know . . . who it is . . . I don't . . . know . . . who anybody is . . . anymore . . ."

Her laughter became sobs. Suddenly she had collapsed against Santomassimo's chest. He steadied her with an arm. Quietly he wiped away the tears.

"Maybe I shouldn't have brought her here," he said to Captain Emery.

"No. We needed her. But take her away, Fred. Calm her down. She's been through a lot."

Santomassimo looked around. There were no bars in this part of town. No places to sit down, except the bus-stop bench, and that was surrounded by teenage boys cracking insults at the police. He took her silently to his unmarked car.

When they got inside, he found a box of Kleenex and she gratefully took one.

He smiled encouragingly at her, but she was very pale and still trembling. He reached into the glove compartment and took out a pint bottle of excellent brandy.

"Aunt Rosa's elixir, remember?" he said. "Don't worry. It's very good."

"I thought police didn't—"

"They don't," he said. "Take a drink. It'll restore life."

She took the brandy and drank it like medicine. She was the first woman Santomassimo had ever met who could down a healthy slug and still look elegant. She shivered again, and pulled her cloth coat more snugly around her. She looked at him.

"You're going to make a drunk out of me," she said.

"Take another. You're still pale."

She took another drink. Her eyes grew stark. The brilliant mind was working again, the panic fading slowly but steadily.

"Was there popcorn?" she asked suddenly.

"Yes. One piece. On the catwalk of the bell tower."

"So it *is* a signature."

"It looks that way. Add another thing. We also found a sealed envelope with five hundred dollars in it. There was another five hundred in his wallet."

"See? The killer's not interested in money. He's only interested in—"

"Killing."

They remained silent. The police vehicles were moving away, leaving a patrolman to guard the church, where distraught priests now denied any knowledge of previous violence to inquisitive reporters.

Captain Emery walked over to Santomassimo's car. He asked if Kay was all right. Kay said she was feeling better, thanks. Emery asked if she would meet with them downtown at the Criminal Courts Building in the morning, before her class, if that was possible.

Kay remained silent for an even longer while, then nodded.

Emery said he'd have a car pick her up, thanked her, and said goodnight. Santomassimo turned the key in the ignition, glanced at Kay, then back at the deserted road, heavily lined with old oak trees. It was late; not even the birds were out any more.

"I guess I'd better take you home."

He shifted into drive, but kept his foot on the brake. She seemed self-conscious.

"Anywhere, Great Saint. Just take me away from here."

She was pale, pale as a statue in the weird light outside the church. Her lips were soft and deep red from crying. Santomassimo's wife had never cried. She had tears of anger sometimes, and from pain, but she had never softened up enough to cry.

"I don't want to be alone tonight," Kay said.

There was a naked urgency and vulnerability in her voice. Santomassimo knew she hadn't meant anything beyond exactly what she had said. Still, he felt self-conscious now, too.

"Where," he asked, "would you not like to be alone?"

"Any place where it's quiet."

Santomassimo nodded almost imperceptibly, squeezed her hand reassuringly, and drove toward the Pacific Coast. The fog and the dark were also reassuring. There wasn't much traffic. She closed her eyes several times but never asked to be taken home.

"We could get something to eat," he suggested.

She smiled. "I'd like that. How about that restaurant over there?"

The flickering neon sign proclaimed it to be: "Little Anthony's Fish Grotto."

Santomassimo's face betrayed a look both haunted and bitter. His voice struggled to say, "I'd rather not."

Kay sensed that something had happened. She looked at him quizzically. "Is the food that bad?"

"Let's just say it's a personal reason."

Kay watched "Little Anthony's Fish Grotto" as they drove past. The clientele had expensive wheels, all gleaming in the parking lot. She focused her eyes on the road ahead, and softly asked, "Your wife?"

Santomassimo nodded.

A small smile edged the corners of Kay's lips. "So that was *your* restaurant," she said. "I'm sorry. I'm sorry people break up. I'm sorry it happened to you."

Santomassimo hadn't talked about Margaret, not even to Bronte, for three years. It made him nervous now. Some things he had hoped were dead. The silence between them became self-conscious. Kay's light laughter defused it.

"You know, it's funny. Out of three thousand restaurants in L.A. I pick the one that reminds you of your wife. How lucky can I be?"

"It's not important."

"Would it help if you talked about it?"

"What's to talk about? After five years of marriage I discovered I never knew her . . . Oh, I knew she was tall. Beautiful. Talented. A dancer. Experimental dance. Jazz. I never understood it very well. She's still in Los Angeles somewhere. I see her name in *The Los Angeles Times* occasionally. She has a dance group of her own."

Kay grew less tense, nestling into the leather upholstery. He glanced at her again, but her face was ambiguous. Softer than Margaret's, but just as mysterious, and a lot more changeable.

Santomassimo reached for a tape and put it on. She smiled.

"Eurythmics," she said. "Nice."

"I don't like most of the new music. I just happened to catch them on K-Joi. Great sound."

"I have their albums."

Santomassimo turned up the volume slightly. Annie Lennox's voice came out, sultry, demanding, superior, infinitely infectious.

"You're wondering about me," Kay said.

He nodded.

"Fair enough. I was almost married. I don't know what happened. I don't think it was my career. Somehow life took us in different directions. I guess I changed a little bit. He—didn't like it."

"Do you still see him?"

"Lots of times. He teaches comparative literature at Ohio State. Sometimes we see each other at conferences. He's changed. He's in the academic pigeon hole. He's let life slip by."

Kay was quiet a long time.

"Men in academia," she said. "Sometimes they remain very young in a funny lost kind of way."

Santomassimo smiled. They were driving toward the beach where several bonfires were raging and teenagers were dancing to the throbbing beat of ghetto blasters.

It would be a matter of minutes before somebody on the night shift was called out to answer complaints from the apartment owners. The long slope ahead led north, past the intersection with Sunset Boulevard, toward Zuma beach and the central California coast.

"Still hungry?" he asked.

"Famished."

"That's my apartment right there. The big block on the rise."

"I guess I can trust you, Lieutenant."

He laughed pleasantly and turned right. She hesitated, however, as she got out of the car. Maybe it was the dark of the garage, or some water on the concrete that had made the footing slippery. Maybe she was suddenly frightened again. She seemed to need to be with Santomassimo and then, as he got closer, she closed off, became distant.

They went up the elevator without speaking. Santomassimo was suddenly self-conscious, and almost regretted inviting her in, and couldn't think of anything to put her at ease. He walked to the door of his apartment feeling that the night had turned into a complicated business suddenly, and they were caught in it.

The dark of his home was illuminated by the amber lights under the John Marin. He had forgotten to turn them off. A smeared kind of weather laid sailboats low in the watercolor, a wild intrusion of weather into civilization's pleasures. Santomassimo began to help Kay off with her coat, but Kay wasn't paying him attention right now. She was transfixed by the lush display of art deco.

"Oh, my . . . What lovely pieces," she said. "Are they original?'

Santomassimo closed the door behind them, flicking the lock into place. He turned on a light switch and two lamps glowed deep in the room. There was a slight intake of breath, an involuntary signal of fascination from her. He smiled and went to her, took her by the arm, and gave her an impromptu guided tour of the living room.

"Every piece is original," he said. "This mahogany chair was made by Paul Tribe in 1912. It's museum caliber. One of a kind."

He walked her toward a set of table and chairs. It felt good, having her hand on his arm. It felt good to share, to be part of something larger than himself in a setting so luxurious, and now, without loneliness.

"Andre Groult made those four ebony chairs in 1925. The table is from Emile Jacques Ruhlman's factory. These two armchairs are his, too."

Kay traced the glistening, undulated surface of one of the lamps that glowed. "And this?"

"Jean Puiforcat."

She walked to the amboya wood sofa, the inlaid ivory gleaming back at her.

"Does one sit on this, or simply stare at it?"

He laughed and sat comfortably, even heavily, on the adjacent chair. "Great furniture is meant to be used," he said. "That's why they become antiques."

She came closer to touch the long edge of the chair and ended up touching his hand, the fingers closing around hers. She broke off playfully, whirled and took in all the living room, even the sumptuous sconces on the far wall.

"All this on a cop's salary?" she teased.

"No way," he laughed. "It all belonged to my parents. They worked in art deco. Collected it all their lives. This was back in 1920s, 1930s, when it was affordable. When they died, my sister got the insurance money and I got the furniture."

He went to a walnut cabinet with turquoise peacocks inlaid along the rails and took out a crystal bottle of the same brandy she seemed to have liked in the car.

"They must have been wonderful people," she said, taking a glass from him.

He poured them a small amount of brandy. They clinked glasses. It was good brandy. It made one smell autumn in unreal countries.

"They were," he said. "Loving, gentle, artistic. And both of them great cooks. Italian, of course. But they hated opera."

"Hated opera?"

"Especially *Pagliacci*."

Suddenly he grotesquely mimed the face of a tearful clown. "Especially 'Vesti La Giubba.' "

She burst out laughing. He took her hand.

"There's more," he said.

"You must be insured for a million dollars."

"Almost. Come on."

"Where?"

"The bedroom."

Santomassimo took her to the bedroom door and opened it. She sensed, in the darkness, the art deco before he even turned on a lamp. She was speechless. An armoire reached the ceiling, delicately patterned with mother of pearl, and long rectilinear lamps of the Mackintosh school stood against a bookshelf of ebony. But the room was dominated by the bed. It was a bed that belonged in a castle. A castle of defined tastes. It was well over eight feet long, with a massive head-board, smoothly lacquered, and a footboard, the whole decorated with exquisite Japanese goldfish and flowering lily pads.

Kay touched the smooth lacquer, the inlay. Ochre water reeds and even green snails were in the watery world described by the artist—a timeless, luxuriant world in which esthetic pleasure bordered on the erotic.

He moved behind her. When she turned, she looked at him plaintively. He wasn't sure what the look meant, but he guessed.

"Have you ever slept on a hundred and fifty thousand dollar Jean Dunard bed?" he asked.

"No. Is it better than on a six hundred dollar Simmon's Beautyrest?"

"Much, much more awesome."

He kissed her, very delicately. She sat on the bed's edge. She was surer of herself now. Relaxed. She looked at him, smiling, and then touched his face, ran her fingers slowly over it just as she had over the art deco furniture, and she studied his eyes. She frowned just a little sadly, or something like sadness.

"Tell me something, Great Saint," she said.

"Anything."

"With such a grand surname, how come 'Fred'?"

He chuckled. He kissed her fingertips. "Well, to tell the truth, I do have a real first name. But I changed it in high school. The kids used to make fun of it."

"Don't tell me. Let me guess. Dominick? Carmine?"

"Worse."

"Angelo?"

He shook his head.

"I give up," she said.

"Amadeo."

Kay was amazed. *"Amadeo?* Ama Deo. Ama Deus. *Love God."* She looked at him, disbelieving. *"Love God Great Saint!* Jesus Christ, Fred, do I genuflect?"

"Whatever you want to do, Kay."

He took her in his arms. She made no countermovements when he unbuttoned her blouse. She smelled fragrant, like a field of flowers. "Anything I want to do?" she whispered.

"Anything."

She laughed, then bent to his lips and kissed him. They lay together on the bed. He felt her heart beating hard against his. She unhooked her bra. They kissed again. His hands easily found her breasts and then her shoulders came close. Lips, tongues, and teeth spoke their mutual language, hot and silent.

"Kay—"

"Yes—please—*oh, please*—Great Saint."

She was exquisitely warm. Santomassimo felt himself become lost in a familiar, yet always mysterious world. There were all the seasons in the world in her, and more love than he had ever believed existed.

Yet he pulled away, lay back alone against the ornate headrest.

She held his hand very tightly, and it was like riding a deep ocean with her, lying side by side, but everything was wrong.

There was a thin film of perspiration on her lip and her eyes were still and wide, watching him. He began to speak, and she reached for his mouth and put her fingers against his lips.

"You don't have to say anything," she whispered.

"Kay," he said, kissing her fingers.

"It's all right, Great Saint. We'll take it slow. Slow as a slow boat to China. That makes it all the better."

He smiled. He sat upright at the edge of the bed, his back to her. When she came close behind him he smelled her warmth again. He needed her, but it was desperately and completely wrong tonight.

"It was her bed, wasn't it?" Kay asked. "Margaret's?"

He nodded. "I didn't think it would matter, Kay."

"Somewhere, deep down, she's there."

"No. Not her. Just the—I don't know—the miserableness of it all—This was where we had such high hopes. But I think we were lying from the very start."

He toyed with a Pierre Cardin robe, a deep navy blue with white bands. He looked shattered.

"I'm sorry, Kay. I feel like a fool."

"And I feel like a sex maniac," she said. "I don't know what you must think of me now."

"Kay, you're the most beautiful, the most wonderful thing that's happened to me—"

"Let's not talk about it, Fred. Let's have that midnight breakfast you promised. Isn't that why we came here?"

She had covered herself in the bedspread. It made her look Japanese, if Japanese women had green eyes. The floral quilt against the lacquer work made an aesthetic object out of her. Santomassimo realized he was in deeper water than he had anticipated. The bedroom was only the beginning, not the end. Complications had a way of blossoming quickly between a man and a woman. Still, he liked the look of her. He liked her mind. And he needed her.

She began to put her blouse back on.

"Do you want me to drive you home?" he asked.

"Am I being invited to leave?'

"No. Never. I don't ever want you to leave."

"Then let me cook. I make a terrific breakfast."

He smiled and kissed her lips. He felt humiliated. He had thought Margaret was dead inside him. Now he believed it was he who had become dead these last three years alone.

Kay went into the kitchen and among the copper pans and spatulas, the spices and rye bread, eggs, and mushrooms, whisked up a full omelette.

"Something I learned in London, while working on my dissertation," she said. "Gourmet eggs."

He set the table with two places, then walked to the window. He was still embarrassed.

"The sunrise is particularly nice here," he said. "You don't see it right away, but the sun comes creeping up over the canyon walls just after the birds start waking."

"Let's do that, Great Saint. Let's wait for the dawn."

He went to the balcony and dragged two chaise longues together, then piled them high with spare blankets. They nestled into the longues and ate their omelettes. They lay together, listening to the dawn birds. He woke several times, but he did not move for fear of waking her. His hand on her breast, under her bra, he felt a calm he hadn't for many years, and was no longer embarrassed.

He half-wakened later, as he heard the black Pacific tide rolling under the piers and against the sandy beaches far below. Kay was fast asleep with her arms inside his shirt, over his chest.

Then, much later, Kay suddenly bolted awake with a gasp. She sat up shivering.

Santomassimo rose, too, and saw she had panicked a second time.

"Easy, easy . . ." he murmured.

Her flesh was full of goose bumps, and cool. She didn't want him to touch her at first.

"I keep seeing that poor dead boy," she whispered. "He was so young. I can't get him out of my mind."

Santomassimo leaned closer, and his warmth against her back comforted her. "I know," he said. "No homicide is pleasant."

She edged away again, thinking. "But that's just it, isn't it?" she said. "We make it pleasant."

"I don't understand."

Now she was at the edge of the chaise. Santomassimo had never seen such a beautiful face, or one so tortured by ideas.

"We play with violence," she said. "And murder. People like me. People like Hitchcock. The people who are fascinated by his films. We dissect it, display it, praise it, yes, we even honor it—as art—" Her eyes grew large and haunted. "We even—love it."

Santomassimo pulled himself backward against the chaise longue. She looked like an alabaster angel on the longue's edge, something sculpted by Jean Dunard.

"It's all just make believe," he objected.

"Not to this killer," she retorted. "*He's* for real. And we're responsible—producers, directors, actors, critics, teachers. We validate violence by rewarding it."

"People always blame themselves, or society, for

violence. It's just one sick killer, Kay. One single psychopath. Living in a private, demented cinema of his own."

"I don't accept that, Fred. Violence thrills us. It excites us, horrifies us. It wins Oscars. We're all to blame for encouraging and—and enlarging this— this—twisted instinct we have—Don't you see? We created a monster."

"You can't make us take the rap for a single psycho," he said.

"One single psycho? There are hundreds out there. *Thousands*. In one damn city alone. Depressed, frustrated, angry, impressionable souls living on the edge of insanity . . . slipping into some crazy universe where there is no morality . . . no decency . . ."

"Kay—"

She moved against his chest. "Oh, God, Fred. How did I ever become involved in Hitchcock's crazy world? I was a simple, striving student, a Chaucerian major at Hunter when, by accident, one rainy Saturday, I ducked into the Thalia and saw a revival of *The Thirty-nine Steps*. I hadn't been much of a movie buff, but I was stunned by the film, by its imagery, by its economy of film language and symbols. It set my blood racing and my mind soaring. It was trickery and manipulation, but it was the new literature, the new art, and I loved it. I plunged into his work with the fascination of a child with a newfound toy. I saw and read everything I could lay my hands on. I became your typical film fan bubbling over with unquenchable enthusiasm. At the end of a month, I switched my master's program from Hunter to NYU; from Chaucer to Hitchcock. Quite a digression, wouldn't you say?"

"Yeah," Santomassimo held her trembling body closer.

"When I told my father about the change, he simply said, 'I never liked his TV shows.' " Her eyes clouded with the memory.

Santomassimo noticed. "I think that's funny. Don't you?"

Kay smiled ruefully. "That's the last thing my father ever was—funny." Her hands clutched him tightly. "Oh, God, Great Saint. Hold me. Protect me. . . ."

She clung to him as though drowning. He began stroking her hair. She began to sleep, holding his arm. He slept fitfully with her while the dawn birds flew past the condominium.

10

Los Angeles had a light fog the next morning that burned off quickly, leaving the downtown court buildings white and gleaming. There was not a cloud in the sky. The buildings that dominated the freeways looked pristine and eternal as the Pyramids.

On the fifth floor of the Criminal Courts Building, Mrs. Jacqueline Randolph, the district attorney, chaired a conference. Next to her was Police Commissioner Terrence McGrath, a heavyset man in his late fifties. Around the long conference table sat Captain Emery, Lieutenant Hirsch of the Central Division, Captain Halleck of the Thirty-third Street Division, and Captain Callahan of the Newton Division.

There was also Preston Wilkins, a slender little man in a severe black suit, from the mayor's office. Wallace Perry, Captain of the Major Crimes Division for all Los Angeles, sat on a straight-backed chair next to Randolph, calmly smoking a pipe.

Kay and Santomassimo sat together at the far end of the table.

Randolph was still good-looking, though the years as district attorney had taken the softness from her face. She had been a good lawyer, an excellent prosecutor. Her ambition now was to be the best D.A. in Los Angeles's history. She talked in a sarcastic drawl, friendly enough, but her eyes were piercing and analytical. She was impatient. She was very self-assured.

Randolph flexed her hands so her chin could rest on them.

"What's going on, gentlemen?" she asked. "Do we have a jurisdictional dispute? Why is Lieutenant Santomassimo appearing in Downtown, Newton, and Palisades?"

Captain Emery nervously cleared his throat. "Lieutenant Santomassimo, who, I would like to state, has won three awards for bravery in the line of duty and—"

"Cut the politics, Emery."

"Right. It seems, in our opinion, that the four recent murders—on the beach, the Windsor Regency, the Lyons furniture store, and at St. Amos's church—are united."

"United?"

"The same killer, Mrs. Randolph."

Randolph exchanged glances with Wilkins, the mayor's representative. She became angry.

"That sure as hell is the impression you've managed to give the city," she said. "The late and unlamented Steve Safran used Lieutenant Santomassimo's unwarranted appearances to create the notion of a major serial killer. There are people now who are terrified to go out in the evenings."

"We didn't create anything, Mrs. Randolph," Captain Emery objected.

Randolph leaned forward. "You had no right, Captain Emery—no right—to send a man downtown to the Windsor Regency—and Lieutenant Hirsch was derelict in letting Lieutenant Santomassimo take the case."

Captain Emery felt the sweat soaking into his collar. Hirsch pretended to be busy with his notebook and then nervously drank a glass of water.

Mrs. Randolph produced copies of *The Los Angeles Times,* the *Santa Monica Journal,* and three supermaket tabloids. *SERIAL KILLER STALKS LOS ANGELES,* read one: *SICK MURDERS THROW SHADOW OVER LA,* read another. *MANIAC PLAYS GOD— WITH CORPSES* was a third. She snapped them back onto the table.

"The media have been banging on the mayor's door," Wilkins added, "asking what he's going to do."

There was a grim silence. Captain Callahan and Lieutenant Hirsch avoided looking at either Randolph or Captain Emery. Captain Halleck, in whose division St. Amos stood, miserably fiddled with his pencil. Mrs. Randolph turned implacably to Santomassimo.

"What, Lieutenant Santomassimo, made you go to the Windsor Regency? Why did you go to the Lyons Furniture Stores? Why did you go to St. Amos's church? Can you possibly explain to me what you're doing?"

Santomassimo coughed to clear his throat.

"The flying bomb that blew up Mr. Hasbrouk, Mrs. Randolph, resembled a scene from *North by Northwest,* which Alfred Hitchcock directed. The intended victim was also in advertising."

Randolph stared at him blankly.

"The electrocution of Nancy Hammond resembled a scene from *Psycho,* in which a young girl was killed in the shower. Also directed by Alfred Hitchcock. Also with a secretary as a victim."

"Is that it?"

"No, Mrs. Randolph. The murder of the college

student, strangled and stuffed into a chest, was exactly the scene in *Rope*. Directed by—"

"Let me take a wild guess, Alfred Hitchcock."

"Precisely. And the death, by falling, of Steve Safran, comes straight out of *Foreign Correspondent*. The victim was also a reporter."

Mrs. Randolph raised her eyebrows skeptically. She looked at the other officers. "And you all bought this?" she said.

The room was silent.

"I'll tell you what I think," Mrs. Randolph addressed Santomassimo. "I think you've been had, Lieutenant. Three divisions have dropped unsolvable murder cases onto your lap. Most murders in this city would resemble scenes in films. Where the hell do you think writers get their inspiration?"

"There's something else," Kay said.

Mrs. Randolph was taken aback by Kay's voice. Randolph studied her face, unblinking. Kay had hardly slept. That and the panic she had suffered at the church had shattered her nerves. Santomassimo put a hand on her arm. Mrs. Randolph noticed it.

"Hitchcock appeared in his movies," Kay said, her voice flat and metallic. "They were very brief glimpses, just bit parts, a walk-on, but audiences expected to see him. They knew his little game. They hooted, they were delighted when they spotted him. It became a trademark of his, like the MacGuffin."

"The MacGuffin?" Randolph asked.

Kay drank from the water in a glass on the conference table.

"Yes," Kay said. "An object. A red herring that started the story, got the story going, but had no real value. In *The Thirty-nine Steps,* the MacGuffin was a secret formula, which precipitates the chase. In *Notorious,* it was uranium in a wine bottle. Both the appearances and the MacGuffin were a kind of signature, like . . . this . . . popcorn . . ."

The district attorney followed Kay's glance. So did the captains, the commissioner, and Wilkins. Four yellowed pieces of popcorn, in a plastic bag, lay in the center of the conference table.

"I can't take popcorn into court," Randolph said decisively.

Commissioner McGrath chuckled. So did Wilkins.

"I can't take *any* of this into court," Randolph said. "I cannot predicate a case for the prosecution of this killer—if you ever catch him—on the kind of evidence you're offering."

She slid the bag and its four popcorn pieces across the table back to Captain Emery.

"You know how much popcorn there is in this city, Captain Emery?" she asked.

"Mrs. Randolph, please, listen—"

"Take a guess. Billions of pieces? Trillions?"

Captain Emery shot Santomassimo an angry glance, as though to say, *You got us into this, damn it. Get us out.* Protocol required, however, that he answer the district attorney immediately.

"I don't think we're trying to make a legal case for you, here, Mrs. Randolph," was the best that Captain Emery could do. "Professor Quinn—who is a national expert on the films of Alfred Hitchcock—is talking about a possible motivation, and I think she's been able to back it up."

"With popcorn?"

"With a peek into a deranged mind," Santomassimo interjected. "Four murders, four pieces of popcorn, Mrs. Randolph. That's a signature. That's consistency."

"Maybe." Randolph turned back to Kay. "All right, Professor Quinn," she said. "Do Hitchcock's films say how to catch him? I mean, if the killer does have this obsession? Got any ideas? Any practical ideas?"

"One."

"Shoot."

"He might make that token appearance. Like Hitchcock. It's audacious. It's crazy. It teases the audience—"

"Audience?" Commissioner McGrath asked.

"Us," Kay said.

"Maybe we could photograph him while he's killing somebody," Randolph suggested. "That would be peachy."

"I meant later, after the crime. He might join the crowd, become an interested spectator. Just to tease."

"Great. Wonderful. We'll develop popcorn consciousness."

The captains chuckled. Wilkins nudged the commissioner and broke into a belly laugh. Kay leaned forward and tapped the conference table, looking into Mrs. Randolph's eyes.

"In *Frenzy*, Hitchcock was a spectator at the wharf, watching the police pull a strangled girl from the Thames River," Kay insisted.

"Maybe he's already *been* photographed," Santomassimo said, coming to Kay's rescue. "Safran was all over the place with plenty of television coverage. We could search his tapes for a recurring face."

"Stay away from the media," Randolph ordered. "Safran was one of their own. They're already mad as hell. And I don't like losing control of cases."

Randolph looked at each face around the table searchingly. While she was not prepared to accept Kay's bizarre suggestions at once, she did want time to consider them. She leaned back and nodded almost imperceptibly to Wallace Perry. Captain Perry tapped out his pipe and dug into a leather pouch for more tobacco.

"If this case cuts across division lines," Perry said, "and mind you, I'm only saying if—then it has to be the baby of the Major Crime Division, downtown. Nobody else has the computer facilities to handle it."

"With respect, Mrs. Randolph," Santomassimo objected, "I'd like to stay in charge of it."

Perry shook his head. "Leave it to Downtown, Santomassimo. You just don't have the facilities."

"I can nail this guy. I can almost sense him out there."

"Why couldn't Lieutenant Santomassimo head up a special task force?" Mrs. Randolph asked Perry.

Perry nodded. "Sure. We could do that. We've done it before. But he'd have to move into the main headquarters downtown."

Captain Emery shook his head. "I need Santomassimo in West Los Angeles. We're cracking under the case load as it is."

"Well, it's impossible. No can do," Perry snapped.

"I want Santomassimo with me," Emery insisted, his eyes darkening.

The captains were at a loss what to do. Mrs. Randolph drummed her fingers on the table. She was thinking. Preston Wilkins whispered to the commissioner. He stopped when he saw Mrs. Randolph glaring at him. She had stopped thinking. She had decided.

"Captain Perry," Mrs. Randolph suggested. "Can you design a task force with Lieutenant Santomassimo reporting directly to you?"

"You mean he would be stationed in the Palisades?

"But he would work under the Major Crime Division."

"It would have to be pretty strict."

"Every move relative to the case would be cleared through your office. All information would flow to you. Any warrants, injunctions, breaking and entering, tailing—everything—"

Perry didn't look happy. "Sure. I can live with that. If you want me to. As long as my office is in charge. I don't want any cowboys running around."

Mrs. Randolph turned to Hirsch, Halleck, and Callahan. "Understand?" she said. "Anything that happens on this case—anything—is handled by Lieutenant Santomassimo under the Major Crime Division."

She turned to Commissioner McGrath, who smiled. He liked her quick politics. Satisfied that she had covered all bases, Mrs. Randolph pushed her notebook and agenda papers into her attache case and snapped the case shut.

"Lieutenant Santomassimo, I want you and Captain Emery to handle the details of the investigation. But Captain Perry will be your supervisor on this case."

"Thank you, Mrs. Randolph."

The men moved to leave the room. Mrs. Randolph remained, and they became still again.

She addressed the captain of Major Crimes Division. "Captain Perry, is this something we should bring SIS in on?"

Captain Perry's face displayed a fractional tension at the mention of SIS, the Special Investigation Section of the Los Angeles Police Department, a nineteen-man surveillance unit that followed and watched known felons but rarely tried to arrest them until and unless they were actually caught in the act of committing a crime, which in many cases turned out to be too late for the victims. To Captain Perry, an old-line policeman, there was an aura of disrespectability about SIS, a taint of KGB.

"I don't think so, Mrs. Randolph," Perry said with careful equanimity. "We have no suspects yet, so there'd be nobody for them to shadow."

Mrs. Randolph thought about this, then said, "Perhaps later," dismissing the entire matter of SIS. She turned a solemn face toward the others. "I want you all to know," she said in measured words, "that the mayor is terribly concerned. His press officer will release a statement to the public this afternoon. I don't have to tell you how much we hate acceding to the interpretation of a serial killer. But I can't refute what Professor Quinn has presented." She paused. "It is vital that you do all you can to catch this obscene maniac. It is vital to the mayor. And to me. And to the people of Los Angeles."

They all congregated in the hall outside the D.A.'s office. Santomassimo conferred with Captain Perry. Mrs. Randolph, looking very worried and very anxious, went into the elevator with Wilkins. Santomassimo rejoined Kay.

"You'll have to excuse me," Kay told him, looking at her watch. "I'll be late for class."

"I'll drive you," Santomassimo said.

Commissioner McGrath blocked their way at the elevator. He smiled pleasantly. "On behalf of myself and the others, I'd like to thank you, Professor Quinn, for your help and cooperation. And for your discretion."

"*Especially* your discretion," Perry added, emptying his pipe in an ashtray.

Kay smiled wanly, turned, and left with Santomassimo. She did not see the district attorney, Jacquelyn Randolph, watching them both from the lobby as they left. Randolph turned to move through a group of reporters and photographers. She kept her head down and ignored their shouted questions.

Santomassimo drove Kay back to USC. He stayed in the lecture hall. She was exhausted, mentally and emotionally, and she took her time opening her briefcase at the lectern. She looked at her audience. They seemed such wholesome, natural people. So eager, so wanting of what she had to offer. For the first time, she began to have misgivings about some of the things she was teaching them.

In the rear, by the projection booth, sat several graduate students in ill-fitting jackets, Kay's teaching assistants.

Kay adjusted the microphone, the lights dimmed,

and one of the teaching assistants turned on the film projector. Behind her on the huge screen appeared an enormous blowup from *Vertigo*. It was an optical enlargement, made in the USC animation department especially for her class. It showed a big closeup of a pair of hands clinging to a rooftop. The teaching assistant held the film projector steady, holding on the stilled frame.

"Hitchcock liked to keep his characters clinging to the edge of things," Kay began tentatively. "Rooftops, train trestles, outcroppings of statues. Here we have Jimmy Stewart clinging from a tenement ladder in the opening shot of *Vertigo*. Let the clip roll, Bradley."

The stocky teaching assistant flicked a switch. The images moved serenely, step-printed to slow down the film's action. Kay said nothing. Nothing needed to be said. Even silent, the kinetic drive of the framing, the pacing, the cruel absurdity of the lethal predicament, filled the lecture hall and dominated it with a subtle sadism presented as art.

CLOSE SHOT: HANDS, NIGHT
Gripping ladder. Jimmy Stewart hoists himself over the top. The MUSIC is driving.
MEDIUM SHOT: THIEF, POLICEMAN, JIMMY STEWART
Chase across rooftop, Jimmy Stewart bringing up rear.
FULL SHOT: THIEF, POLICEMAN, STEWART
Thief jumps from one rooftop to another, barely making it since rooftop he lands on is aslant. Policeman following jumps after him, just making it. Stewart, following, jumps and doesn't quite make it, slipping backward, and barely clinging to the rooftop gutter.
CLOSE SHOT: STEWART
Clinging to the rooftop gutter, which bends under his weight.

MEDIUM SHOT: POLICEMAN
*Turns, sees Stewart's predicament, slides back down
   slanting rooftop to help.*
CLOSE SHOT: STEWART
Clinging, face sweating, gazing downward to see:
HIS POV: RETROGRADE ZOOM
*Dizzying view of ground to describe Stewart's ver-
   tigo.*
MEDIUM SHOT: POLICEMAN
*He carefully slides back down the slanting roof,
   holding onto each small purchase to keep from
   slipping.*
CLOSE SHOT: STEWART
*His face is drenched; his eyes wavering faintly,
   dizzily, in grip of vertigo.*
CLOSE SHOT: POLICEMAN
He extends his hand to Stewart.
                    POLICEMAN
           Give me your hand!
CLOSE SHOT: STEWART
*He is unable to comply, since it would mean letting
   go of the gutter. His breathing is labored as he
   fights to maintain consciousness.*
CLOSE SHOT: POLICEMAN
*Reaching out farther to Stewart, placing himself in
   a precarious position. Then, suddenly, he slips,
   goes flying past Stewart, and goes down eight
   stories to his death.*
CLOSE SHOT: STEWART
*Gazing down in agony, but continues to cling to the
   gutter.*
LONG SHOT: STREET BELOW
*People start to gather around the body of the dead
   policeman.*
CLOSE SHOT: STEWART
Clings and clings to the gutter.
                                    FADE OUT
FADE IN

*FULL SHOT: BARBARA BEL GEDDES'S APART-
MENT.*
*She and Stewart are seated in the cozy, sun-
drenched studio living room enjoying a visit
and tea. The MUSIC is sprightly.*

Santomassimo watched a tall girl writing quickly in
that abbreviated script style, which, by now, he could
read as well.

"Stop the film, please, Bradley," Kay said.

The teaching assistant stopped the clip. Although
the film ended on the frozen image of the gentle tête-
a-tête, the tension was so palpable that nervous laughter, the only release, began to fill the hall.

It was the same fascination with death, with violence, Kay knew, that had also awakened her in Santomassimo's arms last night.

This was the glorification of violent death, exactly
as she had said. Hitchcock, Kay, the students, the film
Vertigo, they were all part of it now.

Was it in such films that the killer learned to glorify
death, to treat is like an entertainment?

"Do you see how Hitchcock plays with the mind,
class?" Kay said. "He brings you to the very edge of
panic—for what can be more panic-inducing than
watching a man who suffers from vertigo clinging to
a rooftop—and then leaves you high and dry with that
devastating image burned in your mind: the dead
policeman below, Jimmy Stewart hanging for dear life,
and simply fades out on the scene with no explanation
of how Jimmy got down. Indeed, Jimmy should have
fallen immediately after the policeman, for how long
could anyone possibly cling to a rotting, defective
gutter even if one had the stamina to keep clinging.
But no, it would not do to have Jimmy fall, for this was
the beginning of the film and no one, least of all
Hitchcock, kills off his star in the first sequence. And
yet, it's a cheat. Hitchcock deceives the audience.

Tension, suspense, terror are carefully honed, carefully maintained, at the expense of reality. The audience thinks it knows the cliches but he always holds back, teases, surprises. He has contempt for the audience. Does that seem a harsh word?" She smiled bitterly.

"Contempt born of the supreme mastery. Hitchcock toys with the soul, damaging the most cherished notions of self. Hitchcock makes permanent impressions—on minds—in ways that cannot be underestimated."

She saw herself walking the dreary rain-filled sidewalks in London, planning her dissertation, planning the book to follow, but needing something more. Something more substantial than the phantom figure of Hitchcock. How had he dominated her these last eight years?

"Hitchcock generates the most profound and irrational fears. I want you to watch his films because that's what you're here for. I want you to learn his film language. But remember, always remember, that what you're watching is insidious. Insidious and dangerous."

The class seemed restless, puzzled. There was a personal warning in what she had said, but they didn't understand.

"Put up the next clip, Bradley," she said.

The next optical enlargement showed a closeup of the actor, Norman Lloyd, clinging to the fingers of the Statue of Liberty, and Robert Cummings reaching down to grab Norman Lloyd's sleeve.

"Our next man clinging to an edge is the actor, Norman Lloyd, who played the part of a Nazi spy in *Saboteur,* a spy who is finally trapped inside the Statue of Liberty by Robert Cummings and Priscilla Lane. The climax takes place inside the statue, in the head, and in the torch area where Mr. Lloyd topples over the railing and just manages to cling to the Lady's fingers . . ." Her voice faltered. She took a sip of water.

Santomassimo seemed to know what she was thinking, because he looked at her with a dark awareness in his eyes as she continued the lecture.

"Robert Cummings attempts to rescue him by grabbing the sleeve of Mr. Lloyd's jacket *but*—in one of the most suspenseful scenes ever filmed by Hitchcock, or anyone else, the sleeve begins to rip."

Kay paused, dramatically, then said, "All right, Bradley, roll it."

The screen became animated again.

CLOSE SHOT: SLEEVE
It begins to rip.
CLOSE SHOT: LLOYD
Fear pervades his sweating face. "The sleeve," he cries, "it's ripping . . ."
CLOSE SHOT: CUMMINGS
Registers shock. Clings tightly to the ripping sleeve arm, to no avail.
CLOSE SHOT: SLEEVE
Slowly, slowly, it rips. Slips off Lloyd's arm.
CLOSE SHOT: LLOYD
Screams as he falls to his death.

A satisfied, delighted murmuring and some applause swept through the room, as the film came to a conclusion. In the flickering light, Kay turned and sought out Santomassimo in the semi-darkness. Her face was an amalgam of conflicting thoughts, as her words were directed solely at him.

"Lights please, Bradley. Well, class, do you see how trite it is? How obvious the film grammar, the cutting back and forth? And isn't that what makes it so frightening in spite of everything? Because Hitchcock has made a joke of death. A sleeve conveniently ripping, a man plunging to his death. Contrivances and coincidences far beyond the realm of reality, and yet it is quirky, and interesting, and neat, and we accept it, and it thrills us even while we abhor it. We leave the theater feeling safe—it's only a movie, we say to ourselves, a sleeve ripping, a man falling to his death from the Statue of Liberty, it has nothing to do with our personal lives, but . . . our brain has recorded the images, and they've been imprinted on our minds . . ." She paused, then softly concluded, ". . . forever."

A few students laughed. But now their laughter was uneasy. It had begun to sink in. They realized there was a lot more to the psychology of Alfred Hitchcock than they had realized, and some of the students weren't so sure they wanted to go much deeper into it.

"Bradley," Kay said to the teaching assistant at the projector. "The lights, please."

The stocky young man with black hair reached behind and turned the lights on. He went into the projection booth and took the tiny film clip off the split reel and put it, yellow plastic core gleaming, carefully into its can.

At the conclusion of the lecture, Santomassimo pushed through a glut of bodies rising and moving toward the doors. Kay looked desperately at him. All through the lecture, she had been fighting the frightened half of herself. Suddenly, she leaned back into the microphone.

"Wait, class!" she said. "I've got one ticket left for the *Scene of the Crime* tour, which, incidentally, will include the Statue of Liberty. We even got permission to visit the torch, which is quite a coup since it hasn't been open to the public since 1916."

Kay looked down at a blond girl, the hair drawn back into a ponytail, white tennis shoes and sweatshirt, giving a sense of athleticism.

"How about you, Cindy?" Kay asked. "I've got three males—give me at least one female."

Cindy shook her head, smiling sadly. "I'm sorry, Professor Quinn, but I can't afford it."

Kay saw the teaching assistant leaving in the stream of students.

"Bradley?"

Bradley turned, his flat face smiling. "I'd love to, Kay," he said, "but I work on weekends."

"Chris?"

A light-haired graduate student, wearing blue jeans and a denim jacket, turned back. "I've already got my ticket," Chris said. "Remember? Me, Thad Gomez, and Mike Reese."

"Oh, yes . . . I'm sorry, Chris, I forgot . . ."

Kay managed to interest three more students, all with pleasant little names like Mark, Steve, Carrie, and Jade, but got no actual commitments. Santomassimo knew why she was pushing the tickets. She was frightened of being alone, here or in New York. The murders had come into the classroom, merging with the ideas and techniques of Hitchcock. They had invaded her life, the same as they had his. And nowhere was it safe.

"Thanks for sticking around," she said when they were alone. "It wasn't much of a lecture."

"It sounded pretty good to me."

"I was trying to tell them all the things we talked about—the glorification—making art of violence—but the right words wouldn't come. In the end, all I did was confuse and frighten them. Bad show."

"I think you're overrating this influence of Hitchcock's," he said reassuringly.

"I think you're the last person in the world who should be saying that."

Santomassimo smiled, and his smile had a sadness in it she had never seen before.

"Can we go somewhere?" he asked. "Maybe I can explain it to you if we're alone."

She threaded her arm through his and leaned heavily on his shoulder. Eyes closed, she nodded. "Far away, please."

"Where to?"

"Take me away from these people, Great Saint. Away from movies and dark caverns. Take me where it's bright and clean and fresh."

Santomassimo took her to the hills over Echo Park. He had stopped for some food, and spread sandwiches, chicken, salads, and fresh fruit on a car blanket in the tall grass under a dry eucalyptus tree. They finished one bottle of dry white Italian wine and he slowly uncorked a second. Down below the freeway cut through the hills, cars glinting in the late afternoon sun, a rushing sound rising through the heat of the meadow slopes.

"Not much of a faraway place, is it?" he said, pulling the cork with a grimace.

"Nonsense. If it weren't for the heavy traffic, smell of smog, billboards, and cocaine addicts all around, you could be in Ohio."

He smiled. "I've been in Ohio. I'd rather be in Los Angeles."

"We've made a mess of the world, haven't we?" she said quietly. "So many wonderful people. So many fine dreams. And we're driven to distraction by crazies. Violent people and crazies."

They drank slowly. She lay with her head in his lap. He stroked her hair, pushing it from her forehead. She closed her eyes. He could see her breasts pushing against the fabric of her blouse as she breathed. He wondered about the man she didn't marry. He must have been a fool of the worst sort. There must surely have been other men. Maybe not. She was fiercely independent. Except right now.

"Crazies come in many shapes and sizes," he said after awhile, hesitating to break the mood. "We don't make them."

"I used to think they were made. I was writing my dissertation on Hitchcock. I lived in London. I lived alone in the top bedroom of a rented two-up and two-down in Knightsbridge. It rained every day that year. I spent six hours every day in the British Museum, the National Archives, private foundations. And in the evenings I used to walk to the East End. It was quite a distance."

"What was so wonderful about the East End?"

"Hitchcock was from the East End." She nestled into his lap again. "I wanted to absorb not only his images, his scripts, what people had said about them. I wanted the man himself, the macabre, elusive, mystery of him."

"Why?" he asked, lighting a cigarette, looking away. To his surprise, she didn't answer right away. "Why?" he repeated. "Why Hitchcock?"

"Maybe I was one of the crazies."

"Oh, come on."

"It's so intense . . . being alone, writing a dissertation in a foreign country. Things happen to the psyche, alone. I needed Hitchcock. Does that sound strange? And he took me over. Lock, stock, and barrel."

"You were young and eager. And good, I'll bet."

She smiled. She relaxed and looked dreamily up at the bland clouds. "Something about him . . . got into me . . ." she said. "I suppose it's that way with all dissertations. Maybe my father . . . oh, the hell with it—"

"What about your father?"

"You wouldn't have liked him. A big man. A university man. Always on the go. Committees. Delivering papers. Discussion groups. Got tenure when he was only twenty-five."

"Sounds impressive."

"He was."

"You sound uncertain."

Kay looked away, suddenly uncomfortable. "He was so successful. So big. So intellectually dominating. He even looked like Hitchcock after he gained weight. He could be cruel. He wounded us, controlled us with his superiority. He died when I was in London."

Santomassimo didn't know what to say. Finally he asked about her mother.

"My mother's alive and well in Pasadena," Kay said. "I see her a couple of times a month. It's strange. The old house with his library, his awards, his books. It's as though he's still alive, trying to control me, making me his marionette."

Santomassimo caught an undertone of hostility that surprised him.

"But," Kay conceded, "I wouldn't have gotten where I am without him. Still, he had fixed ideas. He imposed them. He trained me, you see, from the time I was eight, to teach in the university. I couldn't be other than I am. But he—he could be indifferent. He could blow up without warning. He was obsessed. You never knew what to expect. It was a hard fight, leaving him. Intellectually, I mean." She looked at him. "Does that sound strange?" she asked.

"It wasn't the way my family operated. Italians seem to crawl all over each other. Nobody dominated anybody. It was chaos," he laughed. "Loving chaos."

She rested comfortably against his chest. The breeze was soft and smelled of hot grass. She closed her eyes. She saw her father's library, her father smoking his cigar, approving, disapproving, always measuring her. And in the breakfast nook only the white irises that grew in the garden understood her needs, her sense of fantasy.

Maybe that's what had drawn her to Hitchcock and his work. Something that looked real but had the structure of fantasy. But why the need for such hostile fantasy?

"Be thankful you weren't studying houseflies," Santomassimo said, stroking her hair. "Or you'd have been hooked on them."

She laughed, a pleasant, relaxed sound. "Fred. These crazies. They don't get hatched. They're born and raised and part of raising them is what we celebrate and glorify. And I'm afraid one of the big things we celebrate is violent death. And the trickier, the more violent, the more gimmicky, the better.

"Listen to me, Kay. I deal with these people. They're worse than crazy. They live on Mars. They don't recognize human life the way you and I do."

She nestled more snugly against him. "Okay, Professor. Let's hear your lecture."

"No lecture. It's just that—Well, the seamy side of life is not something people like you know about."

"I'm not naive, Fred."

"No. Of course not. But there are things that happen—violent things—things of such obscenity—you only see them in the police station . . . in the morgue . . . in the back alleys . . ."

Santomassimo finished his glass of wine and poured another. He felt suddenly as though he could never get drunk enough again.

"It isn't just the bruises, the cuts, the wounds, the—beatings—It's the insanity—"

"I've studied psychology."

He chuckled sardonically. "So have I. And not from a textbook. Look, Kay. You read the newspapers. People hear voices. They feel visitations from Jupiter. Long-dead relatives speak to them from trees and make them cut off their neighbors' heads with axes."

He paused. It was good wine. Italian wine. But nothing was taking away his sobriety.

"You know, serial killers are a special sort," he said slowly. "Their impulses come very, very deep inside the psyche. Nobody really understands how their dementia works. Their demands come from frustrations of a very intense degree, humiliations, failures, something missing in the parental environment, maybe something genetic. Who the hell knows?"

She said nothing, but she was listening carefully. She shivered as the breeze worked its way up through the grass. He saw and pulled her sweater gently over her throat. She held onto his hand.

"The worst," he said, "—they listen to Beatles records played backward and hear the commands of Satan. Or they listen to a dog named Sam and kill and kill and kill again. Maybe it's a film they saw, something that strikes too deeply, an actress like Jody Foster—"

"Or Hitchcock."

"Exactly. What triggers these people off, what really makes them kill, nobody knows. The immediate stimulus, say a scene from *Psycho,* is just the catalyst. The problem is much deeper. But we didn't set him off. We never told him to kill."

"I can't help feeling—guilty—somehow. Fred, if you could have seen the look on my students' faces today as I saw them. So trusting. So accepting. And what was I telling them? That murder is an art. Like bullfighting or something."

He laughed. "No, Kay. You're teaching them about *moviemaking,* not murder. Moviemaking is the art."

He settled against the base of the eucalyptus tree. The wine—the bottle was nearly dead—finally was working. He closed his eyes and smelled the fragrant slender leaves overhead. The sunlight, diffused as it was by the haze, filtered unevenly onto his eyelids.

"What's this *Scene of the Crime*?" he asked. "What kind of academic junket have you planned?"

Kay smiled. "It wasn't my idea. My predecessor did it and it became kind of an institution. We do it every semester. Visit an actual location of a Hitchcock movie. Last year two students—"

"Only two?"

"Well, it *is* expensive. And time consuming."

"Okay. What did you do on that field trip?"

"We went to South Dakota and saw Mount Rushmore, where a sequence of *North by Northwest* was shot."

Santomassimo shook his head, disbelieving. "Just don't tell me they got credit for taking a vacation."

She colored. "It's a different experience, seeing the reality and seeing how it was fragmented and recombined, in the camera, in the editing. How the whole thing is given a different psychology by the director, one that you could never see unaided. It's hard work to see that difference and only the best students actually grasp it."

He took her hands and kissed them.

"I'm sorry," he said. "I didn't mean to make fun of your, er, educational journey. Where else have you gone?"

"The year before, we went to Quebec. That's a lovely city, Quebec. That's where *I Confess* was filmed and—"

Santomassimo kissed her square on the mouth.

"Where else did you go?" he asked quietly.

"This year, as you heard, it's New York City. A real Hitchcock bonanza. Four actual locations from four different movies. Greenwich Village. There's an apartment complex there—"

He kissed her neck, and her ears.

"—that the art director, Sam Comer, copied in every detail for the set in *Rear Window*—"

He kissed her throat. She arched her back softly to be nearer.

"What else are you going to see in New York?" he asked.

"Um—there's a mansion on Fifth Avenue . . . where Hitchcock shot exteriors . . . for *Strangers on a Train* . . ."

She felt his hands move under the yellow fabric of her blouse and her hands interceded, then slowly pulled away. His fingers touched along the smooth skin of her breasts.

". . . then, onward to . . . the Canal Street Police Headquarters . . ."

She shut her eyes now, because his mouth was against hers, and his weight was against her, and he seemed to cover her up from the world.

". . . they filmed *The Wrong Man* there . . ."

Button by button he opened her blouse, then kissed her throat, her collarbone, down . . .

From not too far away came hoots of derision. A bearded old man, toothless and lecherous, hooted at them from a path through the hills. Next to him was a sallow, sunken-chested young man who looked bewildered. Santomassimo and Kay pulled apart. She giggled with embarrassment and slowly buttoned her blouse.

"God is determined to keep you a saint," she laughed.

Click . . .

Laughter kept any words from being recorded. The machine recorded laughter. Peals of laughter, bursting out, until tears came to the eyes of the figure seated on the dilapidated couch deep in the heart of Hollywood.

"Oh, Jesus . . . Oh, he was good . . . Perfection . . . I mean, that fat man should have gotten an Academy Award . . .

"Except they don't give Academy Awards to non-actors . . ."

Again, the peals of laughter sent the volume needle against the peg.

"Oh, shit, I'd better calm down. This is serious business, after all. An Academy Award . . ."

Click . . . "Where's a match? Can't smoke a joint without a match. Basic rule. Hell, I'll use the range. Good old range. Should have stuck my head in it a long time ago. Now I'm embarked on this project . . . Well, they're reading about me . . . Trying to give me a name . . . 'The Film Stalker' . . . 'The

*Movie Maniac' . . . 'The Popcorn Freak' . . . Journalists are
such crap . . . Why don't they just call me what I am . . .*

"*. . . The Director . . .*"

The figure sat down, smoked calmly, and deft fingers
opened a bottle of lager. There was the sound of beer being
drunk. And, distantly, the snare drum sound of corn pop-
ping.

Click . . . The recorder rolled forward, recording . . .

"The popcorn killer!" Laughter, then, "That's not bad.
Anyway, as I was saying before . . . Steve Safran, the
television news reporter, who looked like the back end of a
Rapid Transit bus, performed magnificently. Better than
Nancy Hammond. Better even than Charles Pierce, the
overbuilt football goon. Safran was—what can I say—I am in
awe of his talent. A talent he didn't know he was displaying.
He was eager, hungry, greedy, fat and obsequious, so
stupidly clever, and when I hit him, the look on his face—
Jesus—like a pig in a Chicago slaughterhouse. Let me tell
you this right now. If I die tomorrow, if I never accomplish
anything more with my life, I will know that I have directed a
scene to the final inch of perfection and wrought a mounting
tension and orchestrated it with—rare and consummate
panache.

"*Sex cannot be so satisfying.*"

The voice grew thoughtful, confident, in a strange way,
humble.

"Seeing him look back, eyes focusing in on me, while all
the time he was physically falling, just as Hitchcock had
done with the simultaneous zoom in and dolly back . . . Oh,
God, how he splashed against the concrete at the bottom of
the stairwell . . . I've done it . . . I've really done it . . .

"*I wonder if he ever saw* Foreign Correspondent . . ."

Click . . . The figure paced the floor . . . He picked up the
microphone and spoke, urgently and impatiently, into it as
he walked . . . He turned on the tape recorder, recording . . .

"I can't make films . . . They've already been made . . .
And I can't step into the screen and become part of them
. . . So I reproduce them in reality . . . I reproduce the best
scenes . . . of the best director God ever put on this Earth . . .

"It's epic. Truly and mind-bogglingly epic what I've
done."

Click . . . Hours went by . . . The figure came and went . . . It was dark in the apartment . . . It was always dark in the apartment . . . The figure sorted through the mail, throwing the bills onto the floor . . .

"Nothing," he muttered. "Another day, another nothing."

Smells of frying meat filled the room. A hotplate spattered grease onto soiled kitchen walls. He slipped the meat onto a soiled dish and grabbed the bucket of popcorn.

He ate sitting on a couch, surrounded by great, slick posters of Hitchcock films.

Click . . .

"I guess I didn't get the scholarship. Didn't I tell you? I had applied for an AFI directing scholarship, based on the script I wrote in the night class. I guess you have to be the son or daughter of somebody to win one of those. Probably you have to perform sex for them. These scholarships are very high in demand, you know. The competition is cutthroat.

"UCLA is just as bad. Marvelous equipment and some good teachers, at least in the writing department. But all these prima donnas. Egos with no talent. Rushing around making their feminist film, their deconstructionist film, their artsy-fartsy film, not knowing the simplest grammar of what really drives film. It's probably just as well they didn't take me. Got to the interview stage, though. They were impressed by my script. I think they wanted to see who wrote it. They could tell there was something dangerous in it. Something that didn't really conform. No National Endowment grants for my films. That's for sure. Too damn explosive. Too damn angry.

"Angry. Did I tell you I was robbed twice in my Hollywood apartment and a third time on the boulevard? The whole city preys on itself. Drifters, hustlers, addicts, film students, and actors, and all the time sex, drugs, money—interchangeable commodities—and the fourth commodity—the movies. Anything for a chance, even one cheap shot, at the real movies. I received obscene offers, listen, I could tell you about those. Had these guys known anything about film, had they been able to really produce, I might actually have taken them up on it.

"I even took a night course in acting. Because a director

has to know how to handle these poor dumb animals. But the teacher accused me of stealing money. I tore up the prop room in revenge and they arrested me—I could have killed the cocksuckers, but they dropped charges. I think they knew who they were dealing with, the kind of person I was. They could sense the violence in me. They were afraid of me.

"Cal Arts, by the way, was a stinking disappointment. I don't know where they exhume the farts who infest that place. It's also way the hell out in Valencia, which was never good for anything except Magic Mountain and growing oranges. I hated the teachers, and the students, their pristine precision, their commercialism, their goodness. Sure, their films weren't bad, and the animation was terrific, but I wasn't going to end up drawing mattes for some special-effects director. I took two classes there and quit. The dean told me never to try for readmission.

"This town, you see, practices competition at every level. One out of a thousand makes it. Go to Hollywood Boulevard. Go to Sunset Boulevard, Look out my fucking window. You see the dropouts, the failures, still young, still hungry, but dazed by their failure, not comprehending that they've been tossed into the ash can of life, and their only salvation is to go back to Daddy's accounting firm and pray for a job. These schools should be investigated and the deans thrown in jail. There's no place for these graduates. How many ever work in real studios, on real films? One percent. If that. The schools just suck up their tuitions. Unless they're on scholarship.

"There's a reason why I'm telling you about the film schools. I don't shoot the shit for no reason. You didn't think that, did you? Because if you did, you can go to hell right now. No. Everything I say, everything I do, has a function. Like a shot in a film sequence, everything leads to the big climax. So settle down and try to concentrate and maybe some of this will sink in. Of course, it will be too late by then. But that's show business. Ha-ha. I'm telling you about film-school graduates now.

"They inhabit the boulevards like human cockroaches. Ninety-nine percent failures, and the bright-eyed, naive kids still in school don't even see them.

"My cousin had it lucky compared to what's in store for them."

Click . . .

"This meat is rancid . . . I mean it. I'm really going to puke."

After several moments, the figure began stalking the darkness between the Hitchcock posters, microphone in hand, restless, staring out into the twilight as the lights came on over Hollywood Boulevard, and a sleazy glamour grew transcendent. The entire Western sky gleamed with an azure depth, and the facades winked with yellow-and-red neon dots, flashing strobe lights, and the pasty flesh of prostitutes, strangers, cops, and the homeless.

Click . . .

"They're not dumb . . . There's this cop, Santomassimo . . . Interviewed by Safran's replacement . . . I think he knows . . . I sense he knows . . .

"Quinn's pretty bright, too . . .

Click . . . The figure ran to the toilet and vomited. It was a long time later that he washed and came back, staggering badly, almost knocking over a large, covered bird cage. A screech emerged from the cage.

"Sorry, Mathilda. Christ, my head . . . I think I'm disintegrating . . . Mind and body. Especially body. It wouldn't be worth anything on the street now. Ha-ha. It wouldn't be worth anything to Quinn . . ."

Click. The recording light went on . . . The reels turned . . .

"Quinn's very good . . . She knows her Hitchcock . . . intellectual, but visually intense . . . I could have loved her in a different life . . . Now it's too late . . . Maybe I'll dedicate this to her . . . in memory . . . For Kay Quinn . . .

"I saw her with Santomassimo . . . I think they're a sharp pair . . . I also think they're fucking . . .

"I probably forgot to mention that I got into USC. I'm taking Hitchcock 500. It soothes my head. It's a haven, a lair. I dress well. I take notes. I do student things. Meanwhile . . .

"I'm directing . . .

"I think my work's getting more defined . . . Safran was neat. The hunter hunted. Now there are sharper hunters . . . Santomassimo . . . Kay Quinn . . . What kind of name is

Santomassimo? Who does he look like? Farley Granger? His occupation is cop. Hers is teacher. Cop. Teacher. Good occupations . . . good Hitchcock types. These next scenes have to be worked out carefully . . . I need my notebook . . . My storyboard . . .

"Yes . . . my storyboard . . .

"For Kay Quinn . . . deceased . . .

"Cut to black!"

11

Santomassimo drove Kay back to her apartment. The bougainvillea was redder than he remembered, because the sun was setting, and the white calla lilies appeared almost scarlet. A teenager went by on a skateboard. He kicked off the curb and onto the ivy-covered embankment. Then, without missing a beat, he simply picked up the skateboard and walked across the lawn toward the next apartments.

The radio squawked.

"Come in. Come in, Lieutenant Santomassimo," Jim Bishop's weary voice came over the squealer. "Are you there?"

Santomassimo picked up the microphone. "Santomassimo here. I'm in West Los Angeles. I've taken Professor Quinn home."

"Sir? Is that you? Where have you been? You'd better get back here, sir. The captain—"

Suddenly, Captain Emery was on the line. "Damn

it, Fred. We've got an armed robbery, shots fired down on Rose Court, and a maniac threatening to burn himself alive outside the post office. Where the fuck have you been?"

"Echo Park, sir."

"Echo Park?"

"I was on extra duty on the serial murders, sir."

"Look, I don't know what that's supposed to mean, Santomassimo. I didn't enjoy going under the knife with the D.A. And I don't want to see this case cripple the whole damn department. Now get your hide down here or I'll have it removed from your body!"

"I'll be right there, sir."

Captain Emery swore a little and then there was static. He didn't even say ten-four. Santomassimo put the speaker back.

Santomassimo looked at Kay apologetically and said, "Sorry about the captain's language. I guess we're not as refined as some of your professor friends."

"You're not in trouble with your captain, I hope?"

"Not at all. Captain Emery treats me like a son. Come on, I'll see you to the door."

Santomassimo got out, crossed in front of the car, and opened her door. Another teenager went by on a skateboard. This one jumped off and landed on the lawn while the skateboard veered across the road. Santomassimo did not let go of her hand. He became self-conscious. The teenagers were coming back with their skateboards and they saw Santomassimo and Kay holding hands, standing very close together by the Datsun. He moved a short distance from her, looked into her eyes, which at first sparkled in good humor. Then they grew serious. The apartment complex was bathed in a soft orange glow, the palm trees wavering, the fountain loud in the tiled courtyard. The radio sputtered.

"Lieutenant?" Jim Bishop said. "Bronte's found a

suitcase of syringes on the beach. Could you get down here fast? Sir."

"I'd better go," he said reluctantly.

She nodded, then unlocked the courtyard door. The courtyard inside the security door had aqua tiles of peacocks and willows around a ceramic basin crowded with lily pads and reeds. A black catfish lumbered along the bottom. Quicker goldfish darted among the surface plants. The shadows were vague, broken up and blurred by the fronds overhead.

"Isn't it lovely?" she said.

"Looks like my bed."

"That's what I was thinking."

They went up the curving white stairs. It was cool. Santomassimo heard no one in the apartments.

"Who lives here?" he asked.

"Professional people, mostly," she said. "Lawyers. A pre-med student. An importer. And one lonely professor. At least we've never had any trouble with wild parties."

"You've lived here long?" he asked.

"Three years. That's long by Los Angeles standards, I guess. I moved in when I was hired at USC. Before that, it was yearly leases with unpleasant landlords."

"It's like my Uncle Paolo's villa."

"It's very Mediterranean," she agreed. "Very pseudo Mediterranean. Would you like a cup of coffee?"

"I'd love to. But I can't."

"It's good coffee."

"It isn't the coffee I was thinking about."

"You really have to go back?"

"I'm afraid so."

The elevator took them up to the top floor where her apartment overlooked the central garden. As they came to her door, he put his hand on her shoulder. She became still.

"Kay—you know that I care very much for you."

He touched her face. She kissed his hand.

"You've confused me, Great Saint," she said very quietly. "Everything—it's all different now. I don't like seeing you go."

He held her close. She was very soft. He had never wanted any woman so much. She unlocked both locks to her door. The door opened and stood half in a shadow, half in the increasingly vague twilight. Like a sweet, joyous dream, it seemed like everything he wanted in life, inches out of his reach.

"Fred—come inside. Please."

"I can't, Kay. I want that more than anything. But I have to go."

She kissed him on the cheek. She smiled at him.

"When I come back from New York," she said, "we'll make up for lost time."

Santomassimo felt her lips against his. She was pressing the length of her body against him again. He was becoming intoxicated in the fragrance of her.

"How long will you be in New York?" he asked.

"I'll be back Monday night. That's not so long, is it?"

"I'm going to miss you, Professor."

They kissed, long and hard.

"When does your flight leave?" he asked.

"Ten-forty-five tomorrow night. It's the red-eye special. Cheap flight. Cheap food. Cheap hotel . . ."

"What hotel?"

Kay made a sour face. "The Darby, on West Fifty-fifth Street." Her face brightened. "Wanna come?"

"Yes. But I can't. I'll drive you to the airport, though."

"That's a deal, Amadeo."

"You're the only woman in the world beside my mother I'd ever let call me that."

She laughed softly. She went inside and he caught a glimpse of a well-ordered apartment with plenty of books in specially built bookcases, and a few brightly colored modern prints on the wall. She looked at him longingly, almost sadly. She wanted to say something to him, as though there were secret words only for him. Then she became shy and went inside. He waited until he heard both locks click.

Santomassimo walked down from the balcony. He got into his car. He looked around. The courtyard was deserted. But there was an aura of fear, of impending doom in the atmosphere. It felt as though the tiles and lilies, the palms and reeds and goldfish were also afraid of the darkening twilight. Nothing moved. It was completely still. He thought of Kay inside, undressing.

He picked up the speaker. Through the chaos of static and whistles, he heard Jim Bishop issuing commands to the local patrol cars.

"Jim," he said. "This is Santomassimo."

"Sir—?"

"Jim. I want police protection for Professor Quinn."

"Sir, she is out of divisional jurisdiction. Captain Emery would never authorize—"

"Call Captain Perry downtown. Tell him it's the Hitchcock case. Tell him our expert needs protection. 1266 Rosemont Drive. Got it?"

"The captain will have a stroke."

"Move your ass, Jim!"

Kay turned on the lights. In the silence now, she leaned against the door. She thought about the strange new element in her life. That element was a cop. Of all things, a cop. With a hell of a name. Fred Santomassimo. Amadeo Santomassimo. He was angry inside. Angry and hurt. He was afraid of his feelings. But he was warm and unabashedly tender.

The men she had known before Santomassimo had been complicated men. Tense, driven men who played at high stakes in the risky business of professional thinker. They had no skills but their minds. They survived by visual analysis, by concepts. And other minds, equally brilliant, equally aggressive, attacked them in public, in published papers, wherever possible.

They were insecure, suppressed, sometimes alcoholic, nervous, often cruel or brittle.

But Santomassimo was hard. He was hard on the outside, and simpler, because his profession required it. She needed that just as she needed the tenderness.

She turned on the lamp by the sofa. She had a few ceramic pieces but nothing like Santomassimo's extraordinary art deco rooms. She had never been so awed in an art gallery as she had been in his bedroom before the ghost of Margaret intervened. His furniture was massive, bold, and almost ludicrously exquisite. She suspected making love with him would be like that, too.

Her apartment was pristine, a refuge from the clutter, the chaos, of teaching. On the walls were photographs of the old Ealing Studio and a rare photograph of the young Alfred Hitchcock, the grocer's son, the prodigy of East London.

On the floor was a piece of popcorn.

"Dear God—"

She didn't move. Kay kept watching it. She listened. The apartment was still. She slowly looked around. Across the carpet, past the writing desk, her bedroom door was half open.

She backed away carefully until she got to the window and peered down through the blinds. Santomassimo was jockeying the Datsun back and forth, pulling out. She jerked at the window. It was stuck. She turned. The bedroom door wavered subtly. She banged furiously against the glass.

The window had been locked. She reached up and unlocked it, and threw the window open.

Twenty pounds of maniacal shadow emerged from the bedroom, screamed into the living room, swept over the writing desk, and knocked Kay sideways into the bookcase.

"Oh—God—!"

The falcon stank. It clawed her face with outstretched, horny claws.

"*Fred!*" she screamed.

Books cascaded onto her shoulders. She covered her face, but the great bird ripped trails through her hands. She was in shock. She pummeled the air in blind instinct, and her fists caught feathers. A screech filled her ears as the beak jabbed at her neck.

"*FRED!!*"

The wind of the beating wings rushed a warm stench of feathers at her.

The falcon struck at her eyes, missed, and opened a small gash on her forehead.

"*FRED!*"

Santomassimo came to an abrupt stop, slid across the seat, and looked up. He saw Kay as the bookcase toppled over, sending a lamp flying across the living room. He cut the engine and jumped from the car and ran to the security door.

"Kay—!!"

He heard her screaming inside. Another lamp fell and exploded. He heard something else, too; the drumbeats of flailing wings that an enraged bird makes when it is poised for the kill!

"Kay!" he yelled. "KAY!"

He smashed his fists against the security door, then launched himself at it. The door didn't budge.

"*KAY!*"

Inside the living room, Kay crawled toward the door on hands and knees. Her skirt was ripped and little lines of blood soaked upward into her yellow blouse. The falcon spread its wings over her and fell again, jabbing, tearing, reaching for the eyes.

She glimpsed the hooked beak, stuck now with bits

of hair—her hair—and a manic, hostile gleam in eyes
that were too tiny and had burning black centers.

The bird let out a wild, triumphant shriek. She
tumbled over the edge of the long sofa and fell to the
floor. The bird half flew. It crashed into her chest,
ripping, tearing, trying for the neck's big vein.

"Fred—Oh, God—Fred!!"

Santomassimo battered at the door again. It was not
only solid ash, it was reinforced with iron bars. He
turned and ran to the bank of apartment doorbells,
frantically pressing all the buzzers.

"Open the door, somebody!" he yelled into the inter-
com and held his finger on Kay's buzzer. "Kay! *The
door!*"

Kay found a sofa pillow and held it over her face. It
exploded in the bird's assault. Blood—her blood—
smeared the fabric. Her mouth was full of little white
and brown feathers. The falcon lifted off, flapped its
wings, and soared around the apartment.

Between her and the door, the falcon had paused
for just a split second, sitting on the destroyed coffee
table, eyeing her carefully, seeming to judge the secret places over the big veins in her neck. Kay did not
understand where she was. She had an awful feeling
of being in a horror film, a grotesque *grand guignol*.
It was Hitchcock's *grand guignol*. She felt his mocking
presence smiling contentedly on the sidelines as he
watched. The falcon seemed to grin at her. It seemed
to know she had no exit. Then it flew inward at her
face.

"Kay!" came Santomassimo's voice over the inter-
com. "Open the courtyard door!"

She held her forearms over her face, screaming,
knocked backward away from the door by the falcon's
sudden lunge. The bird's scream melded into the
cacophony of Santomassimo yelling through the inter-
com. The downstairs door buzzer screeched in the
apartment, continuous and insane.

"*Kay!*"

"Fred!—Oh, God!—"

The falcon was relentless now. It drove her back toward the bedroom. She threw a lamp at it, a coffee pot, a ceramic vase. Nothing quelled its fury. She felt herself weakening. Her mind fixed—irrationally, absurdly—on the script:

CLOSE SHOT: KAY, NIGHT

Kay struggles, weakening, moments before her death.

A maniac controlled the falcon, controlled her death. For entertainment.

"Fred . . ." she said, faltering. "Dear God . . . Save me . . ."

Santomassimo pressed all the apartment buttons again. Finally, somebody pressed a door release. He pushed the security door open and ran into the courtyard.

An elderly woman in a robe peered from her door. "What the hell is all that racket?"

Santomassimo rushed to the elevator, thought better of it and ran up the steps, three at a time. Terrified, the old woman went inside and slammed the door shut.

He ran to Kay's door and pounded on it. He heard her crying, and he heard the savage beat of wings.

Kay stumbled sideways along the wall. The falcon had adopted a new tactic. It flew away to the far end of the living room, turned, and then, as she tried to retreat, flew down on her with unimaginable speed. It crashed into her, knocking aside her arms, and she fell back onto the writing desk. The falcon sensed victory. Kay's arms were weakened and trembling. She was mumbling hysterically.

The falcon turned, sending a huge shadow rippling across the walls.

"Fred—*Help me!*—"

He pounded on the door. "Kay, try to unlock the door!"

"I—I can't—"

"You've got to! Open the door!"

The falcon struck at her, tearing the chair she had raised in front of her out of her hands. She ducked from the battering wings and ran to the door.

Kay's lacerated hand reached for the double locks. She slid the bolt back at the same time the falcon smashed into her hand, leaving blood splattered against the door.

"Oh—Fred—"

Her voice had a new sound. An injured, fading sound. There was only the chain lock now. Santomassimo smashed against the door. He felt a white shock as something separated in his shoulder. He threw himself against the door with his other shoulder.

Kay's bleeding fingers fumbled, and, reaching up, unhooked the chain.

She crumpled on the floor, blocking the door. He could push it open only enough to enter halfway. But he smelled blood, and saw chaos, and felt, before he saw, the dark, screeching talons that barreled into him.

"Jesus—!" he yelled.

Kay pulled herself from the door. She crawled to a sitting position. She no longer knew where she was. Her pupils were dilated in horror. Her intelligence was clouded by the lethal attack.

Santomassimo punched the air around him. The falcon, enraged, tore at him, ripping up fragments of his suit. Santomassimo reeled into the apartment and the bird pulled him around. Though his fists were lacerated, he punched and slashed at the shrieking bird. Trickles of blood came down his neck.

He grabbed an afghan blanket from the sofa and snapped it at the falcon. The falcon seemed surprised. It withdrew to the fallen bookcase. Breathing hard, jaw clenched, Santomassimo came forward and snapped the blanket again and again. The little nasty pops of the blanket kept the falcon moving backward, hissing and sputtering.

"Don't like that? Have some more—"

The falcon was against the wall. It raised its talons as Santomassimo came relentlessly forward, snapping the afghan. The bird fluttered backward, struck the wall, banged its huge wings. Then it found the open window and flew out.

Santomassimo slammed the window shut. He staggered back to the sofa. Kay moaned and he gently picked her up from the floor. She was incoherent. Outside, the falcon flew from the apartment complex and streaked to a lamppost where it glided smoothly to rest.

"It's all right, Kay, darling Kay . . . oh, God, it's all my fault . . . my fault . . ."

He held her tightly. He brushed his fingers against her face. The wounds were not as deep as he had feared. But she was terrified. Her heart was pounding and she was trembling all over.

"It's over," he kept whispering. "It's over."

But every time he looked up, the falcon was still there, still watching, still imperturbable on the lamppost outside.

"It's over, Kay," he said again and again, kissing her, stroking her hair. "It's all right now."

The great bird left the lamppost. The wingspread blotted out the light and the falcon glided with only the smallest motions of the large front wing feathers down over the road and into the dark.

"Fred—?"

Her voice was pitiful. It had the unnerved quality of someone deep in shock. It was a sound he'd heard too often. He sat her down on the sofa and put his arm around her. He leaned her head on his shoulder. She still didn't know where she was.

"—It tried to kill me—"

"Easy, easy," he kept murmuring. "It's gone now . . . gone . . ."

Santomassimo reached for the telephone beside him on the floor, as he held Kay tightly. He did not notice that the falcon had flown from its perch on the lamp-post.

The falcon drifted through the alley. Its legs spread forward, its wings arched back and the body angled upright. The wing tips fluttered quickly and the talons gripped a black leather glove on a human fist.

A black hood slipped over the falcon's head. It became completely still.

Gradually, the falcon was lowered. Two hands edged the bird into a ventilated black leather valise. The glove was removed, put in a jacket pocket. The hands locked the valise. Then the valise—now a heavy valise—was lifted past a pair of scuffed white high-top Reeboks.

The figure walked away on the asphalt, whistling. It broke the stillness of the night and echoed softly in the alley. Single notes, staccato and distinct, relentless and slow, like a funeral dirge. But sly. It was a march.

The "Funeral March of the Marionnettes," by Gounod.

12

Three squad cars pulled up to Kay's apartment. Whatever calm the neighborhood had had before the screaming falcon had struck was now completely obliterated by sirens. The residents of the apartments spilled into the street and surged toward the patrol cars.

Captain Emery got out of a squad car. He felt depleted. He also felt scared. He had misjudged the killer. Never in a million years would it have occurred to him that the maniac would have turned on them. Not all the caffeine in L.A. could restore his self-confidence now.

Lou Bronte and Detective Haber came from a second squad car. Together, they stood with Emery on the sidewalk. They, too, were frightened. The familiar blue-and-red roof lights swept over their faces and made eerie pastels over Kay's apartment. Captain Perry joined them.

"Looks like we made contact with Hitchcock again," Perry said dryly.

"Yes," Captain Emery admitted. "Looks like he's after his fans now."

An ambulance joined the patrol cars. Red lights swept over the crowd. Patrolmen pushed the curious off the sidewalk. Perry looked quizzically up at Kay's window, which was shut. A dim light penetrated through the sheer curtains.

"I got a question for you, Bill," Perry said.

"What?"

"What movie is this from?"

Emery shrugged tiredly. "King Kong Meets Fucking Godzilla. How the fuck do I know?"

He turned as two medics came from the ambulance, and two police technicians from a squad car. The medics looked grim. They carried little plastic bags of plasma as they wrestled a collapsed stretcher forward. Captain Emery led them through the crowd and into the security gateway. They went up the stairs.

There were a few scuff marks on the walls, scratches, hairline cracks, the kind of thing you see everywhere. It was a well-maintained building. Nothing indicated breaking and entering. Nothing to show how somebody had smuggled a falcon into Kay Quinn's apartment.

"Fred!" Lou Bronte called, running down the hallway. "Are you all right?"

He turned the corner of the partially open doorway.

"Fred?"

Bronte stopped. Under the ceiling light—the only light still working in Kay's apartment—Santomassimo gently washed away the cuts on Kay's arms and legs. There was a small bowl of warm water and cotton puffs. For an instant, it appeared to Bronte like a religious picture. It had that quiet quality, Santomassimo kneeling while Kay sat on the sofa, her hair bright against the light, her face suffused in suffering, that moment of almost—adoration.

Santomassimo saw Bronte standing in the doorway. The men exchanged glances. Bronte understood instantly how badly Kay was shaken up. He walked into the apartment very quietly. Kay didn't even look up at him. Santomassimo turned back to her, washing away the blood.

"Thank God it didn't get your eyes." Santomassimo told her. He applied an eyedropper of antiseptic to a bruise over her eye. She winced and held out her sherry glass.

"More," she said.

Again Santomassimo and Bronte exchanged glances. Bronte knew she was still in a state of shock. He went to the kitchen counter, brought back the half-empty sherry bottle and poured some into her outstretched glass. She still did not look up at him.

Silhouettes blocked out the light at the open door. Captain Emery, Perry, Haber, the technicians, and the medics stood there, staring at the destruction of the room. They looked at Kay. She was so vulnerable, it saddened Emery to look at her. Guiltily, he walked into the room. The medics put down the stretcher and plasma, and went to the couch.

Captain Emery stared down at her with mingled affection and a certain sense of fear he hoped she wouldn't see.

"You all right, Professor Quinn?" he asked.

She looked at Captain Emery but said nothing.

"She's pretty badly rattled, Bill," Santomassimo said.

"Jesus, Fred," Emery blurted. "I should have known—"

"We all should have known."

The technicians invaded her apartment. They went out on the balcony, too, scouring the floors on hands and knees, and bringing harsh flashlights to examine the walls, ceiling, and, back inside, all her furniture, the torn sofa, the broken bookcases, and the smashed writing desk.

They went into her most intimate drawers in the bedroom and her closets, then powdered all the window sills. Men took fragments of blood-stained feathers from her wall with tweezers and put them in plastic bags.

Bronte, without saying a word, lifted the kernel of popcorn from under the television set where it had been kicked, and put it into its own plastic bag. Only Santomassimo noticed.

"The bird sure did a job on the apartment," Bronte muttered.

The falcon had torn apart the upholstery. The curtain was ripped. There were pockmarks in the plaster of the living room wall. Feathers on the floor drifted gently as Bronte walked. Kay submitted to the medics, but Santomassimo didn't like the way she looked; so empty, so alienated.

"She seems to have no concussion," the medic announced. "Some bad lacerations on her hand, face and neck. I'd like her to go to the hospital."

"No hospital," Kay muttered.

Emery beckoned to Santomassimo, who joined him at the window. "What happened, Fred? How did he get this bird in here? Wasn't the door locked?"

"Maybe from the balcony."

"Hell he did. The balcony is fifty feet off the ground. What is he, a mountain climber, too?"

"He's toying with us, Bill. Like the gods tearing the wings off flies. Isn't that what Shakespeare wrote? Like Hasbrouk. Steven Safran. The college kid, and Nancy Hammond. Just a sick game. And now we're the players."

"We?"

"Kay was. Who's next, Bill? You? Me? Bronte?

The medic was disturbed by Kay's refusal to go to

the hospital. He fed her a tranquilizer, left enough sterilized bandages and medication to see her through the night.

While the tranquilizer hadn't taken effect yet, Kay seemed to believe she was safer now. Maybe it was the sherry. But her green eyes were still dark with the horror, and filled with tears.

Bronte went to the window and opened it. The air was cool. They realized they were sweating.

"Fred," Bronte said quietly.

"What, Lou?"

"You got blood on your hand."

Santomassimo looked down. His right arm had twin rivulets of bright red coming from the wrist and soaking through his shirt. It spread darkly down the sleeve of his coat. The back of his left hand was torn up.

"The bird got your shoulder?" Captain Emery asked. "You're standing funny."

"No. I banged it against the door, trying to get in."

"Good thing you're Italian, Fred. They take punishment well."

Neither smiled at the joke.

"I want her protected, Bill," Santomassimo said. "At USC. On the freeway. Everywhere. I don't want her five minutes without protection."

Captain Emery nodded. "No argument there."

More of Perry's policemen came into the apartment, mingling uncomfortably with Emery's. The technicians and photographers filled the living room.

"Hi, boys!" Kay said suddenly, breaking her silence. "Glad you could make it."

She grinned unpleasantly. Santomassimo recognized the panic that had hit her at St. Amos's church.

"Sorry about the intrusion, Professor Quinn," Detective Haber apologized. "We just need to—"

"It's nice to see you again," Kay said sarcastically. "My place this time. Not yours."

The technicians and policemen stared at her. The

tone in her voice was more than edgy. They looked to Captain Emery and Santomassimo, then back at Kay. The medic tried to swab the abrasion but she pushed his hand away.

"Tell me something," she said, her voice rising. "What do you guys do besides pay death calls?"

"Kay . . ." Santomassimo said, coming back to her.

"I mean, all this manpower. My God, the equipment . . . sprays . . . black powder . . . white powder . . . vacuum cleaners . . . What's it for, fellows? What do you do . . ." she finished the sherry. "What the hell do you do except cart away what's left of the dead and leave your mess behind?"

"Take it easy, Kay."

She ignored him.

"Do you ever catch anybody?" she asked, looking at Detective Haber, then at Captain Emery, who seemed to retreat painfully under her stare. "Do you ever actually get lucky and catch somebody? Before they kill the fifth one? Me, Captain Emery. *I'm* number five!"

Santomassimo held her but she stiffened. He could feel her trembling again.

"Please, Kay," he whispered. "Please take it easy—"

"Easy? EASY? How can I take it easy? The son-of-a-bitch almost killed me!" She turned to the rest of the men. She was shouting. "You know why? Because I'm Suzanne Pleshette in *The Birds*, that's why!"

"Kay," Santomassimo said, trying to stroke her face.

Kay's eyes filled with tears. "She was a school teacher, too . . . Oh, dear God . . ."

Santomassimo lifted her firmly to her feet. She swayed, and fought him and clung to him. The medic rose with them.

"I'll help you get your things together, Kay," Santomassimo said. "I want to get you out of here."

"Where? Your apartment? Why? Is the killer scared

of art deco? Don't you understand, I'm marked? I'm part of his goddamn script!"

She turned fiercely to the men.

"Do you know what it's like to be entertainment?" she yelled. "Entertainment for a psycho? I'm the leading lady in his goddamn script."

"That's not true, Kay," Santomassimo said gently. "You know better than anybody that Hitchcock's filmography is long and varied. He's got plenty of characters to choose from besides you. I figure he's got a long list of victims all lined up and ready for action. Probably setting up his next shot right now."

Kay sighed and shrugged and shook her head. "I don't know anything anymore," she said weakly.

Santomassimo glanced at Emery.

"Can I take her home with me, Bill?" he pleaded. "Can we do that?"

"Sure," Emery said softly. "But out the back way, Fred. Damn press and TV've set up shop out front, and we're keeping a tight lid on this. Let the killer think he succeeded, know what I mean? She'll be safer that way."

Kay was crying softly now. She held onto Santomassimo, sobbing openly against his neck.

"Take me home, Great Saint," she wept. "Oh, God, take care of me."

Santomassimo looked again at Emery.

"Get going," Emery barked gruffly.

Captain Emery told Haber to radio headquarters. He wanted a policeman stationed at Santomassimo's condominium. The technicians and medics left. The squad cars took Haber, Perry, and Lou Bronte away. All the way back to headquarters, Bronte worried about Santomassimo. Santomassimo was irrevocably mixed up with Kay Quinn. Bronte wasn't sure what that meant. But he felt uneasy.

Santomassimo opened the door to his apartment and turned on a light. She smiled wanly at the art deco furnishings. It was so improbable, so magnificent. Now the woodwork glowed in the lamplight.

"If you want to stay elsewhere—?" he asked. "A motel? I have a sister in Westwood—"

She squeezed his hand and shook her head. The fabric of his coat was still cool and moist from driving through the misty night. Her fingers played along the lapel.

"No," she said. "I'm safe here. In this palace of art. Do you think he has any taste, our Hitchcock? I'll bet he lives in a tatty apartment with red vinyl chairs."

"Captain Emery has given us police protection, Kay."

"Great. What about my reputation?"

"Well, it will enhance mine."

He brought out the brandy decanter from his liquor cabinet. He held it up for her approval. She did and nodded. He filled two shot glasses with the amber liquor and brought them to her.

Suddenly, she shuddered. "What is he doing to me? What can he possibly want from me?"

"Kicks."

"He wants a performance. He wants a good performance, Fred. But I don't think he got the acting he wanted."

"No. I expect not."

"I was supposed to end up dead."

He said nothing, swaying with her as she moved gently in his arms. She closed her eyes. The fabric of his coat now was warm where she lay her head. She felt his heart beating.

"And I spoiled his scene, didn't I?" she said.

"Exactly."

"So what's next, Great Saint? A retake? A different scene? A different killing from the master's repertoire?"

"Nobody's going to hurt you, Kay. Not here. Not anywhere."

She looked up. She tried to smile. The abrasion over her eye was the color of an overripe eggplant and her hands were wrapped like a boxer's. He stroked her face. "I almost believe you when you say that," she said.

"Believe me. The scene failed, Kay."

Her green eyes kept searching his face, as though for clues as to why he felt safe. His eyes were dark and angry. They reassured her.

"When I saw the popcorn on my floor—"

"Don't talk about it, Kay. It's over. It was a bad movie and the audience walked out in droves."

"I knew—I knew I was going to die. And not all the saints, great or small, were going to save me when that bird hit me . . . out of nowhere . . . and it was . . ."

He kissed her lightly on the lips. They were suddenly cold.

"It was . . . as though . . . I were . . . an actress . . ." she said quietly. "Isn't that what sadists want from their women? Somebody to act out their fantasies?"

She drank the brandy. She was thinking hard. Her intelligence was fighting the panic. For the moment, intelligence began winning.

"I kept thinking," she said, "even as I was fighting . . . for my life . . . trying not to be blinded . . . trying to keep the beak out of my eyes . . . I thought, *he's directing me* . . ." She looked at him. "Is that crazy? Does that mean I'm crazy? The killer was controlling me, through the falcon. . . ."

"Nobody controlled you, Kay."

"Yes, Fred. There *was* a logic. I was caught in it. I can't explain it. An emotional logic. He was the director of that scene."

Santomassimo didn't like the turn the conversation was having. Her cheeks were still flushed. She finished the brandy and so did he. He tried to become professional about it.

"These maniacs are technically clever," he said crisply."That's what makes them so dangerous. And they don't think the way normal people do, so it's hard to figure out what they'll do next."

She looked out over the balcony. Far away, the ocean murmured.

"All during the attack, I kept seeing, in my mind, *LONG SHOT: KAY NIGHT The falcon dives, tearing at her eyes. The falcon rips at her face.* It was awful. It was like a hallucination."

"Kay," he said. "You need to get away from Los Angeles. I'm glad you're going to New York. You need a break."

"I need you, Great Saint. I need your bed of improbable Japanese carp by magnificent gilded lilies. I need your weight, your hunger . . . in a field of mother-of-pearl garlands."

"Yes," he said sincerely, taking the brandy from her hand. "I want to. Very much."

There was a long, slow silence in which the ornate clock under the John Marin was audible. Santomassimo took her hand and led her to the bedroom. She saw the enormous bed and her eyes questioned his.

"It's *our* room, Kay. Not Margaret's. Yours. Now and forever."

He flicked a switch outside the bedroom and the rest of the apartment went dark. He put his hands on her shoulders. He drew her close.

"For as long as you want it," he said.

"Kiss me—"

He bent forward, kissed her neck, and then pressed her closer. He felt her hands against the back of his head. She was warm now. Very warm. Her breath kept thundering into his ear.

"Oh, Fred—" she whispered. "I was so scared—"

He drew her down onto the edge of the quilt and

unbuttoned her blouse. His finger traced the shape of her breasts.

He kissed her lips. She closed her eyes. Slowly, he unhooked her bra, bent low and kissed her throat, where the pulse was beating fast.

"Kay," he whispered. "Kay . . ."

He undressed her. Her breasts were half lost in shadow. He held her on the heavy quilt.

"I love you," he heard himself say.

He was not afraid. He had not trusted a woman since Margaret, but he felt himself falling free, slipping into the familiar dark of woman, where no man, whoever he is, has a guiding light. But he was not afraid. Her fingers pressed on the small of his back.

"Yes . . . please . . . oh, please," she breathed.

He pulled back the quilt, and they slipped under the sheets. Suddenly, he was very hot inside her. Kay lost all sense of herself as he entered her. Things were melting, all the horror, and wounds, the nightmare, all burned in the rush of his warmth.

". . . *darling* . . ." came her voice.

Santomassimo was infinitely tender. A small cry burst from her lips, another, and then a small gasp. She felt herself dissolve with him, like sailing down a broad midnight river, endlessly, wave upon wave toward a great, unknown ocean.

"Kay . . ."

It went on for a long time. He breathed his thunder in her ear. Then he called her name one more time, and convulsed within her, and only very slowly stopped. Then, like her, he was silent. He lay against her and did not move.

A white seagull, curious, hovered at the window.

"Now and forever," she whispered, kissing his fingertips.

They slept through the darkness, body to body. Santomassimo felt he had arrived, at long last, to the place where he had always wanted to be.

They woke when the wind rattled through the balcony. She made love a second time with him. She slept with her arm on his chest. Kay never wanted to waken. She loved the secret place where he had brought her.

Click . . .

"Professor Quinn . . . My dear Kay Quinn . . . The falcon has taught you more about Hitchcock in ten minutes than you learned in four years in graduate school . . . I wonder if they'll give me a degree for this. The third degree. Ha-ha. The third degree. Ha-ha-ha-ha-ha-ha-ha . . ."

The recorder went onward, recording . . . The voice was heavier now, almost toneless.

"I must tell you, for those who think my protestations of talent were bullshit and mere delusion. My script—the script I worked on in New York, reworked in Los Angeles, worked anew in some dumb night class, and worked on some more—that script, I say, into which I poured my reason, my blood, everything I knew about cinema, and about life—and it wasn't all cruel, either, there was love, rejected love, and surprising tenderness—oh, you'd have been surprised at how tender I can be—That same script, I say, found its niche in the industry. But not quite the way I'd intended.

"So listen.

"This script, about blasted dreams and needs that are too real, too sweet for this earth . . . This script, I showed to the C.D.B. Agency, Casso, Dieterling, and Borne. The biggest talent agency in Los Angeles. Probably in the world. I don't start at the bottom, ladies and gentlemen.

"My heart was jumping all over the place. I was disappointed at my lack of professionalism. I was sweating like a pig. They didn't see it, but I knew, and I was ashamed at how much I cared. Because I can tell you, the story was damn good. The characters were complex. You couldn't help but feel for them. And the ending—Jesus—

"Endings like that come to you by the grace of God.

"I registered the script at the Writer's Guild—got their little stamp on the front page—and gave it to a junior agent. That was Miss Howard, a freckle-faced little albino of an intellec-

tual who looked like a white hedgehog—a failed writer. You can tell them. Anyway, she put it on the stack of scripts already on her desk and promised to read it."

"I waited two weeks. I'm not a patient guy. You've gathered that. Then three weeks. I was a nervous wreck. Do you have any conception what doors are opened once that first script heads toward production? Of course you don't. But I do. I can tell you, it's the difference between life and death. I mean, I didn't want to end up in a lightless cubicle like Miss Howard, did I?

"At the end of the month, I went back to the agency and marched into the white one's room. The bitch didn't remember me. But she remembered my script. Get this. The ivory chipmunk had passed the script on, WITH APPROVAL, to the chief reader, a guy called Zelch.

"So I barged into Zelch's office, which had one hell of a view, may I say, and the most beautiful black leather furniture I have ever seen. He must have been gay. He threw me out, of course. But not before telling me he would definitely get to it that week.

"I must have lost ten pounds. I couldn't eat, I only smoked and drank coffee and beer, I was so nervous. It felt like I'd swallowed a lead pipe. You know how it is when the thing you've wanted, what you've always needed, what God put you on the Earth for, is right there, just inches from you, a week, a day, a few hours, like a Christmas morning that never comes, and it's so cruel, because you're so close, so very close you can damn near smell it; the only thing between you and the success you deserve is a person whose judgment you don't respect.

"But there it is. That's the way it is. We're all whores. And, like I've said, the penalties for losing are ultimate.

"Try to wrap your mind around this. Pretend you were gifted with something. And you'll understand, even you, whatever shit you shovel for a living, you'll know this, and know it forever:

"All an artist, any artist, ever wants, is the chance to do his very best.

"That wasn't so hard, was it? I feel you're getting it.

"Needless to say, Zelch never called. His receptionist wouldn't even connect me. I called three times a day. Always *the same story. Mr. Zelch is in a story conference. How many story conferences can an agent have? He wasn't that busy. Finally, I wrote a fake letter, pretending to be my lawyer, demanding an answer within the week. I got a letter back from Zelch's secretary saying he would like to meet with me on Thursday.*

"I kept puking. I couldn't hold it down. I was paralyzed with anxiety and expectation. They would hack at my ideas, sure, but I'd demand and they would concede. They wouldn't understand but they'd give me my rein. They trusted George Lucas. They could damn well trust me.

"I even had my suit dry cleaned. I'd lost weight and looked terrible, but it was the best I could do. I bought new shoes and had my hair done—really done—by Jerry's of Hollywood—These things are important—And I went down to the C.D.B. literary agency.

"It was a beautiful day. It had rained and Los Angeles was clear to the snow-capped mountains in San Bernardino County. I felt reborn. Inwardly, I thanked God—yes. He was there, somewhere—for all the suffering and pain and frustrations because they had given me strength and insight, and the determination to endure.

"I didn't see Zelch. He was in Rome, dealing with Ponti or some Italian bigshot. I was ushered in to see the head of the agency, the big Kahoona, Dieterling, himself.

"Dieterling was a German, a meaty, vulgar Nazi, probably a Jew-killer with distinguished service medals from the S.S. He kept rubbing his bald head until I figured he must have the mange up there.

"He hardly looked at me. He gave me my script—it had been perfect when I gave it to them, but now it was dog-eared. He said it was very interesting. Coincidentally, they were packaging a movie exactly like it.

"If I go to the grave in a thousand years, I will never forget the little smirk dancing around the corners of his mouth.

"I must have blown a fuse. I remember the receptionist coming in with a security guard. Dieterling apparently had a little buzzer under his desk—probably used to this by now— I was screaming, calling him a fascist, a Nazi, a grave robber, a plagiarist. I yelled at him I was going to sue. I would bomb his goddamn agency. I would kill his children.

"And he just smiled. Even as they dragged me down the corridor—my arm bent up hard against my back. Have a nice day, he said.

"Just before the guard threw me out into the street, he warned me that if I ever wanted to work in this town again, I'd better keep my mouth shut because Dieterling has clout with all the other agencies and is intimate with a lot of studio heads. I was pretty small fry as far as Dieterling was concerned. With a couple of phone calls, I could have a reputation so bad I'd have trouble buying popcorn in a movie house.

"Incidentally, I prefer my popcorn buttered with real butter and salted. I can eat mounds of the stuff.

"So that's what happened to my script. I talked to the Writer's Guild. They said I could sue, but who has that kind of money? Besides, Dieterling would make sure to change a line here, a character detail there. There are literally thousands of screenplays floating through this town. Coincidences are bound to occur. No judge would ever find for the plaintiff.

"Ten months later, I saw my film. Landscape of Love. You might have seen it. They'd set the story in New Mexico instead of California, and made the hero about ten years older, and changed his profession. Some other cosmetic changes. But there it was. I quoted the lines, slightly paraphrased, aloud with the actors. Whole passages just slightly altered; still I knew them by heart. Hell, I'd written them. Finally, people behind me told me to shut up and the usher came and asked me to leave. I did, but not too graciously.

"Did they treat Michelangelo like this? Was he some kind of dog turd to be stepped on and scraped off?

"I didn't care. I could see the writing on the wall. Time was passing. My energies were turning elsewhere. I had to direct. You do see that, don't you? I couldn't wait five, ten, fifteen years to fight the system and struggle, always struggle through the labyrinth of the studios and agencies for a chance. For a chance which probably would never come now, because they crucify real talent in this town. It's true. They hate it. Nothing scares Hollywood more than originality.

"I HAD to direct. Some men need sex. Some power. Some chase God. For me, it was a drive that I can only

*compare to trying not to drown in a rapidly moving river.
That doesn't sound very poetic, does it? But that's the way
it feels. If I don't . . . express myself . . . in some way, I
drown. My soul drowns. If you have a soul, you may understand . . ."*

Click.

"Goddamn bird . . . lacerated my arm . . ."

*Click . . . The recorder turned, recording . . . Was it
minutes later? Hours? Weeks . . . ?*

*"Ever shred a falcon in the incinerator? Ha-ha-ha-ha-ha.
Don't get me wrong. I love animals like the next guy. But I
sure didn't want a used-up bird in my way. The fucker kept
flying back to me.*

*" 'Hey, Joe. Looks like a dead bird in the garbage. Must
have been an early Thanksgiving. Ha-ha. Oh, Christ. It's all
garbage."*

"Right on, man! Cut! CUT!"

13

The sunlight filtered through the drawn blinds. Santomassimo sat on a cross-legged walnut chair inlaid with turquoise strips and with a gilded back. He watched Kay. She was nude, wrapped partially in the sheet. She had the rested look of a woman in love. A tiny smile played at the corners of her pretty mouth. He loved to watch it. He reached forward and tucked the sheet around her shoulder. Her warm hand momentarily rested on his.

Santomassimo had seen victims of violent assaults. Their whole sense of reality unglued. They began to doubt the very earth they walked on. Like Kay, after the attack. And even now, a bit.

Santomassimo slipped into his shoes. He wore a white shirt and dark gray trousers with a plaited leather belt. He went to the kitchen and prepared a cup of espresso for Kay. He toasted a slice of bread and buttered it, adding imported jam from Provence by way of the Oceanside Delicatessen, and put it on an ivy-bordered china dish. He poured a tall glass of orange juice. He carried it all on a tray, opening the bedroom door with his foot.

She was up now, wearing his navy blue Pierre Cardin robe. It was much too long for her. She'd rolled up the sleeves and the bottom trailed. She looked like one of the Seven Dwarfs.

"Good morning, Kay," he said tenderly.

"Good morning, darling."

He didn't like the look of the lacerations on her hands, so he rebandaged them with white cotton and anticeptic. She comically flexed her fingers like little puppets.

They laughed. She looked slightly abashed at wearing his robe in his bedroom. They exchanged glances, and Santomassimo saw that the fear had gone away.

"Can we have breakfast on the balcony?" she asked.

"I'd love that."

He took the tray to the balcony. She sat on the white chaise longue. Kay sleepily shook the hair from her forehead and blinked at the superb vista of the ocean in all its shades of blue-green, and the sky, which was blue-white with a distant haze. She had a completed feeling. It was like innocence. A child's innocence.

"*La donna e mobile* . . ." Santomassimo said, swinging the tray to the white table by her side.

She smiled, and took the glass of orange juice in both hands. She knew he was watching her, and it made her self-conscious. He sat on a wicker chair beside her. He leaned forward.

"You're not, are you?" he asked, touching her cheek, his finger tracing the bridge of her nose.

"What?"

"*Mobile* . . . Changeable . . . Fickle . . ."

"No. I'm not fickle. I never was. I never will be. I'm old-fashioned that way, Great Saint."

She closed her eyes and turned her face to the sun.

Her hand closed around his. Again, she was self-conscious.

"Last night was a wonderful conclusion to a frightening afternoon, Fred. Thank-you."

"I loved last night. I loved being with you." He took her hand in his.

"We'll have more nights, won't we, Great Saint? Many more nights like that?"

He kissed her fingertips, one by one.

"Each and every night, Kay. Every night."

He pulled his chair closer. He traced the contour of her breast, under the robe. She neither moved away nor closer. He felt where her heartbeat warmed in the sun.

Santomassimo said, "I want you to put the attack behind you, Kay."

"I'll do the best I can. Actually, I'm glad I'm going to New York. I love New York. It's been so many years since I went to school there. I've truly missed it." She smiled and moved closer, and the robe slipped wider from her. "You still feel guilty about bringing me in on the case, don't you?" she said.

"Yes."

"But then we wouldn't have become involved, would we, Great Saint?"

"No."

Santomassimo leaned back in the wicker chair. Already surfers were out in the waves, bright flashing boards kicking up when they mounted the white crests. Santomassimo's voice was deep, the words carefully chosen.

"I began to care for you. Right away, I cared very much for you, Kay. I wanted to bring into my life. And yesterday, I succeeded in making you a target instead."

"I'm not afraid. I flunked his screen test. I didn't die."

The panic surfaced briefly in her eyes. She suppressed it. Her voice became more intellectual, professional.

"Did they find out how he got in?" she asked.

"By the fire escape leading to the terrace door. It was unlocked."

"Swell."

"Kay, I want to say something. It's about—about us. I want to take care of you. I need to take care of you. Anybody who wants to hurt you will have to crawl through me first. Understand? Nobody will ever hurt you again."

"I believe you. I have to believe you."

He glanced at the espresso cups, then at the marina, and then he turned to her again. She was extraordinarily lovely. A beautiful woman, when she's happy, when a man has made her happy, is a fantastic sight.

"I send a lot of people to prison, Kay. I remember one—Roger MacKimmon—He was shot down in Oregon a year ago, but before that, he'd committed aggravated assault in Hollywood. Assault with a deadly weapon. Armed robbery. I was the one who caught him and he hated me. Just to be sure, I had Bronte keep track of him. He was paroled in two years and I had the computer keep track of him."

He felt it suddenly awkward to speak. She sensed it, and put a hand on his knee.

"I was coming home from the movies with Margaret. It was *Star Wars*. I'll never forget it. Thousands of people on the sidewalk, coming out, going in, coming from the parking lot."

She looked at him. He had grown tense.

"What happened, Fred?"

"He shot. The bullet bounced off a parking meter and came right through Margaret's open window. Grazed her forehead and penetrated the ceiling of the car. I didn't have my gun with me. I tore out of there like a maniac. Margaret was badly shaken up for months afterward. She lost weight, her concentration

. . . started accusing me . . . I don't know. I should have seen . . . should have protected her . . ."

She kissed him. "You worry a lot about your women."

"But, Kay, I knew he was looking for me. In court, he'd told me he would get me."

"You can't blame yourself, Fred. You tried to keep track of him. You did everything you could."

"I had a responsibility. To Margaret. I knew he hated me. I knew he was out of prison. Then why didn't I have a gun? What was going through my mind? When I saw the blood coming down from Margaret's forehead—" He sighed unsteadily. "And, of course, it had already gone sour for both of us. What was in my head, Kay? What kind of risk was I taking? And why?"

She came very close. "Elementary, my dear Watson. When somebody wants to get rid of somebody they also love, they feel terribly guilty if something actually hurts them. Read your Freud."

"Freud, huh? He can explain that because of me Margaret almost died?"

She leaned against him, holding him in her arms. "You're afraid for me, aren't you?"

"Yes. I can't lose you, Kay. You've brought me back from very far away."

She remained on the chaise longue, leaning against him, holding him. She trembled. He moved his hand up and down her back, slowly. He realized he believed in her the way some people believed in religion.

"I'm going to protect you," he promised, his eyes suddenly full. "No risks. Never again."

The telephone rang. Reluctantly, he rose and answered a white wall phone. He listened for several minutes and hung up.

"That was Lou," he told her. "There are a few things I have to check out. You don't mind being housebound?"

"Housebound?"

"I don't want you leaving the apartment."

She thought a moment. "I'd have to cancel my class."

"Cancel it."

He slipped on his tie and knotted it. "Keep the door locked. Don't answer the buzzer. I'm expecting no deliveries. Nobody."

"*Capisco.*"

"*Capisco?* Where did you learn that?"

"Fellini."

He leaned over her and kissed her shoulder. They held hands. He still didn't want to leave.

"There's an officer on duty down in the lobby. There's food in the refrigerator. TV in the bedroom. You know about the booze in the liquor cabinet."

Kay laughed. "No more booze."

"Smart girl."

"Kiss me?" she asked.

Santomassimo kissed her again, very softly on the lips, as though afraid of bruising something. Maybe it was his own hope, he thought. He was afraid of hoping again.

He put on his jacket and closed the door behind him. He heard it lock twice. Double locks had been no help against the falcon. But here, the wall was over a hundred feet high and sheer and the terrace door leading to the fire escape was double-padlocked. There was no access from the balconies, either. They alternated down the face of the building. Kay was safe.

Santomassimo met the police guard below at the door to the lobby.

"Good morning, sir."

"Good morning. I want nobody coming to my door. Clear?"

"Absolutely."

"Come and look at my car, will you?"

"Yes, sir."

Together they spent half an hour inspecting the

Datsun. It seemed untampered with. It started smoothly. Santomassimo ignored the cop's knowing wink and nod toward the apartment. He drove, not to police headquarters, but to where Captain Emery had ordered him to meet Lou Bronte.

A falcon breeder's ranch in the tall grass of Topanga Canyon.

A peregrine falcon climbed into the blue skies, turned, and streaked toward the ground. Its wings feathered out, slowed, then glided against the sun, and came again, diving downward.

A.E. Meredith stood in his khaki work clothes and blew a whistle. It was inaudible, except to the falcon. The great bird swept over the cages and the ranch, around the trees on the knoll, and Santomassimo ducked as, wings out, blocking the sun, the peregrine settled on Meredith's gloved hand. Meredith slipped a black hood over the falcon's head. The bird went still.

Meredith was sixty-three and wiry. His eyes seemed doubled behind thick spectacles. He carried a long knife in a leather holder in his belt. His black leather boots reached almost to his knees.

"That's some whistle," Bronte said.

"Damn right. Only the peregrine can hear it. These birds can hear a rabbit hiccup at two miles."

Meredith was head of the United States Association of Falconry. He was a nervous man. Lou Bronte and Fred Santomassimo listened intently, which made him more nervous. Meredith saw them standing with their urban dress in his corral, and the two policemen looked out of place, sinister.

Santomassimo stared at the falcon's legs and the body, motionless under the hood, the claws squeezing Meredith's black glove. The bird gave him the creeps.

"This is a peregrine falcon," Meredith told them. "Queen of the hawks. Dominant characteristic—attack. It chases. It kills. It devours. Absolutely relentless. It can see five miles. If hungry enough, it will attack an animal as large as itself."

"But not larger?" Santomassimo asked. "Not a human?"

Meredith shook his head. The question offended him. "I have never," Meredith swore, "heard of one attacking a human being."

"Not even from hunger?" Santomassimo asked.

"No."

Bronte studied the bird. It sensed him coming closer and tensed. Bronte retreated. He was fascinated by the talons, which curved out of the knobby grid of hard flesh like dirty syringes.

"The bird was trapped inside a bedroom for several hours," Bronte said. "Maybe all day. Maybe it had been starved before that."

"And it attacked a human being," Santomassimo insisted. "The minute she entered her apartment."

Meredith was stubborn. "No, sir. I do not believe that. The peregrine does not eat human flesh."

"Maybe out of fear?" Bronte suggested.

"No. It would fly away. It only assaults what it eats. Rabbits. Small foxes. Squirrels."

Santomassimo lighted a cigarette. Meredith watched him uneasily. The paddock was full of straw. Horses were around. Santomassimo could smell them. Meredith was worried about the match starting a fire.

The falcon on his arm was heavy.

"Excuse me, gentlemen."

Meredith carried it toward the huge cages inside the paddock. Gently, he eased the talons off his glove and onto a wooden perch inside a wire cage. Meredith locked the cage door. In spite of what he had just said, Santomassimo sensed that Meredith felt easier now the bird was locked up. The men stared at the falcon. Hooded in black like some ancient inquisitor, it sat, alert and lethal, shrouded, inscrutable in its violent instincts.

"Oh, I'm not saying a large harrier hawk or peregrine can't do serious damage to a person—I've got a glass eye, see?—But that comes from mishandling the feet. Errors of judgment. Those talons can lacerate flesh without even trying. But kill? Not in my experience."

"I wrestled with it, Mr. Meredith," Santomassimo insisted. "It wasn't playing."

Meredith shook his head. "With all due respect, officer," he said, glancing at Santomassimo's hand and the cut over his eye. "I sincerely doubt that the falcon was planted in the apartment with the intention of killing."

"The bird did attack," Bronte gently pursued.

"Well, if the falcon had been terribly maltreated, perhaps it might strike at a human, but not to kill— only to frighten."

Santomassimo walked away into the sun. They were on the lip of the long meadow that opened into Topanga Canyon. Far away they could hear traffic. Overhead small birds flew, sparrows perhaps. Lunch for the peregrine. All Meredith had to do was open the cage and take off the black hood.

"Are those whistles hard to get?" Santomassimo asked, irritated by Meredith's bland assurances.

"Anybody can get them. Pet stores. Specialty shops. Our association—"

"Are these peregrines hard to train?"

"Sure. But it only takes a couple months. They're driven by hunger. It's simple. They're just killing machines. For food, strictly."

"And can they be trained to do other things? Say, trained to attack the human face?"

Meredith fell silent. Santomassimo kicked the dirt and watched it float across the yard in the wind. He could smell the falcons in the paddock. They smelled hot and nasty.

"I'm not saying it isn't possible," Meredith finally

said. "You can use bait to train a bird—associate food with a certain shape. Of course, you'd have to be pretty sick to even think of a thing like that."

"Do you sell these birds?" Bronte asked suddenly.

Meredith wheeled to face Bronte. The policemen were thinking alike, getting aggressive. It rattled Meredith. He felt guilty, and he didn't know why. "To members of the Association of Falconry," Meredith said.

"Exclusively?"

"Mainly."

"Could I drive in off the highway and buy one?" Santomassimo asked, taking off his sunglasses and looking hard at Meredith.

Meredith whirled to face Santomassimo. Santomassimo was inches from him. The lieutenant's eyes blazed with a strange anger. Meredith saw again the wound on Santomassimo's face. The lieutenant was right. The falcon hadn't been playing.

"Well, I mean, yes," Meredith faltered. "If you were willing to pay the price. Fully trained peregrines are not cheap, Lieutenant."

"I wouldn't have to be a registered member of the association?"

"Sure you would."

"Would you check on that?"

"I'd ask to see your membership card."

"And if I'd forgotten it?"

Meredith paused. "Membership is sometimes assumed. If you're knowledgeable. And display an awareness of how to take care of falcons."

"How much do you sell them for?" Bronte asked.

Meredith, caught in the crossfire of questions, turned back and forth. He edged against the paddock gate. It was loose, and provided no support. "I've done as well as $5,000," he admitted.

Santomassimo whistled. "Made any sales recently?"

"A few."

"To anybody who didn't belong to the association?"

"I could check. I could go to the office and check."

"I think we'd better, Mr. Meredith."

The peregrine screeched a derisory laughing screech. It echoed over the meadow. A rabbit ran freely through the tall grass. More lunch for the falcon, Santomassimo thought.

They followed Meredith into the cool shadow under the eaves of his rambling ranch-style house, at the front end of which, in a room paneled with veneer and hung with certificates and awards, was his office.

"I've done nothing illegal, gentlemen," Meredith said. "I've sold honestly. I have a reputation all through this canyon. I've been president of the association for fifteen years."

"Just show us the books, Mr. Meredith," Santomassimo said. "Are there any sales not recorded?"

"No, sir."

Bronte examined the certificates on the wall as Meredith pulled a heavy green notebook from a shelf and laid it on his desk. Apparently, Meredith was a member of several fraternal organizations. He was also a champion archer and marksman.

Santomassimo studied Meredith's ledger. Bronte joined them. Santomassimo's finger went down the columns, page after page. Most of the entries were marked *USAF.* A few were not.

"Who was this?" Bronte asked.

"Harriet Senter. She's from Taft, Rhode Island. I had to fly the birds to her by special transport. In some states, they're endangered species, you know. I tell you, the paperwork—"

"Who is she?"

"Harriet Senter," Meredith glanced at the invoice, "481 Jenkins Avenue. 207/555-1173. That was back two years ago. She was English. She was very old and had a passion for Sir Walter Scott."

Bronte pulled out his little black notebook and jotted

down the information. Meredith warmed to the task, remembering old customers, special problems of feeding, environment. Falcons he had known, had raised, had trained. What happened to old falcons? Santomassimo wondered while Meredith reminisced. Were they buried with a ceremony? Did they end up on somebody's barbecue?

"Get to the more recent ones," Santomassimo snapped.

"Certainly, Lieutenant. Here's one from July 16 of this year. Sold to Mitchell Brenner of Inglewood. 2736 Maple Avenue. No telephone number."

"What was he like?"

"Retired Air Force captain. No. I'm thinking of Mitchell Ryder of Memphis. *He* was a retired Air Force captain. And a damned sweet soul, too. Went fishing with him up on the Russian River. Cancer took him. Once it gets in the pancreas—"

"Mr. Meredith, our time is limited. Do you remember what Mr. Brenner from Inglewood looked like?"

"Blond. Youngish. Sort of nice looking. Medium in height. Sure as hell knew his falconry. He had a terrific knowledge of each species of bird, and the lore of falconry. He could have written a textbook. That's why I knew he must be a member of the association. Of course, it's his liability if he's not."

"Take the address, Lou," Santomassimo said. "Is that it, Mr. Meredith? No more falcon sales in the last few months?"

"No, Lieutenant."

"Do you ever rent them?"

"These are living birds of prey, Lieutenant, not furniture."

Santomassimo stared through Meredith's glossy spectacles at watery blue eyes.

"Did Brenner pay by check?"

"No. Cash."

"How much?"

"Three thousand."

Santomassimo made a slight Italian gesture to Bronte. Bronte agreed. The office was as creepy as the paddock. Bronte gave Meredith a card with the Palisades Division headquarters number on it. Santomassimo went to the door.

"If anything occurs to you," Santomassimo said, "about falcons. About Mr. Brenner. About anybody else. Let us know."

Meredith colored and smiled pleasantly. "I'll help in any way I can."

The two men went out into the hot sun. Their black shoes lost their shines in shuffling through the yellow straw toward Santomassimo's car. Bronte's car was parked across the road. Bronte rested against the Datsun's fender and glanced at his friend. He knew he was irritated.

"I didn't like him, either," Bronte said. "I believe him, though."

"You really think he only sold one falcon recently? To a guy in Inglewood?"

"Probably not. But there's no way to find out who else bought one. Who knows? Maybe we'll be lucky."

"Right," Santomassimo said. "Mr. Brenner will fall on his knees and confess."

"So why are you complaining?"

Santomassimo laughed. "It should only happen."

The stood a long time in silence. Santomassimo sensed there was something on Bronte's mind.

"Spit it out, Lou."

"Why a cop?" Bronte asked. "Why you?"

"What? What are you talking about?"

"Quinn. Kay Quinn. A teacher. A professor. Why does she fall for a cop? A wooden-faced, inarticulate, sad-eyed loner like you? Nothing personal."

The question caught Santomassimo by surprise. "I ask myself that, too, Lou. I think it's my eyes.

Or maybe the special way I smile—kinda crooked, boyish . . ."

"Fred, I'm serious. It's real, between you and her?"

"It's very real. What she sees in me—What Kay wants from me—How can I know? How can I understand something like that? I guess I was overdue for something—"

"You're old enough to know what you're doing, I guess."

"You're jealous, Lou."

"You can recover from bullets. Women are permanent."

"*Basta.*"

"Okay. Sure. *Basta.* She's a complicated woman, Fred. Don't say you haven't been warned."

Bronte looked up, letting the sun bathe his face. He scratched the balding place in the back of his head. There was so much he wanted to talk to Santomassimo about. This Kay Quinn was a fascinating woman. Bright. Maybe brilliant. Highly attractive. Sensitive. What was it about her that bothered him? Bronte couldn't think of it. She was vulnerable. Sure. She'd just been assaulted. Maybe vulnerable in a deeper way. She reminded Bronte of his cousin Giovanna who became a nun because she had a secret crush on her priest. Then, after all the trouble she had gone through to be near him, they assigned her to Africa. Maybe Santomassimo was chasing the same lost cause as Giovanna.

"You want me to check out the Brenner address?" Bronte said. "Maybe you should check up on Kay."

"You don't mind, Lou?"

"No problem."

Santomassimo stopped at the condominium. It was mid-afternoon. He looked up at his balcony and didn't see Kay. He went quickly into the lobby. The officer on duty was coming out of the men's room, fumbling with his zipper. When Santomassimo got to his floor, he smelled something warm and wonderfully familiar.

Santomassimo opened the double-locked door. He caught a glimpse of Kay. She had brushed her hair and it was shining. She stood at the range, stirring a pot of tomato sauce. The counter was a chaos of glass bottles, basil, onions, garlic, parsley, and spices pulled from his racks. The sunlight coming through the balcony window struck her, illuminating the skirt and loose-fitting top.

A mixture of incredible aromas flooded toward him. He was transfixed. The odors were delectable, and nostalgic as hell. He shut his eyes and breathed them in. He smiled broadly and, like the Italian he was, exuberantly kissed the tips of his fingers.

"Mamma mia!" he exclaimed. *"Che odora!"*

Kay laughed. Santomassimo came into the kitchen and kissed her on the lips. Then, with one arm around her waist, lifted the top of a pot and lowered his face toward it. He inhaled and sighed in mock delirium.

"Marrona," he whispered. "The gal-a, she cook-a, too!"

"All quite experimental," Kay said. "No fresh ingredients. Canned tomatoes, dried parsley, dried basil, garlic powder, and *no* olive oil. What kind of Italian are you, anyway, using sesame oil?"

"Polyunsaturated," Santomassimo shrugged.

She threw her bandaged hands around his neck and kissed him. Santomassimo felt the abrasive roughness of the bandages even as he felt her warm, responsive lips.

"Come on," she said softly. "I've got a drink waiting for you."

She took him by the arm and led him to the sofa. There she presented him with a tray filled with improvised hors d'oeuvres: anchovies, peanuts, crackers, and a bottle of red wine.

"What a treat," he admitted. "I could get spoiled very easily."

For an instant, it all felt real, so terribly real. He felt almost as if they were married. It seemed everything was possible with her. He almost felt like crying. Instead, he reached out with his glass of red wine and clinked it lightly against hers.

"To you, darling," he whispered.

"To you."

She was much calmer. Probably she had slept during the day. There was a faint flush in her cheeks, which may have been from the heat of the cooking. The bandages on her hands had not been stained by any blood, so the wounds were not breaking open. But they were there, obscene stigmata of the unbalanced mind that had chosen her as its fantasy actress.

"So," she said. "Tell me."

He leaned forward, running a finger absentmindedly around the rim of the glass.

"We found an expert. According to him, falcons can be trained to kill other birds, and small animals, but it's rare that they attack people."

"I guess I'm rare."

"What I'm saying is, he trained the bird to go for humans, then planted it in your apartment to frighten you."

She sat back, not sure what to think. "Frighten me? That falcon wanted to claw my eyes out! Why, Fred? Because I know the Hitchcock connection?"

He nodded. Santomassimo finished his wine and poured more for them both. "He needed to scare you away."

Kay watched him dubiously. "Do you really believe that?"

"That's the falcon expert's opinion."

"And what's your opinion?" she asked starkly.

Santomassimo sighed and gazed at her frankly. "I won't lie to you, Kay. I think he meant to kill you."

There was a deadly pause. Santomassimo held her hand. "There's one positive note. The falconer raises and sells these birds. Recently, a man bought one from him. He could be the killer. Bronte is checking on the address now."

Kay's face turned bland. "What's the buyer's name?"

"Mitchell Brenner."

Kay smiled sarcastically. It had that hard edge he had seen at St. Amos's and in her apartment after the attack: fright.

"Mitchell Brenner is the character played by Rod Taylor in *The Birds*," she said in a voice that was limpid, devoid of inflection.

"Kay—"

"Bronte won't find him at that address," she almost shouted. "He's much cleverer than the whole Los Angeles Police Department."

He gripped her hand. "Kay, I want you not to think about it. I want you to try to put it out of your mind. Trust me, Kay. I won't let him get to you again. Besides, you're leaving town tonight. New York is beautiful this time of year—and it's a nice piece of distance between you and him."

He kissed her.

"Don't hurt yourself by being afraid," he said. "I can see what it's doing to you."

He held her to keep her from crying. But she wasn't crying. She was angry. The crazies win, he thought, even if they don't kill you. Their lunacies stay in your brain.

"I *really* wish you were going with me to New York," she said. "We could have a wonderful time."

"God, I would love that, Kay."

Suddenly, she clung to him harder.

"I'm going to miss you, Great Saint," she said.

She kept kissing his lips. His hand slipped down

her neck, and further under her blouse. She looked at him with a sudden kind of laughter in the green eyes.

"Don't you want to eat first?" she asked.

"Yeah!"

He bent her back into the pillows, where his kisses cut off her laughter.

Dinner was pasta, bread, broccoli, and salad. The sauce was extraordinary. She had improvised well. Coffee ice cream was their dessert, but when the time came, they looked at each other and went to bed instead.

Santomassimo put a candlestick on the bureau. It illuminated their bodies on the massive Japanese quilt. Kay said very little. They lay, holding hands. They saw the sun sliding into the ocean from the bed. The clock moved silently, relentlessly on. They made love, slept, woke, made love, and then slept.

It was seven-thirty. Santomassimo pulled the curtains open. The skies were deep mauve in the waning daylight. Kay stirred, then woke simply. Her eyes opened.

"Is it time to go?" she asked.

"Yes."

"I'm afraid you'll have to swing by my apartment so I can pack."

"I've already allowed time for that."

They kissed, dressed, and ate the coffee ice cream. They felt sleepy, drugged almost, from the lovemaking, from the vivid, eerily lit ocean in the twilight.

He stopped at her apartment. She unlocked the security door. He put his arm over her shoulder, and they went up the stairs together. The apartment was a mess and cold.

Furniture lay strewn everywhere and in the light streaming through her window, they could see the tufts of bloodied feathers and the broken table where she had been trapped.

She packed quickly, efficiently. Santomassimo watched. He realized how little he knew of her, how little he needed to know. He began picturing her as a far more lonely person than he had at first thought. Just because she was beautiful didn't mean she didn't know about loneliness, too.

He studied the terrace door. Though it was closed now and locked, it had been easy access from the black iron escape platform. The killer must have waited and watched the performance down in the alley. A good seat in the orchestra, Santomassimo thought.

She smiled bravely but was anxious to get out of the apartment. It was seven-fifty-five. He carried her suitcase down to the car. He drove quickly out to the Santa Monica Freeway and then toward Long Beach. When they passed Loyola, her face darkened as a thought assailed her.

"How did he even know about me, Fred?"

"Like you said in the D.A.'s office, he must have joined the crowd. That's where he spotted you. With me. More than once. He found out you're a school teacher. You fit the pattern."

"Then he knows we're both onto his crazy game. Like Steve Safran knew." She turned to him. "You'll be careful?"

"Actually, I'd like nothing better than to meet Mr. Hitchcock," he said, hands tightening on the wheel. "I'd like to give him my review in person."

Los Angeles International Airport was busy. The orange-and-blue lights that lighted up the runways reflected off wisps of fog. The glass windows of the terminals showed little pink and dark heads staring out. Rental cars and limousines scooted in and out from the passengers loading at the curbs. Tourists came wide-eyed out of the Pan Am lobby, gawking at the bright lights of Los Angeles.

Santomassimo checked Kay in at the Pan Am desk. They went down the long, carpeted corridors past the security inspection and the airport boutiques. The last call for Pan Am 147 boomed down the terminal. They had enjoyed themselves too much in Santomassimo's apartment, and now had to force themselves to run toward the gate.

The passengers had already boarded the plane. A steward began closing the steel door from the gate.

"Hold it!" Santomassimo called. "Open that door!"

A stewardess saw them running, Santomassimo bobbling Kay's overnight case. Grinning, the stewardess snapped her fingers. Without dignity, Kay and Santomassimo tore into the gate area. When they got there, the stewardess quickly confirmed Kay's ticket and returned her part of the boarding pass.

Kay said, puffing hard, "Are my students on board? From USC?"

"All I can tell you is everyone's on board except you."

"Thank God. Another two minutes—"

"The plane *is* leaving, Professor Quinn."

"Right. Oh, Fred. This is it. You'll be careful? I'll call you. Oh, I'll be thinking of you all the time."

Santomassimo came nearer to kiss her but she backed away.

"I've got students somewhere on that plane."

"Professors have no love life?"

"Not before tenure."

She ran down the red carpet into the 747. Suddenly, she ran back and planted a deep kiss on his lips, then headed back down the corridor. She waved.

"Call you from New York!" she repeated, and was gone inside the plane.

Santomassimo wiped his face with a handkerchief. It was warm and humid in the airport. Sikhs in their characteristic turbans were waiting, and Chinese, Mexicans, Africans—all the peoples of the world seemed to converge at Los Angeles International Airport tonight. Out of instinct, he examined the gate area.

He saw nothing out of the ordinary, and walked quickly back to the parking lot. He checked under the Datsun, started to unlock the door, when he stopped. He thought a moment, then walked quickly back to the terminal. He went to a bank of pay telephones and called headquarters. Captain Emery was working late, as usual.

"Bill? Santomassimo. I just put Kay on the ten-forty-five plane to New York. She'll be staying at the Darby Hotel on West Fifty-fifth Street . . ." He paused, weighing his next words with care. "It's not that I'm worried, Bill, but just to play it safe, would you call Captain Perry and have him notify the New York Police Department to keep an eye on her? . . . Yes . . . I know, I know . . . there's a big bleeding city there, too, but will you please try?" Again Santomassimo wiped his face with his handkerchief, listening to Captain Emery, and nodding his head. "Okay, Bill, great. . . . thanks a lot."

Inside the plane, Kay struggled down the long aisle. Her bandaged hands made it difficult to hold the suitcase. She edged sideways through the business class, and finally into coach. At the far end a familiar figure rose, waving. It was the blond boy in her class, Chris Hinds.

"Here, Professor Quinn!" he called.

She nodded, smiling, still pushing her way forward. She reached her seat, between Chris and another student, Mike Reese. She tried to maneuver the suitcase beneath the seat in front of her, but couldn't. Mike stood and pushed it snugly into the slot. She thanked him with a friendly grin.

"Jesus, Professor Quinn," he asked. "What did you do to your hands and your face?"

"I burned myself in the kitchen."

"It looks terrible. Are you really all right?"

"Of course. It was just some hot water. I was draining spaghetti, if you can believe that."

Now Chris was looking at her bandaged hands. "Are they third-degree burns, Professor?"

"First, second, third—" Kay laughed lightly. "I never can tell which is the worst, but mine are the least, so don't worry about it."

"Wow," Mike sighed.

"We'll take good care of you, Professor Quinn." The voice came from the seat behind her. It belonged to a tall, thin student named Thad Gomez.

"That sounds good, Thad. Thanks."

She peered out into the darkness. There was no hope of seeing Santomassimo. Already she was in the confined, controlled world of the Pan Am 747. She felt as though she had escaped in the nick of time. Her nerves were still shaky. She hoped the stewardesses would bring the liquor around. Or was that a bad image to her students?

"Finally!" she sighed in relief, buckling herself in. "Peace!"

Slowly, very slowly, a hand from behind reached, reached and touched her on the neck.

"Who—?" she exclaimed.

She turned. A face peered over her shoulder. It was the teaching assistant, Bradley Bowers.

"Hello, Professor," Bradley said.

"Bradley—What are you doing here?"

"I bought the ticket at the last minute. I decided I couldn't resist."

"Well, that's great, Bradley. I'm glad to have another on board. You'll be a great help."

"I expect to learn a lot, too," Bradley said. "I'm looking forward to New York. Such fun."

"Yes. It will be fun."

Bradley leaned back and paged through a magazine. It was a film journal.

The 747's engines roared. The plane trembled. It taxied out toward the runway, waited, and then blasted out along the concrete. With a buoyant lurch, it was in the air. It banked, and the marvelous sea of amber lights, stretching to the ends of the Earth, filled the windows on the left side.

Kay ordered a cognac. Bradley ordered a Perrier, Thad had a Coke, Chris had a white wine, and Mike, in football training, didn't drink.

It felt good to be leaving Los Angeles. The case had crippled her life. It had opened a hole under her and dropped her in. New York was a different world. It would stimulate her. It would be like starting over, concentrating on film analysis again. Still, the four young men couldn't know just how much she didn't want to be traveling with them, but with a wooden-faced, warm-eyed Italian cop named Santomassimo.

14

When Kay arrived at Kennedy, the skycaps were on strike. Thad carried her overnight bag and Chris fought his way through the crowds, leading them to the taxi stand. Mike Reese's eyes were red. He applied Murine in the taxi.

"Jesus. What a flight," Bradley grumbled. "I'd have slept better in a washing machine."

The taxi deposited them at the Darby Hotel at 5:15 A.M. It was still dark. The desk clerk paged through a stained register. Mike looked around with horror at the old men sleeping in the lobby. Obviously, they were not residents at the Darby. He could smell them across the moldy red carpet. Kay exchanged glances with him.

"What should we do, Mike?" she asked. "We've got to get *some* sleep."

He smiled gamely.

"I can stand it if you can, Professor Quinn."

"What about the rest of you?" she asked.

"I suppose we can live with it. As long as there aren't any cockroaches," Chris said.

"Thad?"

"Lead the way. I'll follow. Just don't expect me to like it."

"Frankly," Bradley Bowers said. "This hotel is a disgrace. I'll bet it's unlicensed. Look at the filth. Those curtains haven't been washed since the Indians sold the island."

"We really have no choice, Bradley," Kay suggested.

The clerk consulted the register. "Ah, yes. Quinn. 334 and 336. He looked up at Kay. "Ah . . . which . . . that is to say, are you all . . . Who exactly goes with who . . . ?"

"I booked a single for myself and was told there'd be a room for the others," Kay said angrily.

"The room only sleeps three. You didn't say four."

"Can't you get a cot, for God's sake?"

"Sorry. The room is too small. Fire regulations, too." The clerk drummed his fingers on the dirty ledger. He whistled to himself. "So somebody has to stay with you. We *were* advised there'd be only three and you."

"This is outrageous," Chris said. "This is Professor Quinn. She's come all the way from California to lead a tour of—"

"And she can go right back to California, sonny boy. There are dozens of people wanting those rooms. Hotels are busy, even on slow weekends. You're damn lucky we saved them for you. Now make up your mind, do you want them or not?"

"Don't call me sonny boy. Not unless you want the ledger to fit where it doesn't belong."

Kay stepped between them, brushing her hair out of her eyes. She was so sleepy she felt dizzy. "Please," she asked the clerk. "Can we look at the rooms?"

"The rooms are fine."

"We'd like to see them first."

"Look, I don't have to—"

Thad went behind the counter and yanked the keys to rooms 234 and 236 off the pigeon holes.

"Hey—"

"We'll be right back," Thad said, lifting Kay's overnight bag with his own. "Don't disturb your guests," he added, gesturing at the bodies draped over in the shadows on the couches.

The elevator didn't work. The stairs smelled of something like very old broccoli, and the corridors smelled of something worse. Bradley opened the door to room 234. Kay looked in. The 1950's decor was scratched, there was a cigarette burn in the pink-tufted bedspread, and huge areas of wallpaper fell away from the wall. It wasn't dirty, but she didn't feel like touching anything. Even from across the room she could tell the bed was soft as pastry dough. Her back would be completely out. She slept on the bed. Bradley took the club chair. They slept in their clothes.

It was a miserable sleep. Their wake-up call came three hours later. Sleepy-eyed, they staggered down the stairs to the lobby, where a uniformed policeman was waiting for them. He was a burly, Irish-faced caricature of a New York cop. He tipped his visor and smiled winningly at Kay.

"Good mornin', ma'am," he said in a thick brogue. "The desk clerk pointed you out as being Miss Quinn. Is that right?"

"Yes," Kay said, slightly nervous. "Is there any problem?"

"Why, no, ma'am," he smiled, and produced his identification. "Duffy's the name. Officer First Class, Twenty-eighth Precinct. We got a communication from Los Angeles to—well—kind of keep an eye on you during your stay in our city."

Kay felt a chill sweep through her. Was Fred worried about her here in New York? she wondered. Aloud, she said, "Well, thank-you, Officer. I appreciate your concern, but everything seems all right so far."

"Fine, ma'am, fine," Duffy grinned. "Thing is, we've got a big bleeding city out there and more work than we can handle. So we can't exactly be your chaperones, much as we'd like to." He presented her with a card from his wallet. "Here's our precinct's number in the event you have reason to need our help. Call us any time of the day or night."

Kay took the card and put it into her purse. As Duffy saluted and turned to leave, Kay said, as an afterthought, "Oh, Officer Duffy—"

"Ma'am?"

"We *could* use your help in suggesting a better hotel for us."

Officer Duffy thought a moment, then said, "Oh, Miss Quinn, you've hit us at a bad time. For some unaccountable reason, the city is swollen with visitors. I wouldn't know what to suggest to you—"

"That's quite all right, Officer. We'll manage." Kay smiled as Officer Duffy once again tipped his hat and left through the grimy revolving doors.

Bradley and the other students had watched the byplay between Kay and the policeman from a discreet distance. The moment he left, they hurried to her side.

"What's he want?" Mike asked.

"Nothing. Just extending New York hospitality. It's the custom here."

The boys looked at Kay doubtfully.

"Come on," Chris said wearily. "Let's get a cab. He must know where there's another hotel. One we won't die in."

They had to wait for a Checker Cab, which would accommodate five. When they got in, Bradley and Thad sat in the jumpseats.

"What a lousy trip," Bradley said.

"Oh, shut up, Bradley," Mike snapped.

"Everything is so dirty."

The taxi driver took them to the Wilton. It was old, but it had a clean ladies room and a clean coffee lounge off the lobby. They waited for the desk clerk to see what rooms, if any, were being vacated that morning.

There was a smell of car exhaust fumes in the autumn air. Manhattan's rumble never ceased. Kay thought of Santomassimo. He would never tolerate such inelegant surroundings. But Manhattan's energy now began to infect her, and the boys, too. And the tour focused the mind on film again. It was a breath of new life.

She took off the bandages in the ladies room and examined her hands and face by the sink. The wounds had healed somewhat. She re-dressed them and went into the lobby where the four young men had fallen asleep on the red couches. She gazed through the huge windows at the bustling city. Savage and indifferent, she thought, always extraordinary, breathtaking, New York was still the chief city of the world. It might be a pleasant weekend after all.

There was one fly in the ointment. Santomassimo was the new target. She felt it in her blood. Hitchcock had made films about cops.

Who, she wondered, was roaming around Los Angeles, looking for the Great Saint?

Santomassimo slept badly that night. Without Kay his apartment felt empty. He had not closed the curtains and the bright morning sun came onto his face. That and the ringing telephone wakened him. Groggily he fumbled for the receiver.

"Great Saint?" came Kay's faraway, cheerful voice.

Santomassimo instantly sat up.

"Hi," he croaked. Then, more awake. "What time is it?"

"Nine o'clock."

"In New York. It's six o'clock here."

"Well, I thought cops never slept."

"*I* do. I don't go on shift till noon today."

"By then we'll have spent two hours in the Canal Street Police Station following the hallowed footsteps of Henry Fonda in *The Wrong Man*."

He could hear the clatter of dishes in the background, like a cafeteria or restaurant, and the loud chatter and shouts of staff and people going by. He heard car horns on a street outside, a continuous thunder that made him picture the glutted avenues of New York.

His eyes closed. He saw the ragtag remnants of his dream. He was glad she was out of town.

"Fred!" she said. "Are you listening?"

She seemed excited to be in New York. Her voice was eager. That made Santomassimo feel good. He was awake now and in love all over again.

"I really called to tell you that we checked *in* and then *out* of the Darby Hotel. A real fleabag, bleak, foul, and vermin-ridden."

"Where are you now?"

"In the coffee shop of the Wilton Hotel on Eighth and Fortieth."

"Have you checked in?"

"Not yet. We're on standby. Every hotel room seems to be occupied. But the desk clerk is certain he can accommodate us after checkout time. We're on top of the list. Oh, by the way, why did you sic the cops on us?"

"—What?" For a moment, Santomassimo couldn't relate to her question. Then, remembering, he said, "The N.Y.P.D.—they contacted you?"

"Did they ever," Kay laughed. "Sent their finest broth of an officer. Sweet, charmin', and Irish as Paddy's pig. Right out of Central Casting."

"Okay, that's fine. They're there if you need them.

Which you won't Kay. I want you to forget about everything except having a great time. And call me tonight when you're settled in."

"Will do. Now go back to sleep and dream of me. Nobody else."

He sighed and huskily said, "I want you so much, Kay. Last night was a year ago. Come back soon."

He heard her laugh and it was a wonderful sound. Then somebody must have bumped into her because there was a muffled sound and a clatter before she came back to the telephone.

"Don't worry about me, Fred," she reassured him. "I've got four strong males to protect me. One's a football player."

"Great. You're there in New York with good-looking college athletes and I'm stuck here in Los Angeles with Lou Bronte."

Santomassimo was a target, and she knew it. And he knew it. She could tell in his voice. They were so intimate now, they didn't have to say it. Kay became frightened again.

"Be careful, darling," she whispered.

They hung up and Santomassimo lay back in his warm bed. He closed his eyes. He didn't want to dream anymore so he made himself get up and make some strong espresso. He had breakfast on the balcony.

Kay hung up the telephone and maneuvered out of the booth, dodging waiters and busboys. The desk clerk of the Wilton still wasn't sure about the rooms. It was already humid and very bright, and an occasional yellow leaf on the sidewalk outside the windows signified the autumn.

Kay sidled past some tables where men and women were hunched over their food, and came to her own.

Bradley Bowers, Chris Hinds, Mike Reese, and Thad Gomez were jammed into a space meant for two. They were arguing Hitchcock and were only faintly aware of her when she sat down, on a chair, at the head of the table. She retrieved schedules and a pair of half-frame glasses from her purse and studied the finely typed ferry arrival and departure times.

Bradley leaned over the remnants of toast and scrambled eggs on his plate, his dark suit silhouetted against the bright, steamy window.

"Logic," he insisted, forcefully, "was the least of Hitchcock's concerns. His drive—his motivating *need*—was to keep the suspense always rising. Understand? The audience on the edges of their seats, breathless, nervous wrecks—and damn the logic!"

Kay looked up, putting her glasses into their black case and back into her purse.

"What are we talking about?" she asked.

"*Sabotage*," Thad said, brushing the hair back from his forehead. He was as secure in his ideas as Bradley, even more so, but he was less articulate. He felt self-conscious under Kay's green eyes. She thought she saw him color ever so slightly. "You discussed it in class last Thursday—Hitchcock let the little boy get killed by the bomb."

Chris Hinds leaned over. He was excited, invigorated by being in Manhattan. He seemed fascinated by all the ugly types of people everywhere, inside and outside the coffee shop. He enjoyed sparring with Bradley. Now he took on Thad.

"Letting the kid deliver the bomb to the detective," Chris said, brushing his blond hair out of his eyes, "was a mistake. I mean, in allowing Oscar Homolka to use his wife's kid brother to do it."

"Why was that a mistake?" Kay interrupted.

Chris turned to her. "Because the police could identify the boy. Isn't that right? That would lead them straight to the killer."

"Point taken, Chris. What should Hitchcock have done? Logically?"

Chris had no answer. He seemed flummoxed by the

question. Thad smiled and toyed with his spoon in a superior way.

"Hitchcock should have used a boy who was a stranger to Homolka," Thad said shyly, but thoughtfully. "Some kid from a different part of London."

"Wouldn't *he* have been able to identify the killer to the police?" Kay asked.

Thad hesitated. "Not if the killer wore a disguise."

Bradley rolled his eyes and angrily shoved his plate away. "You know what you guys are?" he snapped. "Plausibles! That's what Hitchcock called people who needed everything wrapped up neat and tidy!"

"Okay. Okay," Mike said. "We like a little logic. Is that so criminal?"

"It's shallow film thinking."

"No reason to get personal, Bradley," Chris said, his voice friendly but slightly tense.

Kay realized that she saw these students only in her class, and Bradley only as her teaching assistant. But they shared many classes in the film department, and had been on film crews together. Their relationships were very intense. Sometimes crew members fought like cats.

"It's stupid," Bradly said. "You're not into the genius of the master's imagination! You're—you're still spectators!"

"So tell us, hotshot," Thad snorted. "What about the kid? How does he *not* lead the police to the killer?"

Bradley tore off the napkin he had put around his neck. Bradley was overweight, and he wiped the perspiration from his forehead. He threw the napkin onto his greasy plate. He looked pale. Maybe it was from the long airplane ride, Kay thought, or lack of sleep. Maybe he was claustrophobic, jammed in the corner. Maybe he was intimidated by New York.

"Hitchcock made sure the boy was beyond identifying anybody!" Bradley said, rising triumphantly. *"He was blown up!"*

* * *

Michael Gordon was twelve. He had been hanging out in front of Lucky's Market when a man had come to him with a strange request. Now Michael had been warned about strangers. He lived in West L.A. where the kids knew about deviancy. But he had listened to the fellow. It seemed bizarre. But the fellow was obviously not after Michael's body. A hundred dollars is good money when you're twelve. So Michael agreed.

Now he sat uncomfortably in the rear of a hot taxi. He realized he should have asked for cabfare, too. Still, his profits would be good. Michael craned his neck. His mother had starched his shirt and the skin under his chin was red. The driver kept looking at him in the rear view mirror.

"You know where it is?" Michael asked.

"I know where it is. I know where it is."

"I know about you cabbies. Drive all over L.A. just to build up the fare."

Outside, they drove by palm trees, furniture stores, a leather goods store, and then the long strip of restaurants on Santa Monica Boulevard.

Michael watched the people on the street. Many of them tourists, artists, professionals, and some of them bums.

"Aren't we there yet?" Michael asked.

"Almost."

"I know this area. So don't go out of your way."

"I am taking you direct to the police station, kid."

"Good," Michael said impatiently.

On his lap was a brown wrapped package.

The taxi pulled up in front of the Palisades Division station house. There were several policemen on the steps and a row of shining patrol cars in the parking lot. The city flag flew on a tall pole, the chain rattling in the breeze. Michael stepped out.

"Wait for me," he told the taxi driver. "I'll be right out."

Michael shifted the weight of the package under his arm. He turned to go, but the driver leaned forward and said, "Hold on, kid. A lot of people go and don't come back."

"I'm just delivering this. Honest. I'll be right out."

"I got the meter running. You got money for this?"

"I told you. I've got plenty of money."

"You better."

Michael carried the package into the station. Jerry Rollins, a five-year veteran, stopped him at the desk. Michael walked on past him. Rollins jumped from the desk, grabbed him, and spun him around.

"Not so fast, my little friend," Rollins said. "Who are you looking for?"

Michael looked down at the label on the brown paper. He twisted the package around to read it.

"Lieutenant San . . . San . . . to . . . ma . . ."

"Santomassimo. Give it to me. I'll see he gets it."

"I'm supposed to deliver it to him. Personally."

"That's okay. I'll see that he gets it. Personally."

Michael looked down the corridors.

"Come on, hand it over," Rollins said.

Michael turned back to Rollins. He figured the stranger had gotten good value for the hundred dollars. He handed the package to Rollins. "Make sure he gets it before noon."

"Before noon? Why?"

The stranger had told Michael that. Michael said only, "Please get it to him before noon."

Rollins saw the clock over the doors. It was eleven-thirty. "Yeah, sure, he'll get it," Rollins said.

Michael went outside. Rollins watched him get into the taxi. Where do kids that age get the pocket money for taxis? he wondered. When he was that age, he never had two quarters to clink together. It wasn't Santomassimo's son. Santomassimo and Margaret hadn't had any kids. Rollins peered at the label on the package.

It was a gummed red address label from the USC Cinema Department. It was addressed to *Fred Santomassimo. Palisades Division, Los Angeles Police*. It came from *Quinn*.

Rollins grinned. Quinn was the professor working with Santomassimo on the Hitchcock killings. Rollins had seen Professor Quinn on Steve Safran's news clips. She had legs. There were rumors in the squad room that Santomassimo and she had become an item.

Rollins heard footsteps and turned. It was Detective Haber, coming in through the front door. Rollins held out the package.

"For his lieutenantship," Rollins said.

Haber looked at the label. "From Quinn. What do you think it is, Jerry? Sport shirts?"

"A bit heavy for that. I'd guess a gift book."

"Santomassimo? He can't read."

Nevertheless, Haber sniffed the package, hoping for the fragrance of perfume. All he smelled was brown paper. Maybe a bit of sweat where somebody had carried it.

"A kid brought it. He said Fred's to get it before noon."

"A kid? Who?"

"I don't know. Never saw him before."

"Well, Fred's shift doesn't start until noon," Haber said. "I'll put it on his desk."

Haber carried it up the stairs and into the squad room. The skylights were cleaned after an early morning shower and were brighter than usual. The squad room was crowded. Desks were covered. Detectives against the wall were arguing over a police report, the radio squawked without interruption, and five typewriters were going. Telephones rang constantly.

"Hello, Lou," Haber said, but Bronte was deep in thought and didn't hear him.

Bronte stood and gazed out the window, a coffee cup in his hand. He stared into the bright sun toward the unseen distant beach. Girls in their bikinis would be there, watching well-muscled young men do pull-ups on the horizontal bars. His mind imagined surfers far away playing in a curling wave, falling or diving into the ocean. Bronte sighed. Next day off, maybe he'd grab some deli and spend a few hours on the beach.

Haber came to Bronte's desk, puffing. He was in worse shape than Gilbert. They had finally found Gilbert's ulcer and were removing it that morning at St. Joseph's Hospital. Haber clapped Bronte on the shoulder.

"Too much thinking, *paisano*. Causes gray hairs."

Haber walked to Santomassimo's desk and deposited the package on it.

"What's that?" Bronte asked.

Haber shrugged. "It's for Fred. From his professor girlfriend. Anything happening?"

"The usual. Couple of break-ins. Rape on Eighth Street. Two muggings that didn't pay off. Both victims in the hospital. Broken jaw for one, cracked collarbone for the other. They'll live."

"I meant, from Hitchcock?"

"Hitchcock? No. Nothing so far."

Haber chuckled. "Maybe he takes weekends off. I hope he does. I'm tired. I didn't get a break this summer."

"Nobody did, John."

Haber walked over to the long chart of Hitchcock's films behind Santomassimo's desk. It was secured to the wall with green-headed pins and had become an icon in the squad room. Haber rocked back and forth, hands in his pockets, chewing gum, studying the entries. He peered down the long line of film titles.

"I wonder what movie we'll see next?" Haber wondered.

Bronte glanced at the clock. It was eleven-forty-two. He gulped down the coffee and sat at his desk. He waited for Santomassimo, thinking. Another kinky killing, full of gimmicks, popcorn, and surprises. It would certainly end the boredom of the daily routine.

Santomassimo came into the squad room. Bronte knew by Santomassimo's face he was in love. They must have had some night, Bronte thought, a trifle worriedly. He hoped his partner wouldn't get stung like the last time.

"Hey, Lieutenant," Haber said, turning from the chart, easing himself around on Santomassimo's swivel chair. "You're early."

"Thanks, We need a good timekeeper." He turned to Bronte. "Anything, Lou?"

Bronte shook his head. "Nothing. Hitchcock must be speaking to his writers."

"Wait. You got a package," Haber said. "From your . . . um, your friend, Quinn."

"Kay?"

"Yeah. It just came."

Santomassimo walked to his desk and looked down at it. He frowned. Puzzled, Haber and Bronte watched him. He picked it up, hefted it gently, and then put it back carefully on the desk.

Haber and Bronte stepped tentatively toward the desk and Santomassimo.

"Aren't you going to open it?" Haber asked.

"When did this come in?"

"Not ten minutes ago. Rollins got it from a kid. Delivery service of some sort. I brought it up here. Why?"

"What delivery service?"

"I don't know, Fred. I just got it from Jerry."

"Get Rollins up here."

Haber nodded, somewhat confused, and walked quickly from the squad room downstairs to the guard's desk. Bronte walked closer to Santomassimo. He put a hand on Santomassimo's shoulder but they both stared down at the package.

"What's bugging you, Fred?" he asked.

"This package. Why would she send it?"

"Maybe it's books on the master's files. Maybe she's sentimental. Women are, well, subtle and fantastic creatures."

"I know about women. What's this package doing here?"

Santomassimo walked around the desk, still looking at the package, studying the red address label.

"When did she send it?" Santomassimo asked. "Lou, she spent the last two days with me."

"I know."

"I put her on a plane for New York last night."

"Well—"

Bronte peered even closer at the label.

"Campus mail," he suggested. "She probably mailed it quite a few days ago. It takes a long time for mail to work its way through the university system."

Santomassimo was getting edgy. Rollins and Haber came into the squad room. Haber led Rollins quickly to Santomassimo's desk.

"The kid who delivered this," Santomassimo said. "Tell me about him."

"Just a kid, Lieutenant."

"In uniform?"

"No, sir. Just a kid."

"Wearing what, Rollins?"

"Wearing nice trousers and tennis shoes. About twelve. He took a taxi home."

Rollins's eyes betrayed a quickly developing unease. It was contagious. Bronte saw it in Haber's face, which had grown pale.

"Did you get the kid's name?" Santomassimo asked.

"No." Then, more feebly, "Should I have?"

"It would have been helpful," Santomassimo said sarcastically.

Captain Emery emerged from his office. He saw the men grouped at Santomassimo's desk. Curious, he

approached them. When he got there, he sensed the
nervousness and uncertainty. It made no sense to
him. All he noticed was an ordinary package on Santomassimo's desk.

But he distinctly heard Bronte say, clearly and quietly, into the silence, "You think it's a bomb, Fred?"

Santomassimo's eyes were fixated on the package.
Then he walked to the long chart behind his desk.
The men crowded around. The detectives and policemen left their typewriters, radios, and wordprocessors,
and the squad room fell silent.

"*Blackmail. Number Seventeen. Murder,*" Santomassimo read, his finger tracing the film titles.

In the other columns were the professions of the
victims, and the means of death. "*The Man Who Knew
Too Much,*" he read slowly, carefully, following the
columns. "*The Thirty-nine Steps. Secret Agent.*" Haber, Emery, Rollins, and Bronte hardly breathed. Patrolmen's eyes scanned the wall chart just ahead of
Santomassimo's finger. "*Sabotage. Young and Innocent.*"

"Hold it, Fred," Bronte said.

"What?"

"Look back at *Sabotage.*"

Occupation of victim: *Detective*. Weapon used:
Bomb.

Santomassimo licked his lips and stepped away from
the chart. The squad room momentarily danced in his
vision, as unreal as a funeral notice. Suddenly, he felt
himself sweating and his heart pounding. He whirled
around. The package lay on the edge of his desk.
Ordinary dime store brown wrapping paper.

The patrolmen looked at one another, at Santomassimo, at the wall chart, at Bronte, Haber, and Rollins.
A few inched backward. Captain Emery was still confused, the others paralyzed.

"What the fuck is going on here?" Emery demanded.

Rollins answered obliquely: "The kid said be sure to get it to you before noon."

Santomassimo looked up at the clock. It was eleven-fifty-nine. Suddenly, he grabbed the package.

"Open the window, Lou!"

Bronte hesitated.

"OPEN THE GODDAMN WINDOW!"

Bronte ran to the window, jerked it up and slammed it all the way open. Santomassimo, clutching the package, was wide-eyed in terror, running from his desk.

"Is it clear down there?" Santomassimo yelled.

"It's clear!"

Santomassimo hurled it out into the parking lot. He staggered back from the window, taking Bronte with him. They saw the brown package, twirling slowly, sailing down, down into the center of the asphalt, where it bounced between two empty patrol cars.

And rested there, bruised.

Rollins, curious, came slowly to the window. Haber and Emery crowded them in from behind. Patrolmen leaned out the window. The scuffed package had sand on it now. Emery shook his head.

"I think you're going bughouse, Fred," he whispered.

There was a click on the wall. The patrolmen and detectives, Haber and Bronte, Rollins and Santomassimo turned to look. Even Captain Emery turned. The clock's long, red needle jerked from eleven-fifty-nine. To noon.

Santomassimo turned back and looked down at the package in the parking lot.

A white fireball rocked the patrol cars and skidded them, metal screeching, into the brick wall of headquarters. Fragments of asphalt, upholstery, and hot dirt cascaded, and billowing waves of heat scorched the squad room, shaking the lights and knocking telephones, papers, and coffee mugs off the desks.

Glass blew out from the doors and windows on the

ground floor and Santomassimo heard the reception-
ists screaming. A reeking hole opened up in the
asphalt. Upstairs, the concussion knocked Santomassimo and Bronte clear to the far wall. Captain Emery,
reading glasses ripped off his face, bleeding, reeled
backward, groping for a coat rack for support.

Rollins crashed backward into the side wall. Plaster
showered over him. Then a fluorescent lighting fix-
ture smashed over his legs and in the clouds of smoke
and debris he saw Detective Haber, the pants blown
at the knees, trying to crawl backward, face blackened, desk drawers toppled onto his back.

All over the floor, the patrolmen and detectives
crawled, moaning, dumb and shocked, hands convulsively gripping whatever they had been working with
when the blast went off: telephones, fragments of a
computer, notebooks. One patrolman crawled into the
hall, feeling his body for wounds, and then fainted.

"What kind of insane fucker is this, Fred?" Emery
hissed in rage and helplessness.

Santomassimo held a handkerchief over his mouth.
Oily smoke poured up from where one of the patrol
cars caught fire. He heard shouts outside, and footsteps running, and sirens as the fire trucks came
down Santa Monica Boulevard.

Paramedics ran in but he waved them to the more
badly injured.

There were fragments of the Hitchcock murder
board all over the room, like confetti, curled and
blackened by the blast. Bits of printing were dis-
cernible: *Psycho. Bomb. Salesman. Warehouse. Fifth
Avenue mansion. Empty field. Statue of Liberty. A
Victorian house. Birds. Rope. Gun.* It was all a psychotic pastiche of methods, locations, and professions.
*Sabotage. Saboteur. London. Mount Rushmore. New
York.* Kay was in New York.

Santomassimo stumbled over the stupefied men.
They were sitting, kneeling, crouching, bodies bent

and twisted by the shock and panic, trying to get their bearings. They looked to him for an answer. And he had none. He went into the hall, sucking for air, tears in his eyes.

That was the second time the Hitchcock killer had failed. What next? Santomassimo wondered. *What the bloody fuck next?*

Bronte struggled out of the squad room, coughing. He fixed bloodshot eyes on Santomassimo.

"What do you say, *paisano*? All your important pieces together?"

Santomassimo looked at him but he didn't see him.

Bronte studied Santomassimo, then asked, "What's up, Fred?"

Santomassimo said, "I don't know." The words came out in a dull rasp. He coughed and spit. Then, looking at Bronte, he said, "She's in New York."

Bronte watched him narrowly. "Yeah, I know. So what?"

"*Strangers on a Train* was shot there. And *Saboteur*. And a couple of other places they're visiting."

Bronte waited for more, then prompted. "Okay, that's true. What are you thinking?"

"They're going to visit a mansion on Fifth Avenue. And . . . yeah . . . the Canal Street Station."

Bronte's lips formed a bloody grin. "I'd like to see him try something in the Canal Street Station."

"They're going to the Statue of Liberty, too."

"Again I say, so what? This guy doesn't operate by locations. He knocks Safran off St. Amos bell tower, it should have been a church in London. He fries a girl in a fancy hotel, it should've been a sleazy motel outside Fresno."

"There's only one Statue of Liberty," Santomassimo said.

"Okay. So what you're saying is he followed her to New York. So what do you want to do? Call New York and have them shut down the Statue of Liberty? All on a hunch?"

"I guess that's unreasonable, huh?"

"At this point? Yes. Right now, I think we'd better get our asses down to USC and find out how that package got mailed from the Cinema Department."

15

The humidity evaporated, leaving Manhattan dry and crisp. There was a definite nip in the cool air, with a tinge of something far away and nostalgic.

Kay walked along Canal Street. She formed a compact, intense group with Bradley Bowers, Mike Reese, Thad Gomez, and Chris Hinds. Chris wore a light-blue windbreaker over his sweater, Mike his USC football jacket. Bradley Bowers wore a rumpled black suit jacket and rumpled black trousers. He carefully stepped over dog droppings, sometimes falling behind the group, then walking quickly in front of Kay, then alongside her.

Bradley was nervous. The desk clerk still hadn't confirmed their room at the Wilton, and he dreaded having to spend the night searching for a place to sleep.

The Canal Street police headquarters was half in

sun, half in shadow. A sergeant came lazily out the door, eyed them suspiciously, and went to his patrol car on the curb. Mike stepped out of the way. The car splashed oily water onto the curb.

"*The Wrong Man,* the only documentary film Hitchcock ever made," she said, "was filmed here. The Canal Street police headquarters is the only original existing New York location for any of his films. Except for the mansion on Fifth Avenue, which has undergone a total face-lift."

"What about the Stork Club?" Mike asked.

"It doesn't exist anymore," Kay said. "A great landmark to the cultural life of Manhattan, but it's completely gone."

"Wasn't there the Prudential Insurance Building?" Chris asked.

"Also gone."

"Wait. The home of *The Wrong Man* and his wife," Thad suggested.

"Queens, not Manhattan."

The boys laughed. They often tried to catch Kay. They never did. She had them study the police headquarters.

"How does the building strike you?" she asked.

"Kind of innocuous," Chris said.

"Good, Chris. Exactly. Innocuous. Of course, we *know* that things go on inside that are painful, even tragic. Reports of accident victims, suspects of beatings, forensic evidence of murders. But we don't *see* it in the building itself."

"Until Hitchcock records it," Thad said.

"Until Hitchcock re-images it for us. By his framing, his composition, above all, by the editorial context of tension and suspense."

"So he makes us see it through his imagination," Mike said.

"And once you're in his imagination," Kay said,

"you're in a very precarious place. He toys with your mind."

Chris and Mike drew sketches of the building, and in the margins recalled the framing from Hitchcock's film. It was that discrepancy between reality and the filmed image that Kay wanted them to see.

"Is it true," Thad asked, "that Maxwell Anderson had first crack at writing the script?"

"Yes," Kay said, nodding.

"But he was replaced by Angus MacPhail," Bradley cut in.

"Right, Bradley."

Bradley's one-upmanship annoyed Thad. Thad closed his notebook and stepped closer to the police station. He peered in through the windows. Chris and Mike went to the front door and looked into the hall. More police came out. Kay looked at her watch.

"Listen, guys," she said. "It's almost two. I think we'd better cut our tour of Greenwich Village and see about registering at the Wilton."

"What a bore," Bradley said. "We came here to visit Hitchcock locations and we wind up visiting crummy hotels."

"Now, now, Bradley," Kay pacified. "Tomorrow will be a full day."

They rode back to the Wilton in a cab. Kay's ankles hurt. Her shoes weren't quite right for walking. Mike glimpsed her ankles. He hadn't meant to, but then he couldn't take his eyes off them, either. He blushed. Kay suppressed a smile.

Santomassimo's patrol car's siren split the hot, smoggy air over the freeway. Bronte coughed into a handkerchief. Both men had been patched up by the paramedics. Santomassimo drove eighty miles an hour and even so there were cars going almost as fast. Some of them even stayed in front of him in the fast lane. Roof lights revolving, headlights flashing, the patrol car went slower and slower, as the traffic bottled up, and soon mile after mile of bright cars were filled with frustrated drivers in the unbreathable air, honking miserably in a traffic jam.

The air was even worse at USC; thick with acrid, throat-burning haze. Santomassimo parked at the red curb behind the Steven Spielberg sound stage and ran across a short lawn, leaped a hedge, and entered the courtyard of the Cinema Department.

Bronte followed, breathing hard and sweating, as they rounded a corner and nearly ran into Alice Kahal. Kahal was the Cinema Department secretary. She was forty-five, usually stern, but now trembling. She blinked at the injured men in grimy suits in front of her. A few cinema students turned to look from the internal courtyard.

"Are you the policemen?" she asked.

"Yes, ma'am," Santomassimo said.

"As I told you on the phone, I generally quit at twelve on Saturdays."

"Thanks for waiting."

They followed her into the office. She never stopped talking. She was nervous. There were four desks, each cluttered with papers, arranged in neat piles Friday at the close of work, but all looking disheveled nonetheless. On the walls were posters of film festivals and framed certificates of major film prizes won by students and graduates of the department. Bronte was impressed. They were, he realized, major directors today.

"No packages were sent to your police station from this office, as I told you," she said. "I should know. I do the sending."

"Yes, but the label said USC Cinema Department," Santomassimo objected.

Alice Kahal went to her desk. She opened her drawer and took out a red-gummed label.

"You mean like this?" she asked.

Santomassimo took the label, tilted it so the glare disappeared, and showed it to Bronte. Bronte looked at it and handed it back.

"Yes," Santomassimo said. "Exactly like that. Who else had access to these labels?"

"You must be joking."

"I'm not laughing, Miss Kahal."

"I'm sorry. But everybody has access to these. Faculty, teaching assistants, students. Strangers from other departments trying to get into our program. Even parents arguing with the chairmen. Businessmen from Hollywood—we get a lot of donated equipment, scholarships, and such—Not to mention the secretaries—"

"And they would take a gummed label?"

"They take envelopes, stationery, class schedules, coffee mugs. Posters. Staplers. Anything that's smaller than a bread box and isn't nailed down. We're not thieves here, Lieutenant Santomassimo. But it's hectic and there's an aura of creative chaos all the time."

Bronte and Santomassimo exchanged glances. Bronte mouthed an Italian expletive. Santomassimo hoped that Alice Kahal did not speak Italian.

"Could a—janitor—?" Santomassimo said, faltering. "Absolutely anybody? A fellow faculty member? A teacher—?"

"Certainly."

"Or a student," Santomassimo said with studied calm.

A sinister logic had gradually wormed its way into his brain. The mistake he had promised Kay and himself he would never make, carelessness in not seeing the obvious, had been made again. He felt himself sweating down his back and it wasn't just the sultry air. He became very tense, yet held it in tight check.

Bronte looked at him in disbelief.

"Why not?" Santomassimo said. "Maybe even one of Kay's students."

"Fred—in her class?"

Santomassimo nodded. "HITCHCOCK 500." he said. "Perfect nest for him. A home away from home."

"Jesus, Fred—"

"Miss Kahal," Santomassimo asked, "Do you have a roster of Professor Quinn's Hitchcock class?"

"Of course."

Alice Kahal deftly fingered through neat manila folders. She plucked one out, opened it, and spread it out on her desk. Santomassimo and Bronte crowded around, squinting down at neatly typed, minutely printed computer paper. Bronte could hardly read it. There were long columns of names, college status, major, and faculty advisers.

"There are thirty-six students in the class," she said.

"Where would they be on a Saturday?" Santomassimo asked.

"Those on film crews are usually shooting over the weekend. Midterms are coming, so the writing students are probably holed up in someplace like Bob's Big Boy, memorizing the rules of dramatic conflict. The rest—dorms, fraternities, visiting parents, camping in the San Bernardino Mountains. In short, anywhere."

"Maybe on a tour," Santomassimo said.

"Fred—" Bronte didn't like what he was hearing. It showed in his face.

"Like in New York," Santomassimo insisted doggedly, each word a *mea culpa* litany.

Suddenly his attention was directed at Cindy McLaughlin coming into the office. She was about twenty, with a white sweater and a plaid skirt. Her hair was blond, and her eyes startlingly blue. Like most students he had seen, she looked sweet and vulnerable, but very ambitious.

"I saw the office was open," she said to Alice Kahal. "Can I type my scholarship form?"

Diffidently, Cindy sat down at the receptionist's desk and turned on the typewriter. The stony silence of Miss Kahal and the men didn't bother her. Bronte turned back to Alice Kahal.

"Who went on the tour?" Santomassimo asked. "Do you have a list somewhere?"

Alice Kahal wiped her spectacles, flustered. In truth, she didn't know where she had put the list. Around midterm, things had a way of getting misplaced. She turned to Cindy.

"Cindy would know better than I," Alice said. "She's taking the class. Cindy—"

Cindy looked up. Eyes soft as a doll's but Bronte saw the drive in them.

"Cindy, these are policemen," Alice Kahal said. "They need to know which students went to New York with Professor Quinn."

"Thad Gomez, Chris Hinds, and Mike Reese," Cindy said.

Bronte scribbled the names into his notebook.

"That's all?" Bronte asked.

"That's all. Wait. I ran into Bradley Bowers, the TA. He said he might go at the last minute. I don't know if he did or not."

Santomassimo had a memory of the slightly stocky, overweight teaching assistant. Something in the impatience of the young man's face, the rumpled darkness of his clothes that were not quite clean, made Santomassimo positively ill now.

"Do you know where they were staying in New York?" Bronte asked.

"Sorry," Cindy said. "Nobody told me."

Santomassimo suddenly hit his hand on Kahal's desk in frustration. "Shit."

"What is it, Fred?" Bronte asked.

"I know where. At least I did. Kay called this morning—They'd checked out of one hotel—it was the Darby—and were trying to check into another. They were on standby."

"Which hotel?"

Santomassimo shook his head, desperately irritated. "Christ, I can't remember, Lou. I was half asleep when she called. *Wyland*. No—*Wheeland*. It began with a *W*."

Bronte walked back to Kahal's desk and rummaged through the folder. There was nothing there but the computer sheets of the students' roster. "Miss Kahal," he asked gently. "Did Professor Quinn give you an itinerary of the tour?"

"No."

Cindy finished typing and ripped the scholarship form from the typewriter. "They were going to the Canal Street Station in the morning and Greenwich Village in the afternoon. Tomorrow it's the Statue of Liberty in the morning and a mansion on Fifth Avenue in the afternoon. No, no—" she corrected. "It's the mansion in the morning and the Statue in the afternoon." Her eyes became vague. "—I think."

"These four students," Bronte asked. "Do they live on campus?"

"I'd have to check the residence roster," Kahal said.

She went to a rack of upright folders. She pulled out a dog-eared manila folder, opened it, and showed them the contents. All kinds of notes were pasted inside. Obviously, some of the students were transient.

"Thad Gomez and Mike Reese," Kahal said, reading. "Mike's the football star. He's only a freshman but he runs the hundred in—"

"Miss Kahal. Please," Santomassimo said. "This is urgent."

"Mike lives at the Psi Delta Chi fraternity house. It's a good address, Lieutenant Santomassimo. And Thad lives in married students housing. He has a wife and a little boy."

"Mike's not in trouble, is he?" Cindy asked. "He's really terrific."

Santomassimo grabbed the roster from Alice Kahal's hands. He and Bronte looked down the list.

"What about Chris Hinds?" Santomassimo said. "And the teaching assistant, Bradley Bowers? Where do these guys live?"

"In apartments."

"What addresses?"

"They don't seem to be on the computer list. Well, it's the computer's fault, not mine," Kahal objected.

"Miss Kahal," Santomassimo said. "It is absolutely vital that we find those addresses."

"I—I think there must be a record in the Admissions Office. They keep up-to-date records there for scholarship purposes, and—"

"Is someone there today?"

"Yes. Dean Reynolds is likely to be there. Mrs. Wilson works on Saturday. I'll take you there. But I'd have to telephone or they won't unlock the doors."

"Please, Miss Kahal. *Hurry.*" He swung around to Bronte. "Lou, call Captain Perry. Tell him to call the New York Police Department and issue an A.P.B. to intercept Kay and her students, and hold them for questioning."

The lobby of the Wilton was teeming with people. A convention, sent by an overbooked sister hotel, had taken over the entire premesis. Charts and displays of harvests, farm machinery, tourist sites, yachting harbors, and vineyards sprouted in the hotel foyer like surreal, gaudy flowers. Men wearing plastic I.D. tags gathered at the bar, smoking and discussing investments.

Thad was appalled at the density of people. Even the packed Amphitheater in Hollywood had an airiness about it. Humidity and darkness of so many bodies jammed together in what should have been a

decent hotel was horrible. It made him claustrophobic.
Kay battled her way into the lobby. Then came Mike,
carrying her suitcase as well as his, and then Chris
and Bradley Bowers.

"Haven't seen anything like this since I visited the
Chicago slaughterhouse," Mike shouted.

Nobody heard him in the crush of people and the
clamor. Kay elbowed her way to the front desk. She bit
her lips, worriedly. The desk clerk gave keys to a trio
of conventioneers. He didn't see Kay and when he did
he didn't remember her, kept referring to her by a
number of other names not even close to her own.

"Quinn," she yelled. "You said you'd give us rooms."

"Do you have reservations?"

"Don't you remember? There were five of us. At
nine o'clock this morning?"

"I don't have any rooms reserved for Quinn."

Kay leaned on the desk, cutting off a Rotarian or a
charter member of the Hee-Haw Society. "But,
damn it," she said, "you promised you'd take care of
us!"

"I'm sorry, Miss," the desk clerk said, wiping his
neck. "Look. I was mistaken. Many of the people we
expected to check out, didn't. Have you tried the
Darby? They generally have space."

"Sure they do, because the place isn't fit for pigs.
We checked out this morning."

"You shouldn't have."

Exasperated, Kay turned to Mike. But he had no
idea what to do. Bradley was worse than useless. He
had been pushed from the desk by a gaggle of ladies,
now he sulked among the worn couches and ashtrays,
despising the mob.

Kay tried politeness. She turned to the desk clerk
again.

"Please," she said. "Can't you help us? We've come
all the way from California. We've hardly slept in two
days. I am Professor Quinn of the University of

Southern California, and these are my students. We desperately need a place to stay."

The desk clerk, a short man with a rounded face, as though something had sat on it in his infancy, smiled. It was a smile born of fatigue. He didn't like being confronted by this Professor Quinn. In a week of cigar-breathing businessmen and slightly alcoholic, overbearing women, it was a very pretty face to be confronted with, but he had had it up to his neck with irate confrontations.

"Try the Hospitality Center at Penn Station," he suggested.

Kay shoved the ledger back at him. He caught it as it toppled over, sending reservation cards twirling.

"Thanks for nothing!" Kay said. "Hospitality Center! Maybe we could sleep under the Brooklyn Bridge! Come on, Mike. Get Bradley. Let's get out of here!"

Led by Mike's tall and forceful figure, they went through the lobby to the street and the warm September evening. Once on the sidewalk, Kay looked miserably at the fierce indifferent bustle of the island: taxis, buses, cars, pretzel vendors on the corners, ludicrously huge black limousines with smug foreigners in back, and thousands, millions of ordinary people walking quickly past the shops and restaurants everywhere.

"I feel so damn homeless," Bradley said. "It makes me so damn mad."

He held a handkerchief to his nose. It bled because he had gotten caught in a crowd in the revolving door and had been pushed against the Wilton's display case of New England harvest products.

Kay felt lifeless.

"What are we going to do, Mike?" she asked.

"Find a hotel, I guess."

Uncertain, Mike stepped to the curb to hail a taxi. Even the taxis ignored them.

* * *

Judge Robertson was a genial man, portly and addicted to expensive cigars. He lay in his heated pool under the sun, reading a crime thriller, while his feet lazily dangled from an inner tube. Perry and Emery came across his living room, led by his maid, and stood blocking out the sunlight by the diving area.

Judge Robertson shielded his eyes.

"Wallace?" he called.

"Yes, Henry," Perry said. He and Emery came around to Robertson's inner tube. "Henry . . . we have a pretty bad emergency."

"I assumed as much. Else you wouldn't be here on a Saturday."

Judge Robertson handed Perry his crime thriller, then eased backward like a bloated seal, slid underwater with surprising agility, and climbed out on a steel ladder. He covered himself with a terrycloth robe and combed back his jet black hair. He gestured to white, webbed pool chairs under an umbrella. As they walked there, he dried his face in a white towel.

"What's the matter, Wallace?"

They sat. Wallace Perry steeled himself uncomfortably under the umbrella despite which the late afternoon sun still managed to make a blinding halo in his eyes. "Henry, this is Captain Emery, in charge of the bureau of the Palisades Division." Judge Robertson and Emery shook hands. "His lieutenant, Fred Santomassimo, has headed the task force on the Hitchcock killer under my supervision."

"Ah yes, Hitchcock," Judge Robertson said. "What can I do for you?"

Captain Perry spoke first. "We believe there is a good chance that the killer is a film student at USC and is now on a tour of New York with Professor Quinn."

Captain Emery leaned forward. "There are four students on the tour, your honor. All males. We don't know which one it is. We need break-in and seizure warrants to investigate their quarters, look for possible evidence that would link one of them to the crimes."

Judge Robertson's eyebrows raised slightly. "Four of them?"

"Yes, sir."

"I need some information."

Perry showed the judge Santomassimo's list of specifications, plus the gummed label from USC's Cinema Department. Judge Robertson glanced at it with distaste. "You expect me to let you break into a man's home—four men's homes—with this sort of thing?"

"The mayor—" Perry began.

"I don't play politics with civil liberties," Judge Robertson snapped. "The whole damn state—the whole country, for all I know—is watching us. I'm not going to let you start smashing doors down on such flimsy—"

"Then you'll have him at large in Manhattan," Perry said brutally.

"That won't sit well with Americans. Or the media," Captain Emery added. "Your honor, we have reasonable cause to suspect that at least one life—Professor Quinn's—is in danger."

Judge Robertson handed the papers back to Perry. "It isn't enough, Wallace," he decided. "Anyone could have had access to these labels."

"We know," Captain Perry said tiredly. "We are currently interrogating the cinema faculty and all the people who work in the Cinema Department. But our belief—and I'll admit, Henry, it's only a hunch, is that one of the students with Professor Quinn in New York City at this moment—is the killer."

"Your honor," Emery added strongly, "a bomb, intended for Lieutenant Santomassimo, destroyed half the west wall of my headquarters!"

"I read the papers. I watch the news, Captain Emery."

"How many more people does he have to kill?"

Emery protested. "How many more people does he have to put in his psychotic fantasy films?"

Judge Robertson pulled a fat cigar from an inlaid mahogany case. He tried lighting it three times, gave up, and simply chewed on the end until it became black and moist.

"It's flimsy," he said. "This information you gave me. It's flimsy."

"They busted Watergate on less," Perry said.

"We don't have much time," Emery said.

Judge Robertson grunted, stabbing his cigar into an ashtray, even though it had never been lighted. He picked a piece of tobacco from his teeth. "I wish you hadn't landed me in this mess, Wallace," he said.

"We're all in it, Henry. Hitchcock seems to have lots of extras working for him now."

Judge Robertson grunted again, went to his bedroom, and dressed quickly. They drove to the courthouse downtown. It took him half an hour to sign the four warrants.

Mike Reese's room at Psi Delta Chi was Marine perfect. The fraternity secretary, Roy Peters, wore tan shorts and tennis shoes. He was worried but eager to help. Word had gotten out about the cops in the building investigating the serial killings, and the publicity could prove embarrassing for the fraternity. He watched as Santomassimo explored the room. Neat. When he tested the bed, he felt the sheets, too. They were tucked in, military fashion. The shelves had very few books.

"Doesn't this guy study?" Santomassimo asked.

"In the library," Peters said. "Mike stays out a lot. Studying."

"You ever study with him?"

"No, sir."

"*Anybody* ever study with him?"

"Mike's kind of a loner."

Santomassimo peered into the kitchen cabinets. Reese was also a fanatic on high fiber. The refrigerator had pints of yogurt. In the corner of the room were some weights. Reese was lifting heavy iron.

"How often does he work out with the football team?" Santomassimo asked.

"Oh, every afternoon. Psi Delta has five men on the football squad. That's tops here at USC. Yes, sir. Mike works out every day, and Saturday mornings."

"What does he do when he isn't studying and tackling dummies?"

"He watches movies."

"What kind of movies?"

"Laurel and Hardy. Chaplin. He wants to be a comedy writer."

"Is he funny?"

"Mike? No, not at all."

The detectives came back from the bathroom. They shrugged and looked at Santomassimo with a blank expression. Santomassimo still felt uneasy. The room was *too* neat.

The Emergency Squad found nothing in the bedroom, the closets, or in the storage cabinet assigned to Reese in the hall. Santomassimo rummaged through Reese's desk, looking for telephone numbers, items suggesting falcons, wire-stripping tools, model airplanes, the numbers of antique stores, a photograph. There was nothing. He slammed the door, and snapped, "Who's next on the list, Captain?"

"Thad Gomez."

Married students housing turned out to be a block of concrete. There was a small lawn in front, with slender light poles on the paths. Though the sun had set, there were still a few women pushing baby carriages and chatting. Santomassimo and Captain Emery led the men up the stairs and knocked on a metal door. A very pretty brunette looked puzzled, holding a boy in her arm.

"Thad's not home," she said hesitantly, in a Mexican accent.

Then, seeing how many men there were, she became alarmed and retreated. Santomassimo showed her his police badge. Her eyes widened. "He's not hurt?"

"No. May we come in? We have to ask you a few questions about Thad."

Reluctantly, she let them in. Santomassimo saw she was thinking quickly.

"He don't do coke," she said. "He don't do those things."

"I'm sure he doesn't, Mrs. Gomez."

The apartment was cluttered with the baby's playpen and yellow-and-red plastic caterpillars, and ducks on the floor. Rings and plastic oblongs hung over the dining room table. The family's photographs were stuck on a cork board. The apartment smelled of Mexican food.

"Mrs. Gomez, we want to know if Thad's been home every evening the last few weeks."

"Why?"

"Please, Mrs. Gomez. Does Thad go out?"

"No. He studies in the bedroom."

"Every night?"

"A few nights, he goes for a walk."

Mrs. Gomez didn't like the police going into her bedroom. The detectives came back and shrugged. Santomassimo turned to Mrs. Gomez again. The baby was getting anxious, kicking and drooling.

"Thad must feel a lot of pressure," Santomassimo said.

"Sure. Being married and going to school is hard. He worries a lot. He tells it to his diary."

"Diary?"

"He says it's a diary. I never read it. He doesn't let me. I don't even know where it is."

"He just spills his thoughts onto paper?"

"Paper. Whatever. He goes off on his walks and after a long while he comes back. He gets intense, you know. He needs to get it off his chest. He comes back and he feels better. Film school is no joke."

"No, Mrs. Gomez. I'm sure it's not."

The detectives went through the rest of the small apartment carefully; kitchen, living room, closets, finding no diary, no chemicals, no weapons, just a neat, homey place to live, redolent of Spanish stew and sweet baby smells.

"Have you talked to him since he left on the tour?"

"In New York? Why? Is something wrong?"

"Some husbands call their wives as soon as they arrive in a strange city."

"If something goes wrong, he'll call."

Santomassimo smiled. "I'm sure he would, Mrs. Gomez. Do you have a photograph of Thad?"

"Sure. Lots of them."

They left with an eight-by-ten portrait of Thad Gomez, which Captain Emery promised to return to her as soon as they could make copies.

"I don't know about him," Captain Emery reflected quietly as they walked across the lawn to their cars. "Diary? Walks at night? Why is he so intense? Is school that hard? To me, it was just boring."

The other men exchanged glances. Captain Emery was trying to make a connection, but they had nothing and they knew it.

"I think we'd better find Bradley Bowers's apartment," Bronte said nervously.

— 16 —

Bradley Bowers surveyed the lobby of the old building with disgust. It was the New York YMCA. Positioned on Ninth Avenue and Thirty-third Street, it was noisy. It was night, and the day had been half shot with the hotel mess up. Headlights from honking vehicles outside flashed over the Ping-Pong room in the lobby. Bradley didn't trust the clean-cut men who read in the small library. An aura of mustiness permeated the entire premises.

"Foul," Bradley said to Chris. "Don't you think it's foul, Chris?"

"Live with it, Bradley."

Chris left Bradley to stew by the reading room entrance. He went back to the others standing with the luggage among the brown vinyl chairs and couches. Mike looked at the lobby, sighed, and smiled gamely.

"At least it's clean," he said.

"And fairly quiet," Thad added. "In comparison to the Wilton, which was worse than a Mexican cockfight."

Kay walked back from the desk. The desk clerk wore a white T-shirt tight around bulging biceps and pectorals, a perfect specimen who could be counted upon to keep order in an understanding but firm way.

"It's all arranged," Kay told them. "You'll have to sleep in one room, but they tell me it's clean and comfortable. Anyway, if you're as beat as I am, you'll sleep well. I'm off to *my* Y. I'm sorry, guys. I promise tomorrow will be a hell of a lot better."

"Don't worry about it, Professor Quinn," Chris said. "It wasn't your fault."

"Anyway, we did get a good look at the Canal Street Police Station," Thad said.

"Right." Kay looked at her watch, "My God, it's nearly midnight! Goodnight!"

"Goodnight!" Mike, Thad, and Chris chorused.

Kay waved farewell. Bradley waved, too, and she went out to the sidewalk.

The women's "Y" was uptown on the eastside and was much too far to walk to, especially at this hour. She waited for a passing cab. None came. She went farther down the sidewalk. For several seconds, she looked toward Ninth Avenue for taxis before realizing a heavy form breathed behind her. She turned. It was Bradley. The neon made his face glow red, half disappear, and glow again.

"I'm sorry if I startled you," he said. "May I escort you to the YWCA, Professor Quinn?"

Kay cursed silently. Bradley's coming up meant she had missed a cab whose red taillights now flashed, turning a corner, heading uptown. "Please don't bother, Bradley. I can get a cab at the corner."

"It's no bother, Professor Quinn."

"I'm just as happy getting it myself. Thanks."

She smiled at Bradley, walked away toward the cor-

ner, and waved frantically at a cab that went sailing by
southward. Again Bradley followed her. He leaned
slightly forward, over her, as though scrutinizing her
face.

"It isn't safe on the street, Professor. Please. Let me
take you to the Y."

"Bradley—I'd really prefer that you didn't. I've had
it up to here with movies and movie talk and New
York City. I just want to be by myself and get some
sleep."

He noticed her hands. Even scarred they were
lovely. He even noticed them trembling.

"Of course," he said. "I understand."

Kay smiled. She was pale, she was so exhausted.
"Goodnight, Bradley. Thanks. Please don't misunder-
stand. I really am tired. And please tell the boys to be
ready at eight sharp. The boat leaves at nine from
Battery Park."

"Yes, Professor. I'll tell them."

"Thank you. Good night, Bradley."

"Goodnight, Professor."

Bradley went back toward the YMCA, shoulders
slumped, kicking a crumpled coffee container.

Kay hefted her overnight bag and stood on the
corner. A mist was falling, warm and humid despite
the chill air. The neon and headlights reflected off the
slick black, oily streets. For a moment, all the hectic
crowds of hotel lobbies, falcons, art deco furniture,
and Pan Am terminals swirled into her mind. She felt
momentarily disoriented by the stress of the last
weeks. Then she shook her head clear. Kay tried vainly
to hail a cab, but it was full of passengers.

Bradley stood before the YMCA entrance.

The red neon illuminated his face, the unshaven
jowls, the ring of dirt on the once white collar, and
the small nose that had bled that morning. Bradley's
eyes were dark slits watching the scene on the corner
of Ninth Avenue where Kay had moved farther down

the sidewalk, trying to catch a cab. His eyes impinged on her restless figure caught in the harsh light of a street lamp. Between red glows of the YMCA's exterior light, Bradley's face cut into the darkness and back out of it, like the flicker in old-time silent films—an early Chaplin, or Melies.

North of Hoover Boulevard in central Los Angeles, about a mile from USC, a four-story apartment building stood. It was painted pea green and its fire escape a pastel peach. The cornices still bore the floral designs of a previous era. Telephone wires sagged at the exterior wall.

Inside the lower corridor, Santomassimo entered with Captain Emery, Bronte, two policemen, and three men with axes from the Emergency Squad. The manager of the apartment, a small Greek named Eliasis, stood before them on the first step leading to the floors above. Captain Emery showed his badge and the court order.

"You don't destroy no doors," Eliasis begged. "I run a clean house, and nobody never complained."

"Mr. Eliasis," Santomassimo said. "We're going to need to get into a room upstairs."

"Sure, sure," Eliasis said, backing up the stairs. "Only I ain't insured for no ax damage."

The surge of men clattering up the stairs caught Eliasis by surprise. He backed into the railing as they passed and then ran after them, up three flights of stairs.

"No axes!" he shouted.

On the fourth floor, the corridor was dark, running straight to a door at the far end, which let in a diffused twilight, full of neon signs. Santomassimo saw the tops of boutiques and warehouses, and then the dark, washed-out colors of traffic passing on Hoover.

"This door, Fred," Bronte said.

The men walked quickly to the door nearest the fire

escape. The silence unnerved Eliasis. The axes were poised. The men were tense. But they were waiting.

Santomassimo snapped his fingers, pointing to George Schmidt, the lock expert.

Schmidt produced a ring of keys from his hard leather case. Some were near misses. Schmidt tried a smaller shank size. Santomassimo's eyes, like Bronte's, kept going to the door onto which a small white sign had been fixed.

POSITIVELY NO ADMITTANCE.

It was hand-printed. Below was a second sign. *This means YOU!!!!* Then came a small but fastidious signature.

B. Bowers.

"Hurry up, George," Santomassimo whispered.

"I'm hurrying, Lieutenant. I'm damn well hurrying."

Eliasis bent over Schmidt. Bronte pushed him away.

"Don't destroy no doors," Eliasis pleaded. "Please. Don't destroy nothing—"

"Get over by the wall, Mr. Eliasis," Santomassimo said. "You're in our light."

A policeman held the flashlight closer to Schmidt's hands. Finally, the bolt clicked. Schmidt pushed and the door swung slowly. Santomassimo and Bronte were in before Captain Emery moved.

Santomassimo flicked on the light switch. The policemen blinked and carefully studied the room, then stepped over fallen books on the carpet and crossed the threshold.

Bradley Bowers's apartment was filled with rotted fruit, magazines, unlaundered clothing by the radiator, even autumn leaves that had somehow drifted in through the window. The small bed opened from a tattered red couch. There were neither sheets nor pillow cases. Only an Army blanket served as bedding. A mouse crawled along the baseboard.

"Lovely," Captain Emery said, wrinkling his nose. "Fuckin' palatial."

The kitchen was a hot plate on a counter by a sink clogged with dirty dishes, opened cans, and crawling roaches.

The rust in the toilet had turned to black, and the shower curtain had holes. Santomassimo looked around with Bronte who shook his head. "Get the name of his decorator," he said.

The apartment was depressing as hell. The filth and disorder had an aura of unspeakable loneliness. Santomassimo looked under the rollout bed and behind a broken armchair. He found more film magazines: *Screen, Sight and Sound, Film Quarterly,* and coffee-stained copies of *Variety.*

"Think he's your killer?" Captain Emery finally asked Santomassimo.

"I don't know, Bill. I don't know what to make of this garbage."

Captain Emery walked gingerly around the mess. From the window, he could see a parking lot below and the back of a movie theater.

"Nothing in here says he's abnormal," Emery said. "A slob. Yes. A pig wouldn't live here. But a killer . . .?"

Captain Emery saw Bronte opening dirty pots on the stove to peer inside. Bronte opened the refrigerator and checked the freezer. Bronte had a stong stomach, Emery thought.

"What do you say, Lou?" Captain Emery asked.

"Maybe. I'm not convinced, though. Just a pile of film magazines. Any film student would have something like that."

Bronte looked at Santomassimo. He saw the wretched anxiety on Santomassimo's face.

"I think we'd better open another door, Fred," Bronte said.

"Yeah, Chris Hinds."

* * *

The Manhattan night lights reflected from the oily streets. Limousines passed like huge sleek fish, headlights glaring. Buses roared down Ninth Avenue. Kay stepped from the curb hailing taxis, but those that came had passengers or their "Off Duty" lights on.

Distraught, Kay stepped back onto the curb. It was after one in the morning. She had a terror of being stranded in New York at night.

"Here—Over here—! Oh, damn—"

An empty taxi went by, ducked into a sidestreet, and crossed toward Eighth Avenue.

The light changed. She crossed the street. Hordes of young people, their hair very short and dyed, bumped into her. They were energetic, laughing, some half dancing on the pavement. The night was theirs. Kay struggled through them and made her way to the corner of Thirty-second Street.

Tennis shoes, jogging shoes, black patent leather, even sandals, passed by over the wet asphalt, a symphony of walking, disembodied voices, fragments of conversations, coats, faces, eyes. It was all part of Kay's half-waking state. Her body felt like concrete. All that kept her going was the mental image of bed, a nice clean bed at the YWCA. She crossed the street at the corner.

Reeboks crossed after her on the wet asphalt.

Kay saw an empty taxi and ran into the street.

"Taxi!" she shouted. But the taxi didn't see her and continued down Ninth Avenue. She walked down to the middle of the block. Night lights of a large hardware store made a pool of brilliance. There she would be visible.

Reeboks followed, silently. They paused.

At a cross street down the block, cabs were coming through from the west side. Relieved, Kay walked quickly into the intervening darkness.

The Reeboks followed, right through oily puddles, determinedly.

* * *

The ax point shattered Chris Hinds's door. Splinters of dark solid wood exploded up past the faces of the Emergency Squad and showered into the corridor. Santomassimo and Bronte shielded their faces. The point man of the Emergency Squad struck again and again, and again. A slit opened in the door.

"Fucking oak—" he grunted.

He swung again with all his strength. With an explosive groan, the door buckled inward. Santomassimo lowered his shoulder and smashed through it. He stumbled into Chris Hinds's room. Bronte followed, tearing the door panel apart with his bare hands.

The point man brought in a flashlight. Captain Emery crowded behind them. The detective and Schmidt, the locksmith, came in afterward. The flashlight beam played slowly over strange configurations in Chris Hinds's room.

It was a museum of Hitchcock. Postcards, publicity photographs, posters, videos of his films, even mock-up sets in crude cardboard, neatly labeled and mounted on rickety wooden tables, crowded the tiny apartment. The bookshelves curved under the weight of volumes devoted to Hitchcock.

Santomassimo walked gingerly into the room. It was messy, like Bradley Bowers's room, but there was a method to it. It was not the mess of a lazy slob. It was the creative chaos of someone who worked fast and hard. Bronte turned the crank of a rewind set on a shelf. He flicked on the light of the 16mm viewer into which the film was threaded. Captain Emery watched, too. A flickering, strangely hypnotic, terrifyingly familiar scene unrolled in Chris's silent 16mm film viewer. A scene from Hitchcock's film, *Sabotage*.

A little boy carried a package on a bus. A clock ticked away the seconds. Caught in Picadilly Circus traffic, the bus waited. The little boy fingered the package on his lap unsuspectingly. Then the bomb went off. In the slow, hand-turned frames, splinters, smoke, and fragments of the bus blew up. Captain Emery rubbed his face. His thin scars were still painful on his cheek.

"That's close to what happened to us," Emery said, amazed. "Second for second."

Santomassimo searched through folders littering the floor. They were filled with bits of scripts, pitiful letters to producers and to studios, offering his services as a scriptwriter, a hack writer, even as a delivery boy. It was evident nobody had even answered. There was a copy of a term paper for Kay. It was on the techniques of illogic in the suspense film. She had given him an *A*.

"Captain. Lieutenant," Bronte said, gesturing.

Beside a rusted Bunsen burner on a table in the closet were retards, pipettes in neat wooden racks, vials, glass tubing and copper wire in loops, and a large chest of chemicals. Bronte bent down and peered, eyeball to glass, at sediments in the bottom of a beaker. It stank. In a plastic bag, thickly wrapped, was a flesh-colored substance. A policeman began unwrapping it. Bronte put a hand on his arm.

"*Plastique*," Bronte said quietly.

The policeman backed away. "That's enough to blow this room to Pasadena."

"I guess he had some left over," Bronte said wryly. "The producers will like that. He comes in under budget."

Bronte caught Santomassimo's eye.

"A little bit of nitro, too," Bronte said. "Probably for Hasbrouk's plane. Your bomb was timed to a clocked charge. Hasbrouk's was designed to go off on impact."

Bronte tossed the copper wire and few tiny batteries back onto the table in disgust. He turned. Santomassimo stood before him with a stainless steel pot.

"What's that?" Bronte asked.

"Open it. Have some."

Santomassimo took off the cover. It was popcorn, heavily salted, heavily buttered, and it was now rancid. Santomassimo put the cover back on.

"He makes the shit in quantity," Santomassimo said.

"Well, that's the signature, all right," Emery said.

Alfred Hitchcock looked down at them from the wall. The fat genius, insouciant as a baby, sinister as Jack the Ripper, watched every man, and every man felt it.

"Turn on the light, Lou," Santomassimo ordered.

The overhead light went on. Santomassimo pulled huge black portfolios from under Chris's bed. He untied the black cloth strings and opened the first portfolio. Inside was a drawing, meticulously rendered, of *North by Northwest*. Where the crop duster flew down on Cary Grant in the middle of a corn field, Chris had sketched in surf and sand. The plane was circled and the word *miniature* was penciled in. There were other, smaller sketches: diagrams of the plane, and the placement of the explosive, the rotary shaft, the speed of the toy plane, calculated at impact.

Chris Hinds was an excellent draftsman. He had a quick, precise style, and a sure hand.

In the next portfolio were more storyboards. A naked woman appeared in a shower. A sketch showed a naked foot touching wire. Santomassimo looked at the copper wire on the chemistry table. There were diagrams of lead pipes and grounding the current. The woman in the sketches was naked and very beautiful. She looked somewhat like the young Janet Leigh.

"I've seen enough," Captain Emery growled.

"Fred—" Bronte said.

Santomassimo turned. Bronte stared at a tape recorder by Chris's easy chair. It was a professional instrument—a battered Nagra. The reels were threaded. The take-up reel was about three quarters filled. The men stared. The recorder glinted in the light.

"Turn it on, Fred," Captain Emery said quietly.

"Suppose it's booby trapped?"

"He wouldn't expect us to be here."

Bronte stepped to the recorder and put his face inches from it. He tilted his head to look at the base and sides.

Santomassimo looked at Captain Emery, then at the detective and the Emergency Squad men, who were backing toward the door.

"Get me some wire, Lou," Santomassimo said.

Bronte found some on the work table and gave it to him. Santomassimo slowly passed it under the tape recorder. It was very heavy and the wire ate into his hands as he lifted. When it was tilted toward him, Bronte peered under the machine.

"Nothing," Bronte said.

The tiny screws were still covered in dust and a suggestion of grime. Nothing showed the recent use of a jeweler's screwdriver.

"Anybody who wants to," Santomassimo muttered, "get out into the hall."

Nobody moved.

Santomassimo turned the power switch. A red light glowed. He set the machine into *Play*. The tape sagged, then the reels stabilized. All held their breaths, waiting for some sound to emerge from the small speaker, but nothing came, except for some static and room noise, and finally dead air.

Santomassimo snapped off the set; quickly pressed the *Reverse* button. The tapes whirred for a few seconds before a high-pitched soprano voice rapidly speaking backward was heard. Santomassimo pushed the *Stop* button, then the *Play* button immediately after. Again the tapes fluttered and stabilized. The wobbly sliding voice focused into Chris Hinds's.

"I'm sorry, but I'm forced at this point to interrupt my narrative. I have to go on location. Quinn's wop knight came to her rescue. So I have to work out another scene for her.

"I'm sorry I won't be in L.A. to see the Santomassimo sequence. It would have been fun to watch them scrape him and his cohorts off the station house floor. Ah, well, directing in absentia isn't exactly pleasurable. I guess I'll have to read about it in the New York Post.

"Didn't I tell you? I'll be in New York. I'm taking Professor Quinn's Scene-of-the-Crime Tour. But the scene we'll be doing together is from Frenzy, *one of Hitch's finest thrillers.*

"CUT! That's a wrap!"

Santomassimo stopped the machine, and grabbed the telephone. He punched information for New York City. There was static and squeals then, just as he was ready to redial, he heard the bored, rude accent of a New York operator.

"Operator, this is an emergency call."

"What is the nature of the emergency?"

"It's a matter of life and death. My name is Lieutenant Fred Santomassimo. My badge number is 6540, and I am in charge of the homicide department of the Palisades Police Division in Los Angeles."

"What is the nature of the emergency?" the operator repeated.

"I have to locate someone."

"What is the name, sir?"

"I want you to read me the listings of every hotel in Manhattan that begins with the letter *W*."

"We don't do that, sir."

"*W*. As in William."

"Sir, there are many hotels in New York."

"And it is a felony to obstruct a police inquiry. I am ordering you to give me those hotel names."

Santomassimo heard the *clackety-clack* of a keyboard. Then a long pause. Then another operator began reading names from a screen. Santomassimo scribbled the names, addresses, and telephone numbers as fast as he could.

Bronte looked up. Over the chemistry table was a huge poster of *Frenzy*. Face twisted in blind hatred, the actor Barry Foster strangled a young woman with his necktie.

17

Chris Hinds's face moved out of the lights. The skin was chalk white, then it flickered into silhouette. Only his eyes kept their steady, hard stare. Ahead of him, Kay walked through a well of darkness, toward the lighted intersection far in the distance.

Kay walked steadily. She shifted her bag to the other shoulder, brushed her hair from her forehead, and walked on. She heard the squeak of shoes—a man's rubber-soled shoes—behind her.

Thirty feet behind, Chris Hinds quickened his pace. He slipped the tie from his collar.

Kay stumbled on the uneven sidewalk. She stopped. The footsteps stopped. She was too terrified to turn back and look. In Manhattan? Who could possibly be following her, stopping when she stopped, going when she went, except a mugger? Or worse? She moved on quickly.

CLOSE SHOT: KAY, NIGHT
Kay stumbles down the sidewalk, hearing footsteps
behind her.

Kay giggled. It was like studying for finals, this tour, this Hitchcock class. Fragments, facts, and spurious images came to mind. She saw herself, scripted and story-boarded by the master, walking down the nightmare streets of the world's most inhospitable city.

KAY'S POV: THE INTERSECTION, NIGHT
The intersection toward which she walks is high-
lighted by store windows. But behind, OFF
SCREEN, we hear the steady squeak of a man's
tennis shoes.

Kay giggled again. It was a cliche, but so right. She was so scared, overtired. There were half-baked film sequences running amok in her head.

In her path, a tiny curb rose. She didn't see it; stubbed her toe. It hurt and she stopped. In the silence she heard the footsteps behind her also stop. She began walking again, more quickly toward the bright intersection. The footsteps followed quickly, keeping pace with her.

"Oh—dear God—"

Now it became real. Too real. She heard the soft-soled shoes coming faster. She began to run. Behind her Chris also ran. They were still in the darkness of the side street and he clutched the tie like a noose.

She saw nothing behind her because she refused to look. And she was running faster now, her shoes clacking down the pavement, the tennis shoes following faster, faster, gaining . . . while in her mind she saw:

CLOSE SHOT: FEET RUNNING, NIGHT
INTERCUT shots of feet running: woman's low-

*heeled pumps running faster and faster; man's
Reeboks following even faster.*

A taxi crossed the intersection in the distance.
"Taxi!" Kay shouted.

*KAY'S POV: TAXI
Taxi pulls away from the intersection. Behind, OFF
    SCREEN, we hear killer's tortured BREATH-
    ING coming on.*

"Jesus—" Kay whispered.
Was this how it ended? Not with a bang, not with a
whimper, but as a victim in a trite melodrama?
"TAXI!"
But now there were no taxis, not even cars in the
intersection ahead. It was very late. Before her mind's
eye the scene played:

*KILLER'S POV: KAY RUNNING
FROM BEHIND we rapidly follow Kay as she runs
    desperately toward the intersection, waving
    her hands.*

As Kay ran toward the corner building the thought
flashed through her head, insanely: what would
Hitchcock do with the script at this point?
Of course, there would be no taxi to rescue her. The
tension must be maximized, he would declare. And
then the horrifying thought that she might not be the
star of the movie, only a supporting character, one
who was meant to be caught and killed.
But no, she thought then, Hitchcock *would* have a
taxi pull up. It would provide the illusion of safety.
She would get in and be saved—to be assaulted later.
That was Hitch's method. Kay ran to the curb of the
intersection.
A taxi pulled up to the corner and she climbed in.

Chris came to a sudden stop on the curb. He jammed the tie into his fist and ducked back into the shadows. She was still visible in the taxi as it pulled out, wheeled into main traffic and gained speed up Eighth Avenue.

"Lucky bitch," Chris said, smiling sardonically.

He licked his lips. His throat was dry. His body slumped, and so did the tie in his hand. He walked disconsolately back to the YMCA.

"Need a place to hang that tie, honey?"

He turned. In the deep recess of a storefront stood a young woman with her cheeks heavily rouged. She was short, with black curly hair. She wore tight jeans and a revealing red sweater. Chris stopped dead in his tracks. She smiled and came out of the dark recess. He seemed to her to be a stranger. He looked naive, maybe a college kid, a young man with urges. She came forward onto the main sidewalk. She licked her lips and smiled.

"Huh?" she coaxed. "What do you say? What are you going to do with that necktie?"

Chris looked down at the crumpled necktie. His fingers convulsively tightened around it.

This guy will come in three seconds, she thought. He's wired like a piano string.

"Come on, honey. I'm cold all alone. I can tell you're hot. I can tell you need somebody."

She beckoned him with her head. Chris nodded slowly and came forward. His eyes had brightened, as though she had given him a fantastic idea. His hand grabbed her arm hard.

"You don't have to play so rough, friend," she said. "I know what you can do."

Instead, he shoved her into the dark recess of the store.

"Hey—"

"How the hell do you know what I can do?" he hissed.

"Now, come on—easy—"

Chris slammed her against the glass door and pressed against her. She became frightened.

"C'mon—you don't wanna do it here. Standing up like a poodle. I got a nice warm room—"

"What's your name?"

"Carla . . . Carla Mendoza . . ."

"Wrong! Your name is Anna Massey and you're a barmaid as well as a whore!" Chris slipped the tie over her head. He pulled the knot tight.

"What are you doing—?"

Terrified, she yanked at the tie. Chris slammed her head back against the glass. Both her hands pulled at the tie. He pulled it tight, and she kicked, high heels crashing against a garbage can lid.

"You're in the movies, kid. You've got the second lead in *Frenzy!*"

"Please—no—" she begged.

Her voice was blocked. Her painted fingernails scratched at his eyes. Chris ducked and pulled hard. It was exhilarating. She squealed like a shot rabbit. Her eyes rolled up and her lips became blue. She grew limp. He took no chances and kept pulling on the tie as hard as he could.

She became heavy and slumped to the tiled floor. He felt no pulse. One eye of the whore stared upward at him. Chris stepped off her, breathing hard.

He dragged her to the garbage can, where he covered her with newspapers and cartons. Then he reached into his pocket, pulled out some popcorn, munched some, watching her, and tossed a kernel of popcorn at her feet.

"Not bad," he said smugly. "Nice bit of action." And he started backing away slowly—a slow zoom back from the corpse in the dark recess.

It was a lousy night for Larry Dixon. First they had put him on the graveyard shift at the Wilton Hotel desk, and then they had overbooked the place with rowdy conventioneers, some of whom were worse than drunk college kids on a spree. Already three of them had vomited on the Wilton's front steps. God knew what was going on inside the rooms. Literally. Dixon was a devout Methodist. Left up to him, he would have preferred to burn the sheets in the morning.

People were sleeping in the lobby, waiting for cancellations. Was this a way to run a hotel?

In New Jersey where he lived, you could grow vegetables in a real garden. You could feel the peace of ground that was earth, not stone. There were churches there where the voice of God was manifest. In New York, Jesus was strictly on the defensive. Being a Methodist here was like carrying a candle into the hurricane.

The telephone rang.

"Wilton Hotel," he said.

It was long distance. He could hardly hear the man's voice at the other end.

"Who? What? This is not a private residence, mister. This is the Wilton Hotel."

He began to hang up but the man was insistent. Dixon put the receiver back to his ear.

"Quinn? Like Anthony Quinn? Who? What? Can't you speak louder, mister. I'll look."

Dixon moved his thumb down the fine lines of the hotel register. It was just as he thought. "Nope. Sorry. There's no Quinn registered."

The second desk clerk, Ray Velos, leaned forward.

"Wait, Larry, don't hang up."

"Hold on, please," Dixon said into the telephone. He turned to Ray. "It's the police. In California," he said.

"Give me the phone."

"Why?"

"Don't be an obstructionist. Give me the fucking phone."

Dixon did. He didn't know as many big words as

Velos and felt slightly intimidated, even though Velos
was a P.R.

"Hello?" Velos shouted. "Did you say the name,
Quinn? A woman? Right, sir. She was on our standby
list. No, we couldn't accommodate her. That's right.
Four male students. They left mid-afternoon. No, I'm
sorry. We don't know where they went . . ." Velos
listened. "There's really no space anywhere tonight,
Lieutenant."

He hung up and went back to reading the racing
form. Dixon went for a cup of coffee. A drunken
salesman wheeled into the lobby, crashed over a
stand-up festival schedule, and staggered sleepily to
the elevators.

Santomassimo and Bronte walked fast toward the
LAX boarding gate. As they walked Bronte read from
his little black notebook.

"Your plane arrives at five-thirty-six in the morning," he said. "The police will meet you at Kennedy.
An Inspector Markson. And Captain Perry has gotten
them to issue the all-points-bulletin throughout Manhattan. And Thad's photo's on the way to them."

"Good."

"Starting at dawn, they'll have stakeouts at the
Statue of Liberty and at the mansion on Fifth looking
for a young woman and four male students. They'll
spot her, Fred."

"*If* she's alive."

Santomassimo checked through security. Bronte
accompanied him to the gate. The last of the passengers were boarding. Impulsively Bronte gave him an
Italian send-off: a quick embrace.

"Be careful, Fred," he whispered.

"Say an *Ave* for her, Lou."

Santomassimo squeezed Bronte's arm and went
quickly down the ramp into the TWA plane.

Bronte scrutinized the boarding area. It was easy to do. He was the only person in it.

Kay's YWCA room was spartanly furnished. There was a bed with a clean white tufted bedspread. An oval braided rug was on the wooden floor. The bathroom was old, but neat and immaculate. The window looked out onto a dark, empty side street.

Kay pulled her overnight bag onto the easy chair, closed the curtains, and locked the door.

The sound of the soft footsteps behind her on the street still unnerved her. She wanted a brandy. It wasn't just the brandy she wanted. She wanted Santomassimo. She sat on the edge of the bed. She picked up the telephone and heard the switchboard operator.

"I'd like to call Los Angeles, please," Kay said.

The operator dialed. Kay heard the telephone ringing in Santomassimo's apartment. It rang twelve times. She knew where the telephones were. There was a white telephone on the balcony wall, another white telephone on the kitchen counter under the spice cabinet, and a third pale green telephone by the bed. She visualized the entire apartment.

"I'm sorry," the operator said. "There doesn't seem to be any answer."

"Thank you."

Kay hung up. She stared into the darkness. She undressed, went into the bathroom and showered. The wounds on her hands had almost entirely healed. She rubbed her face and neck with a scented cream.

She called Santomassimo again. Again there was no answer. She hung up. Where the hell was he? she wondered.

Kay drifted into an unpleasant sleep. A montage of images and voices, voices and images, played in staccato cuts in her mind.

Footsteps . . . a falcon . . . a man dead under a bell tower . . . a face grinning up, stuffed into a trunk . . .

and footsteps again, following her down the dark New York street.

And then the dream segued into another dream—a familiar dream. She walked into a darkened parlor. Her father snored softly on the couch. She was very young, about as tall as the couch. She walked over a deep-piled scatter rug and touched him. He remained sleeping. She shook him, but nothing woke him from his sleep.

She shook her father repeatedly and suddenly she noticed blood running down from the couch and forming a pool on the rug. He was dead, yet he snored. Outside, workmen came to dig his grave, uprooting the lilacs and goldfish pond. There was a revolver on the floor, her little toy. Horrified, she ran for her mother, but she was playing bridge with three other women in the sunny breakfast nook and did not hear Kay pounding on the sliding glass door.

Everything had a black-and-white look, grainy, like an old film.

Kay awoke. Her heart was pounding. Had her whole life become a *film noir*? Who had killed her father? Why was it a film? Who the hell was trying to kill her and Santomassimo?

It was three-fifteen. She dialed Santomassimo but there was no answer. She lay back in the chair by the window and started to cry.

"Dear God," she wept. "Let this be over. Please please please."

But God made her go to sleep in the chair and the dream continued. Her dead father, angry at being disturbed, rose from his grave (the couch was now his grave, replete with headstone) and slapped her.

She jerked awake. Her head was splitting and her mouth was dry. She desperately needed a drink. She had always been afraid of her father. What was he so angry about? That she was independent? That she had chosen her own life? That she was in love with a man who needed her?

Her father's dogmatic self-righteousness had been instinctive. He never saw the wounds he drilled into her. He never saw the hysteria he had created. She loved him, the essential him, but he remained a fantasy figure, larger than life, and it had repressed, no, denied, her sexuality.

That was why he pushed her academic career. It neutered her. And the men she had met had been, somehow, equally neuter. But now, with Santomassimo . . .

Kay telephoned again, and again there was no answer. She tried reading. But reading under the dim bed lamp only made her drowsy. The dream came rampant, bringing ferocious images. She was in a darkened theater. There was a film screening, and she was in it. Masked men in a carnival of freaks threw pies and slipped on banana skins. The clowns had daggers and revolvers. Suddenly Kay had to direct the scene. Behind her, a man, a huge man like her father, kept screaming to do it again, do the scene again.

It was Alfred Hitchcock, not her father. *"Kill the cop!"* the fat man screamed. *"Kill the cop!"*

Kay now saw, behind the balloons and arcade wheels, the all-too-familiar silhouette of the obese, dictatorial figure. On his right arm perched a falcon. Behind it was a trunk with rope dangling out of it. Kernels of popcorn sprouted from a red-and-yellow machine under bright lights.

Kay had to direct the scene, but she didn't have the script and didn't know the characters. Suddenly she saw Santomassimo carrying a revolver, looking for a killer, not seeing that the clowns throwing whipped cream pies and blowing party whistles also had knives.

LONG SHOT: SANTOMASSIMO, DAY
Unsuspecting, the cop enters the bedroom. The place
is filled with clowns. He does not see the killer
behind the door.

Kay visualized the script in her nightmare. Suddenly the clowns dropped their pies and stabbed Santomassimo. The confetti ran red with his blood as he crumpled in pain. She screamed, "NO!"

But Hitchcock kept shouting to do it again, kill the fucking cop like the script said!

ANGLE ON SANTOMASSIMO
Under repeated thrusts of the clowns' knives Santo-
massimo writhes in pain, slipping to the floor,
sliding in whipped cream and party favors.
ARCADE MUSIC SCREECHES. His body
shakes in shock. The clowns kick him viciously.

"Retake!" Hitchcock screamed. "Stab him in the belly! Like the script says!"

Kay was sweating as she rose to full consciousness. She had been half awake during the nightmare. It was more a hallucination. She looked in the mirror and what she saw frightened her. She saw a haggard, desperate woman, pale and tear-streaked, hair unkempt, living a nightmare on both ends of the American continent.

Frantically she called Santomassimo. There was no answer. She asked the telephone operator to check if the line was out. It wasn't. She hung up.

In the quiet room she was afraid of the nightmare. It seemed to want to unroll in garish color, full of sadism and surrealism. She didn't want to know what it was about anymore. She didn't want to watch. She didn't want to be in New York. She didn't want to be on the tour. She just wanted to be with Santomassimo.

It was four o'clock. She washed her face, dressed, put on eye shadow and lipstick and went down the corridor and into the ALL NITE COFFEE SHOP, her ears still ringing with Hitchcock's screams.

Why did Hitchcock—or anybody—want to kill Santomassimo? Where was Santomassimo? Kay drank coffee, and dismissed sleep. The flickering fluorescent lights cast sick hues over her face. There was no one around but a busboy and someone mopping the far end of the floor. And someone who looked like a prostitute at the counter.

In London, once, she came close to suffering a mental breakdown. She had worked twelve weeks in the British Museum with little rest, seeing no one, talking to no one, eating alone in her tiny flat at night. She had thrown herself into the Hitchcock dissertation with a fanaticism that ruined her health. Then she received a telephone call that her father had had a stroke in Los Angeles. She stayed by the phone, unable to sleep, waiting for word. It had been an awful wait. Images of her father's death had paraded through the flat like savage little monsters, torturing her. Caricatures of doctors experimented on him, doped him up, stuck tubes and needles up all his orifices in a pornographic charade. Then the call came announcing his death. She remained in London. Her mother had felt it unnecessary for her to attend the funeral.

Gradually, the images died. A long time elapsed before she felt somewhat calm again.

Until tonight.

Tonight's nightmare had an incandescent hostility. As if something were getting ready to explode.

Kay stirred her coffee. It had whipped cream and was sprinkled with cocoa, the kind of coffee that had comforted her in London. But no comfort came now.

But then, at four-twenty in the morning in a coffee shop in Manhattan, not many things looked sane. The lights were on in the streets, but the sky had lost its black and was turning deep indigo.

Hands shaking, she nursed the coffee cup and didn't care what the busboy and cleaning boy thought.

A falcon's talons . . . a bell tower . . . Norman Lloyd's grotesquely enlarged face . . . a man's tennis shoes behind her on the pavement, coming, coming forward—

Kill—like the fucking script says!

The TWA 747 droned through clouds over Utah. Stars shone through dark patches of sky.

Inside the coach section Santomassimo gratefully took a brandy from a stewardess.

"Thanks," he said, and leaned back, closed his eyes and drank.

He had left Bronte with instructions to liaise with Captain Perry if necessary. It was now two-fifty-six New York time. In about five hours Kay would be starting the day's tour with students from USC.

He stared out the window. Utah disappeared under thickening clouds. Everything he knew hinged on intercepting them in time. Before they got to the mansion on Fifth, or the Statue. *If* Kay were still alive, he thought, then quickly wiped the thought from his mind. She *had* to be alive! But why? the devil within him asked. If Chris Hinds meant to strangle her with his tie, why would he have to wait till morning? Why select either site on the tour, which would take place in broad daylight? What more convenient place to enact a murder than a dark alley in the nighttime city. Who would hear? Who would care? Manhattan was renowned for being uncaring. Lying among the homeless, who would find Kay's body, report her death—?

"Dear God," Santomassimo prayed, "let her be alive! Save her. For me."

Then he surreptitiously made the sign of the cross, signaled the stewardess, and ordered another brandy. This time a double.

* * *

Four cots were crammed into a tiny room. The neon sign of the YMCA had long been turned off. A steady blue-white light from a parking lot shone through the window. Bradley Bowers, unable to sleep, sat upright on his cot, wearing a stained striped bathrobe, reading *Stories They Wouldn't Let Me Do on Television* by Alfred Hitchcock.

Thad had taken off his shirt, which he had crumpled into his laundry bag. He wore black trousers. His feet were bare and he wriggled his toes as he sat at a small table. Opposite him Mike Reese hunched over a hand of cards, shielding his eyes from the light overhead.

It was 3:15 A.M. Tired though they were, sleep seemed to elude them.

"Gin," Mike announced, spreading out his aces and heart sequence.

"You've got to be cheating, Mike," Thad mumbled.

"The world hates a sore loser," Mike chuckled. He counted his winnings. "That's twenty-eight bucks you owe me, Thad. At this rate you'll pay back my air fare."

"That's not funny. I should have known better than to play with you. That's all you jocks do, play cards."

Mike laughed pleasantly, scooped up the cards, and shuffled. The door opened behind them. Chris Hinds, his shirt open at the collar, came in carrying a bulging shopping bag. Thad looked at the cards Mike had dealt him, grimaced, and then threw them onto the table.

"Shit!" Thad said. "What the hell are we doing in here, anyway? We're in New York City for Christ's sake! Let's go out on the town, have a ball!"

"Why not have a ball right here?" Chris asked.

Chris lumbered to the table and pulled out potato chips, Fritos, pretzels, Oreos, six-packs of Budweiser, and from his suitcase two bottles of tequila. "Anyone for a tequila shooter?" he offered. Mike and Thad fought for the bottle. Chris snapped open a metal can, poured it into a cup and popped a straw into it. He offered it to Bradley Bowers with a smile,

"Here, Bradley. You don't drink hard stuff, do you?"

Bradley looked up and peered into the cup. "A Coke! Gee, thanks, Chris. What is this? You got a guilty conscience?"

Thad poured seltzer over his tequila, then covered the glass with his hand and banged it on the table. The fizz was explosive. He drank it in one gulp. Grinning dizzily, he asked, "Hey, Chris, where did the tequila come from?"

"Part of my traveling kit. I never leave home without it."

Mike pulled out a bag of Twinkies. "God," he said, mouth full, "this is disgustingly wonderful. We wondered where you went after Professor Quinn left."

Chris smiled his boyish smile. He sat on the edge of the cot. He watched Bradley Bowers, Thad, and Mike pass around the bags of chips, pretzels, nuts. And popcorn. Chris had only a little popcorn.

The 747 rumbled through the darkness over America. Most of the passengers slept. Santomassimo was wide awake. He sipped his third brandy. At this hour it kept him going better than coffee. He looked at his watch. It was twelve-forty-five Los Angeles time. He adjusted his watch to read New York time. 3:45 A.M.

The panel above him lighted. Santomassimo heard a musical *bong*. He looked up. The *No Smoking* sign was on. So was the *Fasten Seat Belts*. He buckled his belt and finished the brandy.

The captain's voice came through the 747's internal speakers.

"Pardon me for waking you, folks," he said. "This is Captain Wilson. We are experiencing a slight electrical problem in our number two engine. There's nothing to worry about. But for safety reasons we've been cleared to land at Sedalia Army base to have it checked out."

"Oh, Jesus—"

"On behalf of TWA we apologize for the delay. Your stewardesses will come through with complimentary beverages to help shorten the wait. In any case, we don't expect the delay to be very long."

Santomassimo looked at the other passengers. Some groaned, some resigned themselves. Some slept on and had heard nothing. Others already craned their necks for the free drinks.

"Oh, holy mother," Santomassimo muttered, and sank back in despair.

It was 4 A.M. in New York.

The YMCA room was getting warm. Bradley Bowers opened a window. Thad gathered the litter of empty bags and beer bottles into a heap. He dumped it into the wastebasket. The smell of beer evaporated.

"I'm worried about Professor Quinn," Mike said.

"What?" Chris asked.

"I don't know. She seems jumpy. Nervous. It isn't like her."

"It's the pressure of tenure," Bradley said. "Will she make it? Won't she?"

"I don't know," Mike said. "Something's on her mind. She sure isn't with this tour."

"And who was the guy with her?" Thad said. "Always wears a dark suit. Looks like a Greek. I think she's mixed up with him."

Mike lay back and put his hands behind his head. "Well, he'd better be something special. Because she sure is."

"How about a little sleep, fellows?" Chris asked. "I'm pooped."

Ten minutes later Bradley had fallen asleep in a sitting position, the Hitchcock paperback on his knees. Chris smiled and put the book onto the table.

He draped the blanket over him. Mike fell asleep almost instantly, snoring loudly. Chris covered him with a blanket too.

Thad moved his lips in a prayer, then rolled over once, and slept. Chris covered him, too.

"Good night, sweet things," Chris said. "Sleep soundly." He turned off the overhead light.

It was quiet around the YMCA. There were no radios or TVs and little traffic noise outside. Chris pulled off his shirt and pushed it into his canvas bag, then slipped off his trousers. He coughed. He looked at the sleeping boys and shook his head. *What fucking little angels*, he thought.

He lay on his cot. He didn't bother to cover himself with the blanket. He thought of nothing, absolutely nothing at all, except the next morning's scene.

At Sedalia Army Air Base the 747 wheeled from the main runway, pulled by a yellow tow tractor. It parked the plane near the terminal, where a crew in gray overalls stepped out on a crane platform and began working on the number two engine.

Santomassimo went into the Officer's Club and found a telephone. He dialed, one eye on the 747 and its repair crew beyond the plate glass windows. He heard the telephone ringing.

"Come on, Lou, Goddamn it!"

In Los Angeles Bronte turned away from the ringing phone. His wife, Terri, opened her eyes and nudged him.

"Lou. The phone."

Bronte groaned, rolled upright, turned on the lamp, and blearily picked up the receiver. He had a premonition it was Santomassimo even before he heard the voice.

"It's me, Lou," Santomassimo said.

"Where the hell are you?"

"Sedalia, Missouri. The pilot had to land. Something wrong with the electrical system."

"Shit."

"There's no other plane out of here, Lou. It's an Army base. They tell me it'll take an hour to fix it. That means I'll be arriving in New York around eight-thirty."

"Okay. I'll call them, let them know. I'll keep Perry informed."

"Did you contact Canal Street?"

Bronte shook his head to clear it. "Yes. Negative. Nobody remembers seeing a teacher and four students. And there were no photos of Kay at the university. But I got one of Mike Reese, the football player. I got it from the team publication. I faxed it to New York."

"Thanks."

During Bronte's report Santomassimo remembered the voice on Chris Hinds's tape. Cocky, insanely cocky. Manic and creative. Unpredictable.

Other images interceded: Kay on the knoll, her own strange need and devotion to Hitchcock, her fear of him now. In the lecture she had tried to warn the students, tried to tell them things she herself hardly understood, all the while an enormous blowup of an actor leered at them from the screen behind her.

"Lou."

"I'm here, Fred."

Santomassimo was almost afraid to ask. "A-Any other . . . news—?"

"No, Fred. No reports on bodies strangled with a necktie. At least not as of 2 A.M."

"Call Markson's headquarters. I want a chopper when I hit New York. Right at the airport."

There was a slight pause at Bronte's end. "Where to?" he asked.

"The Statue of Liberty."

"The Statue, Fred?" Bronte paused. "Markson's supposed to take you to the mansion on Fifth. That's their first stop. Remember what Cindy said, the mansion in the morning and the statue in the afternoon."

"Cindy wasn't sure, Lou. And anyway, I can smell the way this asshole thinks. The Statue is unique. It's awesome. It's inspiring. Pure Hitchcock! All my instincts point to the Statue. That's where our boy is going to distinguish himself."

"The police have the Statue covered, Fred."

"I know, and I'm glad. But they're fishing with a torn net. They don't know what Kay looks like. I can spot her in a cast of thousands."

Bronte knew better than to argue with a superior officer with strong instincts.

"I'll tell Markson."

"Thanks, Lou."

Bronte nodded dully. He hung up. He sat, depressed, on the edge of the bed. His wife reached out for his hand. He smiled but in the pit of his stomach he felt a fatalistic sense that it was all too late. That Chris Hinds would succeed in completing his film. He picked up the phone.

Santomassimo leaned against the wall, rubbing his face. He stared through the fogged window at the crippled 747 and then sat down in a lounge chair. He closed his eyes and saw Norman Lloyd, Hitchcock's actor, staring back.

18

The sun broke sharply over the city. The day was clear. Autumn was unmistakable. Windows dripped with cold dew. Geese flew overhead, V-shaped formations going south against the skyline.

The street lights were still on. An unmarked police car stopped across the street from the mansion on Fifth Avenue and Eighty-second Street. Two New York detectives, plainclothesmen, settled themselves inside the car. The stakeout at the mansion began.

Far away a helicopter tilted over dark water, banked, and slowly lowered, skimming over the waves. The chopper carried pilot, co-pilot, and detectives. The men looked out the side windows. They were awed in spite of themselves. Magnificent in the slate gray dawn, half-blue, half-green, tipped at the top with the morning sun's rays, the impassive lady, the Statue of Liberty, stood against wheeling birds in a swirling sea mist.

The helicopter sank gracefully down onto a concrete landing pad at the base of Liberty Island.

The detectives jumped out and sped toward the ferry dock. One stood on the concrete debarking apron, two stood on the path leading to the base of the statue, and the fourth paced on the lawn. All wore sunglasses. All waited for the first boat to arrive.

The stakeout of the Statue of Liberty was in place.

Kay wore a white blouse and russet skirt, and put a matching russet sweater over her shoulders. She telephoned Santomassimo again, and again there was no answer. She considered calling his headquarters but decided not to. It seemed too possessive an act, pursuing him at the workshop. She hung up the phone and stepped out of her room. She had no trouble getting a taxi to Battery Park.

The Battery pier was thick with tourists. It wasn't as packed as the height of the season, July or August, but the crisp autumn and warm air were still bringing them in from neighboring states. Five ferries were in operation. Blue pennants fluttered from their masts and from ropes leading to the sterns. Voices rose everywhere.

Before Kay even finished paying the fare, Chris Hinds was peering at her through the window. He wore tan slacks and a light brown jacket. She didn't see the others. He opened the door and she stepped out.

"Where are the others?" she asked.

"They're not coming, Professor. They're still asleep."

"Asleep? That's crazy! Let's go back and wake them up!"

She started to re-enter the cab, but Chris blocked her way.

"I'm sorry, Professor," he said. "But they're really knocked out. They went out last night after you left."

"Out? Where?"

"I don't know. One of the discos. They got Manhattan fever, I guess. In fact, they got back only an hour ago, totally sloshed. Bradley threw up. They're dead to the world, Professor."

Kay shook her head in disbelief. "Oh, my God. This tour is turning into a nightmare."

Chris smiled sympathetically. "I'm ready to go, Professor," he said. "And the boat is almost ready to leave."

Kay sighed. "I can't believe it."

"This is the part of the trip I've really been looking forward to," Chris urged.

Kay stared miserably at the boat. "What a mess," she said. She turned to him. "Okay, Chris," she agreed. "I guess it's just you and me and the great lady in the harbor."

Chris grinned. As they made their way to the dock, Kay studied Chris. He was not one of the students she knew well. He had never come to see her to talk about exams. She had never been alone with him before. She glanced at him. He had a boyish enthusiasm and a clean-cut smile. But something suggested he was more experienced than he looked.

The line at the ticket booth was long. Chris took Kay's arm and guided her quickly to the end, neatly cutting off a party of tourists.

The dawn was muted at Kennedy Airport. Mail handling carts moved sluggishly in a humid, diffused orange glow. The TWA 747, three hours late, taxied toward its terminal. Rumpled, sleepy businessmen lumbered into the entry ramps.

Santomassimo shouldered them out of his way and elbowed through a group of salesmen reminiscing, laughing, shaking hands and exchanging addresses.

"Excuse me. Sorry, this is an emergency—Excuse me. Sorry—"

Santomassimo struggled down to the gate. He was the first out of the ramp. He took out his wallet, opened it, and held it over his head, showing the police badge. Buffeted by the crowds, he circled toward the incoming escalators.

Inspector Daniel Markson of the New York Police Department pushed his way through the crowd from the opposite end.

"Santomassimo!" he yelled.

Santomassimo turned. Markson was a big man with a scar over his left eye. Santomassimo ducked past a group of servicemen.

"Right here," Santomassimo yelled. "Let's go!"

Markson turned and he and Santomassimo ran down the long corridors. Markson narrowly missed a cart mountainous with luggage. They careened into the porter, jumped a lost poodle, and ran into a short corridor. Beyond the plate glass doors Markson's helicopter waited on a slab of concrete.

The pilot of the New York police helicopter had not turned off the rotors. He waved Santomassimo and Markson on. They ran across the concrete and ducked into the wind. Santomassimo climbed aboard and felt himself hauled up into the front of the dark blue chopper.

"Move it, Joe!" Markson yelled.

The helicopter tilted off the concrete.

Liberty Island lay south of Manhattan, a distant, greenish mass in the morning reflections of grass, sky, and water. Into the clear, bright day the Statue of Liberty rose, massive bronze arm raised with its torch, impassive female face looking across the harbor.

Passengers, cameras clicking, walked up the gangway onto *The Liberty Belle*.

Kay walked in their midst with Chris Hinds. Chris politely but firmly pushed their way into the crowd.

Kay felt uncomfortable. Chris hadn't said a word during the interminable wait in line for the tickets.

"Step lively," the boat attendant called.

Chris and Kay stepped onto the deck. Five more passengers followed. The boat attendant threw off the mooring rope, jumped back on, and hauled the rope onto the deck. He doubly secured the slender safety chain.

"Your first time in New York?" he breezily asked Chris.

"I was here once before. It was a lousy experience."

The attendant kept smiling. Some tourists were grouchy. They shouldn't get up so early. It was all the travel, the rich food, too much excitement. They should stay home, just send their money in.

"Well, we'll try to give you a better experience this time," he said.

Kay felt a cool breeze and pulled the sweater back over her shoulders. There was a lurch. Tourists squealed and laughed. *The Liberty Belle* chugged into deep water.

The YMCA attendant was beside himself with fury. A scandal of this proportion was a violation of everything the YMCA stood for. Residents, strangers—curious faces pressed against the doorway, peered in. But he was even more worried about the condition of the three young men in their beds.

His supervisor examined Thad Gomez. Thad's eyes were unfocused, looking upward at the ceiling. The supervisor held the eyelid open. He passed a penlight back and forth across the pupil.

"Still dilating. He's alive. Just."

He felt the young man's pulse at the wrist and again at the jugular. "It's awfully faint, Jim, like the others. They've probably O.D.'d on something."

"Are they going to make it?"

"Get an ambulance," was all the supervisor said.

Frightened, the attendant ran back to the telephone at the main desk. As he did he cast one quick glance back at the room. Thad Gomez, Mike Reese, and Bradley Bowers lay like inert heaps struggling to breathe.

The New York Police helicopter swept at an angle over the trucks and electric carts below.

Santomassimo was jammed against the pilot. Markson was jammed in the rear compartment. The helicopter rose still higher, cutting across Brooklyn on a direct course to New York City's Upper Bay. They could see the tip of Manhattan Island on their right, and the Verrazano Narrows Bridge on their left. Ahead in the distance, murky in the morning haze, stood the deserted docks of New Jersey and, in the center of the Bay, the vague form of the Statue of Liberty.

The pilot pulled a lever. The struts of the helicopter shuddered. Santomassimo saw their shadow race across Brooklyn's tenements, garbage dumps, marshes and reeds where gulls fluttered up beneath them, wings flashing in the morning light.

The pilot adjusted his sunglasses. Santomassimo checked the gun in his shoulder holster.

The Liberty Belle churned a white wake, rumbling toward Liberty Island. The gaily dressed passengers now crowded the front of the boat. The huge Statue seemed to glide closer, the great haunted face serene in the brightening morning. Kay saw the streaks leading down from the face of Liberty. She had never realized that the face was melancholy.

"It's different from *Saboteur,* isn't it?" she said. "How would you define the difference?"

Chris licked his lips, smiled. "It's more, I don't know, impassive."

"Yes. That's a good word. It has no qualities."

"Until Hitchcock makes us see it as dangerous."

"Exactly."

At least she had got him to talk, she thought. Kay

leaned forward at the railing. The great crown—a tiara—of the Statue had tiny black openings, windows from which people could view the harbor below.

"You know," Chris said, loosening up now that they were close to the island, "when you think about it, Professor, *Saboteur* was the predecessor of *North by Northwest,* and basically utilized the same format as *The Thirty-nine Steps.* Structurally, they were all identical."

Kay looked at him. She didn't know what to make of him. One moment he was dour and silent, the next voluble as hell.

"In what way, Chris?"

"Picaresque spy plot, transcontinental chases . . . but, of course, *Saboteur* went east by northeast, moving from California to New York and ending inside the head of the Statue of Liberty instead of at the presidential faces on Mount Rushmore."

She let Chris ramble. Like the others, he tried to impress her. It was vaguely pleasant, at first. He *did* seem to know a lot about Hitchcock. But his voice grated. She half listened as she looked up at the shadowed side of the statue.

"In any case, *Saboteur* was the inferior film," Chris continued. "Don't you agree, Professor? Robert Cummings and Priscilla Lane were good, but not strictly Hitchcock types. And the story line. Jesus, so unbelievable. All those highly convenient delays to heighten suspense. Car runs out of gas, plane forced to land. So desperately phony, so false—like the dialogue. Even Dorthy Parker couldn't make it work. It was purely synthetic. Bashed together. Forced. Plodding. With all those kitchy encounters—the circus troupe with the oddball freaks, a dead steal from *Murder,* don't you agree, Professor Quinn? And being handcuffed like Donat in *Steps.* Imitating oneself is masturbation. If you'll excuse the word, Professor Quinn, but then we have no reason to be coy, do we?

We understand Hitchcock too well not to call a spade a spade. Even the scene in the moviehouse, in front of the flickering screen, when Norman Lloyd shoots it out with the police to the horror of the audience, is identical to the scene in *Sabotage*. Even I could have done better. I *have* done better."

Kay found him irritating. His words had a way of throwing a net over everything. It was hard to think with him spouting off. Suddenly he was silent.

Chris looked up at the Statue's head, which seemed to revolve slowly as the boat bumped alongside the dock. Then boat and statue were still. The head, the torch, the merciful eyes were serene. They were supreme, inscrutable. They had seen so much. Would see more.

"And that final scene in *her* head . . ." Chris said. "The villain's escape up the arm and onto the torch, then ludicrously pitching over the railing and falling to his death as the music rises and the screen fades to black. My God. How puerile. How infantile—It's terrible that Hitchcock was forced into that compromising position."

Kay turned to Chris. His eyes seemed to change between hazel and green, depending on the reflections of water and skies. She had to bring him down to Earth.

"Forced?" she asked. "By whom?"

"The moguls! The censors! The Hays and Breen Offices! The guardians of public morals and public tastes. Who always, may I say, indulged in the most hideous urges themselves, behavior that would make Hieronymous Bosch blush for shame. Professor Quinn, Hitchcock was forced to pander to what *they* considered acceptable for public consumption."

"I don't agree, Chris. Take the moguls. Who do you think the moguls were? Hitchcock owned twenty percent of Universal at the end of his career. He benefited greatly from the studio system. He was a very powerful man in Hollywood. Nobody told him what to do."

"The censors—"

"Hitchcock was always best suggesting the inadmissible. Trying to state it directly was a sign of flagging creative powers."

Chris smiled, trying to light a cigarette in the rising breeze, cupping his hands. "Got to hand it to you, Professor. You got one hell of a brain."

"Well, you know one hell of a lot about Hitchcock, Chris. I didn't teach you all that. Oh, I think we're docked."

The mooring ropes were looped onto the embankment. The boat attendant dropped a narrow gangplank, let the chain drop, and leaped to the concrete. One by one, smiling nicely, helping the elderly, he eased them onto Liberty Island.

Two ambulances, sirens wailing, preceded by a motorcycle cop, barreled up Eighth Avenue. Traffic moved grudingly aside. The ambulances turned the corner and squealed to a stop at the YMCA.

"Hurry up, damn it!" the YMCA attendant screamed. "The tall one's shaking all over.!"

Far above Manhattan, Santomassimo looked down on the choppy waters of the harbor, where black-hulled freighters were docked, and he could see the stevedores handling enormous pallets heaped high with bales, and cranes lifting tractors and crates.

Inspector Markson tapped Santomassimo on the shoulder. Santomassimo turned. Markson pointed out the right window of the helicopter. In the near distance stood the Statue of Liberty, fragile somehow, and the water around it was crisscrossed by the wakes of dozens of small craft. Santomassimo saw to his horror that a ferry had already docked on Liberty Island.

"Can you make this machine go any faster?" he shouted at the pilot.

"You want to die?"

Nevertheless, the pilot banked the helicopter and the struts began shuddering. The helicopter streaked over the cold water.

Up in the YMCA room, the ambulance attendants didn't bother with diagnosis. They took one look at Bradley Bowers, Thad Gomez, and Mike Reese, and bundled them as fast as possible down the elevator and into the ambulances.

The three were strapped down. Nylon oxygen tubes were inserted into their nostrils. Electrodes for the electrocardiogram were jellied and taped onto their heaving chests. Two of the pulses were erratic.

"Move!" an ambulance attendant shouted at the driver. *"Move!"*

When the ambulances streaked into the emergency entrance of Bellevue Hospital orderlies rolled the three bodies inside. Another orderly cleared a path through the crowded hospital corridors, and the three boys were rushed into the emergency room.

The eyelids of Thad Gomez kept fluttering open, but Thad Gomez saw nothing. Not the pink curtains drawn around his gurney, not the nurses, not the injured and dying in adjacent beds—nothing.

The tourists walked off *The Liberty Belle*. The pressure of their bodies pushed Kay and Chris along the gangway. The four plainclothes policemen studied the line of people as they debarked. Chris recognized them by their sunglasses, their set faces, their posture, and the small bulges under the breasts of their suit jackets.

Chris covered his nose and mouth with a handkerchief, coughing. The detectives carefully scrutinized each person filing past them. They tried to be incon-spicious, which made them obviously conspicious.

Chris slapped at his pockets.

"Oh, gosh, Professor Quinn, I think I dropped my map at the railing."

"We can get another, Chris."

"No. You go on ahead. I'll be right there."

Chris turned and hurried back through the press of people. They grunted as he stepped on their toes.

The detectives' eyes roamed the debarking crowd. From all angles they watched for four young men with an attractive woman. They held in their hands small reproductions of the photographs of Thad Gomez and Mike Reese.

A detective stopped a tall, dark-haired athletic young man, but he turned out to be a German on holiday who spoke no English.

"Ja, ja. Bitte," the German asked. *"Ist alles in ordnung?"*

"Fine. Fine. Everything's fine. *Gut.* Very *gut.*"

The German smiled, mystified, and put his passport back into his hand-carried wallet.

Chris saw the German tourist go. Then, still pre-tending to look under the benches, he peered between the slats and realized the detectives had photographs in their hands. And the size and coloring of the German tourist told him who one of the photographs probably belonged to.

Chris rejoined the last of the tourist group of elderly women struggling with canes and walkers down the gangplank. He assisted them. The detectives looked past him, past the elderly couples, and saw that the boat was empty. Chris smiled as he went past. He joined Kay on the walkway.

"Did you find your map?" she asked.

"Silly me! It was in my pocket all the time."

Kay and Chris walked toward the shadowed en-trance to the base of the statue.

* * *

In Bellevue's emergency room, Dr. Ira Robard finished listening to Thad Gomez's heart.

"They took one hell of a dose of pheno," Dr. Robard said. "But they'll be okay."

Bradley Bowers moaned on one of the gurneys. A nurse took his blood pressure again. It had improved. Dr. Robard joined the motorcycle officer at the desk. The officer read from a slip of paper.

"These names?" he asked Robard. "The orderly got them from the YMCA?"

"Yes. That's how they were registered."

Dr. Robard saw an uneasy expression in the officer's eye. Dr. Robard brought the medical tray from one of the gurneys. Among the paper cups, wrapped hygenic syringes, and check-in status card; the officer saw a slim, black leather wallet.

"We found it in this one's pocket," Dr. Robard said.

The officer picked up the wallet and opened it. It had $45, a single credit card, and receipt of an airplane trip from Los Angeles. The officer plucked out a laminated card.

"Thad Gomez," he read. "The University of Southern California. Department of Cinema. Los Angeles, California."

"Poor kids were tourists," Dr. Robard suggested. "Somebody on the street introduced them to phenobarbital."

But the motorcycle officer didn't hand the identity card back.

"Is there a telephone?" he asked.

"You can use the one at the emergency desk."

The officer clomped to the telephone in his knee-high boots, leaned over, and, holding the card in front of him, began to dial.

The helicopter lowered unevenly onto the cement landing pad of Liberty Island. The rotors slowed. The helicopter groaned and settled down on its struts. Santomassimo unstrapped himself and jumped to the pavement before the helicopter's engines were cut.

The four detectives ran to meet him and Inspector Markson.

"I'm Lieutenant Santomassimo. What's happened?"

"One boatload of tourists," said a detective. "Nobody matching the photograph Sergeant Bronte wired."

"What about the woman?"

"No group of five."

Santomassimo took the photographs of Thad and Mike from the detective. Reese smiled blandly; eyes squinted at the Southern California sun. He wore a football jersey. It didn't look like much of a photograph to identify anybody by.

Santomassimo looked up at the huge statue. It dwarfed them. It dwarfed the people filing toward into it.

He handed the photographs back. "Fuck," he said simply.

White gulls wheeled around the last of the tourists entering the massive base. From the Battery more tourists' boats were coming, two of them, between tugs and a barge.

"How long before these people come back down?" Santomassimo asked.

"Ten minutes. Twenty," a detective said.

Santomassimo and Markson walked to the path. The plaincothesmen took up their sentinal positions. Santomassimo searched the distant harbor for a sign of the next ferry. And his lips moved. Markson barely heard but he understood enough. The lieutenant was praying.

19

It was cold inside the enormous hollow body. There was no way of knowing one's position relative to the external features of the Statue. The circular stairwell ran up into the high shadows of the Statue's interior. Daylight came in through high windows and electric lights were strung along pipes jutting from the walls. Kay looked past Chris and saw, far above at a metal platform, streaks of rust coming down from the tiara section floor. Puffing, climbing tourists, their nervous giggles and coughs, resounded in the vast stairwell.

Heads clumped together, foreshortened in Kay's vision, they all headed for the light far above where the windows opened out from the great tiara.

"Are you okay, Professor?" Chris asked.

"Just fine. Not in as good shape as I thought I was."

"You're in plenty good shape, Professor,"

To Kay, it was like climbing up inside a green, damp

death vault, a limbo of echoing noises and ambiguous shuffles straight out of Dante's *Inferno*.

The sounds of the tourists and their metallic echoes sent memories of heavy wings thundering around her head. Memories of what? From where? Other dreams, perhaps.

"Come on. Take my hand," Chris offered.

"Thanks."

She took his hand. It was warm, dry, and strong.

They got to a small landing and self-consciously let their hands drop. Kay caught her breath. Chris watched her carefully. It seemed to Kay that everyone watched her carefully, the tourists and a tour guide. A kind of paranoia came to her, probably borne of fatigue and lack of sleep, she thought.

What was she doing here, conducting a tour, a film seminar, when her whole mental equilibrium hung by a thread?

"Only one more flight, Professor," Chris said.

"Go ahead, Chris. I'll follow."

As Kay climbed she began to feel trapped. There were people in front, people behind, and a sheer drop over the curving metal rail. She heard the flapping of a falcon's wings.

"Jesus," Chris said. "Somebody puked."

He pointed at a disgusting stain on the steps. Kay kept climbing. She pulled herself up by the rail. An elderly couple stopped to catch their breath. These were the decent people of America, Kay thought. The slightly bent forms of the old man and his wife, with their tourist buttons, matching turquoise sweaters, white sun hats, helping each other. Were they immune to the secret terrors of psychopathology? What did Hitchcock stir up in their subconsciouses without their even knowing it?

Or in hers, she suddenly realized, who had spent ten years in detailed analysis of every frame of his perverse films?

The old couple moved on. Chris and Kay followed up, up, always up the narrow metal stairwell.

"Come on, Professor," Chris called gaily.

Chris climbed higher, up increasingly narrow steps. He seemed impatient. He kept looking around, as though calculating, as though there was something he had to do here. He came to the tiara section floor, turned and extended his hand to Kay. Kay ignored him and stepped at last onto the floor.

In that instant she was drawn to the astonishing panorama through the windows and a fierce, cold wind rushed into her face.

Suddenly through the tall reinforced windows she was looking out at the greatest harbor in the world, and it struck her with all the force of a vision of infinity.

"How magnificent—" she blurted.

The blindingly bright horizon curved far, far away, beyond a landscape of warehouses, highways, tenements, more highways, wastelands, whole cities, and beautiful blue lagoons. The fresh air whistled through the holes in the statue's tiara. Her hair blew about her face.

People crowded to the openings, transfixed.

"How lovely," Kay whispered. "How truly peaceful."

"Yes," Chris said nervously, looking around.

"I feel like I could fly," she said gently.

"You wouldn't like it," Chris said, trying to be charming, but the voice growing tense. "Remember, a gnat isn't hurt, a fly bounces, a bird breaks a wing, and a man splashes from a height like this."

She glanced at him. There was considerable anger bottled up in Chris. It came out in short, uncontrolled bursts. Now, abashed, he went to a far window, breathed steadily, and watched the sparkling on the harbor waters far below.

"Hell of a location for a murder," Chris said. "Only

it wasn't really a murder, was it? More an accident. Well, the film ended in death. That's what counted."

As Kay looked out she remembered the little girl she had been, the girl who had grown up in Santa Barbara and played on the beach with her grandparents, under the same shade of blinding white-blue heaven.

But though she tried to hang onto the thought, the memory faded.

The tourists adjusted telephoto lenses and took photographs of every angle of the immense view below. The tour guide explained the dimensions of the view, the tons of bronze inside the statue, the problems of disassembling it in France, shipping it to Liberty Island, and reassembling it.

"So spectacular, so corny," Chris confided to Kay. "That was the master's way, wasn't it? Places like here, like Mount Rushmore, sucking in the patriots. Toying with the dreams of decent people."

Chris waited impatiently until the tour guide led the elderly tourists down the dizzying circular stairway. Just below them, arms folded, a guard in uniform stood before the gate leading to the arm of the statue. He studied Kay and Chris speculatively, then inquired: "You the teacher who got permission to go up to the torch?"

"Yes," Chris answered quickly. "This is Professor Quinn."

"Shouldn't there have been five of you?"

"Yes," Kay replied tautly. "There should have been. But they were detained."

The guard nodded and unlocked the gate.

"I'll have to accompany you," he explained. "It's dangerous up there. The wind blows hard."

At that moment, on the stairwell below, there was a slight commotion. An elderly woman had slipped and was nursing her ankle. The guard gazed down with concern.

"These old people," he said sadly. "Bones like chalk. Sorry, folks. You just stay put and I'll be right back."

The guard went down. His footsteps paused and they heard his kind voice encouraging the old woman to test her weight carefully on her ankle. Seized by a sudden concern of her own, Kay walked to the head of the stairs. The unnerving events of the previous night had taken their toll.

"I think we should go, Chris," she said. "I'm worried about the others."

"Not yet," Chris snapped.

Surprised at the tone of his voice, she stopped.

"It *is* awesome up here," she conceded, "but we aren't tourists. We're analyzing the difference between reality and filmed images. And we have the mansion to visit."

"I'd rather not leave."

"Honestly, Chris. We should go."

Kay turned back to the stairs. Chris jumped from the tiara windows and grabbed her arm.

"Professor . . . !"

Startled, she jerked her arm back. She stared into his face. It was handsome but the eyes showed strain.

"Please," he said, trying to be charming. "Can't we stay here until the next boat comes? It shouldn't be more than another few minutes."

"I'd rather not, Chris. This *is* a serious tour, in spite of our three friends—who should be awake by now."

She stepped onto the metal flange of the stairs. Chris moved in front of her.

"It hasn't been much of a tour so far, has it? First the hotels turned out to be a disaster, and then Bradley and the others got stewed. I'd really like to spend a little time here. And we do have the torch to see."

"Chris, how can we? The others have a right to be in on the tour, too. They're expecting to visit the mansion. They may be waiting for us there already."

"I don't think so."

The tourists' voices disappeared, going down, down, back to the interior of the statue's base, and out onto the lawn and embankment far below. The guard and the tour guide nursed the elderly woman down the flights, joking and lifting her spirits. Up in the tiara section the wind soughed around the metal. Kay felt a terrifying coldness and it wasn't from the wind but something deep inside.

Chris grinned and stared hard into her eyes.

"Think, Professor, here . . . among the memories of Priscilla Lane, Robert Cummings, and Norman Lloyd. Can't you sense them? Hear them? See them? For all its faults, *Saboteur* was a hell of a film, wasn't it?"

"Yes. It was."

"Then let us pay our—homage—"

In some subtle way that she was loath to examine she was afraid of Chris. Or afraid of herself. Afraid of coming apart, as she almost had on the dark New York streets.

"Okay, Chris," she sighed. "We'll take the next boat."

"Thanks. I appreciate that, Professor."

Kay went to the windows. She rested against the sill. She tried to recapture that feeling of calm innocence. When she closed her eyes against the sheer drop and immense panorama, she suddenly saw a bell tower, and a man falling. From *Foreign Correspondent*. Only it was Steve Safran. God, these images! Please make them stop!

She felt a hot breath, and it was Chris, looking out at the harbor just behind her. He had moved around to her window. She shivered.

"Some scene," she said weakly.

She felt as fragile as etched glass.

"What a terrific place to direct," Chris said.

Santomassimo stood in front of the *American Eagle*. The ferry boat was packed with tourists, gaily bedecked with red, white, and blue pennants. A loud-speaker disgorged information about Liberty Island. It was a noisy boat. Boy Scouts and a group of Puerto Rican kids from the Bronx hooted and ran around the decks.

Markson and the plainclothesmen walked on the second dock. The *Queen of the Harbor* chugged in the distance toward Liberty Island. Groups of tourists, some elementary school teachers and their students, looked admiringly at the statue ahead. Half a dozen Japanese families in black clothes, smiling, leaned over the white rails, the sun bright in their faces, taking pictures of each other against Liberty Island.

The children and schoolteachers of the *American Eagle* went down the gangplank. Santomassimo stood directly in their way, arms folded, right hand ready to reach inside to his shoulder holster. He looked hard at the boat attendants. They looked like weathered sea-men—the sort of faces you'd see in a Navy melodrama. No woman remotely looked like Kay.

"Any luck?" he asked Markson, when the school-children were safely on the embankment.

Markson shook his head. "No groups of four with a female teacher." We've searched the boat, too."

"What about that first group, from *The Liberty Belle?*"

"All on board. One of the elderly women sprained an ankle. That's her on the park bench."

Santomassimo looked up at the great bronze face of the Statue of Liberty. It slanted just slightly, it seemed to him, half in shadow. The windows of the tiara were dark. He hated the idea of the several hundred people now crossing the paths of the island.

The situation was getting out of control.

"Is the tiara clear?" he asked.

"Want to take a look?"

Markson handed Santomassimo a pair of binoculars. Santomassimo looked through them and saw, in the dense, compacted air, the bright bronzed arm and torch, a slight fence around a slender platform. The platform was devoid of people. Below, in the tiara section, he thought he saw a vague motion in a black window. It must have been birds. He watched a long time and nothing moved. He handed the binoculars back to Markson.

"They don't allow people up to the torch, do they?" Santomassimo asked.

"No. It's been closed for years." Markson looked at Santomassimo, who seemed very worried. "I'm sure everybody from *The Liberty Belle* must have come down, Lieutenant."

Santomassimo nodded appreciatively, though Markson's words were small comfort. He knew that in Chris Hinds he was dealing with a maniac who had attacked Kay with the falcon, and who had attacked Santomassimo himself with the delivered bomb. He now had a terrifying intuition that Hinds was preparing something spectacular as a topper. Maybe even a mass murder? Where were Kay and the three other students?

"Do you have any sharpshooters?" Santomassimo asked suddenly.

"Wilson. The tall fellow."

"Does he have a rifle?"

"In the helicopter. Do you want me to get it?

"Not yet. I don't want to panic all these people."

Santomassimo turned back toward New York, shielding his eyes. Ferry boats were filled with tourists but they had not yet left their docks. Santomassimo turned back to Markson.

"Inspector, did you ever see a film by Alfred Hitchcock that ended in the Statue of Liberty?"

"It was an old film, wasn't it? Black and white?"

"I think so."

"I saw it once. Strange film. Had to do with Nazi spies, didn't it?"

"Do you remember how it ended?"

"Somebody got killed. Probably the bad guy. Isn't that how all films end?"

"That's how they used to end," Santomassimo said ambiguously, and walked back to the park bench to confer with marksman Wilson.

In *Psycho* Hitchcock had electrified audiences by killing off the star, Janet Leigh, only minutes into the film.

What strange narrative twist was Chris Hinds plotting, Santomassimo wondered, now that he had found his favorite actress?

Far above, leaning from the shadow, Chris looked down onto the sheer drop of the embankment, which was now in full sun. From the tiara windows he saw a man's figure, conservatively dressed in a black suit, nervously slipping his right hand in and out of the bulge under his jacket's breast.

Santomassimo?

Though he couldn't be certain from this distance, Chris involuntarily moved to the side of the window. For a long time he stayed in the shadow, ashen and trembling. Was it possible he was still alive?

"How the hell did he survive?" he whispered.

"What?"

Chris came to. "Nothing, Professor. Sorry. Just thinking of the movie. Hell of a fall, isn't it?"

He suddenly grinned unpleasantly and turned to Kay. "Would you stand by that window, Professor?" he asked.

She looked at him quizzically. "Why?"

"Then we'd be standing in the exact positions as Priscilla Lane and Norman Lloyd before Robert Cummings and the police came to get Lloyd."

Chris looked ill. Or was it her own discomfort projected?

"You certainly have gotten into the spirit of the tour, Chris," she said.

"Please—"

Kay reluctantly stood at the window. There was a sudden rush of the wind, bringing panic. It ran through her nerves, gathering speed. It blossomed. Everything darkened suddenly and she was overwhelmed in a single, unmistakable film image as a sudden *deja vu* flashed through her mind.

MEDIUM SHOT: PRISCILLA LANE, NORMAN
    LLOYD, DAY
Priscilla Lane stands in close proximity to Lloyd at
    the window inside the tiara of the Statue of
    Liberty.

It was sharp as a projected film. It *was* a film. It was *Saboteur*. The image of *Saboteur*'s reality. Only she was in it. Or was she watching it? As in the dream the night before, she both watched and participated, unfree, unable to escape, and it was both around her and inside her, a mental manipulation overwhelming her like a fish net.

"What's the matter, Professor? The height got to you?"

"No—Fatigue, I guess—"

"I'm sure it's been a difficult semester for you."

Even Chris's voice seemed to have a sarcastic edge, as though he and the hallucination came somehow from the same place.

"Yes, I—Maybe I should sit down."

But there was no place to sit down. She leaned against the window. Her head swayed and her forehead leaned against her hand. The cold hardness of the stone helped restore her sense of place. Her pulse slowed, but was still fast. What had it been? A film image born of fatigue?

Chris's obsession was contagious. She talked to deflate it, to deny its reality.

"You realize, of course, Chris," she said, "that *Saboteur* wasn't shot up here. It was shot on a sound stage in Universal Studios."

"Right. But this is more real, isn't it, Professor? Isn't that what we've come to learn? The difference between movies and reality?"

Again, under the influence of his damned enthusiasm she saw flecks and graininess, and even Chris began to fade into something in black and white. Kay held onto the window ledge. The sensation passed. But she was frightened.

"I—I'd like to go now, Chris. Please—"

"Sure, Professor. In just a minute—"

"Not in a minute—"

"Just a damn second!"

Chris peered carefully out the window again. Santomassimo ran down the docks and the plainclothesmen searched the water line, revolvers drawn.

"The stupid little kid," Chris whispered. "Probably never delivered it. I hope he's spread all over Beverly Hills."

"What are you saying, Chris?"

"*Sabotage*. A different movie, a different scene."

Suddenly Santomassimo whirled around and Chris ducked deep into the tiara's shadow. Kay watched Chris narrowly. Chris stood with his back to the stone wall, trembling.

Santomassimo felt a deep depression, fearing that Chris Hinds had somehow slipped through. Santomassimo's guilt clouded his mind like a dark shade. He knew damn well he himself had drawn Kay Quinn into the Hitchcock case. His love for her might end up killing her.

"*Santomassimo!!*"

He whirled. The helicopter pilot waved frantically to him.

"New York headquarters, sir!" the pilot shouted, holding up his yellow earphones.

Santomassimo ran to the landing pad. He climbed into the helicopter and jammed the pilot's earphones on his head.

"Lieutenant Santomassimo here," he shouted into the microphone.

Lieutenant," cracked a voice, *"We have picked up three young men at Bellevue Hospital, emergency admittance, on overdoses of phenobarbitol. The names are Mike Reese, Thad Gomez, and Bradley Bowers. All from USC, all from the cinema department."*

"Hinds!" Santomassimo yelled. "Where's Chris Hinds?"

"No idea. The YMCA attendant said Chris Hinds must have checked out early."

"Early?"

"Yes, Lieutenant. Before the other three were discovered."

"Any idea where he is?"

"None, sir."

"Any idea what he looks like?

"Sort of All-American, apparently. That's what Bradley Bowers said. He's still pretty groggy."

"Okay. Keep interrogating the boys. Find out anything they know."

"Roger. Out."

Santomassimo rubbed his face. Ideas, plans, procedures, seemed cut loose from their moorings. His guilt swirled on the rampage. Kay was with Chris. That was obvious. But where? The ferry boats had been searched. Except *The Liberty Belle.* Markson and the detectives had only photos of Mike Reese and Thad Gomez to make comparisons with the passengers, and no idea of what Bradley, Chris, or Kay looked like.

Santomassimo looked up at the Statue of Liberty.

The head was bright, immense, and magnificent in the full morning sun. Again he thought he saw movement in the windows of the tiara. And suddenly he knew.

"Oh, Jesus!" he blurted. *"He's up there! With her!"*

From high above Chris saw the men become animated. They were all drawing out their revolvers now. One of them brought a rifle with a telescopic sight from the helicopter. Santomassimo ran toward the statue and the others followed, pushing tourists aside.

Chris saw it all. He knew by their frenzied run why they were coming. It was part of the script. He was scared, but exhilarated. He backed into the shadow and bumped into Kay.

"Sorry—"

Kay jumped. She wondered why Chris had grown so pale. She followed his gaze and looked down. Far below, a man, more silhouette than man, but an unmistakable silhouette of the body she knew so well, came running over the concrete. It was Santomassimo. She neither moved nor spoke, but began to tremble, seeing in her psyche's moviola:

MEDIUM SHOT: PRISCILLA LANE, NORMAN LLOYD, DAY
Priscilla Lane, terrified, and Norman Lloyd stand at the window of the Statue's tiara, watching below.
THEIR POV: ROBERT CUMMINGS, POLICE, DAY
Viewed from high overhead, Robert Cummings and the police dash across the lawn and into the base of the Statue.

The hallucination faded slowly. She felt as though it came from Chris, from the statue, from some far distant, omnipotent place. It was Santomassimo, she knew. And now she knew exactly who Chris was.

For a long time, a terribly long and awful time, she
looked down, afraid to look at Chris. Even as Santo
massimo and the detectives ran toward the base of the
statue, their echoes faintly audible, she neither moved
nor spoke.

"You okay, Professor?" Chris asked metallically, cru
elly.

"Yes, thank you," she said in a voice she barely
recognized as her own, flat and emotionless with
terror. "I guess I've overdone it, going without sleep
so long."

"Yeah. Pity about the hotels. After a red-eye special
and all."

Chris grinned at her. She was helpless as a rabbit
trembling right against the tiara windows in front of
him.

He saw Santomassimo and his cohorts as they dis
appeared into the base of the statue. Santomassimo
must have flown all night, Chris thought.

"Well, well, Professor," he finally said. "Seems your
boyfriend's still alive."

"Alive?" she whispered, refusing to look at him.
"What do you mean?"

She was pale and couldn't swallow. She felt him
come very close, casual, too casual, and his shadow
fell over her.

"The bomb must have gone off too soon. Well, that's
one obnoxious kid fragmented."

"Kid? Bomb?"

"Just like *Sabotage,* Professor. Remember? The de
tective was saved and the kid was killed. How corny!"

Chris moved behind her, blocking the way to the
stairs. She turned and made herself look at him. His
small eyes were direct and piercing, like a falcon's,
she thought.

"How Hitch would have loved this," Chris said,
looking at her deeply. The paralysis of fear electrified
her hands, arms, and legs. Her life in danger in the

very city she had run to for refuge. Trapped in the
very symbol of liberty.

Kay saw deeper. She understood the dispensability
of her life. Her career, the books and articles she had
written, the colleges she had attended, having loved
Santomassimo—everything was dispensable as dust.

Because this was reality. Not a movie. She saw it in
the grin on Chris's face.

Again an irrational montage of images catapulted
into her mind. Suddenly they congealed.

*MEDIUM SHOT: PRISCILLA LANE, NORMAN
     LLOYD, DAY*
*Priscilla Lane, terrified, backs away from Norman
     Lloyd as he closes in on her, smiling sinisterly.*

The hallucination did not fade this time. *Saboteur*
hung like a visual curtain. Through it she saw Chris
watching her minutely, still in his boyish good looks,
his jacket, half student, half the actor Norman Lloyd.

Suddenly they heard the metallic clicking of footsteps far below climbing the interior stairs.

Chris's ears perked up. "Listen, Professor," he
sneered. "The white hats are coming to the rescue.
Just like in *Saboteur*. Of course, Norman Lloyd should
have killed Priscilla Lane. Right here, on this spot—"

Chris's hand reached into his pocket. He began
chewing yellow buttered popcorn.

"—But no! Norman Lloyd didn't kill her! He couldn't
kill the heroine. You're the heroine now, Professor.
But in the movie he couldn't kill her! Right? Ha, what
a laugh! Hitch must've vomited everytime he thought
about it.

"He *hated* happy endings because he knew that life
doesn't work that way. That it's all a sick joke!"

Kay watched the popcorn go into Chris's mouth
with increasing rapidity. She had once thought his
face handsome, in a boyish, All-American way. Now it

was hideous, taut with tension, mania, and an obses
sive cruelty.

"I've transcended the limitations—the bullshit, th
pandering to mediocrity. Real people, Professor, goo
people, have succumbed! I carried out his true, mos
heartfelt intentions! I created for him in reality wha
he was not allowed to do in film! I fulfilled his genius!

"Y-You're crazy . . ."

Chris flinched. *"That* line is unworthy of you. *H*
would have hated it."

"What—What are you?" she stammered.

He smiled, but coldly. "I am a director," he sai
with a chilling sincerity.

And to her disgust and repulsion, she knew, in hi
perverse logic, it was true.

"What did you do to Mike and the others?" sh
demanded.

"I told you," he laughed. "They're dead to th
world."

"Kay!" came Santomassimo's echoing shout fron
below. "CHRIS!!"

Chris jerked around. He looked down the stairwel
Far, far below could be seen Santomassimo, Markson
the detectives, six tiny dark figures climbing up th
metal steps.

Santomassimo stopped dead in his tracks. He didn
recall Chris Hinds from the class, and judged him t
be about six feet tall, slender, pale, as though physi
cally run down, overwrought. Nothing a professiona
law enforcement officer couldn't easily deal with. *If h
could separate him from Kay.*

"Come down the stairs, Chris!" Santomassimo or
dered.

"Fuck off, cop!"

The marksman Wilson knelt to aim his rifle bu
Santomassimo suddenly saw that Kay was right be
hind Chris.

"Hold it," Santomassimo said. "She's right behin
him."

He paused, and then, with surprising speed, began running up the metal stairs at Chris.

Chris grabbed Kay by the arm and dragged her across the tiara floor. She fought as another hallucination hit her, pulling her into fragments of *Saboteur*, splotches and light streaks, forming a montage of quick cuts of faces, feet running to speeded-up, high-pitched sounds of the film track.

LONG SHOT: ROBERT CUMMINGS, POLICE, DAY
Seen from high above, Robert Cummings leads the
    policemen running up the spiral staircase of
    the statue.

Chris slapped her and dragged her by the hair. Kay screamed. It sounded to Santomassimo like a person screaming for sanity.

"WE'RE UP HERE!" Kay yelled.

Santomassimo saw her disappear just beyond the floor level of the tiara, fighting Chris. His heart sank in fear and his footsteps faltered.

Chris threw her at the stairway to the torch. She fell against the cold metal floor and sprawled in the dust.

"Come on, get up!" Chris commanded. "We're going up to the torch!"

"W-why?"

"Because that's where the last scene took place. And this is the last scene!"

"No—"

"Let's give these assholes a *real* Hitchcock ending!"

A six-inch blade glinted like white mercury from a knife in his fist.

"No—" she pleaded.

"You do what the director tells you, little lady!"

Chris slashed the knife at her. Kay gasped, scrambled backward, and fell against the iron railing leading upward to the torch.

"No—" she pleaded. "You don't want to end the film that way!"

"Why the hell not?"

"Because it was Norman Lloyd who died!"

Chris turned. Santomassimo pounded up the stairs.

"It was Norman Lloyd who panicked!" she shouted.

"What the hell are you babbling about, Professor?"

The tiara section grew grainy. Chris's jacket turned dark. His hair turned dark. Suddenly Kay wore the fashions of a by-gone era. The forearm she held in front of her own face for protection was white as ivory, like an old film, and everything else shimmerd in tones of gray and black.

MEDIUM SHOT: ROBERT CUMMINGS, POLICE, DAY

Robert Cummings and the police dash closer up the metal stairs.

CLOSE SHOT: NORMAN LLOYD, DAY

Panicked, Lloyd turns and dashes up the iron stairway alone.

"See? I told you!" Kay said.

"Told me what?" Chris seized her and pushed her roughly past the unlocked gate and to the iron ladder, which was nearly vertical.

"Priscilla Lane didn't go up to the torch! Norman Lloyd saw the police coming and ran up alone," she uttered stridently, as to a recalcitrant student.

He swung the knife and it struck the rail, sending sparks into the cold air.

"I break the conventions! I direct the scenes Hitchcock *wanted!* Now get the fuck up there!"

He prodded her up the ladder with the knifepoint.

The iron door to the torch opened, revealing an infinite cold sky, infinite and indifferent as death itself. Kay believed she was in a different time and place. The man behind her was a foreigner.

He was Norman Lloyd, the Nazi spy. And she was explaining the film to her students at USC. Madmen, she was telling them, never figure in Hitchcock's films. The audience can never sympathize with completely psychopathic characters. Hitchcock insisted on sympathy for his murderers.

Then all illusions faded. Chris backed her onto the bare, open platform around the torch, with only a waist-high fence between them and the embankment two hundred feet below.

"KAY!!" Santomassimo yelled, coming onto the tiara floor.

A piece of popcorn lay on the floor in a patch of sunlight streaming through a window. He stared at it, silent, unambiguous, taunting. Santomassimo tightened his grip on his revolver.

"The door to the torch is closed, Lieutenant," Wilson said, gripping his rifle.

"We'll have to rush him," Markson said.

"I can put a hole in the kid's head," Wilson promised. "Honest I can."

"No," Santomassimo said grimly. "She's with him. I'll go alone."

Santomassimo quickly climbed the iron steps. He raised his head slowly. The iron door was inches ajar and through the slender opening he saw Chris bent over Kay at the railing, an arm hooked around her neck. Chris's knife flashed in the silver sunlight.

Santomassimo lay on his belly on the cold metal and inched his revolver into position. Chris held the knife point at Kay's throat. As they struggled Kay's head kept moving in front of Chris's, making a shot too risky.

Astounded, Santomassimo made out their words through the rush of cold wind. Was Kay buying time? Or was something else going on?

"Don't you agree Hitchcock would have preferred it this way?" Chris shouted.

"It was the killer who died, Chris!" she yelled.

"Phoney! Phoney!"

"It was right that he died! He was a spy! A murderer! Without any conscience!"

"Bad guys get it! Lovers tootle off to their marital beds. Crap!"

Santomassimo hunched forward. Kay had bent back, against the fragile railing, revealing Chris's head, but then Chris yanked her back and was shielded again.

"What's wrong with a happy ending," Kay yelled.

"It's shit! It's not real! Life ends in shit!"

"If Cary Grant had been killed by that cropduster, there'd have been no movie!"

"So what?"

"Hitchcock always delivered what the audience wanted!"

"Hitchcock mindfucked them into accepting what he hated!"

"People need—"

"Even on TV he had to apologize every time the bad guy got away with murder."

"It was his style—"

Suddenly Chris perfectly imitated Alfred Hitchcock's lazy, sinister, insouciant cockney drawl. " 'The killer was caught later by an overzealous cop fresh out of the police academy'—all pablum, and he knew it!"

They were talking a different language—a private arcane language of their own. With a sense of horror Santomassimo realized that the terror of the serial killer, which he had drawn Kay into, had unbalanced her.

"CHRIS!!" Santomassimo shouted and jumped up.

There was an explosion of metal. Chris whirled. Santomassimo had slammed open the iron door and Chris saw a black revolver aimed at his eyes. Santomassimo's fingers trembled with eagerness. Kay moved to Chris's side. One shot from the lieutenant at fifteen feet would split Chris's forehead.

"Drop it!" Santomassimo roared.

Chris hesitated, blinking back, disbelieving. "Well, Sir Galahad, the white knight, the oldest formula in the book."

"*Drop it!*"

"Who wrote this script, Santomachismo? Because it sucks!"

"DROP IT!!"

Chris saw the barrel, rock solid, aimed right between his eyes. He sighted up the barrel and saw Santomassimo's fierce eyes. Cops who have been sent bombs, whose lovers have been pursued by falcons, suffer severe failures of senses of humor.

Chris smiled like an angel. What the hell, he thought. Improvise. He stepped back and dropped the knife onto the platform. It bounced once, clattered, and rolled to Santomassimo's feet.

"All right, Mr. Policeman," Chris grinned. "I dropped it. Now what?"

Kay crumpled against the metal wall in a wind so fierce that it blew her hair around her face. Kay watched Santomassimo but he saw a dark look in her eyes that filled him with infinite remorse.

"Put your hands behind your head and step over here. Slowly," Santomassimo ordered.

"That's good," Chris said. "But could we try it again? This time speak from the diaphragm. It's much too nasal the way you deliver your lines."

"GET YOUR ASS OVER HERE, PUNK!"

"Oh shit. He's improvising."

Santomassimo came even closer. He was furious. The black revolver was still pointed between Chris's eyes. But the lieutenant kept watching Kay. She was tense and her eyes were black with rage and a kind of horror he had never seen. She did not bolt for liberty.

She did not come to him. She backed away, seeming to see things that weren't there.

"Oh, God," he muttered. "Kay—"

But Kay, backing away, didn't even see him anymore. What she saw flickering through the sprockets of her mind was:

MEDIUM SHOT: NORMAN LLOYD, DAY
Norman Lloyd pitches backward over the railing,
*   screaming.*

"Fall!" she commanded. "Now!"

Chris, startled, swung around to face her, his expression betraying confusion and a rictus of fear.

"W-What?" he stammered lamely.

"That's how Nazis die!" Kay shouted angrily, and rushed at him.

Panicked, Chris fell against the railing, lost his balance and pitched backward over the side. It happened so suddenly that Santomassimo was unable to seize Chris before he toppled downward, slipping, grabbing at metal outcroppings, screaming, cascading down the massive torch base. Finally, Chris was able to grab hold of the Statue's hand, between the thumb and the forefinger, and held on tightly in a bizarre handclasp.

Crazed, he seemed to thrash in a dream. He was suspended now, several hundred feet over the lawn and concrete. Murmurs rippled through the tourists below. The murmurs turned to screams as hands pointed at the diminutive, dark figure hanging from the Lady's fingers, high overhead.

LONG SHOT: NORMAN LLOYD, DAY
Seen from the waterfront, Norman Lloyd's diminu-
*   tive, dark body hangs from the torch arm high*
*   over the tourists.*

The scene flashed through Kay's fractured brain. She saw it all, grainy, macabre, inevitable, a relentless parade of Hitchcock's images.

"P-P-Professor—Help me—" Chris's pathetic cry was scarcely audible in the high wind.

"I can't," Kay explained calmly, almost sadly. "The scene was written this way."

"No—Please—D-Don't let the film—end—like this—"

Santomassimo tucked the revolver into his belt and climbed over the fence after Chris, whose face had gone chalk white. Kay's delirium was contagious to them both.

"H-Help me—Professor—!" Chris cried.

"It's not in the script!" Kay shot back.

"GET AWAY FROM THE RAIL!" Santomassimo roared at Kay.

Kay looked at Santomassimo, puzzled, confused. Santomassimo looked at Kay and saw something in her face more frightening than panic. He didn't even have a name for it. It was a dreamy, grim wonder, a bright-eyed giddiness that he had seen before in the eyes of the aged, whose minds have lost the ability to focus on objective reality, who remain locked hypnotically onto a tiny wedge of memory. What was Kay seeing now, he wondered, as he watched Kay's total concentration impinged on Chris.

Markson and the detectives pushed through the metal door and eased their way across the platform to the railing. They stood beside Kay.

Astonished, they watched Chris hanging by his hands far over the sheer drop, and Santomassimo bending over farther and farther, reaching down.

And Chris now looked at Kay. And knew what visions played before her.

MEDIUM SHOT: PRISCILLA LANE, POLICE, DAY
Prisiclla Lane and the police. They gaze starkly over
*   the railing down at Cummings and Lloyd.*

She was directing the ending of *Saboteur*.

Suddenly the absolute terror in Chris's face faded to an accepting understanding. He looked at Kay's distraught face. "You're directing, huh, Teach?" he asked in amazement. "You see it, don't you?"

"Leave her alone, Chris," Santomassimo snapped.

"Oh, no," Chris laughed, sure now he knew. "She sees. She feels. She knows what it's like to direct!"

Kay backed away, shaking her head to clear it, desperately attempting to wrest herself from the clutch of illusion that gripped and pulled her back into its nightmare cinema.

"Come on, Professor, admit it! Admit it!" Chris intoned in an hypnotic mantra. "You see it! You feel it! You know! You know!—"

"I—I—" Kay stammered weakly, caught on the cusp of fantasy and reality. "—I—yes, yes—I see it—I see it. God help me! I feel it! I know—!"

"KAY!" Santomassimo yelled. Then to the detectives: "Get her out of here!"

But Kay slipped from them and moved down the platform floor. Their actions only served to re-energize the illusion. She moved down to where Priscilla Lane had to stand on her mark, at the rail, to watch and react to Norman Lloyd's death. *Saboteur* was rolling again. The images were running through the aperture gate. The fate of the film was fixed. No one could change a film once it began running. And what she saw now was:

CLOSE SHOT: ROBERT CUMMINGS, NORMAN
*   LLOYD, DAY*
Robert Cumming's hand slowly extends to Norman
*   Lloyd's sleeve.*

"Grab my hand!" Santomassimo shouted.

"No!" Kay objected. "You've got to grab his sleeve!"

"SHUT HER UP!" Santomassimo exploded.

Markson and the detectives didn't know what to make of Kay's delerium. It was like nothing they had ever experienced. Astonished, they watched Chris hanging by his hands far over the sheer drop, Santomassimo bending over farther and farther, reaching down, his hand bypassing Chris's hand and reaching down for the jacket sleeve.

Kay watched critically, caught in the scene's lethal hypnosis.

CLOSE SHOT: ROBERT CUMMINGS, NORMAN LLOYD, DAY
Robert Cummings reaches for Norman Lloyd's sleeve.

Santomassimo's powerful hand seized Chris's sleeve. Chris's face was white.

"P-Please—don't let go—!" The words were choked out of him.

Santomassimo braced his shoulder. Gripping the railing and the sleeve, he put every ounce of strength into pulling Chris up to the railing. But the kid was a dead weight. Santomassimo felt the blinding white flash from his shoulder, the same shoulder he had separated at Kay's door. He groaned and clenched his teeth.

"I'll get the helicopter!" Markson shouted.

"Forget it!" Santomassimo shouted back. "The airstream'll blow us both off. Get a rope!"

Markson ran down the stairs.

Santomassimo grasped the jacket sleeve tighter. Suddenly the terror made a mask of Chris's face.

"Hold on! HOLD ON!" Chris whimpered. "My sleeve won't tear like his did!"

Kay leaned forward over the low rail, waiting for the inevitable.

CLOSE SHOT: NORMAN LLOYD'S SLEEVE, DAY
Bit by bit, slowly at first, Norman Lloyd's sleeve begins to tear at the arm. Gradually the stitches begin to open.

"Yes, yes—" Kay gasped, her hand to her mouth.

CLOSE SHOT: NORMAN LLOYD'S SLEEVE, DAY
The torn sleeve unravels and slowly slips off Norman Lloyd's arm.

As Kay watched breathlessly, Chris's sleeve didn't rip. A sense of loss gripped her. The scene's momentum was off. The sleeve should rip! Now! Kay shouted to Santomassimo but he barely heard in the wind. When he did, he heard a disembodied, alientated voice:

"Rip! Rip! . . . "

She was a director issuing orders on a set, he realized as a chill went through him. "GET THAT ROPE UP HERE!" he bellowed.

But her voice came again, shrill and flat, perfunctory, through the howling wind.

"His sleeve must rip," she insisted. "It *must!* He's a traitor! A spy!"

Grinning maniacally, Chris stared upward at Kay.

Santomassimo looked from Chris's tormented face to Kay's, inseparably locked in the same hallucination. A detective held her from behind.

"That's it, Teach—!" Chris grunted, holding tightly onto the statue's fingers. "Direct this f-fucking climax right—!"

Kay looked at him from far away, with a distant sense of desperate purpose.

"I'm trying," she pleaded. "But I'm no Hitchcock."

"Well, he couldn't have directed it any better than you, Professor," Chris congratulated. "Sorry I can't be of more help, but my sleeve seems to be holding up." Then, a flicker of amusement brightened his eyes, as the solution came to him. "Here! Your last image, director—!"

MEDIUM SHOT: NORMAN LLOYD, DAY
Normal Lloyd falls screaming to his death.

Chris let go of the statue's hand.
"*I never wanted to be born, anyway!*" he shouted to the world.
"—you crazy shit—" Santomassimo blurted.
The release of Chris's grasp added sudden strain. The white flashes in Santomassimo's shoulder exploded again.
"Okay, Professor!" Chris's hoarse gutteral shout rose above the screaming wind. "ACTION!"
Chris Hinds slipped from Santomassimo's grasp.
"ZOOM—ZOOM!"
   "—Zoo-om—
      "—zooo——m—!
         "—zooo——oo—mmm—!"
His body turned over and over, hair flying up, jacket streaming out, tie billowing from the pocket. He tumbled in a half somersault, straightened, and smashed into the concrete in the form of a swastika.
The body of Chris Hinds hit the concrete at almost two hundred miles an hour and splashed blood, flesh, and bits of teeth as far as the park benches on the embankment.
Tourists screamed and scattered. Markson, running back from the helicopter with the rope looped around his shoulder, stopped, sickened, and watched.
Tourists had been eager to look, but when they saw what was left of the once handsome face now, they looked away.

"Step back, please!" a dazed policeman said automatically. "Please step back!"

Where the wrist was broken, several pieces of yellow, buttered popcorn lay scattered in the sun.

Santomassimo leaned back against the statue's metal and close his eyes. He was frightened. Not of falling. Not of anything in the real world. But of Kay. Santomassimo was terrified of what he had done to her.

For a long time, Kay stared down. Her lips silently formed the word "Cut!" Then, sensing Santomassimo's eyes upon her, she turned to him with a tiny smile.

"How about it, Great Saint?" she asked. "Want to wrap it up with a clinch and a kiss?"

A trickle of nervous laughter escaped her lips. It grew into uncontrollable laughter. Santomassimo was chilled to the bone. He did not move. Her insanity was his purgatory.

"Some hero," Kay shouted. "Come on—where's the clinch?"

Santomassimo remained where he was.

"Come on, dummy! The film is over! You've got to kiss the leading lady! Haven't you been on a set before?"

Santomassimo swallowed hard. The detectives, afraid she would jump, grabbed her from behind.

"Let me go, you bastards—"

She hammered at their faces, bit their wrists, and dug at their eyes. They ducked and held her tighter.

Finally Santomassimo climbed back onto the platform and grabbed her. Whatever he had done to Margaret, however he had wronged her, was nothing compared to what he had done to Kay Quinn.

"*KAY! FORGIVE ME!*"

He pressed his head against her face. "I beg you, darling, forgive me. It's over now. It's over. Over . . . over . . . "

"He had to fall. He knew it. I knew it. Why couldn't you see it, you stupid Italian cop?"

"No more films, Kay. Believe me—believe me—"

"You said that before."

The accusation struck Santomassimo hard. He held her closer even as she fought him. "I love you, Kay. More than I've ever loved any person in this world. Believe me, it's over now!"

"You're crying, Great Saint. Cops aren't supposed to cry at the final clinch."

"This isn't a film. Kay—"

She tried to smile but suddenly Kay burst into tears. She broke apart in his arms.

He began kissing her over her neck, face, and hair. Tears streamed down his face. "Easy, easy," he soothed.

"I dreamed I saw—It was a dream—I *was* Hitchcock—and this was *Saboteur*—and I was condemned to watch it, and act in it, and direct it—"

"I know—darling—I know"

She wept unashamedly now. "Oh, God," she cried. "I was in hell . . . "

He rocked her for a long time. "It's over. It's over. It's over."

"Hold me . . . Hold me . . . " she wept. "Tell me I'm all right. Great Saint . . . Tell me I'm all right . . . "

You're all right, Kay. You're fine. It's all over now."

The detectives watched Santomassimo hold tightly onto her. It seemed that the two held each other hours before they descended the long interior stairwell of the Statue of Liberty. But none of them, even then, felt cleansed of the Hitchcock nightmare.

—20—

Click . . .

. . . *The voice was changed . . . not so tense, almost sweet . . .*

"I remember on Christmas in Nebraska—I was about seven—the snow was eleven feet high in drifts. You couldn't see the neighbors, our windows were blocked with snow. And I went out—and it was so brilliant, like the first day of Creation.

"I walked down the road, because the sidewalks were not shoveled yet. And I felt clean as that snow, that one brief moment when nobody was fighting, nobody tormented me because of my differences. How can I explain it? Even Nebraska was God's paradise then.

"Where was I going? What was I doing? I'll tell you, because it was the turning point of my life.

"I was going to Greenbaum's Department Store. My parents had not been able to think of one single thing to give me for Christmas. They gave me a $5 bill in an envelope

*and told me I could buy myself anything I wanted at Green-
baum's.*

"Can you believe parents so emotionally tight, so unimag-
inative, so parsimonious with their affection? Even a goddamn pair of socks—anything—that they'd have taken the
trouble to wrap and give me, I've have cherished. But no, I
went by myself to Greenbaum's.

"I was raised pretty strict. Church people. I told you.
We're not here on the Earth for fun. That sort of thing. So
they wanted me to pick out something worthy. Books, a tie.
Socks. That sort of crap. Practical. I wanted games. I
wanted to live, have fun, shit, it was Christmas, wasn't it?
But they expected me to give up any weird ideas. Like fun.
This was their cruel little test, see. I knew it.

"And I got so depressed. I realized how alone I was, and
how there was nothing that they could give me—were prepared to give me—nothing of what I needed.

"I knew, that Christmas, that I was like an orphan and
always would be.

"Greenbaum's had a charity box in the basement. That
was where the poor families came and paid next to nothing
for cast-offs and donated clothing and broken toys. I felt at
home among the rejects. I found something in that box: an
8mm spring-wound Bell & Howell camera.

"Was it God or the devil led me there? You have your
opinion. I have mine.

"When I picked it up, I felt a compact power that could
destroy the civilized world. I knew it. It was natural to me. It
gave me life. And my reason eventually foundered on it. But
I have no regrets. And neither should Hasbrouk and all the
others.

"Because from that day, I created myself from nothing. I
lived in film. I existed only in film. I saw life as poorly made,
undisciplined film. And being constructed like that. I met
Hitchcock and he became the single, most powerful influence on my life.

"I suppose you feel my life is a sick joke. Of course, you're
right. But I didn't make it that way. I was crippled by the
force within me . . . I was bottled up . . . castrated . . . in
rooms without doors . . ."

*Click . . . Sounds of bumps, things being packed . . .
something fell . . . The tape rolled on, playing back . . .*

"Hitchcock taught me to hear the horrid laughter of death and insanity behind the ordinary realities of trivial people.

"I dedicate my life, and whatever significance it may possess, to Alfred Hitchcock."

Click . . . Click . . . *The voice became tense again, as though trying to break through, trying to make contact . . .*

"Hitchcock visions tormented me. I made them real. I made them eternal. Priests understand this principle of life, of serving the greater. Of HOMAGE."

Santomassimo turned it off.

They were in King's Canyon, high in the Sierras. He had rented a park cabin and had it outfitted with firewood, canned foods, wine. Now they sat on the floor in the firelight. The altitude was over six thousand feet and the wind made rushing noises through the sequoias, dark ponds, and twisted firs on the hillside outside. Now, with Santomassimo's tape recorder turned off, the wounds of the last month seemed to bring a guest: silence.

Kay wore a loosely hung sweatshirt and tan pants. Her feet were bare and her hair freshly shampooed. Santomassimo had been cutting the wood and wore heavy denims and a rough turtleneck sweater. He didn't feel like much of a camper but he was glad to be out of the city.

"Maybe I shouldn't have brought it," he said. "I found it in Chris's apartment labeled *For Professor Quinn. In Case of Failure.* I felt you had a right to hear it."

"Thanks."

"I'll burn it now. There's no point in hearing from him anymore."

He reached for the tape but she put a hand on his arm. He sat back on the rug. The logs burned brightly behind the recorder, little lights glinting from the last remnants of Chris Hinds's torment.

"I'm not afraid of Chris Hinds anymore," she said,

letting him stroke the back of her neck. "And it's pointless to try to run away from what happened."

But Santomassimo was still horribly guilty, and tentative, afraid of what he had done to her.

"Poor Chris," she said. "He had talent. In a perverse way. He researched his subject brilliantly. He should have gotten a degree."

"Are you serious?"

"Why not? I've seen them given for less. Who knew more about Hitchcock than Chris Hinds?"

She smiled at him. Santomassimo was glad to see the flash of humor in her beautiful eyes.

"It'd be the kind of ending Hitchcock would have loved," he conceded. Then, unexpectedly, he made a crude attempt to imitate Hitchcock's cockney drawl, lazy and macabre, down to the slow, labored breathing. "Chris Hinds, having proved his expertise in a hostile world, received a Master of Arts in Film Studies at a highly respected university in California, but lamentably, the certificate had to be delivered—posthumously—to his uncle's home in a significant wheat-producing state in the the Midwest where it is currently on display on the mantel."

Santomassimo and Kay laughed, but Kay's laughter was tepid, unsure. He stroked her arm. She seemed to flinch.

"Fred. I still feel . . . fragile . . ."

Santomassimo pressed his lips against her neck. He felt sure his clumsy attempt at humor caused her to slip back into the nightmare of the statue.

"It was a frightening experience, which almost killed you. Of course you feel fragile."

"There was such . . . power . . . in those film images . . ."

"Insanity can be contagious."

"I was as insane as Chris Hinds."

"The first time I was shot at, I felt myself pull away from myself," Santomassimo said. "I saw my own death written in a pulp paperback. I did. Even as the bullet ricocheted past my head."

She watched him closely. She seemed reluctant to believe that everything could be all right again.

"It's fear, Kay," he said. "Fear splits us from ourselves."

She pulled away. They had a jug of red wine and he poured some for her. She reached for the poker and jabbed the logs. Fiery red sparks spit out.

"And I was indeed split. I was the perfect foil," she admitted. "Hitchcock fascinated me totally. Like Chris, I was totally vulnerable."

She looked from the fire and the tape recorder to his patient, smiling face, and the patience in his eyes made her heart ache. "Bear with me, Great Saint. I've said it all before, but I must say it again, and again, and again . . . Film is mental manipulation. Chris was right. It's mind control. It's directing people's emotions, desires, ideas through visual techniques they know nothing about."

"Are you trying to tell me that Hitchcock killed Nancy Hammond, Steve Safran? Hitchcock killed Hasbrouk early in the morning on the beach?"

She nodded slowly.

"That's what I believe."

Santomassimo hastily finished his glass of wine and poured another.

"That's like blaming the Beatles for what some deranged psycho heard in their lyrics."

"People who have been stripped of their defenses are capable of anything. And that's what film tries to do."

"To murder? I don't agree with you, Kay."

"To strip bare the souls of their characters. To subject them to grotesque and terrifying situations, using every dark, horrifying cinema trick and art—"

"Kay, it's called theater, and it's been going on for centuries. People today pay six, maybe seven bucks for an hour and a half of entertainment. They get a few vicarious thrills, sure, but that's all."

"Really? Then why was I trapped like an image in an

old film? I couldn't get out. I was held by Hitchcock's strings, like a marionette—a marionette in his funeral march. And I could have killed, too. Do you understand. I *needed* to see that figure fall! It was in the film and I couldn't stop it!"

Kay's fierce eyes caught Santomassimo unexpectedly. It sent a chill through him.

"Kay—"

"Up there on that torch there was very little separating me from Chris Hinds. And from who knows how many crazies, seeking something, too much maybe, from films."

"Okay," he agreed. "For some reason you wanted too much from Alfred Hitchcock. You got infected. Like a disease. But the boil has been lanced, Kay."

Kay watched him, trying to see if he understood. Curious, he watched her, the lovely womanly form half silhouetted by the fire, soft as a kitten, silent now, and he waited.

"I'm not going back to USC," she said perfunctorily.

He raised an eyebrow. "You got a better offer somewhere else?"

"No."

"What are you going to do?"

"I can write. Maybe a novel. But I'm not teaching film again."

"Kay. Give yourself time. Be sure of yourself."

"I am sure," she said. "I'm more sure than I've ever been about anything. Film is insidious. Subtle, charming, hypnotizing, and insidious. For too many people it has too much power. And I'm not going to teach it."

Santomassimo knew better than to argue. He sighed. It left a huge question in the air.

"Kay," he said softly.

He pulled her to him and looked into her eyes. She felt suspended, infinite in a sudden way. He kept looking into the deep intelligence of her green eyes, the troubled eyes that he had caused to see too much, know too much.

"I love you, Kay. I need you."

He leaned forward and kissed her, slowly. At first she responded, her warm lips moist and supply. The she moved away slowly.

"I—I need time, Fred," she said.

Then, trying to make a joke instead of crying, she said, "I can hardly keep one person together, much less a relationship." Then she was crying. He held her.

"I can keep us both together," he said. "Kay, without you . . . I . . . I . . ."

Suddenly his eyes were moist, too, and he found it difficult to speak.

"Can I call you Amadeo?" she asked.

"You can call me anything you like."

"Amadeo. Amadeo, Amadeo," she chanted, laughing, crying. He held her harder, and felt her tears, warm and wet, against his neck.

"Can we swim in your art deco bed, Amadeo?"

"We'll do anything and everything in our art deco bed."

"I still see him in dreams . . . I see the falcon . . . the Statue . . . and Chris . . . falling . . ."

He clung to her tighter. "The film's over, Kay," he said gently.

"Is it?"

"The audience has gone home."

"Have they? Is any person's death, like Chris's, ever really over?"

"If a new life begins."

"Yes—if a new life begins. I need that—"

He let her cry, a refreshing cry. It was half laugh, half cry, a lovely sound like spring rain against lilacs, gentler now because there was a last, final release.

"Amadeo. Hold me, Amadeo."

"I'll never let you go. Not now. Not ever."

"Amadeo—"

"Cry, Kay, cry," he whispered. "It's a beautiful sound."

Santomassimo knew, and he knew Kay knew, that for ᵐ a new film was beginning.